SURVIVE THE UNIVERSE

PHOENIX PHIL MORLEY

Written by Phoenix Phil Morley

Edited by Laura Carley-Read

Cover Art by Steve Horry (www.stevehorry.com)

This is a work of fiction. Names, characters, businesses, places, events and incidents are either the products of the author's imagination or used in a fictitious manner. Any resemblance to actual persons, living or dead, or actual events is purely coincidental.

Unless, of course, I have actually been blessed with 'the gift' and all of this is actually a wild premonition.

Second print edition 2023.

Get all the news and scoops here:

phoenixphilmorley.com

And/Or come find me here:

Email: phoenixphilmorley@outlook.com

Twitter : @PhoenixPhilM

Facebook : Phoenix Phil Morley - Author

DEDICATION

Dedicated to my beloved Laura for inspiring the dream and
keeping it alive
...and Coco for being the Mother of all Molines.

SURVIVE THE UNIVERSE #1

DISTRACTED IN VASTRID

Chapter One

THE CIRCLE IN THE SKY

The day was done, the battle had been lost, and as he clutched the crimson wound on his chest, Christopher Macy sensed the next death to occur was likely to be his own.

Forcing tired footstep after tired footstep, Christopher dragged himself through the cold, cobbled streets of New Maven, a small market town in the southern reaches of Vastrid. A light rain had started to fall, and Christopher kept his eyes down, focusing on the streetlamp reflections on the ground beneath him.

He was a born and bred Vastridian, thirty-two years old, and had garnered quite the reputation over the past decade or so. He was many different things to many different people: a noble warrior to those he had protected; a source of great frustration for his enemies; a fountain of wounded wisdom; the gregarious life and soul of the party. But as he stumbled down Halifax Street, he realised all of his valiant victories, starry-eyed romances and celebrated accomplishments hadn't amounted to anything that would help him escape this fatal evening.

Billowing smoke and torrents of dust from the aftermath

of the battle scattered through the streets, following Christopher as he slowly and agonisingly made his way through the panicking crowds. As he passed, the sounds of shock and screaming rang his ears ragged as the din rattled against the surrounding brutality and loss.

Eventually, Christopher found an abandoned café tucked away down a side road and slumped onto its stone steps. Both of his hands were full, his left holding the wound on his chest and his right clasped around a long stick. The stick in question was more than just a walking aid; it was, in fact, a weapon – a bo-staff made of solid oak and blessed by a power from beyond the stars. It was a weapon used only by a select few; members of a mysterious order known as The Sentry, the protectors of the past and the guardians of the future.

Pushing through waves of pain, he slowly eased his left hand from the torn flesh on his chest and the bullets buried deep within. He had instinctively placed his hand over the wound to stem the bleeding, but it had now become more of a comforting cradle. He straightened his bo-staff and began turning the weapon quickly between his two open palms. He knew his actions were against the oath he'd sworn, but he had to find out if his fate was sealed. Rather than shine with the bright light required to self-heal, his eyes crackled with short, flickering sparks, and Christopher begrudgingly accepted defeat.

Christopher had been born with a curious nature, and instead of dwelling on his injuries, he carefully positioned himself against the wall and gazed up at his surroundings. He wondered how old the doorway around him was; the last ten thousand years had seen roads, buildings, streets and cities raised, levelled and built again in a cycle spun without due care or concern by the greedy ambitions of humankind.

After the most recent war laid waste to much of the planet Earth, The Shadox Corporation had decided to start

again from scratch. It destroyed the details of past civilisa-
tions and the dynasties that thrived within them. They
claimed it was to create a new era of peace; a welcome opportunity for humanity to start again without the baggage of the
past. As the decades rolled on, many began to realise that it
was just one of the tactics the Corporation had employed to
seize complete control.

The Sentry were amongst the number that opposed The
Shadox Corporation's grasp. In addition to their insidious
power plays, Christopher Macy and his allies knew that
Professor Shadox, the head of the Corporation, held far
darker secrets and ambitions.

Tonight was supposed to have been the night that The
Sentry overthrew The Corporation, but instead, they walked
right into a trap. Unprepared, outnumbered, beaten. As
Christopher's fingers traced the cracks in the ground, he
wondered if they had been betrayed or merely naive. He
glanced back up to the main street – crowds of people still
rushed past, jolting and pushing and shouting, but his focus
returned to his surroundings.

A soft creaking sound had caught his attention, and
Christopher squinted at a pile of wet rubbish bags in the
shadows, readying his bo-staff to shoo away rats. His eyes
searched the darkness, and his heart sank as he began to
make out shapes - first shoes, then legs, then the silhouette of
a body slumped amongst the trash. Christopher leaned
forward and stared at the still stomach area as he watched for
any signs of movement, breathing and life. There were none,
and he sighed with relief.

The creaking sound came again, this time louder and
accompanied by the rustling of bags. Christopher watched in
horror as the legs of the body stretched out, and the chest
began to rise and fall in time with a slight hiss of breaths,
slowly wheezing from the mouth. The figure unsteadily eased

itself up from the rubbish bags and shuddered to its feet. There was no time to waste - despite the pain he was in, Christopher knew he had to act fast. If he was to die this evening, then it had to be on his terms. After all, he had just dragged himself away from the battlefield to ensure that the Corporation couldn't seize his body. Christopher had seen the remains of his comrades bagged up and loaded onto trucks and shuddered to think what was in store for them.

Christopher tried to lift his bo-staff but found he could no longer grip. Weakened by his wound and exhaustion, his arm fell by his side. The staff clattered to the ground, causing the figure to turn towards Christopher and begin staggering forwards. Sounds of sinew scraping and bones grinding snaked through the alleyway as the body stretched its arms out, and the nails on the hands attached to them started to extend. Two green pinpoints appeared where the eyes should have been, and the figure let out a sour, malicious hiss.

Groaning in agony, Christopher clenched his left fist as hard as he could, and tiny sparks once again fizzled from his eyes. He stuck out the index and middle finger of his right hand and made a sweeping gesture towards his bo-staff on the floor, causing the weapon to launch itself towards the creature in front of him just as it was about to pounce. As the bo-staff struck the silhouette, its form dissolved instantly, leaving only the tattered clothes it had been wearing. Christopher's staff rolled back to him, and he dragged himself to his feet. He had no power over when his final breaths would be, but he could at least aim for something more inspiring than a pile of trash bags for his final view.

Christopher had hoped to get to the banks of the River Taisteal. As he made his way there, not stumbling now but drifting, he noticed that the screaming, panicked clutches of New Maven locals were gradually replaced by looters, arsonists and thieves eager to take advantage of the chaos and unrest. Reaching the top of Lea Hill, he realised he could go no further and leaned heavily against a wall, gazing out across Magna Harbour below. To his right, a small, run-down bar called The Endless Knot was still open, its landlord trying desperately to shepherd his customers out and lock up for the night before the looters arrived.

Most of the pub's customers who spilled out of the double oak doors hurried away, eager to find safe passage and distance themselves from any trouble. However, one figure, a young woman with long, unkempt hair, stood motionless in the crowd wearing an expression of sorrow as she stared at the man slumped against the wall.

'Kendra?' Christopher croaked as his eyes met hers. To his surprise, he felt a wave of relief wash over him at the sight of a familiar face. It had been months since they had seen each other, and neither of them had forgotten the harsh words spoken. He knew the tears that streamed down her cheeks weren't for him. Seeing the bottle in her hand, he guessed that she'd been trying to drown her sorrows as her sorrows increasingly drowned her.

A kind of resolve came to Christopher as his peripheral vision caught something deep in the night sky. He smiled softly; he'd been surprised that his wound had allowed him to reach this far, but he now understood that fate had secured his arrival at this exact place and at this exact time. All of those valiant victories, starry-eyed romances and celebrated accomplishments - they had been part of a journey culminating in this one final moment - the moment to fulfil his life's purpose and deliver this message.

Fighting for his final breaths, Christopher lurched towards Kendra, who dropped her bottle of ghost alcohol and managed to catch him as he slumped to the ground. Christopher's bo-staff slipped from his fingers and rolled a metre or two away, eventually nestling in the curb.

'Kendra,' he murmured, but as he lay gasping in Kendra's arms, he found himself unable to push any more words out. Instead, Christopher stretched out his right arm and traced a perfect circle against the night sky.

'I... I don't understand.' Kendra searched his face for answers, but as his body fell limp in her arms, she knew she would receive none. With a near-silent sigh, Christopher's final breath left his body.

Kendra gently laid him down and began gathering dry sticks and foliage for the fire. She may no longer have been a member of The Sentry, but to leave a blessed body for The Corporation to find and do whatever it was they did to them was unthinkable. Noticing the bo-staff lying in the road, Kendra reached out and picked it up. A sense of security and purpose flowed through her. It had been a while since she'd held a bo-staff, but Kendra had never felt a connection like this with one before.

Her mind raced back to Christopher and the circle he'd drawn in the sky. *What could it mean?* Kendra looked out over the grassy peak of Lea Hill, past the mossy rocks and tiny villages that led down to the sand and shore of Magna Harbour. She could hear the rumble of the Vastridian Royal Guard's fleet advancing towards the harbour to intercept the looters from Baker's End. The Baker's End mobs responded in kind by escalating their efforts, emptying shops and stores of stock then burning the buildings to provide enough chaos and distraction to escape.

Despite the uproar around her, the sky that rested overhead was peaceful and still. A sprawling, deep blanket of space, serene and clear, graced only with the stars peppered throughout.

Kendra raised her index finger and repeated Christopher's movement, mapping a circle over the same patch of sky he'd highlighted. The stars twinkled back at her, and Kendra sighed. She closed her eyes and breathed deeply, trying to silence the fear clattering in her mind. Focusing her eyes again, Kendra stared deep into the night's sky precisely where the centre of the circle she'd drawn had been. Hurtling towards Vastrid were two blazing, luminescent orbs. They looked a little like comets but were brighter and seemed to be constructed of pure light. As the two shapes began their descent several miles from Kendra, glittering shards of silver, blue, pink and purple sparked around them.

Kendra knew what they must be but almost couldn't believe it. She thought for a moment as she constructed and reviewed plans in her head, then nodded and muttered the name, 'Calvin.' He wouldn't want to help her, but she knew he was the only person who could. Kendra fumbled in her pocket for matches and silently bid Christopher farewell. She picked up her discarded bottle of ghost and threw it into the fire, watching the pale blue flame flare up then vanish, before walking off through the night until it became a new day.

Chapter Two

HER 15TH DISTRACTION

On a Thursday morning a decade and a half later, Callie Haywood was squeezed between armpits and baggage in a carriage full of commuters. The crowded subway train stood static in front of a red signal while her thoughts began to travel far.

Callie's eyes felt strained and irritated by the artificial light. She began to blink repeatedly; at first, she saw only the darkness of her eyelids when her eyes closed. On the fourth blink, however, came a bright, bewildering light. This pattern continued; darkness, darkness, darkness, light, repeating until the flash of an image appeared. It may have only been there for little more than a second, but it was there – her bedroom on a stormy night. Illuminated briefly by a bolt of lightning striking the sky, her window lay wide open as if to invite in the magic and malice she sensed waiting on the other side.

Callie dragged her hand over her face and shook herself back into the present. She sensed that if she allowed herself to focus on the images in her mind, she would start to detach from the world around her and become consumed in an internal moment, as terrifying as it was fascinating.

Callie didn't know what to make of this, but it wasn't a new experience for her; this was the fifteenth time it had happened.

With the monotony of her commute returning to the centre of her thoughts, Callie sighed with relief and frustration. She'd escaped being overwhelmed by whatever was going on in her mind but was still stuck on a train, wishing away the seconds until it arrived at Charterton station, where she could escape the suffocating presence of other passengers. As an officer of the Vastridian Royal Guard, she officially had to refer to her daily shifts as 'duty'; however, in terms of what the role meant to her and how it occupied her time, it felt more like 'work'.

Callie craned her neck and peered around the carriage until she found a thin wedge of daylight emerging from a window. She squinted out at the Caspian City skyline. As the largest and busiest city in the Kingdom of Vastrid, Caspian City was comprised of several distinct sectors. The imposing skyscrapers that dominated the financial district of Charterton were clustered on the city's western edge. This was also where a large section of the Royal Guard was based, and as the train finally pulled into the station, Callie squeezed her way past the other passengers and tumbled out onto the platform. She swept her dark hair out of her face and took a deep breath, pushing her backpack straps back onto the tops of her shoulders.

Despite the hustle and bustle of other city dwellers swarming around her on the platform, a lone, voluminous voice sailed over the surrounding din and caught Callie's ear. 'Stay classy, Haywood.'

She glanced up to see Dev Khatri, a fellow Royal Guard and Callie's patrol partner. He was a tall, stocky man, rarely seen without a huge grin on his face and always eager to share a joke.

'Stay classy? What's that supposed to mean?' Callie replied, edging her way past the last clutch of commuters.

'Don't act like you didn't just mouth abuse under your breath at those Shadox suits taking an age to get off the train.' Dev chuckled and shook his head as he bounded towards the exit.

Callie quickened her pace to keep up with him. 'They should be thankful that a mouthed insult is all they got. I had to spend the whole journey listening to them chattering on. And seriously, who doesn't just walk through a door when it opens with a crowd of people behind them? Idiots and sociopaths, that's who.'

'Ha-ha, you don't like Corporation types much, do you?'

'Nope.'

'C'mon, don't be so judgy; some of them are ok.'

The pair made their way up the escalator, away from the cramped, grey concrete of the Outer City Line and on to the clean, red-bricked pavements and marble walled streets of Charterton.

'Dev, think about every member of the Guards that we've known who's left to go and work for the Shadox Corporation. What do they all have in common?'

Dev stopped in his tracks for a second or two. 'They're all idiots and sociopaths?

'Exactly.'

'Fair enough,' Dev shrugged. 'Anyhow, how are you doing? You ill or something? You look awful.'

'Well, that's lovely,' Callie replied in a sarcastic tone, 'You're not hitting on me, are you?'

'Hitting on you? Nah, you're out of my league. Too intelligent. I like to be the smart and sophisticated one in a relationship. I don't want to be with someone who'll look down on me.'

Callie widened her eyes in mock concern. 'That must really limit your choices.'

'Seriously, you have no idea,' Dev nodded. 'It's been a good long while since – '

'Alright, no need to over-share.'

'Well, someone's gotta share something. You never dish from your diary. Your life outside of the Guards is either so boring that you have nothing to talk about or so wild you daren't. What do you want us to do, walk to work in silence?'

Ideal as this sounded to Callie, she realised how rude it would be. And besides, she did like having Dev as a friend and colleague, even if she could do without his booming banter at this time of the morning.

'With the extra shifts we have to do to make ends meet, I don't have a life outside of the Guards. Speaking of which, what is it today? Litter picking? Traffic management? Searching through the marshlands for something that almost certainly isn't going to be there?'

'Nah, first up, we're at the flight simulator.'

'Really?' Callie groaned.

'I thought you loved the flight simulator?'

'I loved it when we got to use it, not try and teach a bunch of rooks who either won't fly, can't fly or worse than that, the ones who can. We get to watch the ones who don't come from money end up doing the same drudgery shifts that we have to do, then sit there all smiles when they announce the rich kids who have been drafted to the Astro regiment. I mean, I hate to bring it up, but I did get the highest test score ever last year and did I get to join the Astros? No, I did not.'

Dev shook his head. 'You're too cynical. You know the Astros don't have any vacancies at the moment. It's not all bribes, backhanders and nepotism around here.'

'Isn't it, though? Name one person in the Astros with a parent who's not tight with King William.'

'Yeah, alright, I can't. But still,' Dev stopped and turned to Callie with a mischievous twinkle in his eye, 'I hear that you might have a royal connection soon. That should help you get a transfer.'

'What in the name of Vastrid are you on about?'

Callie knew exactly what Dev was on about and instantly regretted inviting him to explain.

'Prince Alistair, right? I've heard he likes you. In fact, since that time our squadron escorted him to swimming practice, he's personally requested you be in his security detail twice.'

'So what? That doesn't mean anything. It's not like anything happened between us,' Callie said, pushing the Prince's attempts to flirt with her from her mind and refocusing the conversation to their next assignment. 'And look, here we are.'

Tall fences lined the narrow pathway ahead of them, the lenses of security cameras and infrared scanners occasionally glinting in the sunlight. At the end of the path stood the vast white building of the Astro Academy, topped with an olive and blue domed roof and flanked on either side by expansive runways.

As they approached the entrance, Callie and Dev were met by two middle-aged, tired-looking guards. Despite Dev's best efforts and to Callie's relief, the guards had little time for small talk and begrudgingly got on with scanning their retinas and handing over the site passes.

Once cleared, Callie and Dev received a nod of approval from the security guards and made their way through the reinforced steel-lined doors into the main foyer. As they walked towards the elevator, they saw Dev's older sister Nyra.

She had her arm around a crestfallen young cadent and was leading him towards a side door.

'Alright sis, who's that you were with?' Dev bellowed as his sister turned back towards them. 'Tanya's little cousin, Zacharias, wasn't it? Is he alright?' Callie felt a familiar tension in her shoulders and was suddenly unsure of how to hold herself. Most Vastridians were part of large families, often living close to each other and sharing their lives through news and gossip. Having lost her parents at a young age, Callie had no family of her own and always felt somehow detached and unprepared when these kinds of conversations sparked up, as though hearing a language she only half-understood.

'Yeah, just failed his flight test, nothing earth-shattering,' Nyra chuckled. 'Anyhow, I would love to stay and chat, but I'm already late for my next shift.'

'What have they got you doing next?' Callie asked. She liked Nyra and was keen to try and establish a friendly rapport with her.

'Off on a wild goose chase. There's been a supposed Lomax sighting near Mockingbird Road. Are you ok?'

The words "Mockingbird Road" sent a strange tingling sensation down Callie's spine, causing her to shudder and jolt.

'Ah yeah, sorry, it's just... well, I live there. On Mockingbird Road, I mean. It sort of caught me off guard.'

Callie's unease was lost on Dev, who was a step or two behind in the conversation. 'What's a Lomax?'

Nyra frowned incredulously at her brother. 'Seriously, Dev, don't you watch the news?'

'I'm not getting out of bed early for anything or anyone, let alone to watch Good Morning with the McClouds,' Dev snapped.

'I like Tobias and Millicent McCloud,' Nyra muttered, looking a little hurt. 'Anyway, Lomax. Kendra Lomax.'

Dev let out a hoot of laughter. 'What, as in The Sentry and all that? Haven't they all been dead for years?'

'Yeah, that's my feeling too. Like I say, probably a complete waste of time.' Nyra turned to Callie and placed a reassuring hand on her shoulder. 'I'm sure it's nothing to worry about.'

Callie smiled weakly at Nyra, but the odd sensation she was experiencing continued to make her body clench and tremble, and the feeling of strain and irritation in her eyes rose up again.

'I'm so sorry; I need to use the bathroom. Nyra, lovely to see you. Dev, I'll catch you inside the test centre.'

Finding the nearest toilet cubicle, Callie barged past the door and collapsed on the seat. The methodical blinking pattern returned; darkness, darkness, darkness, light. Darkness, darkness, darkness, light – then the same image she'd seen whilst on the train.

This was not just a recollection of her bedroom. Callie found her mind concentrating and focusing on a moment in time that she couldn't place. She saw herself ill at ease and alone on a stormy night, a sense of inescapable terror in the air.

This state of mind was more lucid and tangible than a dream, yet more abstract and surreal than getting lost in everyday thought. Despite common sense telling her to snap out of it and get back to her shift, Callie found herself pushing further and further into her thoughts and imagined walking slowly towards the bedroom window. The white lace curtains that graced the sides of its frame flew around in the breeze like anxious angels before gently brushing past Callie's shoulders and folding behind her, urging her closer.

Beyond the window, she saw a small number of synistrails rampaging through the city square. Callie had seen one of these creatures before, during a patrol; the palest of skin

14

tones and eyeballs that had all but rotted away, leaving only luminous green pinpoint pupils. Sores and blisters covered their faces, dark veins pulsing and pushing some kind of life force through their bodies. These foul creatures were corpses that had somehow risen, deemed by the kingdom's scientists to be a strange and unwelcome evolutionary step for humankind. The Vastridian High Council continued to deny their existence and discredited or ignored sightings. However, in the shadows and out of sight, the number of these creatures had grown ever larger and ever stronger.

Staring down at the synistrails below, Callie felt her heartbeat increase as the Academy slipped further away. She stepped back from the window, but as she turned, Callie found herself face-to-face with a synistrail. As an active officer of the Vastridian Royal Guard, she was trained to deal with situations like this – her hand reached out and grabbed a nearby desk light. However, as she raised her arm to strike, it suddenly went limp, causing the lamp to fall to the floor and smash.

She saw the pale-skinned creature in front of her seize its chance, hissing and then hurling Callie across the bedroom. As she imagined smashing against the wall above her bed, images and sounds began to fill her head with increasing speed. There was a blinding flash of light, and the figure of a young man stood at her open window framed by billowing curtains, surrounded by the night's sky and the lightning that rode within it. The figure was backlit by moonlight, leaving his features hard to distinguish. Callie could see a bo-staff in his hand, and then suddenly, his eyes began to glow, full of bright, white light.

Another flash of light and Callie was now sitting on her bed, which was rising into the sky. She peered over the edge of the mattress and realised that it was unexplainably perched on top of a rapidly growing tower. Callie somehow knew the tower – a magnificent construct made from ancient masonry, with a strange meter-long horizontal slot near its top. At the foot, Callie could make out the grasping arms of more synistrails, scrabbling up the walls.

Callie gasped for air and squeezed her eyes shut, trying desperately to steady her nerves. She breathed deeply for a few seconds then forced open her eyes; there was nothing. The tower had gone, the synistrails had gone, she conceived herself alone on her bed, floating in empty darkness.

A split second later, Callie realised she was looking out at the city square. She shook her left arm and found that it was no longer numb, then glanced to The Soteria Archway in the square's centre and saw the enigmatic figure from her window emerging from it. Her heart was racing; it was clear now that something more significant than the life she had lived until this point was about to happen. Callie squinted, trying to make out his features as the young man walked towards her. As his pace increased with each step he took, her heartbeat quickened to match it. Just as he began to come into focus, the distraction was shattered by the sound of Dev calling her name and banging on the cubicle door.

'Damn!' Callie sighed, surprised by her disappointment that the threat and the excitement of her distraction had faded away. She'd never fallen that deeply in, and to be pulled from it as it blossomed left a deep sense of yearning. The distraction had offered prospects of danger and romance, two things that Callie usually found unappealing in her day-to-day world, but both seemed so enticing when played out in her mind. Ignoring an itch that had suddenly appeared near her shoulder blade, Callie looked at the time on her Cuff-Linq and noticed she had been in the cubicle for over twenty minutes and was running late for her shift.

'Sorry, Dev,' she called out, 'I just had a funny turn. I'll be out in a minute.'

'What I said earlier, y'know, about you either being boring or secretly wild? Well, locking yourself in a crapper, thrashing about and refusing to answer ain't exactly the actions of someone boring.' Dev's voice turned to one of soft concern. 'Is everything ok?'

Thrashing about? Callie had always presumed that her physical presence remained still during these distractions, and she found herself quickly trying to recall whether the previous episodes happened in public places.

As a child, she'd been known as a sleeptalker, sleepwalker, and pretty much a sleep-everything-except-still-and-silent type and Callie told herself that these distractions were just a different sort of dreaming. Her heart knew differently, though; there was more to it than that.

Callie took a deep breath in and steadied her voice. 'It's alright, Dev, you go and start the session. I'll be up in a minute.'

A pang of remorse echoed in her chest as she heard the door close. She wished that she could talk to Dev about these experiences, but she had never shaken the feeling of being somehow out of step with those around her. Sometimes, Callie felt so removed from day-to-day life that she wondered if she could ever connect to a time, place and person in the physical world the way she could with those in her mind.

The sound of the morning patrols taking to the air outside interrupted Callie's thoughts. She stood up, splashed some cold water in her face and straightened her uniform in the mirror. 'Get yourself together, Haywood,' she muttered, 'you've got work to do.'

Chapter Three

UNEXPECTEDLY AWOKEN

Little did Callie know, across the city at the Royal Academy's library, a young man named Ryan Tyler had just stirred from a similar distraction.

Ryan had been born in the slums of Vastrid. While his habitat may have been surrounded by criminal activity, he'd managed to avoid any of the entanglements with local crime families or the Vastridian Royal Guard that usually swamped the lives of those living there. Ryan was a cautious, humble young man, and although this approach had kept him safe from harm, he had never reaped any tangible benefits from these characteristics. He had grown up into an unassertive and somewhat anxious nineteen-year-old with little money and fewer prospects.

Aiming to escape a life in the slums, Ryan had managed to secure a clerical job in the Royal Academy library. Gaining employment at the Academy and striving to show enough promise to be considered for promotion was the standard way of escaping the slums for young Vastridians born to poorer families.

Grateful as he was to work in the Library, Ryan had

always held dreams of being in the Royal Guard. He had never been much of a fighter but thrived on the invention of combat moves during Augmented Training Module sessions at the Holodome. Ideally, he wanted to do the standard five-year stint in the Royal Guard then move to a job creating new hand-to-hand combat techniques that would be taught by stricter teachers to stronger pupils. The fact that such a job didn't currently exist was, admittedly, a stumbling block, but Ryan had to dream of something to distract his mind from filing dusty maps.

At the top of a twenty-foot ladder, Ryan had been hard at work retrieving an assortment of long-forgotten journals and documents. These items had been requested by retired soldiers of the Savior War who now had little to spend their time on except tasking the library staff to retrieve artefacts to help them relive their glory days. Ryan had been escaping the mundanity by allowing his thoughts to wander through a series of abstract visuals when suddenly an old reference book flew through the air and bounced off the back of his head, causing him to look up with a start.

'Wakey wakey,' a voice hollered. Ryan followed the sound to find his cousin Jayden grinning back at him.

'Alright, alright,' he chuckled, 'I'll be down in a second.' Ryan adjusted his reading glasses, slid down the rails of the ladder and bounded towards his cousin. Jayden was one of the few to have made the transition from the slums to the Academy and then the Royal Guard. She was the only person Ryan knew not to suffer any backlash or change in personality from this. In many ways, she was his hero. She was also his only friend.

'Hey there, cousin! How you doing? Have you only just staggered in for duty? Out partying again last night?' Ryan smiled.

Jayden rolled her eyes before throwing an arm around

Ryan and walking with him to the doorway. 'It's not against the law to have a good time off-duty. There's no shame in coming home at one in the morning.'

'...Or three, or five or six.'

'Or seven. Or even just stroll on through the dawn and walk straight into the morning debrief,' smirked Jayden. 'Maybe you should go out more; it might loosen you up a bit. Anyhow never mind all that, I've got news. The Academy Grid Test is going to be sprung on applicants within the next twenty-four hours.'

The duo stopped walking as Ryan turned and faced his cousin. He was suddenly ashen.

'Twenty-four hours!'

'I know, isn't it great? Just in time for the debutante ball. Imagine all the girls swooning at my little Ryan, all spruced up in a Guards uniform. It's not right that a nineteen-year-old boy like you has never had a girlfriend.'

'I have had a girlfriend. Don't you remember Bernadette?'

Jayden frowned. 'Do you mean Sour Bernie?'

'Um, yes, I believe that's what certain cruel people may have called her,' Ryan replied, cringing at the memory.

'No, no cousin, she wasn't an actual girlfriend. She was more like a bully, albeit a bully who sometimes held your hand. Also, wasn't that, like, five years ago now?'

'Three years,' sighed Ryan, remembering the stress of his one and only, thankfully brief, romantic relationship to date. Still, compared to the rush of anxiety the Grid Test news had given him, the days of courting a girl known as Sour Bernie seemed somehow preferable.

Jayden placed her hand on Ryan's shoulder. 'You'll be fine in the Grid. You just need to beat those nerves of yours and CON-CEN-TRATE, Mr Sleepyhead. Once you've passed this test, you'll be a member of the Royal Guard, and then there'll be plenty of time for falling asleep on the job.' Jayden straightened her jacket and turned to leave, then glanced back with a smile. 'Like I do after I crawl in at seven for the debrief.'

With a sigh and a shake of the head, Ryan returned to finish his shift.

Several hours later, Prince Alistair Hawthorne arrived at a high-tech Caspian City Gold Line subway station. After a resounding victory at the annual Ocean Olympics, he was returning home hungry for the praise and approval of his fellow Vastridians. As the prince passed through a turnstile and walked onto the platform, a crowd of admirers flocked around him. Despite his position as heir to the throne, Alistair was secure in the knowledge that he was completely safe in this environment.

To ride on this section of the subway was an expensive privilege; it was mainly used by his wealthy friends or The Royal Guard, who received a free pass to aid their duties. Security staff monitored the station, and the advanced weaponry detection rays that swept through the platforms and trains continually scanned all commuters. If any of these people wished to do him harm, there were easier ways to go about it. And besides that, the young prince thrived on the attention.

Still feeling a vast swell of pride from his sporting victories, Alistair shook hands, posed for photographs and eventually boarded a train before noticing Callie Haywood sitting in the carriage. The prince was acquainted with Callie as she had been assigned to a series of training exercises and field trips with him before he'd set off to the other side of the world for the Ocean Olympics. She'd proven more challenging to get to know than most, but this distance had only served to make her all the more intriguing to him. Hoping to surprise her, he crept forward and bellowed, 'CALLIE! Guess who's back?'

Unfortunately, he hadn't noticed that Callie was catching up on some much-needed sleep. She was exhausted after her long morning of training at the Academy, not to mention the intense distraction that had overtaken her mind. As the prince's words flowed into her ears, she woke with a start. In a split second, her brain had decided that she was under attack, and she flung out a punch, powered with the explosive frustration of a person awoken too soon.

As Callie rubbed her eyes and focused, she noticed that Prince Alistair was clutching his cheek with a pained expression on his face. Callie's blood seemed to pump both panic and embarrassment around her body. 'Oh... my. I'm so sorry. Please forgive me, Your Highness'.

Alistair stopped rubbing his face and leaned in with a slightly seedy grin on his face. 'That's ok, Callie; I've always admired your fiery nature.' The prince moved her belongings from the seat beside her and sat down.

'I'll forgive you, of course, but you must stop calling me Your Highness. I expect us to become friends, good friends, in fact. Please, call me Alistair.'

Callie wasn't sure she wanted to becomeanykind of friend to Prince Alistair, let alone a good one. Sure, Prince Alistair was a handsome young man and a sporting hero. He was also kind and just, and he had more integrity and intelligence than the rest of the jocks and egomaniacs usually found within the higher ranks of the Royal Guard. But, and it was a big but, Callie just didn't feel a spark with him.

'Tell me', Alistair asked, doggedly pursuing eye contact with Callie, who was trying to avoid it, 'who are you going to the Debutante Ball with?'

'Oh, I'm not going to the ball', Callie replied. 'It's not really my kind of thing.'

'Well then, it's lucky that I like a challenge,' Prince Alistair threw an arm around Callie, 'and the way I see it, I have the rest of this twenty-minute train ride to change your mind and convince you how it could become your kind of thing.'

Callie sighed a curse word under her breath and rolled her eyes as the subway train sped towards the city centre.

Fifteen miles away from Prince Alistair's attempt at wooing stood his home, The Royal Palace of Hawthorne. Most Vastridians perceived that the building looked like a distinguished historical monument despite being constructed less than fifty years earlier. This was due in part to it being the first building of note to be built after The Saviour Wars. The destructive war had been lengthy and had effectively closed the first chapter of human life on Earth.

Before the war had begun, planet Earth was dying, with many of the planet's resources all but used up. Humankind had struggled on with hydropower for a while, but ultimately the changing climate rendered this close to useless. Floods destroyed power stations, and poverty and desperation raged across Earth as the oceans devoured the land. Millions of lives were lost as nations fell, leaving new, ungoverned states to form on the scattered pieces of land that remained above water. It appeared that all was lost.

However, far away in a deep, uncharted realm of space, an ancient yet powerful life form made of small astral sprites had begun a journey. The first astronomers to learn of this life form's presence named it The Tide due to its path towards Earth ebbing and flowing in line with the same gravitational forces that also affected the planet's sea levels.

Upon discovering The Tide, the astronomers were spellbound by its beauty and the unique light surrounding it, but they lacked the understanding to comprehend what it was. Little did they know, it was far more than a newly discovered nebula; it was alive and had been travelling the universe looking for a planet to settle on and evolve.

While entering our solar system, Earthborn microbes caused a virus to develop within The Tide. The disease corrupted and contorted half of the Tide's sprites and split the life form in two - a Tide of Light and the Dark Lethe.

Although weakened by this, The Tide of Light still intended to reach Earth and fulfil its purpose. However, the Dark Lethe's destructive, lightless Tide developed an appetite for matter and wished to consume the whole universe and so began to attack its purer half. As the virus further mutated its form, The Dark Lethe became increasingly obsessed with destroying the light Tide before moving on to eliminating all of creation.

During this lengthy celestial war between The Tide's two fragments, the Dark Lethe sent some of its dark sprites down to Earth to create a physical form that could gain power on the planet's surface. The first attempt to do so failed, as The Dark Lethe sprites tried to use the bodies of recently deceased humans as vessels. The mixture of ravenous greed from the Dark Lethe and the human bodies' decaying remains created the Synistrail race. As deadly and vicious as they were, the undead creatures lacked intellect and control. The Dark Lethe realised that it would require an intelligent and powerful representative on Earth.

With its escalating hunger for control on Earth, The Dark Lethe melded many of its sprites into a pure power source and encased it in an ancient monument located near the country of Parnasia. This fragment flooded the monument, influencing the building's structure and turning it into a modern labyrinth that ultimately led to a tall tower that held the secrets and the Dark Lethe's power.

With Earth facing its most desperate hour, a group of the world's most exceptional scientists teamed together to help find a way to save the planet from escalating environmental chaos. Upon discovering the strange, alien labyrinth located in the largely abandoned country of Parnasia, they led an expedition there to study its enigmatic form and seek to harness the power it possibly held inside. After entering the labyrinth, all communication with the team was lost. For several weeks it was presumed that they had perished, but eventually, one survivor returned - a stern and ambitious professor named Maxwell Shadox. His face had aged considerably since his journey into the labyrinth, and his manner carried an increasingly sinister air. Those who questioned the professor's account of his teammates' deaths via a chemical explosion inside the maze were largely ignored, as he now had what the world most needed – access to a new power source.

During the eight years that followed, Shadox used his knowledge and access to the Tall Tower in Parnasia to draw power from the Lethe and convert it into a new fuel source known as Saviour. The profits from this could have made him a very wealthy man; however, he always ploughed his money back into the Shadox Corporation. Money didn't interest him, but power did. Soon he owned and controlled every tradable commodity on the planet. With Earth under his control, Shadox turned his attention to the sky and broke new ground in space travel and off-planet housing.

As his power grew, he found a way to communicate with the Lethe and utilise its ability to control the few Synistrails that roamed the planet, using them to bring chaos to specific areas when it suited his own needs. However, his master-stroke was the manipulation of the remaining political powers of Earth. He tricked them into entering a destructive ten-year war against each other over Saviour fuel that left Earth ravaged. The Corporation had become the sole political superpower on a tired and order-free Earth, resulting in Maxwell Shadox gaining complete control of the planet.

To ensure that order was maintained on Earth, he awarded a popular war hero named William Hawthorne a kingdom. He bestowed the largest habitable area of Earth to the new king, who christened the area Vastrid. Despite its grandeur, The Kingdom of Vastrid was far from autonomous; Shadox Corporation retained control of all energy and produce. If the kingdom didn't obey The Corporation's wishes, it would run the risk of being plunged into poverty.

King William had always been aware of this and had secretly hoped that Shadox's advancing age would eventually give him a get-out clause when the Professor passed away. However, after over four decades on the throne, he found himself still bound to the Corporation's wishes.

Shadox began to slowly withdraw from public appearances until most presumed that he had retired. The business side of The Corporation was now run by his niece, Rachel Stone, who was as cruel and, in a calculating way, more ruthless than her uncle. She had a sharp face and spoke her vicious words in a slow, condescending manner. She had no time for failure or disappointment and had built up her own private fortune over the past decade and a half; she had married three powerful, wealthy men and killed them as they were sleeping while framing enemies for the murders.

At The Royal Palace, King William sat with his back to his desk, gazing out across Caspian City. He'd been holed up in his study for the past two weeks, thinking about the life he'd led and the damage it had caused. Initially, turning a blind eye had appeared to be the best thing to do. He had believed that humanity's recovery from the war would lead to a more civilianised age where guilt and reason would breed enough compassion to end conflict. However, with the divide between classes increasing and the stranglehold of The Corporation tightening, he had been proven wrong.

Almost half a century's worth of guilt burned inside the

king's stomach. He knew that standing down as monarch would result in little more than his assassination, but he was tired, and it was time that this ever-growing spiral of shame ended. The king opened his video memoir. He confessed everything he knew, either from first-hand experience or reliable informants, from Shadox's manipulation during the Saviour Wars to Rachel Stone and The Corporation's recent activities.

When the recording had finished, he sent it to several people he knew would make good use of the information. Some of these people were once enemies, and it was to them he directed the conclusion. 'I concede that, on behalf of my kingdom, I backed the wrong horse. I apologise for the pain and suffering that the Kingdom of Vastrid has caused. I humbly ask that you take this information to make right what I assisted in making wrong.'

Luckily for humankind, the recording contained all the information that would be required to strike back at Professor Maxwell Shadox and his Corporation.

Unluckily for King William Hawthorne, Rachel Stone was watching.

Far away in a lavish private office aboard the Shadox Corporation's floating space station Shadox VI, Rachel Stone paused her visual of King William's message.

'Oh dear,' she smirked to herself. 'Willy has really gone and done it now.'

She called her assistant Private Holmes on the telecom. 'Fetch Mr Nox. It's very important.'

'But... but...M-m-Mr Nox – he normally meditates at this time of day,' stammered the voice of Private Holmes. 'You know what happened to the last person who disturbed him.'

'No excuses,' Rachel snapped. 'Tell him that the Repossession of Vastrid must be brought forward.'

Rachel swung round in her chair and slowly teased the power lead out of the back of her monitor. As the paused image of King William faded, she waved at the screen and pulled her face into an exaggerated pout. "Bye-bye, your highness."

Chapter Four

DOOR TROUBLE

In Caspian City, Prince Alistair and Callie made their way out of the subway station and into the bright afternoon sunshine. The train journey had ended, but Prince Alistair's badgering of Callie had not.

'You know it makes sense. Even if you're not interested in the glitz and glamour of the ball, it's still a night out as my guest.'

Callie stared expectantly at the prince as though waiting for him to finish speaking. He coughed.

'Of course, you may wish to treat yourself to a new gown – paid for by me, naturally.'

'You mean paid for by your father,' Callie quipped back with a scornful smile on her face. 'Alistair, you're a nice guy, but I'm just not princess material.'

'Fair enough,' Alistair replied, his tone suddenly flat. 'Just promise me you'll think it over.'

The two of them walked without another word spoken for the next minute or so. Callie desperately scanned around for something to remark on and break the silence, internally cursing her lack of small talk skills. She was relieved to see that Alistair didn't look hurt or annoyed but lost in thought as he pondered how long he should leave it before asking Callie's friend Tanya Masters to the ball instead.

Nearby, Ryan had been left to lock up the library. This was all he needed. He was already feeling anxious, having learned that the Academy Grid Test would be sprung on him tomorrow, and now he had to contend with the library's finicky lock system. Ryan had realised a few weeks ago that he was the only staff member to struggle with the doors, and this nagging fact only made the task harder.

He had been struggling for over ten minutes when, after much tutting and sighing, it appeared that the doors were finally locked. Now all he had to do was remove the key, but it wouldn't budge. He gripped the door handle and tried twisting and turning the key in various directions. Eventually, he felt a satisfying click and yanked the key out with such force that he flew backwards and landed on the floor, only to glance up and see the door slowly creak back open.

Ryan's head fell into his hands just as Alistair and Callie rounded the corner of the library building.

'Haha, what do we have here?' said Alistair, in a muffled whisper.

Callie looked down at Ryan, but instead of wondering whether he was injured or not, she was trying to work out why she recognised him. She rarely visited the library, and yet he seemed familiar. While she was pondering this, Alistair attempted to help in the only way he knew how.

'Are you OK? Has someone broken into the library?' Alistair paused and searched for something else to say. 'Are you crying over a girl? She's probably not worth it. Um, just who are you, anyhow? I hope you have a security pass.'

Without looking, Ryan dusted himself off, stood up and

found himself face to face with Prince Alistair Hawthorne. Feeling shocked and embarrassed, Ryan was astute enough to know that this incident would soon be a humorous anecdote for the prince's friends, despite his well-meaning concern. Ryan's eyes focused and darted to the left of Prince Alistair's shoulder, and then, for a brief moment, he gazed at Callie. Callie was still trying to figure out who this boy from the library was when she realised she was looking deep into his eyes.

Noticing the eye contact, Ryan blushed and made his glance hit the floor. He had seen Callie walking around Caspian City a few times since he had moved away from the slums. He had no idea of her name, but he knew her as the girl with the dark hair who seemed different from the others at the Academy. There was something about her that produced a strange rush of flutters inside of him.

Ryan decided the best thing to do was mutter that everything was alright and go back to trying to shut the library while making as little eye contact as possible.

'What a strange boy,' said Alistair, hoping that a bit of one-upmanship would impress Callie as they walked away.

'Being strange isn't such a crime,' Callie answered with a smile as she glanced back at Ryan, still struggling with the library door.

In her office aboard Shadox VI, Rachel Stone glared at the ticking clock on the wall. It had been several hours since she had assigned Private Holmes the task of bringing Mr Nox to her office and her hand hovered over the button on her communicator. Just as she was about to press, the body of Private Holmes came crashing through her office doors like a rag doll tossed across a nursery.

A beaten and bloodied Private Holmes crawled towards

the desk. He attempted to speak but only managed a croak before passing out. 'Ah!' Rachel clapped her hands together and stood up, looking towards her now doorless doorway.

'Well, well, Udo,' she smiled brightly. 'That's a new door and possibly a new assistant you now owe me.'

The sound of heavy footsteps preceded a tall and muscular figure dressed in a sharp suit. His long hair was slicked back, the ends gently brushing the handle of a sword carried in a strap across his back.

'Firstly, I will never owe you anything,' answered the figure as he walked into the office. 'And secondly, you should call me Mr Nox.'

'No. You can call yourself whatever you wish; I'll continue to use your name as I see fit. My uncle can tell the public that you are the – ' she squinted into the distance as if trying to remember something, ' – Head of Territories, Political Compliance and General Enforcement of Corporation Policy. To me, you're just a glorified bodyguard.'

She turned towards the cabinet beside her desk and opened it, pausing to trail her fingers along the bottles thoughtfully for a few moments before selecting a wine.

'I must talk to you about a disturbing development.' Rachel glanced up at Nox as she poured and noticed him staring at the glass.

'Oh, don't worry. As much as I don't appreciate your ambition or your ego, you must realise that I need you and your department's support if we are to seize Vastrid. Murdering you would be oh-so-very inconvenient.'

'Believe me, Ms Stone, your weak Earth-born poisons would not affect me. I was merely ensuring you weren't doing anything to get on my bad side. Your butchered corpse would be very hard to explain to the board of directors.'

A condescending smile spread across Rachel's face as she handed Nox a glass. 'It appears that King William is keen to bite the hand that has fed him. He has sent a rather damaging video to some of our key enemies. We must bring the repossession of Vastrid forward.'

'I see,' said Mr Nox finishing his wine in one gulp. 'I'm ready to go, but I will require a battalion of Corporation troops. If the King is set to betray us, he will have his Royal Guard ready to protect him.'

'Colonel Bron will be leading an initial troop of a thousand to take out the Kingdom first, with additional squads deployed to secure the rest of Vastrid.' Rachel took Nox's glass and placed it carefully back on the desk. 'I want you to aid Colonel Bron and his men.'

Nox smirked. 'Bron? So you want me to go to Vastrid to look after your boyfriend?'

Rachel took a deep breath to dampen the anger swelling inside of her. 'The Colonel is a decorated soldier and, admittedly, a good friend. Your crude and childish label does him an injustice and only serves to make you look naïve and jealous of his military career.'

'OK then, I'll re-brand him; he's your lover, and he is the man who betrayed the Kingdom of Vastrid for a better position with the Corporation. Is that a less "naïve" description of the not-so-good Colonel?' retorted Nox.

'Colonel Bron's change of employer is one of the reasons you're standing here now, in more ways than one.'

As if on cue, Colonel Bron arrived, striding into the office. 'Ms Stone, you called for me.'

'Ms Stone? Do you make him call you that in the bedroom as well?' Nox asked Rachel with a grin.

'Let's get something straight,' barked Bron, getting in Nox's face. 'I don't have a problem with the burden of you coming along as a tourist to our little massacre, but don't think for a second that I'll turn the other cheek if you dare to disrespect me. The fact that you're Shadox's golden boy doesn't mean a damn thing to me. It means even less on the battlefield.'

Nox turned away, laughing to himself. 'On the battlefield? On. The. Battlefield? You truly are a miserable relic lost in memories of scuffles won and lost a generation ago.'

'Mr Nox, I urge you to leave it!' ordered Rachel, slightly overlapping the end of Nox's last sentence before Bron softly brushed her aside.

'No! Let's hear the titan talk.'

Nox continued his slow steps away from Rachel Stone and Bron, but his speech's tempo and volume had increased. 'What you fail to understand, Colonel Bron, is that the definition of pain and conquest have recently gone through some changes.'

Mr Nox spun round with his sword drawn and his eyes glowing red. 'Pain and conquest now mean me."

Bron dropped to one knee and drew his rifle, fixing the targeting laser directly on Nox's forehead. At that moment, the communicator on Rachel's desk chimed and caused a break in the rising hostilities. An aged yet stern hiss emerged from the speaker. 'Bron! Go and prepare your men. Mr Nox and Ms Stone, I seek counsel with you both immediately.'

Rachel, Nox and Bron all answered in unison. 'Yes, Professor.'

'Some other time,' Bron grunted at a smirking Nox as he left the room.

'Shall we then?' Nox turned to Rachel, making a sweeping arm gesture towards the door.

'OK, let's go,' said Rachel, quickly adjusting her hair as she stepped over the twitching, groaning body by her feet. 'Oh, and Private Holmes? Please sort yourself out. You're making my office look untidy.'

Chapter Five

THE GRID

Professor Shadox was resting in his chambers. Since his retreat from the public eye, his torso had become fully consumed by the Dark Lethe. His body shape was still that of a human, but it hovered in a dark cloud. His flesh had been scarred into a dull, moribund grey while his eyes shone a wicked shade of crimson. The changes to his physical appearance were not the only reason that he had retired from his role as the public face of The Corporation. Shadox had merged almost completely with the Lethe and now spent most of his time plotting and planning with the strange alien power that flowed through him.

He had just concluded one of these communications when Rachel Stone and Mr Nox arrived.

'Welcome, my friends,' Shadox hissed, 'I think we all know why we are here. The time has come to seize back The Kingdom of Vastrid. It has become a troublesome device, especially since Hawthorne's change of heart.'

Rachel stepped forward. 'The plans are in motion. Bron and his men will arrive in Caspian City and replace the monarchy with something much more agreeable, namely, us. We have, of course, prepared evidence to make sure we get the public's support.'

'Excellent work, my niece. There is, however, another concern.' The cloud surrounding Shadox began to darken and slow as the volume of his voice lowered, 'I have sensed a steady increase of unanticipated power in Caspian City. It recalls the days of The Sentry. We must find this new Child of the Tide and ensure they are unable to hinder our operation.'

'I'm sure this is Lomax,' Rachel replied, a sour expression falling across her face. 'After all, she was never caught; her body has never been found. There have been recent sightings of her reported to the Vastridian Royal Guards. We need to be mindful of this as we proceed.'

'Kendra Lomax is either dead or a washed-up drunk. She poses no threat to us,' growled Nox.

'No, this new power is different from the power of Kendra Lomax and her scum Sentry friends,' replied Shadox. 'Younger.'

'Very well,' replied Rachel Stone, 'I shall pass the information on to Colonel Bron. He will find this new threat and bring them in for examination.'

Shadox nodded his head. 'Thank you, Ms Stone. Please return to your duties.'

As soon as Rachel had left the room, the features of Shadox's face transformed from that of an elderly gentleman to the shape of a warped, demonic skull.

He turned to Nox and hissed, 'Meddlesome witch! Once she has played her part, we can dispose of her. Soon we will be able to put our true plans into action, and this cluttered galaxy will be free of the frustrating form that afflicts it. There will be no more existence. There will only be the divine clarity of the Lethe.'

Nox grinned in approval and headed for the door, malice burning deep within his eyes.

Back on Earth, it was morning. Ryan Tyler wearily dragged himself into the library, safe but not at all comfortable, in the knowledge that his trial for a place at the Royal Guard Academy would happen at some point that day. The tests took place in a large building that contained a maze-based assault course known as the Grid. To pass, applicants had to reach the only exit in the building within ten minutes. This task was made harder by the multitude of traps scattered throughout the Grid.

Being a young man of a slightly pessimistic nature, Ryan assumed that he'd be called to the Grid just as he was about to take his lunch break. As such, he wasn't surprised when the clock struck one o'clock, and two Royal Guards greeted him at the library doors.

Ryan was led to a waiting room where an incredibly calm receptionist, only a few years older than Ryan, advised that his examiner would 'be along in a minute'.

She spoke in a calm and relaxing way that only served to make Ryan's nerves worse. There was an agonising ten-minute wait as Ryan sat in silence with nine other candidates.

Eventually, the receptionist came out once more and gently advised, 'Sorry for the wait; your examiner will be here very soon.'

Ryan fixed his gaze on the wall in front of him and tried to concentrate on his breathing. He inhaled as slowly as possible, held for a moment, then quietly exhaled, hoping that no one was noticing. It suddenly occurred to Ryan that the increased focus on his breath was drawing his attention to the thumping panic in his heart, but before he could follow the thought, the door to the waiting room clicked open. Ryan saw a flicker of relief cross the receptionist's face as the examiner arrived, and he turned to see Prince Alistair striding into the room.

It's ok, Ryan thought to himself; *he doesn't remember the library door incident – just relax. There's no way he'd remember me. Maybe I'll look sort of familiar, but how many people does Prince Alistair Hawthorne meet? Stay calm, Ryan. This is not a problem.*

'Hello there, bored with the old library, are you? Best of luck.' Alistair smiled broadly at Ryan as he made his way over to shake his hand before nodding at the assembled group and motioning for them to follow him into the next room.

The candidates found themselves in a small staging area, facing an immense set of steel double doors, at least fifteen feet high. Alistair stood on a riser and addressed the room. The Prince explained that they would have ten minutes to escape the Grid and warned of the various kinds of traps that the construct held. Ryan, however, wasn't fully listening as his mind was still going over the embarrassing library door incident. He shook his head and forced his attention back into the room.

'Although I am the chief examiner,' Alistair was saying, 'I will have some help from assistants who shall observe you from the viewing gallery and make sure any time penalties are calculated.

Ryan looked towards the viewing gallery, hoping that his cousin Jayden wouldn't be there to witness his certain failure. He saw a rather generic jocular squaddie type; a girl he recognised as his cousin's friend, Tanya; an athletic, muscular guardsman and then finally, the girl with dark hair who had witnessed the library door incident. She looked beautiful. He felt terrified. And somewhere in the middle of that burning juxtaposition, his attraction to her began to grow.

Ryan was still gazing at Callie when she happened to look

down and catch his eye. She smiled at him, but Ryan turned away. Callie felt a pang of rejection but quickly dismissed it. Observing the Grid try-outs was her final task of a long shift, and in all honesty, she just wanted to go home and sleep.

Ryan, on the other hand, felt dizzy as the rush of nerves, attraction and fear coursed through his body. As the large doors to the Grid opened, images of Callie smiling at him flooded Ryan's mind. His anxiety peaked, and Ryan's body was besieged by nausea and trembling nervousness as he made his way in, past Prince Alistair. Inside the Grid itself, Ryan looked around at the immense room lit primarily by blinding flashes of spotlights scanning back and forth. The sound of alarms and klaxons attempted to deafen his ears while a series of giant clocks were beamed onto the walls, counting down the remaining time.

The other applicants began sprinting through the Grid like machines ready for war, leaving Ryan no option but to follow them. Despite the stress flooding his body, Ryan was able to leap over pits that appeared suddenly in the floor and somehow managed to vault over a wall. As he did so, he broke a sensor beam, triggering two darts loaded with tranquillisers to fire at him. Instinct took over Ryan's reflexes, and he back-flipped out of their path. This newfound agility was a surprising development, and in shock and confusion, Ryan blindly stumbled into one of the other applicants.

'What's wrong with you? Get out of my way,' screamed the boy, pushing Ryan into a wall that spun around, leaving him in a corridor with a dead end. Blocking his way out were two snarling guard dogs.

'Good doggies,' pleaded Ryan, but it had no effect as the hounds raced towards him with a hunger for flesh in their eyes. Noticing a sensor beam nearby, Ryan waited until the dogs were close before breaking the beam with his hand. The dogs leapt at Ryan, but he managed to jump higher, and the two darts triggered from the trap shot out and hit the dogs in their necks, knocking them unconscious.

Fearing that his time was running out, Ryan sprinted out of the cul-de-sac only to find himself back at the beginning of the Grid. His heart sank, and a surge of frustration turned to upset and anger. Suddenly, Ryan felt a fire grow within him, and he attacked the assault course with all of his might. Ryan bounded over the walls that obstructed his path and somersaulted over the pits on the floor. Despite knowing some basic gymnastics, he had no idea where these new skills had come from, but he was immensely grateful that he had discovered them now.

Just as the Grid exit came into view, Ryan was stopped in his tracks by the sound of a fellow applicant screaming. Ryan spun around to see a young man with his leg caught in one of the Grid's sliding walls.

'Help me!' screamed the young man. 'It's tearing my leg off.'

Ryan looked towards the exit. He knew he would pass the test with flying colours if he just sprinted out of that door. A golden opportunity for a rare personal victory was staring him directly in the face in the form of an open door, but Ryan's conscience simply wouldn't allow him to move towards it. Ryan raced back to the fallen, wailing applicant and managed to push the door open long enough for him to crawl out.

'Can you walk?' asked Ryan. The wounded young man attempted to stand before collapsing with a groan.

'I guess not,' sighed Ryan, putting the man over his shoulder and walking towards the exit, breaking several sensor beams in his path and triggering a flurry of tranquilliser darts.

Dart after dart pierced Ryan's skin as he stumbled towards the exit, and he felt his eyes begin to close. Collapsing to his knees, the last thing he heard was the wounded applicant groaning, 'please, whatever you do, don't drop me.'

Everything went dark for Ryan Tyler.

Chapter Six

COMPROMISED INVITATIONS

Ryan awoke in a hospital bed to find a nurse standing over him, removing a needle from his arm.

'Don't worry, Mr Tyler, you're perfectly safe and well. To be honest, I'm surprised that you've woken so quickly.' The nurse glanced at Ryan's confused expression. 'After all, most people would be out for days after being hit with,' she picked up his chart and scanned it for a moment, 'numerous tranq darts.'

Ryan's groggy mind followed the information trail it had been given: Hospital? Woken? Tranq darts?

Suddenly Ryan jolted up and screamed in a half-conscious slur, 'Oh my stars, the test! I must get back to the Grid!'

Ryan slung himself out of the hospital bed before feeling his legs turn to jelly. Rather pathetically, he collapsed face-first to the ground, knocking over a medical tray in the process. With his face against the cold bleached floor of the ward, Ryan heard the nurse sigh and tut as she bent down to collect the fallen items.

A second voice emerged. 'That's the thing about the darts in the Grid – they're filled with Betanex Perphenazine, which is a slightly bottom-heavy tranq. Your mind will be willing a long time before your legs are.'

The voice belonged to Prince Alistair, who crouched down and helped Ryan back onto his bed. While Ryan was trying to process yet another embarrassment in front of the prince, Alistair continued.

'Of course, we use these tranqs for purely selfish reasons. We can't take risks with a candidate's mind. Many of those that fail the Grid reapply and pass the following year. We can't risk sending tranq-brained rag dolls into battle now, can we?'

'I guess not,' said Ryan, partly out of confusion and partly out of a desire to bring the prince's visit to an end as swiftly as possible.

'So then, Ryan Tyler,' said Prince Alistair in a slightly more formal manner, 'you're probably wondering about the results of the Grid, aren't you?'

'Well, I ended up unconscious in a hospital bed. I'm guessing I failed,' Ryan replied.

'The thing is,' said Alistair, placing his left and right index fingers together and raising them to his lips, 'becoming a Royal Guard isn't always as simple as passing or failing the Grid'.

Ryan felt a strange sense of optimism. Could it be that he'd get through the test on some kind of technicality? Maybe he was just the kind of maverick the Royal Guard had been looking for. Goodbye poverty, goodbye Slums, goodbye boring library. Hello success, hello status and yes, possibly at long last, hello romance.

'You mean, I passed?'

'Not exactly.'

Along with his brief-lived optimism, Ryan's heart sank, and his mind tried to process what the result could be. If he hadn't passed or failed, then what?

Noticing the concern on Ryan's face, Prince Alistair decided to explain the situation as quickly and simply as possible.

'We can't pass you because you didn't manage to escape the Grid. However, you did have the opportunity to do so, and you sacrificed your own gain to aid someone who was in danger of losing a limb. With that in mind, we can offer you a six-month trial secondment with the Royal Guards.'

Ryan was halfway through thinking, *I suppose that's not too bad,* when Alistair continued. 'Of course, you'll still be on the same wages that you're on now during the six-month trial. Your first post will be policing the Slums. You'll be on duty in four days time. Your acceptance letter, daily duty orders and a uniform coupon will be delivered to you later today.' Ryan's heart sank like a stone.

The Prince watched Ryan's face for a delighted reaction and, finding none, patted him on the shoulder and bid him goodbye. As Prince Alistair went on his way, Ryan slid under the hospital bed sheets and prayed that his failed career gamble was all part of some awful nightmare or a hallucination brought on by the tranq darts.

Aboard the Shadox VI, Colonel Bron sat alone in his room. Unusually, for a high-ranking military man, the room was devoid of expensive furnishings. Nor was it decorated with medals, photos or ego-boosting artefacts celebrating his military career. In fact, it was barely decorated at all and could hardly be described as comfortable. It was as basic as the living quarters the rookies stayed in and not all that different from The Corporation cells. Colonel Bron liked his room this way - cold, harsh and uncomplicated. It was a room he understood. He was sitting on the edge of his bed, cleaning his rifle, when Rachel Stone arrived at his door.

'Survived the dressing-down from Shadox then, did you?' said Bron, his eyes focused on the mechanics of his gun.

'Actually, I received some vital information,' Stone smiled as she walked towards him.

'Oh yeah?' Come on then, let's hear it. Let's hear what's so important you don't even need to knock.'

'Colonel Bron', Rachel whispered, running her fingers over Bron's weathered face and making him rise to his feet, 'I didn't know you were such a stickler for manners. After all, you don't mind if I fail to knock when I come to your room late at night for *social* calls.'

'Fair enough', Bron replied with a grin. 'Pleasure aside, how may I assist you with this news from Shadox?'

'It appears that the old boy has had another one of his conversations with outer space. Normally I would dismiss or ignore his demented ramblings, but this time it could be something. It appears that he has sensed a new power in Caspian City.' Stone paused and looked deeply into Bron's eyes. 'This power reminded him of the Sentry.'

'Lomax?' asked Bron as he sat back down on his bed. 'It can't be Lomax. She hasn't been seen or heard of for years. Even if it is her, there's nothing to worry about. I've gone toe-to-toe with Kendra Lomax before and survived to tell the tale.'

'Shadox seems to think the power is younger than Lomax's. I need you to try and find this new threat during our repossession.'

'Not a problem. I shall leave no stone unturned.' Bron went back to tending to his rifle, and Rachel shook her head, perplexed.

'You haven't seen Shadox in years. Does it not bother you?' she asked.

'How do you mean?'

'Well, you never ask questions about him or about what he's become. Are you not curious? Or worried?'

Bron looked up at Stone again. 'The way I see it is, you need my muscle to help you make your fortunes, and I need your fortunes to allow me to use my muscle. Personally, I don't have time for that galactic mumbo-jumbo that Shadox puts so much stock in, but he's always given me free rein to hit the enemy as hard as I like, so I'm prepared to let him get on with whatever stargazing he feels he has to do. And let's face it – the more stargazing he does, the more he vanishes from the public eye, making our power play all the easier.'

'You don't worry that Shadox, or Nox for that matter, could use his powers against you? Against us?'

'Admittedly, Shadox has truly frightening abilities, but he's losing the focus to use them instantly,' replied Bron. 'As for Nox, he's a skilled bodyguard, sure, but I've not seen anything from him to suggest he could survive a squad of my boys opening fire on him. And believe me, the lads are more than willing to do it.'

'Then we bide our time and speak no more of it. We must focus on the task at hand.' Rachel tapped her fingers together, nodding to herself as her thoughts took shape. 'We'll need Shadox and Nox onside until Doctor Davron can perfect his Synistrail collars. I don't fancy going up against the old man and his boy if they can control those diseased corpses, and we can't.'

'Wise move, those creatures are savage and unpredictable. I'll brief the troops on searching for this new threat in Vastrid. If it is Lomax, I suggest we do something to flush her out.'

Rachel's eyes lit up. 'Get some of your men to burn down a school in the slums. An infant school, during the day. Make sure the doors are sealed; we'll need fatalities. I'll get our media boys to run some news stories implicating "feared terrorist Kendra Lomax". If she is indeed hiding in the slums, she'll soon be hounded out, or else, the bereaved families will take care of her for us.'

Bron nodded in agreement. 'Plus, all the news reports and hours of angry mourning will distract the Vastridians in the days leading up to the repossession.'

Rachel turned to leave. She moved towards the door, then stopped and turned back to face the colonel.

'Oh, before I go, I must inform you that I'll be back again later tonight for a social visit, so please make sure you've finished cleaning your weapon by the time I arrive.'

In Caspian City, Callie had finished her long shift, and after completing her dreaded weekly grocery shop, was finally on her way home to relax in a hot bath.

As she walked, she thought about the incidents at the Grid. Firstly, there was that peculiar librarian boy, who had arrived looking like a nervous wreck and then gone on to pull off incredible feats of athletics and survival. Then there was the matter of the mechanical glitches that had smashed that poor candidate's leg. The Grid had been in use for as long as Callie could remember, and there had never been an accident or malfunction – she couldn't shake the feeling that something wasn't right. Before she could think about the events any further, she was distracted by a voice calling her name.

'Hey Callie', cried Tanya Masters, catching up and falling in step beside Callie. 'I think you were too busy to chat earlier.'

Before Callie could work out whether she had been told a statement or asked a question, Tanya spoke again. 'So I hear Prince Alistair has asked you to the ball?'

Tanya Masters was a fellow member of the Royal Guard and was known amongst her comrades for being the life and soul of the party. Callie liked her, but only in small measures, and she certainly wasn't in the mood for socialising after such a long day.

'He has indeed asked me,' replied Callie. 'That doesn't mean I've said yes, though.'

'Are you mad? You've knocked back the wealthiest, best looking and most desired bachelor in Vastrid.' Tanya's eyes widened in bemusement. 'What's wrong with you, girl? I'd say yes in an instant.'

'Well, if you like him so much, you're welcome to take him off my hands,' Callie said with a smile. 'I know he's good looking and successful. I know he can be kind and occasionally funny, in a dumb playboy kind of way, but I just don't have any romantic feelings toward him.'

'You'd only be going to the Debutante Ball with him,' laughed Tanya. 'You don't have to marry him.'

'I know, I know. I just don't see the point of starting something that I'll then have to finish.'

As if from nowhere, Prince Alistair suddenly joined Tanya and Callie in the street. Noticing the sudden silence and awkward look on the girls' faces, he went in with an opening gambit. 'I do believe my ears are burning. I guess Callie's telling you all about how I shall be taking her to the Ball?'

'Actually,' said Callie, 'I was just telling Tanya that I thought you and her would make a cute couple.'

Realising that he wasn't going to win Callie's heart anytime soon, Alistair decided to seize the opportunity to ask Tanya to the Ball instead. He hoped that seeing him with another girl might make Callie a little jealous and awaken the hidden feelings for him he was sure she had.

'A cute couple? I must agree,' said Alistair, reaching for Tanya's hand and laying a gentle kiss on it. 'I would be delighted if you would allow me to escort you to the Ball.'

Tanya squealed in delight, seemingly unaware or unconcerned with the fact that she was his second choice, and excitedly threw her arms around a suddenly terrified Prince Alistair.

Callie rolled her eyes and began to walk away, but before she was out of listening range, Prince Alistair yelled, 'Don't think for a minute that you now don't have to go to the Ball. I'll need you there on duty, as my bodyguard.'

Callie turned to face Alistair, still with Tanya draped all over him. 'A bodyguard? Don't worry,' she said, 'I'm sure that you don't need protecting from Tanya.'

'You'd better be there, Haywood. That's an order!' Alistair's voice echoed the street as Callie walked away, grinning to herself.

Chapter Seven

SHENANIGANS AT MURPHY'S

On the outskirts of Caspian City, Jayden Tyler sat by the bar at Murphy's, sipping her drink. She had been sitting alone for twenty minutes, waiting for her cousin Ryan to arrive. Looking down at the time on her cuff-linq, she disguised a disapproving tut with a sigh.

'Believe me, sweetheart, whoever it is, they ain't worth it,' said the barman in a voice that sounded smokey and worn.

'You may be right,' smiled Jayden, 'but it's not like that. I'm waiting for my cousin.'

The barman nodded, noticing traces of Jayden's slum-based childhood in her accent. 'Well, I hear cousins as sweethearts is all the rage where you come from, so forgive my mistake.'

Jayden decided to laugh along with the barman for a while, but he seemed to enjoy his joke much more than anyone else in the bar, so she grabbed her drink and moved to a seat by the window instead.

In the corner of Murphy's, a vid-screen was showing the evening Newscast, and by the look of concern on newscaster

Tobias McCloud's face, it was clear that something serious had occurred.

'Oi mate, turn it up, will ya?' cried a ruddy-faced man. His name was Lee Rudd, but he was known, for obvious reasons, as Ruddy.

The barman grumbled something about the holo-control being broken as he reached up to the screen and poked at the settings.

'Citizens of the Kemsley district are still reeling from the shock of an arson attack at a local preschool during lessons today. Many parents wait nervously for....'

Jayden, Ruddy and almost everybody else in the bar turned to pay attention to the news report. There were, however, two patrons who didn't seem interested. One sat at the far end of the bar, alone. The hood of a large rain-cloak covered their facial features, and they seemed oblivious to the shocking report, despite the volume of the video screen. Unfazed, they sat silently staring down through the steam that flowed from a coffee cup.

The other person was a young man with a short, stocky build. Unfortunately for the patrons of Murphy's, he was utterly unable to sit quietly. Dressed in a dark grey hooded top, he leapt from his barstool and motioned with a pointed finger towards the barman. 'No! No! No!' he cried. 'Anything but the bleakin' news! I mean, this is a bar, right? Not a bleakin' library or something. You've got SensualSound speakers here. Go to channel 45; I think they show the Star-cuties' Beckoning Show on Thursdays. Come on, let's set the mood! Some of us here are young and desirable and hoping to find a little magic in the night,' he glanced over at Jayden and threw a wink in her direction, which she was quick to deflect with a scowl.

A chorus of 'tuts', 'shushes', and cries of 'shut up' echoed around the bar.

'For goodness sake, Scudder, can't you just sit down and shut up for ten minutes of your life?' The barman glared at the young man.

'Alright! Settle down!' he replied. 'Firstly, my name is Key-C and secondly –'

Before he could finish speaking, the barman interrupted. 'Firstly, I don't care about the fake gang name you're so keen to go by; I know that your real name is Caleb Scudder. And secondly, I don't care what your secondly was going to be. Now sit down.'

Caleb Scudder retreated onto his stool as the patrons of Murphy's went back to watching the news report. As soon as they were distracted and the bar's atmosphere was one of calm concentration, Caleb ran back to the vid-screen, hitting the mute button.

Jumping up onto a stool, Caleb began again. 'And secondly, I know for a fact that the news is all faked-up anyhow. My cousin's mate saw the school on fire, but everyone escaped. Some homeless woman apparently turned up and smacked several shades of crimson out of the Corporation security. I bet they're only putting it on the news to frame her. You gotta be careful these days, what with the graphics and holograms and erm... stuff that they have.'

The patrons of Murphy's stared in silence before the sound of their communal anger at Caleb's declaration began to rise.

'Good lord Caleb you've tried to sell us some nonsense in the past, but this takes the biscuit,' snarled the barman.

'No, no, it's true!' Caleb pleaded, more than a little hurt that his revelation had inspired such hostility rather than making him appear intelligent and worldly.

'It's almost as good as the time he reckoned that he had a chip in his head that stopped him swearing,' another punter added, nodding sagely.

'I do! I do! There is a chip in my bleakin' head,' said Caleb,' which is why I say bleakin' instead of b-b-bleakin'.'

'Swearing? What's swearing?' asked Ruddy.

'You know, like how they used to talk before the Savior War.' The barman cleared his throat. 'Like, "How do you futting do? I can't believe there's a bladdy man walking on the moon".'

The patrons fell about laughing.

'No, no,' said Caleb, 'that isn't what swearing is about at all.'

'Why would anyone want to talk like that anyhow? It makes you sound like an idiot.' Ruddy shook his head. 'Anyhow, why would the royals pay all that money to put chips in people's heads?'

'They don't like people like us swearing; they reckon it makes us too rowdy,' Caleb explained. 'Oh, and it wasn't the royals who put the chip in my head. It was the Shadox Corporation.'

'The people who make vid-screens?' The whole of Murphy's filled with the sound of people mocking and jeering. As Caleb tried in vain to settle the noise and put his point across, Ryan walked in and edged his way through the crowd until he found Jayden.

He slung his bag on the empty chair and slumped down opposite her.

'I take it the Grid didn't go well then.'

Ryan brushed his hair from his eyes and sat back with a sigh. 'It went ok, I suppose. I sort of passed.'

'Sort of passed?' asked Jayden. 'How do you mean, sort of passed?'

'Well, I was doing good until a door shut on another candidate's leg. I had to rescue –'

'Please, Ryan,' said Jayden gently, reaching forward and

taking his hand. 'I'm your cousin; we grew up together. There's no need.'

Ryan jolted back, offended. 'I'm not making this up! The wall started closing and wouldn't stop.'

'My dear cousin, the Grid has not injured a single person since it was brought in as a test over a decade ago. It's ok to admit that you didn't manage to pass it. I didn't pass first time; it takes most people two attempts.'

An uneasy silence followed before Ryan spoke again. 'Well, believe me or not, I've got a six month trial with the Guards.'

Jayden leapt up and hugged him. 'That's great news!'

'Hardly,' sighed Ryan, 'I'm still going to be on the same pay.'

'Pay? Who cares about the pay? This means that you get to come to the Debutante Ball.'

'Settle down, Jayden; I'm not going to any Debutante Ball, so you can scrub any ideas you may have about setting me up with one of your scary friends.'

A huge grin emerged on Jayden's face. 'Ha! Dearest cousin, what you don't seem to know is that a newly appointed member of the Royal Guard has to honour their first formal invitation.'

'Or?' sighed an already-defeated Ryan.

'Or you get suspended from duty and fined for being disloyal to Vastrid.'

'Ok, I'll go,' Ryan sulked. 'But don't expect me to do any dancing.'

'Oh, it's also deemed treason not to dance.'

'Really?' asked Ryan, his eyes widening in panic.

'Oh yes, you'd get fined for not dancing,' said Jayden, before bringing her drink to her lips and muttering, 'probably.'

Ryan looked over towards the edge of the bar. The vid-screen showing the Newscast was still losing the fight to be heard over Caleb Scudder's attempts to explain his conspiracy theories to a sea of heckling faces.

'Look! Look at this!' demanded Caleb, drawing people's attention back to the vid-screen. The news report was now showing footage from a security camera, in which a woman with an athletic build and long unkempt hair could be seen breaking into the school and setting the fire. The voiceover explained that the footage had been restored by The Shadox Corporation's top digital lab due to fire damage.

'See! See?' Caleb shouted, wagging his index finger at the screen and searching the crowd's faces for a reaction.

'Yeah, what of it?' scowled the barman.

'Can't you see? The footage is clearly faked. All schools are sponsored and funded by the Shadox Corporation, right? So they'd surely get their security cameras from Shadox too.' Caleb stared at the barman, whose expression remained unchanged. Caleb continued. 'Shadox security products are pretty much indestructible. They'd easily withstand a fire that happened metres away from the lens.'

Ryan was watching with great interest and wondered if this mouthy stranger may have a point. Some of the punters standing around Caleb began to mutter in reluctant agreement. Ruddy, however, disagreed. He peered closely at Caleb. 'How comes you know so much about Shadox security products?'

The barman raised an eyebrow and replied before Caleb could. 'Oh, if anyone knows about security systems, it'd be him. Caleb Scudder is infamous in some sectors of the slums for being quite the thief.'

'Oh, that's unfair,' protested Caleb. 'I've never stolen anything from anyone's home, ever.'

'No, you haven't,' the barman agreed, 'but you've certainly aided those who have.'

'I'm simply a locksmith who hasn't always screened his customers very well,' said Caleb, his voice trailing off as he saw the barman staring at the Commerce Box behind the bar, which was now open and empty.

'Scudder!' bellowed the barman. 'All the takings are gone. This is your doing – come here!'

'Well! I don't have to put up with allegations like those.' Caleb glanced around the bar for support and found none. 'I'm off. Goodnight.' He hopped from the stool he had been standing on and fled out the door, the barman hot on his heels.

Jayden nudged Ryan. 'Come on, soldier, let's go and arrest your first troublemaker.' Both grabbed their jackets and took off after Scudder and the barman.

Ruddy turned to address the other punters. 'So I'm guessing that Scudder was the distraction and the actual thief is still in here.' The clutch of people by the vid-screen all muttered in agreement and looked each other over.

'She's been very quiet,' said a tall man with a scar across his chin.

He motioned towards the figure in the rain cloak who, until this point, had been all but forgotten.

The mob approached the stranger. 'Yeah, you've been very quiet, ain'tcha? Just who are you, anyhow?'

'I'm just someone trying to enjoy a hot cup of coffee during a cold stretch of night.' The hooded stranger stared down at the cup. 'I appreciate your concerns about the landlord's takings, but if you are keen to employ some mob justice on a petty crook, I suggest you start with him.'

The hooded stranger lifted their arm and stretched it out, pointing an index finger directly at the tall man with the scar on his chin.

The accused man pulled out a knife and hissed, 'You shoulda kept quiet, hobo'.

He charged forward, ready to strike, only to feel his arm caught tightly in a clenched fist below the cloak and then thrown hard against the wall of Murphy's.

The crowd stared in shocked silence for a moment before Ruddy turned to the figure and spoke. 'You shouldn't have done that, stranger. This is our bar, and we don't take kindly to outsiders declaring the rules.'

'What? So he steals from your beloved barman, and I'm a villain for noticing? Really? As there's no benefit in arguing with numbskulls, I apologise.' The hooded figure stood up and faced the mob. 'So then, can I go? Or does anyone else have a problem with a stranger drinking in this bar?'

Ruddy shook his head angrily and gathered the mob. 'Ok guys, let's show this tramp how we do things here.'

A block away from Murphy's, Ryan and Jayden had lost all trace of the barman and Caleb. Jayden sat on a low wall, catching her breath.

'Hey Ry, do you know what that slum-rat claimed his name was?'

Ryan looked at her with a smile. 'No, what was his handle?'

'He called himself Key-C!' she laughed. 'Those rats really are running out of stupid names. Oh well, not much else we can do tonight, cousin. Shall we just go home?'

Ryan nodded. The news about having to attend the Debutante Ball had left his body and mind consumed by unhelpful feelings of dread and exhaustion.

The Tyler cousins walked back past Murphy's, unaware that a bar brawl was occurring inside.

They were just out of earshot when Ruddy's body crashed through the bar's front window and landed with a thump and a groan on the paved street outside.

Back inside, the hooded stranger stood alone beside the twitching and unconscious bodies of the bar's patrons, staring at the news report. A holographic image flashed onto the screen.

'...*digital artists have managed to create from reconstructed security footage retrieved from the scene.*'

The face in the picture was that of a woman. Long, wild hair framed her features, which were worn from years of combat and alcohol abuse.

'*We are urging the public to use extreme caution and not approach the suspect, who is believed to be infamous terrorist Kendra Lomax*'.

The hooded stranger turned and walked to the exit, each step crunching through broken glass scattered across the floor.

'Looks nothing like me.'

Chapter Eight

AS THE PAST CATCHES UP

The hefty wooden doors of the Royal Palace's study swung open, startling King William from his thoughts.

'Father!' Alistair bellowed as he strode towards him, his arms outstretched. 'What a pleasure it is to see you on this fine morning.'

The monarch of Vastrid shuffled in his chair, trying to find the words to use. Despite his expertise and experience in finding the right words for the right occasion, he was struggling. The burden of his time in service to the Shadox Corporation and the inevitable repercussions of his change of heart revealed itself in the crow's feet that adorned his sad, anxious eyes. 'Ali, please sit down. I need to speak to you about something important.'

'It's ok, all the arrangements for tonight's ball have been made,' interrupted Alistair, oblivious to his father's sombre manner. 'Everything is going to plan. Tomorrow night will be a fabulous celebration of Vastrid's young.'

'No, my son, I don't want to talk about tomorrow's ball. If anything, we should perhaps cancel it.'

Alistair stopped abruptly and frowned. 'What? You can't

cancel the ball. It's a tradition. Think of the broken hearts of our people.'

'Please, you must listen to me.' The old man's voice was reduced to a near-whisper. Alistair pulled a chair towards the desk and sat down, leaning forwards to hear his father.

'I've made some terrible mistakes in my life. After the war, Maxwell Shadox urged me to be the monarch of Vastrid. At first, I was unsure whether I wanted to be the figurehead of a brave new world. I was scared of the responsibility that came with being the man in charge of rebuilding civilisation. Shadox told me that I'd be fine, that I should follow his lead and promote his actions in a favourable light to our people. For years it seemed to work, but I put too much trust into the Shadox Corporation. I would give an inch, and they would take a mile. I trusted them when they persuaded me to neutralise dissidents on the outer world colonies. I trusted them when they said the Sentry was a threat, and our troops supported Shadox's efforts to wipe them out. Now I sit here powerless, forced to take orders from Rachel Stone, and belittled by threats from Nox. In the time it's taken me to wake up, they've built up an army that's twice the size of ours. We're now powerless to fight back. I've led our people into a cul-de-sac, and I'm struggling to find a way out. I have so much guilt I can't shed − there's blood on my hands. The only way I could cleanse my soul was to confess everything and send the evidence to the chief revolutionaries in the hope that the hidden truths I know about the rise of Shadox may help them overthrow his Corporation's stranglehold on the galaxy.'

The colour had drained from Prince Alistair's face. He glanced down at his hands, which were gripping the arms of the chair. He'd always believed that his father was a war hero and a champion of the people. The image of his father as a man that had built the kingdom of Vastrid from scratch, implemented a new era of civilisation and seen off destructive threats from non-conforming colony dwellers, synistrails and the Sentry was shattered.

'Alistair,' the king waited for his son to look up and nodded at him softly. 'I will be assassinated soon. I know too much, and my dissatisfaction with Shadox is clear. Don't fear for me or mourn me. Should I die, at least I shall go to the grave knowing that despite the blinkers I wore for too many years, I tried to do right at the end. I'm afraid that this will leave the redemption of our family name and the kingdom of Vastrid to you, my son. It will be up to you to lead humanity against Stone, Nox and Shadox – if he's still alive. I haven't spoken to him directly in years; as far as I can tell, nobody has. Son, all the info you will need is hidden in the computer in our section of the contingency cavern. Genetic profiling along with palm print and retina scanning can access the data. It's important that you keep yourself safe and out of trouble. The kingdom will need you.'

'Father, I will not fail you.' Alistair rose to his feet, trying to hide his shock and upset behind a dutiful stance. 'If you should fall, I will protect your dream of a new civilisation away from the Corporation's control.'

'Ali, you've been a good son, and you'll make a great leader. I'm very proud of you.'

Alistair bowed to his father. 'Thank you, but the credit belongs to you. I am the product of your raising, after all.'

As he turned to leave, Alistair paused and turned back to his father. 'And the Debutante Ball?'

The King looked up with a sad smile, 'Oh go on then, the ball is still on. Who's the lucky girl this year?'

Alistair glanced at his reflection in a glass cabinet. 'They all are.'

On Shadox VI, a trooper began to back away slowly from

the escalating volume of his superior's angry voice. This aggressive barking of dissatisfaction was Colonel Bron's immediate reaction to the news that the mission to burn down a school had failed.

The skin across Bron's knuckles strained white as he clenched the Sergeant's throat, pinning him against a wall. The entire squad, battered and bloodied, had been summoned by the colonel for the mission debrief.

Bron spoke slowly, leaning into the less swollen side of the Sergeant's face. 'What do you mean it didn't go to plan?'

'W-w-ell,' he stammered, 'we were about to light the fuses, but.... but... .'

'Go on,' ordered Bron.

'But suddenly, someone in a rain cloak just appeared from nowhere and threw us all over the place.'

'And you just let this happen?' Bron barked.

'No sir, we went into attack formation 4Q as per protocol, but – '

'But what?' Bron clenched his fist tighter as the Sergeant's eyes widened in panic, his speech reduced to gurgles.

'She had a bo-staff, sir.'

Bron turned to the squad as a young trooper limped forwards and spoke.

'Yeah, a bo-staff. Well, she came at us with it, twirling it all over the place. It seemed to have this light surrounding it whenever she swung it around fast.' Bron released the gasping Sergeant and slowly paced a few steps away from the squad.

'It can't be,' he muttered to himself. 'Not after all these years. It can't be.'

'Sir,' continued the trooper, suddenly feeling more confi-dent as Bron looked increasingly anxious, 'before we knew what hit us, me and the lads were scrambling back to our feet, all beaten and bloodied. We had no choice – Serg ordered us to retreat.'

They were interrupted by the sound of slow, sarcastic clapping. Mr Nox emerged from the shadows with a huge grin on his face.

'Well, well Bron,' he said, 'your boys are quite the heroes, aren't they?'

Bron was too angry to even look at Nox's smug face, let alone dignify his taunts with a response. Realising that Bron wouldn't play along, Nox turned his attention to the Sergeant.

'What's your name, Sergeant?' asked Nox in a lighthearted manner.

'Sergeant Dollis, sir,' he replied, his voice hoarse. 'It's an honour to see you down here, sir. I must apologise for our failure today, sir.'

'Apology accepted. Life is all about surprises. So this stick-waving lunatic, was she a tough woman to be in combat against?'

'Indeed she was, sir', answered Dollis. 'Like we said, she was waving this bo-staff around, and it was deflecting our bullets. Plus, she was so fast we didn't have time to know what was going on.'

'Sounds like a difficult and unexpected challenge,' replied Nox. 'Why did you retreat so easily? Did you panic?'

Sergeant Dollis nodded along frantically. 'Well, in a situation like that, it's easy to lose your head – '

Nox drew his sword and decapitated Sergeant Dollis with one swift slice.

'Indeed it is,' he smirked, his eyes glowing a sinister shade of crimson.

Dollis' headless body fell limply to the floor as his head rolled towards the cowering squadron.

'Clean up that mess and get out of my sight,' Nox sneered at the troopers before glancing down at the headless torso and muttering to himself, 'Dollis? What a stupid name.'

'You didn't need to do that.' Bron snapped as he hurried to catch up with Nox in the corridor outside.

'Oh, but I did have to do it, Colonel Bron,' declared Nox proudly. 'I promised myself that if he relayed the story to me and said that he lost his head, then I would slice off his noggin and make some witty aside.'

Nox paused for thought before declaring, 'Admittedly, I did manipulate the conversation to make him say it, but all is fair in love and failed arson missions.'

'I don't buy into your supposed manipulation skills,' growled Bron. 'You claim you can control the world with your words, but it becomes clearer to me every day that your ego and abilities are nothing more than a blight on the Corporation's mission.'

Nox smiled, a flash of red lighting his eyes again.'Bron, I could make you my puppet in seconds, but honestly, your often-monosyllabic, angry little critiques of my work give me a strange sense of satisfaction.'

'I hope that you get all the satisfaction you can take when you finally prove your heritage by eliminating Kendra Lomax,' Bron snarled. 'That is *if* you're able to defeat her.'

'The question is not if I can defeat her, but how soon?' Nox was focusing now on his sword, wiping the blood from the blade and placing it carefully back in its sheath. He looked up at Bron.

'You see, the big, big difference between you, your men and me is that I don't fear that woman. The myth of Kendra Lomax is just that; a myth, a fairy tale, folklore. When all the ghost stories are through, and Ms Lomax feels the harsh reality of both my blade and my fury, then we shall see that Mr Shadox was correct in his patronage of me.'

Bron's voice shook with fury. 'Afraid? How dare you claim I'm afraid of her? I don't need to remind you of my history with Lomax. I had her at my mercy once. I could've slaughtered her. I could've finished all of this Sentry nonsense off there and then, but I had my orders. And the fact I carried out those orders are the reason why you're standing here in front of me today.'

Nox had enough self-awareness to know the role a brawl between Bron and Lomax a generation ago had played in his legacy but was damned if he'd give Bron any credit.

'Forgetting Kendra Lomax for a moment, we should agree on a strategy for tomorrow night. I feel the situation is too risky for us to allow the Hawthornes to live. If they should escape our custody and return to Vastrid, they could win the support of the public and lead the peasants into rebelling against us.'

'Very true,' answered Bron, 'but imagine the control the Corporation could harness if we were to capture them in one piece. Manipulated images for the media; enforced confessions. The repossession of Vastrid could be explained and receive support from the public instantly.'

Nox shook his head. 'No. They must be slaughtered, and that's an order.'

'Well, if it's an order, it's an order.' Bron shrugged lightly and turned to leave.

'Colonel Bron.' Nox stopped him. He knew Bron well enough to be suspicious when he backed down easily. 'We take them out quickly and hidden by confusion. While any member of the royal family lives, we risk a lengthy and inconvenient war that wouldn't be cost-effective for the Corporation.'

Bron strolled away from Nox, a smile breaking across his face. 'A lengthy and inconvenient war? Well, we wouldn't want that now, would we?'

Chapter Nine

BAKER'S END: ENTRANCES & EXITS

Through a damp, musty alleyway in the Vastrid district of Kemsley, the slouched figure of Caleb Scudder edged towards a fence made of corrugated iron. The barrier divided the ill-reputed area of Kemsley and the lawless ghetto of Baker's End. He glanced around to ensure that he hadn't been followed before dragging a wooden crate toward the fence.

Hopping up onto the crate, Caleb hoisted himself over and landed clumsily on the other side. He dusted himself off and took a long look around at the tin huts, bonfires and barking dogs that made Baker's End a less-than savoury place to visit, let alone live.

'Oh well,' he said to himself with a heavy sigh, 'there's no place like home, I guess.'

Despite the failings of Baker's End, Caleb was glad to be there. His recent criminal forays on the outskirts of Caspian City had been a four-day-long disaster culminating in the bungled robbery at Murphy's earlier that evening.

He had thought he was onto a winner for sure. All he had to do was distract everyone while the guy he met from another bungled robbery the night before did the tricky part of stealing the money. The plan was to split the cash an hour later, after which Caleb hoped to be enjoying a nice, long nap in a warm hotel bed. Instead, he ended up running for his freedom from an angry barkeeper and two Royal Guards who, Caleb had quickly realised, were far fitter than he was. His knowledge of various shortcuts and hiding places had saved him this time, but he had to wonder how much longer he could live like this.

Caleb sighed and looked up as he passed the row of tin huts where his cousins lived. They were far better equipped to deal with life in the underworld. They hit their victims hard and with malice and enjoyed using their power to rob and hurt people. They would operate locally in the slums to keep a steady income generated through fear and bullying. Caleb preferred to target the city, where people were too distracted by the lights and their busy lifestyles to realise what they might miss. A more introspective thief could waste hours pondering whether this gave them a moral high ground or whether such tactics were born out of cowardice. Still, Caleb wasn't one for navel-gazing at the best of times and right about now, he just wanted to sleep.

Caleb yawned and stretched out his tired body as he walked, imagining how sweet it was going to be to rest his head on a pillow, bring a blanket over his body and shut out the noise of Baker's End. As he approached the door of his shack, his daydreaming was interrupted when he noticed his oldest half-brother Lee standing in the doorframe.

A shot of despair hit the pit of Caleb's stomach. Although his cousins were bad, his four half-brothers and two half-sisters were worse. They had grown beyond simple thievery and torment and were now more concerned with controlling the crime that occurred in the slums. They also had little tolerance for Caleb's unique approach to the lifestyle. Caleb knew that Lee's presence in his doorway could only be bad news.

'Evening, little bruv,' Lee smiled. Caleb gazed at Lee and wondered, not for the first time, how he managed to convey such malice in his expression.

'Lee! What a pleasure and surprise. I'm guessing that you need to have a word with me.'

Lee put his arm around Caleb and led him into the shack. 'Oh, little bruv. Unluckily for you, it ain't me that you'll be having a word with.'

Caleb peered into his shack and saw a barely-lit group of figures standing around the shadowed outline of a seated woman in the centre of the room. As Caleb edged forward, the shadowy figure became recognisable to him and said in a croaked voice, 'Well, well, look what the cat dragged in.'

The colour drained from Caleb's face.'Oh my, Mother Scudder!'

Mother Scudder leaned forward, maintaining eye contact with Caleb. She had a thick mane of smoky yellow hair that framed her worn face in its own unique style. In her hand, a solid steel cane. Mother Scudder's cane was an artefact of legend in Baker's End; she used it to help her walk, which was ironic considering the number of people she'd crippled with it over the years.

'Welcome 'ome son,' cackled Mother Scudder. 'Now, please tell me that you've made your old mum proud and brought a little something for the family pot?'

Caleb looked around for some form of escape, but he was cornered. Every inch of his shack was filled with family members, all of whom glared at him with venomous contempt.

'Erm, my dearest mother. I did have some jobs lined up, but I was let down – let down by other people, you understand. I escaped two Royal Guards today, and well, I'm not much of a thief anyhow; more of a locksmith. I can unlock anything you want, but....'

Mother Scudder pounded the floor with her cane, not only silencing Caleb but also making him jump back in fear.

'Caleb, it's quite a simple question, even for you,' she croaked in a hushed tone. 'I wanna know; do you 'ave anything for the family pot?'

With his hands quivering, Caleb fished about in his pockets and finally held up fifty Vastrid credits in crinkled, dirty notes.

'What's that supposed to be?' hissed Mother Scudder, her glare burning into Caleb's frightened eyes.

'My contribution,' he whispered, 'for the family pot.'

Without warning and with a viper's speed, Mother Scudder whacked his hand with her cane, causing the crumpled notes to fly into the air before falling tattily to the ground. Caleb yelped in pain and grabbed his injured hand screaming, 'BLEAK!' several times.

'Watch your language in front of mother,' spat Lee, pushing the staggering Caleb back into the centre of the room.

'I've got a chip in my head; all I ever do is watch my language,' Caleb cried. 'Although I don't actually watch it as such - I mean, it doesn't take any effort, or does it? Perhaps I'd be better at other stuff if my mind didn't have a chip to work around all the time. But then again – '

'Shud Up!' Mother Scudder snapped, cutting him short. She looked him up and down, her mouth curled into a sneer. 'You've failed us again.'

'But I offered that money,' pleaded Caleb.

Mother Scudder leant forward. 'True, but how did you get it? Gambling, I'd bet.'

Caleb laughed at his mother's pun. 'Haha, I get it. Gambling, bet – classic!' His demeanour suddenly changed back to one of cowardice as an unamused Mother Scudder raised her cane.

'OK, I see, it wasn't meant to be a joke. But no matter how I got the money, it's still money, ain't it?'

'Oh, but it does matter,' said Mother Scudder, slowly rising to her feet. 'This is Baker's End, boy. This is where the League of Thieves rule and thrive. We are the Scudders - the royalty of all scoundrels. What we don't have, we steal. What we don't want, we steal and then destroy. And that's the problem, Caleb; you ain't ever stolen anything.'

Lee stepped forward. 'You're bringing our family's bad name into good repute. If we all died tomorrow, the family name, Scudder, would mean nothing but idiot locksmiths. Our bloodline ain't survived since before the war just to be known as locksmiths.'

Caleb stared down at the ground, willing their scorn to end so he could draw this disastrous day to a close and get some rest.

Mother Scudder spoke. 'With that in mind, Caleb, we're casting you out. Out of Baker's End, and out of the family.'

'What? You can't cast me out,' Caleb cried. He looked around, but the stony faces on his kin were as much evidence as an 'idiotic locksmith' would need to prove that they could indeed cast him out and intended to do so. Caleb decided to let them sleep on it and try to come up with a plan during the night to win them back around.

'OK, fair enough, I'll be gone by morning,' he shrugged his shoulders and began to move towards his bed, only to feel Lee's fist punch him hard and fast in the cheek. Floored and dazed, Caleb crawled forward.

'You're out tonight, my boy,' cackled Mother Scudder, 'and don't come back until you've stolen something. Something that money can't buy. Something the family can use; a weapon, a Royal Guard I.D, something that'll make your old mum proud.'

'But where will I go? I'll need money,' pleaded Caleb, 'and the Royal Guards are after me.'

'Not our problem,' Mother Scudder shrugged before grabbing Caleb by the front of his hooded top and pulling him close. 'And if we see you again without something to redeem yourself, Lee will have no choice but to wipe you out of our family tree for good.'

Without a moment's hesitation, Lee picked Caleb up and hurled him out of the shack, sending him crashing into the rain and mud outside. Caleb cried out in shock and then looked back through the open door at Mother Scudder's cold expression. A tear ran down his cheek as he spoke. 'But you're my mother.'

Mother Scudder walked to the front of the shack and gazed out at the driving rain before glancing down at Caleb again. 'True, but you're not my only son.'

And with that, the Scudders' closed the door of Caleb's shack, leaving him with no other option than to walk out into the night with nothing. Wiping his eyes and trying to steady his breath, Caleb looked up into the late-night sky for inspiration. There weren't any stars, and there wasn't any magic. There was just trash and filthy gutters and rain pounding down on him, forcing his head to face towards the muddy turf.

A more introspective thief may be inclined to spend hours on end weighing up if this was to be their lot in life. Pondering whether they would ever get to see stars and magic or if they would be forever trapped in poverty, lamenting the skills and characteristics that didn't come naturally to them. Caleb, however, wasn't one for navel-gazing at the best of times and right about now, he just wanted to sleep.

· · ·

As Caleb left Baker's End, wading through mud and trash, another person involved in the brawl at Murphy's hopped past him over the rattling iron roofs of the shanty huts. The mysterious woman in the rain cloak bounced from one plat-form to the next with an uneasy mix of grace and heft; her footsteps all but drowned out by the sound of rain hammering on the roofs.

As the figure leapt from the last remaining roof in Baker's End and landed on the better side of a fence into the neigh-bouring borough of Swanstree, she let out a sigh of relief.

'I don't know what's louder: the sound of you thumping from one roof to the next or the sound of you catching your breath,' said an elderly man standing in a doorway nearby.

'After all these years, Calvin, I thought you'd be glad to see me.'

'I've seen too much of you on the news lately to be feeling nostalgic,' Calvin replied. 'You'd better come in, Lomax. We have much to discuss.'

Kendra lowered the hood of her rain cloak and entered Calvin McGuire's small living quarters. Calvin busied himself shuffling pieces of paper aside, making room for his guest. Once he had cleared space, he gestured for Kendra to sit down and asked, 'Something to drink?' As soon as the words had left his mouth, his expression darkened, and he awkwardly straightened himself. 'Tea perhaps, or water?'

Kendra ran her hands through her short, scruffy hair and then over her face. 'Calvin, how many more years do I have to stay dry to convince you that my drinking isn't a problem anymore?'

'Lomax, you know it isn't just the drinking; it's you. The self-pity, the excuses, the lack of ability. I think of all the blessed that died while you of all people survived, and it breaks my heart. What have you achieved in the past fifteen years?'

spent the past decade and a half receiving
from Calvin, but they hadn't lost their ability
steadied herself before presenting her case.

I've tried to do my bit. I was the youngest of
; I wasn't meant to be left here alone to take on
everything the Dark Lethe could throw at us. I'm still not
ready now, let alone back then.'

'Yet more excuses,' Calvin sighed. 'I wish I had been
blessed with the gifts from the Tide like you were. I believed
in everything the Sentry stood for. I'd at least have made sure
that the boy was on course to fulfil his destiny.'

'This is where you and I will always differ. Who says that
he must sacrifice everything to follow a bunch of old folk's
delusions?' Kendra got up from her seat and began to pace
the tiny living room. 'They grumbled about the world ending
before, and life goes on. I'm not saying that things are good at
the moment or that what's happening is right. But the boy
doesn't know any better. Can't I just let him live in ignorance
rather than ask him to give his life for our cause?' Lomax
turned to look at Calvin, her face searching for answers to
questions she had asked herself a million times.

'Lomax, come here,' Calvin said, beckoning her to the
kitchen window. 'Look out over the estate, look deep into the
shadows, and you will see.'

Kendra squinted into the darkness and saw torsos jittering
with movements she recognised all too well.

'Synistrails,' she sighed.

'And lots of them. Too many for you to take on alone,
especially at your age. They thrive in areas like these: the
areas occupied by the poor, the areas left alone by the
pampered Royal Guard. Of course, as the number of their
victims increases, so does the number of their kind. They are
slowly but surely on course to becoming the dominant species
in this district.' Calvin shook his head and turned to Kendra.

'Shadox and Nox will soon have an army of these creatu_ control and destroy human resistance to the Lethe.'

Before Kendra could respond, the sound of breaking glass and a man screaming interrupted them. A sea of hissing echoed the estate, and Kendra and Calvin ran outside into the eerie fog and darkness.

They stood together and listened. Amongst the hissing came the anguished sound of the man's increasingly desperate screams. Calvin closed his eyes and held his hand up, signalling Kendra to wait while he tried to determine which direction the sounds came from before pointing towards a narrow alleyway. Kendra sprinted ahead, just in time to catch a glimpse of the man's legs on the ground, disappearing into the darkness. She pulled out her bo-staff and ran towards him, only to find herself shrouded in fog as the sounds of the man's screaming, his body being dragged, and Synistrail hissing reached a piercing crescendo.

Disorientated from the lack of light and escalating sounds, Kendra fell to her knees. As she collapsed on the ground, the screaming stopped, the hissing faded, and finally, the sound of the dragging disappeared into the night.

'Do you see?' said Calvin minutes later, once Kendra had joined him back inside. 'This war we've been fighting for a generation is coming to its resolution, and the boy is too late. I believe he has been accepted into the Royal Guards, despite my advice?'

'How do you know about that?' Kendra snapped.

'I may not have a bo-staff or otherworldly abilities, but I have my sources and my ways. As I said, Kendra, the Tide should have blessed me. As an aide, I am forbidden to become involved physically; my oath decrees that I leave the hands-on stuff to those that have been blessed. If it weren't for that oath, I would take this matter out of your clumsy hands in an instant.'

'I'm sure you would,' replied Kendra. 'I did all I could to make sure he stayed in the library. I tried to sabotage the Grid, but it seems they've still offered him a trial. I overheard him talking to his cousin at Murphy's. He's going to the Debutante Ball tomorrow night.'

'You must find him there tomorrow and ensure that he doesn't fall in with the Guards. Through cruel circumstance, we've already lost the girl to them. If we lose the boy, then we cannot win this war.'

Calvin paused deep in thought before leaning in close and laying his final card on the table. 'Needless to say, you have a separate interest which a blessed apprentice may help you finally resolve.'

As smug and irritating as Calvin was, Kendra knew that the plan of watching and waiting would now have to become one of action. 'Calvin, you're right. I shall find him tomorrow and lead him to his destiny.'

Calvin drew a circle in the air with the forefinger on his right hand. 'Blessing you, Kendra Lomax.'

Kendra rolled her eyes. 'C'mon, are we still doing this Sentry kinship stuff after all these years?'

She received the answer to her question through the hurt look on Calvin's face and thought it couldn't hurt in the troubled times they were facing. Kendra smiled and made the same gesture.

'Blessing you, Calvin. I'll see you around.'

Kendra slipped out of the front door and disappeared into the night. Calvin sat down in his easy chair and turned off the lights. Alone in the dark, he listened to the tragedies of the night unfold in the side streets and alleyways outside. The smile on his face that had said farewell to Kendra slowly morphed into a frail frown. He pulled a blanket over his body and could only hope that the boy the Sentry had put so much faith into could bring an end to all this sorrow.

Chapter Ten

BAD NIGHT AT JENKINS

'It's dreadful, truly dreadful,' cried Callie from behind a changing room curtain.

She had been persuaded by Tanya Masters to 'wear something nice' to the Debutante Ball. Her outfit last year, consisting of terrain boots, flight jeans and a sleeveless t-shirt, hadn't been well received by senior staff at the palace. Only her exemplary track record with the Guards had saved her from facing a sterner disciplinary.

Tanya had also persuaded Prince Alistair to ensure that Raynard, the head tailor of a boutique called Jenkins', open the store much later than usual so that Callie could have a private fitting before her next shift began. As well as being the official supplier of Vastrid Guards uniforms, Jenkins' offered well-regarded tailoring and dressmaking services. With the clock about to strike eleven p.m, it had taken the promise of an extremely generous tip from the Prince to convince Raynard to do so.

Raynard was a fussy, middle-aged man with a bossy demeanour that hinted at a class and grace level far above his actual social standing. Raynard prided himself on his appearance and was never seen in anything less than immaculately tailored clothes, with both the hair on his head and the pencil-thin moustache above his top lip straightened and styled with fierce accuracy.

Many of Jenkins' customers had received a barbed comment on their appearance or an unexpected critique of their manners during Raynard's tenure. Ever graceful, his venom was hidden in the light tone of his voice, while his flowery vocabulary often left his customers unsure if they should be offended or not.

On this occasion, he would have loved to have vented his frustration at the annoying girls who had spent the past hour discussing his stock in great detail. However, with the heir to the throne in his store, he found himself biting his tongue.

Luckily, Raynard had a handy whipping boy to take his frustrations out on in the form of his storeroom assistant Spillet, and just as the verbal back and forth between Tanya and Callie increased in volume, the sound of boxes crashing to the ground drowned everything out.

'Spillet!' screamed Raynard, 'You clumsy buffoon, do I really have to go back there and teach you how to stack?'

Raynard tutted and re-adjusted his hair before taking a deep breath and spinning on his heels to refocus his attention on the customers.

'I hate it!' Callie said, still behind the curtain.

'I'm sure it looks beautiful,' assured Tanya. 'Ali, please tell Callie to stop being so shy.'

In theory, Alistair had tagged along with the girls to buy his outfit for the ball as well, but in reality, it was just an excuse to spend more time with Callie. She was such a beguiling mystery; the conversations they shared stayed with him, and life around her felt like a fresh start - as if the world around him had grown to be something more than his duties and privileges.

Of course, that's not to say that he wasn't also attracted to Tanya, though this was in a more conventional way for the Prince. He certainly found her physically attractive and easy to be around, but the Prince knew from experience that his interest could not always be held for long. A fleeting romance with Tanya might ruin any chance he had with Callie for good. But Tanya did seem keen, and Alistair was in the mood for courtship. Alistair enjoyed the distraction of weighing up both sides.

Throughout the shopping trip, his mind had been preoccupied with his father's recent confession to him. Alistair would typically deal with troubling news by ignoring it and instead focusing on a glory within his reach; in this case, to further romance the girls arguing about dresses. However, chances for flirtations increasingly passed him by as his mind kept drifting back to revelations of Vastrid's secret history and the potential threat of an attack from the Shadox Corporation.

As the girls continued their somewhat circular conversation behind him, Alistair let out a heavy-hearted sigh and did something that always helped him let off steam – he threw a hard and fast boxing jab and let it connect with the chest plate of his servant, who he'd brought along to carry the shopping home.

The servant staggered back a little way before losing his balance and falling to the floor. He was odd in appearance; his skin was a hybrid of light brown and orange that had faded over the years. His eyes seemed to take in everything, and yet the lack of expression or reaction on his face created an eerie distance in his general manner.

'Whoah-yeah!' hollered Alistair. 'That was a good one.' He looked down at his servant and asked, 'Probot, report - what was the speed and instantaneous force?

'Speed equalled 39.377 kilometres per hour. Estimated impact force equalled 453.581 kilograms', Probot reported.

The sound of Probot's fall distracted Tanya, who broke off from persuading Callie that she looked good in her dress and approached the pair with a look of disgust on her face. 'I don't know why you brought that thing along,' she said to Alistair. 'It totally gives me the creeps.'

'Which is why they didn't sell,' Alistair nodded. 'Oh, and then, of course, there were the astronomical retail costs. I was sent this one when they first launched. Can't say that I've ever bothered to learn how to program the thing, but it's good to have around for carrying, cleaning and, of course, punching.'

'But look at him - that wavy hair and the creepy paint job on his skin. And the way he just keeps staring.' Tanya shuddered, and Alistair threw his arm over her shoulder and laughed.

'Indeed, he isn't the best looking chap, but you know, at the end of the day, despite it being expensive and occasionally useful, it's just a toy.'

'Just as well,' Tanya scoffed. 'Looking like that, I don't think he'd have much luck at the ball.'

Alistair and Tanya laughed as Probot stared at them impassively. Beyond his blank stare, every detail of every moment was being monitored and recorded. If they had asked, he could have told them the pitch and decibel reading of their laughter, he could have recited every word of their mockery, and he could have even suggested wittier insults. But they never asked, so he never told.

Alistair and Tanya were still laughing when they heard a loud, 'AHEM!' behind them. They both turned around to see Callie in her final choice of gown.

'Well, will this do?' Callie snapped. 'Please say yes, I had a long shift today, and I've got another ahead of me, but more importantly than that, I'm tired of playing dress-up.'

The dress fitted to perfection. It was cut from cream silk with a navy blue lace trim around the cuffs and collar. Callie had also found some rather old-fashioned navy blue lace gloves tucked away in a stock box that had been left in the changing room. She probably wasn't going to tell Alistair and Tanya that the gloves weren't officially part of the ensemble, and she certainly wouldn't mention her plans to trim the fingers off them.

'Oh Callie,' Tanya yelped, 'you look beautiful! It's a bit different, but it's so you. Tell her Ali, tell her.'

The Prince was lost for words. She did indeed look beautiful, but there was also something else about the dress she'd chosen. It captured her spirit. It captured her edge. It captured all the sweet contrary elements of Callie Haywood that he was attracted to and presented them in an elegant way that was pleasing to the Hawthorne ethos. He immediately felt annoyed that he hadn't persuaded Callie to go with him to the ball. He then felt regretful at having settled to have Tanya on his arm. As this selfish dissatisfaction grew, he realised that he had been staring straight at Callie for a little too long. He turned to face a furious Tanya Masters.

'So do you like the dress?' she said. 'Or just who's inside it?'

'I'm... I'm sorry,' stuttered Alistair, 'my erm, mind wandered.'

'Your mind wandered?' mocked Tanya. 'You'd better hope that your hands don't, or you'll be in trouble.'

Callie looked embarrassed and uncomfortable. This was exactly the sort of situation things like the Debutante Ball seemed to spawn, and exactly the sort of situation she didn't like being part of. With her mind running blank about how to respond, she said, 'Maybe this isn't the right dress. I'll try something else on.'

'No, no,' Raynard cried, hurrying over to Callie and smoothing a non-existent wrinkle from the fabric. 'I declare it looks and fits you perfectly.'

Callie looked unconvinced and turned to a now-sulking Tanya. 'Really?' she asked softly. Raynard hovered over the situation, his mind screaming at these annoying people to leave his store so he could close up for the night.

Tanya swallowed her pride and smiled. 'Callie, you look amazing. If you don't wear this dress, it'll break my heart. Just promise me that you'll let me steal the show at the next ball, ok?'

Callie still looked uneasy and had begun to talk herself out of buying the dress. 'Well, it's very long, isn't it. And what about the sleeves? Too puffy?'

'Ball gowns are meant to be long,' reassured Tanya, 'and your puff sleeves are tiny. You wait till everyone sees mine; I'm going to redefine puff sleeves.'

Alistair's heart sank as he imagined arriving at the ball with Tanya wearing some puffy-sleeved horror, and his face couldn't hide it. Raynard leaned over to Alistair and whispered, 'I'm so very sorry.'

Alistair shook himself out of his sulk and took charge of the dress discussion. 'Ok, are we decided then? Excellent. Raynard, put it on my account.'

Callie started to object, but the Prince cut her short. 'No, Callie,' he said, taking her by the arm and leading her back to the changing room. 'I insist. Raynard, bag the dress up, and we're out of here!'

Alistair turned around to see Tanya had sprung into action and was holding several expensive dresses up to her body and smiling a 'pretty please?'

Raynard sloped back to the counter while his internal

monologue laid out a bitter rant about the phrase 'bag the dress up' and how an heir to the throne should have a more dignified grasp of language and retail etiquette. His thoughts were interrupted by the sound of yet more boxes tumbling over in the storeroom.

'For Vastrid's sake, Spillet! What is wrong with you? One more incident and I swear I'll fire your incompetent backside,' Raynard screamed beyond the counter before turning to look at Alistair and Tanya with a quickly adopted expression of calm. 'My apologies.'

Nearby, Ryan was walking through town on the way home from his evening out with his cousin. Exhausted from his busy day at the Library, the Grid and the hospital, Ryan had not only managed to get on the wrong bus but had also fallen asleep on it.

He had said goodbye to his cousin over an hour ago and was now making his way back to his apartment on the east side of the city. He had so much on his mind and so little energy to think about it all. As he passed the many closed boutiques of the Ivy Lane shopping district, the realisation dawned on him that he would need to acquire a Guard's uniform before the ball, and he only had a couple of hours in the morning to do so. Ryan sighed and decided to take a short detour past Jenkins' and check the opening times, and as he turned a corner towards the store, he was surprised to see the lights still on.

He darted across the road, but just as he reached the door, Raynard slammed it shut and turned the sign from 'Open' to 'Closed'.

Ryan thumped on the door, begging to be let in. Just as his fifth rat-a-tat-tat was about to connect with the glass, it swung open, and Tanya bustled past him with a giggled, 'Oops, excuse me!'

One by one, Probot, Tanya, Callie and Prince Alistair filed

out of the shop. Callie recognised Ryan from the Grid and smiled hello before suddenly panicking that he probably had no idea who she was. Wishing to avoid any more awkwardness this evening, she quickly averted her eyes and rushed past.

Alistair studied Ryan for a few seconds then let out a joyous chortle. 'Oh, it's you. Good to see you back on your feet. Are you looking to pick up your uniform now?'

'Um, yeah, but I think I'm too late.' Ryan pointed to the closed sign on the door.

'Leave it to me, junior,' Alistair said, jabbing Ryan on the shoulder. He lent back through the door and caught Raynard's attention. 'One more, if you don't mind.'

'Of course not,' sighed Raynard, trying his hardest to keep his cool. 'This way, sir,' he motioned to Ryan.

Ryan stepped through the door and looked back to offer a quick 'Thank you' to Alistair and a shaky-voiced, 'Goodbye' to Callie.

As the door closed, Ryan felt Raynard's frustration looming over him. 'Yeah, sorry about that. I've just passed the Grid, well sort of, well it's just a secondment really but I – '

'I take it you require a Guard's uniform?' interrupted Raynard. 'Tailored or surplus?'

This took Ryan by surprise as he presumed he would just turn up, and they would hand him the uniform. 'I don't understand. What's the difference?'

'Well, by the look of you, I would guess that you don't have the money to have a uniform tailored from scratch. I'm also guessing that the only form of currency you have in your pocket is the basic voucher attached to the bottom of your acceptance letter.' Raynard arched his eyebrow at Ryan. 'Hmmm?'

Ryan felt a compulsive urge to check his pockets for money even though he knew they were empty. As he did,

Raynard heard the solitary sound of the voucher crunching against Ryan's hand.

A smug expression flooded Raynard's face. 'A voucher only entitles you to the items on the surplus rail. Which you will find over there on the left.'

As Ryan made his way to the rail, he noticed that the jackets looked rather large. He looked through the selection twice, studying each label for a measurement that was a little closer to his medium frame. He was about to go for a third look when he heard Raynard call out, 'Sir, please make your choice within the next minute as we are about to close.'

'But there's nothing here in my size! Every jacket on here is – '

'Built for the strong, athletic bodies of the Royal Guard,' Raynard interrupted, looking over Ryan's somewhat boyish physique before pulling a face that conveyed disgust and disbelief at the same time.

'Well, what do you suggest then?' Ryan asked despairingly. Raynard was about to suggest that Ryan take one of the larger jackets and attempt to grow into it when his eyes suddenly lit up.

'Actually, I have just had a *won-der-ful* idea.' Raynard smiled and began to rummage beneath the shop counter before dragging something out with a victorious flourish. 'Try that on', he said, throwing it towards Ryan.

Ryan caught it and held it up to himself. Whilst looking like a standard Royal Guards jacket, the arms were noticeably longer than the body, which also differed from a traditional Guard's jacket by having a slanted hem at the front.

'It's not been cut right,' protested Ryan.

'Sir,' Raynard gasped. 'This is a modern play on a tradi-tional military hem. Try it on.'

Naturally, Raynard wasn't going to admit that this was one

of Spillet's tailoring failures and that Ryan's predicament was a useful way of offloading wasted material.

Ryan slipped it on and was surprised to find that the jacket was quite comfortable. Admittedly, the arms did cover his hands slightly, and the unusual cut made it seem shorter than the standard-issue ones. However, it was the best option available, so Ryan took the jacket and shuffled out of the store, unsure that he had done the right thing.

Raynard sighed with relief and went about finally closing down the store for the night. Suddenly there was another crash in the storeroom.

'For Vastrid's sake, Spillet! That's it! Come out here this instant.' Raynard stood with his hands on his hips for the next ten seconds while Spillet failed to emerge from the stock room.

Raynard felt a shiver down his spine. 'Spillet? Spillet, where are you?'

With his heartbeat starting to increase, the uneasy silence began to play on Raynard's mind. After all, Spillet was so clumsy that even the way he dragged his feet when walking left an audible trail. Raynard took a step forward and heard a short hiss, followed by a sizzling sound. All the lights in the store went out.

Raynard's mouth went dry as he asked again, 'Spillet? Are you there, Spillet?' Another hiss came from somewhere in the endless darkness ahead of him.

Raynard edged towards the table at the front of the shop, where some scented candles sat. His hands quivered as he wrapped them around the largest candle and then reached inside his pocket for his silver monogrammed lighter, snapping it alight and lifting it to the long wick of the candle in the other hand. The frenzied panting of Raynard's breathing rose and fell with the pulsing flame from the candle.

'Spillet?' he whispered as he raised the candle high and

caught a glimpse of his reflection in the window ahead of him.

The small glow surrounding his reflection confirmed that there was somebody, or possibly something, standing behind him. Another hiss emerged, this time coupled with a cold, damp trail of breath that prickled and jabbed at his ears and neck.

Raynard started to weep, and with no options left, he turned to face whatever stood behind him. As he turned, the flickering flame illuminated a seven-foot-tall, green-eyed synistrail. The creature hissed at an ear-piercing pitch and threw up its clawed hand to attack.

Raynard whimpered, 'No... please,' before falling to his knees in fright. As he fell, he dropped the candle, and its flame extinguished.

There was one final scream in the darkness before the store fell into complete silence. It had been a busy night for Raynard and one that would turn out to be his last.

By this point, Ryan was several streets away and was weighing up whether or not to put his new jacket on. On the one hand, the time was edging ever closer to midnight, and a cold chill rode through the city sky; however, on the other hand, he would need to walk past Craydon's Corner, and he'd get enough grief from the Wise Guys who hung around there as it was.

As dark clouds drifted across the maroon sky and the escalating chill of the night's change travelled through to the breeze on the street below, Ryan's quandary answered itself, and he put the Guards jacket on.

Ryan shivered as he pulled his jacket in close and glanced up at Craydon's Corner ahead. As usual, a certain type of young man had come to hang out, haggle and hustle. The Wise Guys lacked the savagery of the Baker's End gangs and instead relied on their intelligence and social standing. They possessed an aura of confidence that, by some unspoken law of nature, made them prey on the uneasy and uncomfortable.

As expected, Ryan was greeted with a wolf whistle and cry of 'Oi! Soldier-Soldier!' by a tall, platinum-haired Wise Guy wearing a sharp silver suit.

Ryan made his glance hit the floor, only to hear the platinum-haired Wise Guy sing out louder, 'Soldier-Soldier, wontcha marry me?' as his gang cackled in encouragement behind him.

'I don't think he 'eard you, Tone,' one of the gang said, laughing and nudging the ringleader.

Tone ran his fingers through his silver quiff and nodded in agreement. 'Looks like soldier-soldier got his jacket but lost his manners.'

Tone stepped out in front of Ryan's path, stopping his progress as the gang of Wise Guys gathered around, smirking.

'Excuse me, please,' Ryan said quietly.

Tone looked Ryan directly in the eye. 'Only if you marry me with your musket, fife and drum.'

The gang of Wise Guys laughed like a pack of hyenas as Tone noticed the unusual cut of Ryan's jacket. Picking up one of the lapels, he ran his fingers down to the bottom of the hem and motioned to his gang. 'Lads, would you look at the state of this? What's going on 'ere soldier-soldier, are you just playing dress-up or what?'

'No, I passed the Grid, but....'

'He got stuck with a knock-off jacket, what a plum!' another Wise Guy bellowed in Ryan's face.

'Nah,' croaked Tone, 'I don't think he is actually a soldier-soldier. And to think I wanted to marry him. Oh, my broken heart. Were you trying to trick me soldier-soldier?'

'No, I just want to get home,' sighed Ryan, but Tone was unrelenting.

Stepping forward, Tone looked straight into Ryan's eyes and, with menace, asked again, 'Were. You. Trying. To. Trick. Me?'

With each word, Tone pushed Ryan back a little way with the palm of his hand. Ryan stumbled backwards, and through a combination of his instincts trying to correct his balance and sheer frustration, he lunged forward, knocking Tone off his feet.

Humiliated at his slip, Tone scrambled back up and rolled up the sleeves of his silver jacket, clenching his fists. 'Oh, you're gonna get it now, soldier boy'.

Ryan scrambled backwards, holding up his hands. 'Look, I'm sorry, I just want to get home – leave me alone,' but it was to no avail as Tone marched towards him, backing him against a brick wall. Tone unloaded punches from both fists as Ryan clumsily attempted to block them with his forearms. Ryan began to sink down the wall when all of a sudden, something changed.

Ryan's right arm thrust forward, and his hand wrapped around Tone's throat, flinging the Wise Guy face-first into the wall. Tone's face connected with such force that it split his forehead wide open. As he crumpled to the floor, blood erupted from the cut on his head, seeping across his platinum quiff.

Ryan turned to the remaining Wise Guys with his eyes glowing pure silver light.

'I SAID, LEAVE ME ALONE!' he howled as they ran for their lives.

The light from his eyes faded as quickly as it had appeared, and Ryan fell to the floor, trembling. 'What happened?' he whispered to himself as he looked over at

Tone, who was lying in the corner, covered in blood. 'What have I done?' Ryan picked himself up and fled into the night.

Watching Ryan run, Tone dragged himself to a seated position against the wall. 'Yeah, that's right, Soldier-Soldier, go home to your mother,' he bellowed. 'Next time I see you, I'll kill you!'

'Nah, I don't think you will.' Kendra Lomax emerged from the shadows and strolled towards Tone before stamping down hard on his right leg and shattering it in two places. 'Well, not for a month or two, anyhow.'

Tone howled in agony and attempted, with shaking hands and gritted teeth, to reach for a flick knife concealed in his jacket. He whimpered for a moment and then finally passed out.

'Bloody kids.' Lomax shook her head and sighed. She reached inside her rain-cloak and pulled out a flask of coffee, humming the Soldier, Soldier tune. While she warmed herself, she pondered all of the things that had been erased and forgotten from the past: religious concepts, key moments in history, the names and boundaries of countries. However, a song dating back centuries before the Saviour Wars had somehow managed to stand the test of time.

Lomax looked far into the distance and watched Ryan disappear into the dark. Introductions would now have to wait until tomorrow night at the ball. Ryan was in no state to have the truth revealed to him, and Kendra was far too tired. She took a sip from her flask – it might help keep her awake, but no amount of caffeine would help her devise a plan of how best to explain everything to the poor boy.

A few streets away, Ryan walked back to his bedsit, turning the events of the last few days over in his mind. Everything seemed to be moving so fast. Until now, his life had been going nowhere – a boring, safe existence. As the rain fell, Ryan realised that he was at a turning point. He questioned whether he was brave enough to jeopardise everything. Little did he know, he would soon be required to risk more than he could ever have imagined and fulfil a destiny that sat far beyond all other human achievement.

Chapter Eleven

SPARKS AND SIGNALS

The following morning, Ryan woke suddenly. The rain had passed, and the sky, which had been a strange shade of maroon, was now clear sunlight. The change in the weather, however, wasn't what had stirred him.

Ryan was used to sleeping with his blinds open. Daylight was the first stage of his three-tiered alarm system to ensure that he'd be awake in time for his shifts at the Library. Instead, he had been woken by the sudden end to a reoccurring dream. As his body slept, Ryan would find himself wandering through the same scenario in his mind. It would always begin with him chasing after something he could only describe as a spark.

Bright and bewildering, the spark would fly away from him in a perfectly straight line. Driven by something he couldn't understand, Ryan would chase the spark through fragments of his memory. People and places from his short time on Earth would flash and melt around him as his physical form was slowly eaten and erased from behind by a strange, dark substance. As the spark accelerated, two-dimensional images of Cardea Gardens would drop down in front of him as if projected onto a screen. Eventually, the spark would join these two-dimensional images of the Gardens before stopping short of The Freedom Arch. Ryan would then reach out to touch the spark; however, his physical form had been all but devoured by this point, leaving just his face and the fingertips on his right hand. In the dying moments of the vision, Ryan would feel the remains of his body disintegrate as the spark diminished before his eyes.

Following these dreams, Ryan would sit on the edge of his bed in a state of confusion and fear as he tried to make sense of the images. But on this specific morning, he glanced at the calendar on his wall and groaned. 'Eurgh, it's the morning of the day that ends with the Ball.'

The previous day had been so hectic that until this moment, he hadn't fully considered how he was going to survive the whole awkward affair. Ryan's heart sank as he tried to remember where he had left his invitation; it had been waiting in his mail locker when he'd returned home the previous night, but after that, his mind ran blank.

Stumbling out of his bed, he made his way to his dresser. While reaching around in the top drawer, he pulled out a hundred Vastridian Credit note that he had tucked away for emergencies and promptly forgotten about.

'Nice!' Ryan grinned, then glanced over at the guard's jacket hanging on the back of his door. 'Although I could've done with this last night at Jenkins.'

Ryan was about to put the emergency funds back in the drawer when the trees outside caught his eye. Something about the way the sunshine hit the leaves instilled a flutter of joy inside his heart. Ryan looked at the note and smiled. 'If I'm to be bound by guard's duty for the next six months, I think you should accompany me on a trip to the Market Square.'

This elation was temporarily halted by Ryan's realisation

that he was in his underwear, talking to a piece of paper, and the whole spectacle was being witnessed by a shocked window cleaner who had been cleaning the room's side window. Ryan cleared his throat, grabbed some clothes and dived into his bathroom, praying that the window cleaner didn't know anyone he knew.

After fifteen minutes or so of hiding, Ryan finally left the bathroom, slipped on his guard's jacket and set off towards the Market Square.

The Market Square was one of Vastrid's most profitable and charismatic trading areas; however, due to the less-than-legal status of the goods for sale, it preferred to remain under the radar. Most of the Vastridian noble classes had turned their noses up at the Market Square years ago. Those that hadn't were loyal customers who were more than willing to turn a blind eye to buy their wares from somewhere other than the Shadox Corporation.

The market was one of the few places where Ryan felt truly comfortable. There was something about the atmosphere and the people the market attracted that allowed Ryan to feel confident in himself. While perhaps not the most academically gifted boy in Vastrid, Ryan's fascination with the relics and oddities for sale in the market over the years had made him something of an expert, and several of the traders found his company fascinating. Ryan's favourite vendor was named D'Rekk Creel, and beneath the cover of his spare computer parts stall, he primarily sold Flex-izdats.

Flex-izdats were small, flexible disks that contained audio and image files recorded before the war. Some of the audio was said to be centuries old, but that was open to debate. Following the war, it had been decided by a committee of world leaders that, as most of the historical records had perished, any remaining evidence of human existence couldn't be trusted to be an objective record of the truth and should be destroyed to preserve the new era of peace. Despite the strength and influence of the Shadox Corporation, not even they could wipe out centuries of text, audio and images. The things that slipped through the cracks and survived found their way onto Flex-izdats. These ancient artefacts were collectively known as the 'secret echoes'.

Ryan's favourite Flex-izdats were those which contained music, especially the 'Rawkenrawl' ones, as D'Rekk described them. There was, of course, music produced by the Shadox corp, but it was generated by reactive computer software that scanned listeners and adjusted arrangements, pitch and tempo accordingly. The music found on the Flex-izdats sounded as if human beings had produced it, and Ryan found this thrillingly bizarre.

When D'Rekk saw Ryan approach, he cracked a huge smile and bellowed, 'Eh there, laddie! Long time no see.' D'Rekk leapt out from behind his stall and touched the lapel of Ryan's jacket.

'Ooooh, very nice. You passed the Grid, then? I trust you haven't come here to arrest me?'

'No, of course not; with the amount I've bought from you over the years, I'd be locked up too,' Ryan laughed. 'I come with good news. I found some money in my drawer, and I'd like to exchange it for an interesting listen.'

'Well, of course you would, laddie, of course you would,' D'Rekk beamed. 'Alas, I don't think I have much rawkenrawl that you haven't heard already. There is, however, some more stuff relating to our theory about what a rolling stone was. There's a new song that's cropped up - shocking audio quality I'm afraid, but it's about someone's father being one of them. It's something to do with some kind of ancient cult. The Sentry of their time, I'm sure.'

'What about the song where they sing of being on the cover of the rolling stone?'

'Maybe a cover is like a bed cover? Perhaps they wore bed covers like they were a kinda rain cloak or somesuch'.

From the back of the stall, D'Rekk's wife Randa smiled over at them. 'You boys with your theories. If you spent less time thinking and more time doing, we could be dining with the Hawthornes instead of being stuck here in the Market Square!'

'Hey!' protested D'Rekk, looking towards Ryan for support.

'Believe me, Randa, we're having a better time here,' Ryan replied. 'And I say that as someone who has met Prince Alistair on more than one occasion.'

'Really?' D'Rekk asked. 'Tell me, laddie, what's he like? Proper full of himself, I'd wager.'

'He's not so bad, I guess. Annoyingly good looking, over groomed, and yes, a bit full of himself. But he has shown me occasional acts of kindness. For instance, I only managed to get this jacket in time for the ball because he arranged for Jenkins to stay open a bit later for me.'

'Rich man's guilt,' D'Rekk grunted. 'So you've got the ball tonight, have ya? You must be excited. This is where it all begins. No more dusty old maps for you, son. You could create the life you'll go on to lead at this ball.' D'Rekk looked fondly at Randa before turning back to Ryan. 'You never know – you could meet your wife.'

Ryan blushed. 'Oh, I don't know about that. I don't have much success when it comes to matters of the heart. I'll stick to my Flex-izdats, I think. They capture my heart and stay kind to it. I don't need the drama of it all, and even my simple life's busy enough.'

'Fair enough,' smiled D'Rekk, rummaging under his stall for the few Flex-izdats that Ryan didn't have. 'I used to be the same, but when I met Randa, it was strange how fast my philosophies changed. Anyhow laddie, that'll be fifty-three credits, please.'

Ryan surveyed the market as he waited for his change, breathing in the morning air and enjoying the hustle and bustle. Suddenly, just ahead, he caught sight of a familiar uniform.

Ryan's heart sank as he quickly turned back to D'Rekk. 'Oh, that's great – I've only been a Royal Guard for five minutes, and already I'm going to get a disciplinary. I'm going to have to run.'

D'Rekk handed him his change, and Ryan fled as the two guards arrived. In his panic, Ryan hadn't noticed that one of the guards was Callie Haywood, who was attempting to say 'hello' to Ryan as he rushed past.

'Callie! Dev! What a pleasure. Forgive young master Ryan; he presumed, wrongly of course, that you were here to arrest him. It looked like youse were going to say hello.' D'Rekk leaned towards Callie and, in a mock-salacious tone, asked, 'Are you two acquainted?'

'I barely know him!' Callie spluttered. 'In fact, I don't think I've ever said more than two words to him. He always seems so awkward.'

'Ah, Ryan's a top lad. He's been coming to this stall since he was just shy of sixteen years old. True, he's a little hard to get to know, but he's a good friend when you do. And he knows almost as much as I do about the Flex-izdats.'

D'Rekk leant across the stall counter and examined his nails before glancing up at Callie with an exaggerated casualness. 'And he is very single, if that's what the real burning curiosity in your heart is.'

Dev hooted with laughter. 'Could it be that the Guard's very own ice queen has a crush on the Grid tumbler?'

Callie shot them both a warning look. 'Stop this now, you two. I'm really not looking for any kind of boyfriend. I just like to do my shifts and get back to my quarters. Now then, please just give me the latest Flexi!'

'It's funny,' D'Rekk said, rubbing the stubble on his chin. 'He doesn't want a girlfriend. You don't want a boyfriend. Love has overcome bigger hurdles in the past. Look at it this way, my dearie – at least if you got together, you could save a fortune by sharing the Flex-izdats.'

Dev was in hysterics at this point. 'Ah, stop it, man, I can't take much more.'

Seizing his moment in the spotlight, D'Rekk raised an eyebrow and delivered the punchline. 'Maybe with the money you save, you could buy him a jacket that actually fits.'

Callie attempted to speak but had become so flustered from the teasing she just let out an exasperated gasp.

Dev collapsed against the stall, holding his stomach. 'It's too funny, man. I'm going to get some big laughs when I tell the squad about this tonight.'

'Oh, for Vastrid's sake,' Callie turned to face Dev. 'I would have expected a little more support from my academy buddy!'

D'Rekk held up his hands and smiled. 'Sorry for the teasing, Lady Callie – it's just my way. By way of an apology, I'll sell you my two latest Flex-izdats for eighty credits and throw in a copy of Flexi LV-29 for free.'

'It's a deal,' Callie said, fishing the credits out of her money pouch. 'LV-29? I thought that was obsolete!'

'Ah, now that just depends on whether I decide someone needs a copy or not.' D'Rekk slid the disks across the counter.

Callie held LV-29 up and examined it, a huge smile spreading across her face. 'I can't believe I've finally got a copy of this. I've heard such great things about it. What was it that made you decide that I need a copy?'

'Well, it's young master Ryan's favourite, and I figured it'd give you something to chat about at the ball tonight.'

Callie's face turned to thunder. She slammed the Flex-izdats into her satchel before letting out an angry 'pfft' noise and storming off.

'That girl just can't take a joke. See you later, man,' Dev grinned at D'Rekk as he took off after Callie.

D'Rekk watched as they disappeared into the crowd, only to be replaced by two of the Kingdom's Royal Planners marching towards him.

'It seems that the uniforms can't get enough of the marketplace this morning.' D'Rekk shook his head and started to rearrange the items on his stand in a vague attempt to look less conspicuous.

As he finished muttering, he looked up and found the Royal Planners standing directly in front of him. The taller of the two was flushed red from rushing; he placed his hand on the counter and motioned at D'Rekk to wait a moment while he caught his breath. His colleague hung a little further behind and glanced around nervously.

'They got to my stall quick enough,' D'Rekk mumbled to himself. He looked disdainfully at the fitted breeches that the planners were wearing and shuddered, 'I would have thought that wearing trousers that tight would have slowed them down.'

'Are you or are you not D'Rekk Creel?' the flustered planner asked as his silent partner stood beside him, avoiding eye contact with anyone or anything.

D'Rekk grinned and leaned in towards the visitors, answering the question with one of his own. 'Well, that would depend, wouldn't it. What do you need him for?'

The planner sighed. 'We have been tasked with securing the services of a gentleman named D'Rekk Creel. We need his technical expertise to fix and program our Melodium.'

'A Melodium, eh? Will youse two be needing it for the ball tonight?'

'Well, of course we need it for the ball tonight,' the planner replied in a pitch somewhere between bluster and fluster. 'The Melodium seems to be damaged from the recent cold weather. It needs its broken parts replaced; the timings need tightening, the Meloquins need syncing and – '

'The tonal selections will need to be loaded,' D'Rekk interrupted, a plan forming in his mind. He grabbed his coat and an old burlap bag from under the counter. 'Well, consider me the one and only D'Rekk Creel. It'll cost youse a pretty penny for the labour, but I'll give youse a good price on any parts I need to change.'

'Fine, fine. Just please hurry. We need to get the Melodium working before the start of the evening.'

'No worries, pal,' D'Rekk stepped out from his stall then stopped suddenly. 'I have just one condition.'

The planner rolled his eyes.'Name it.'

'I'll need to work alone. I get dead nervous if I have people watching over me.' D'Rekk looked at both planners and mimicked his hands shaking to emphasise the point.

The silent planner sheepishly looked over at his more assertive partner and muttered to no one in particular, 'Imagine that.'

'Very well, you can work alone, but we must be on our way. Time is running out.'

D'Rekk smiled and patted his bag. 'Lead the way, my good man. May the Melodium generate heartbeats amongst the young tonight.'

Ryan, meanwhile, found himself in Cardea Gardens. His plan of heading directly back to his room to enjoy the new Flex-izdat had gone awry when he had become lost within an internal monologue.

It had begun with some simmering fear that now he was a

seconded officer, he wouldn't even be able to browse the marketplace without being recognised by other members of the Royal Guard. This then led to some regret and reflection over the scuffle he'd got into with the Wise Guys on Craydon's Corner the previous evening and concluded with a self-pitying lament about the cut of his guards' jacket.

Ryan held up his arms in front of his face, his fingers barely visible beneath the long sleeves. He sighed to himself. 'What was I thinking? It'll have to do, I guess.'

Ryan could have wasted the rest of the afternoon feeling sorry for himself; however, as he glanced between his raised arms, something caught his attention. It was the Spectraqua Fountains which, in the right weather conditions, could shoot out multi-coloured jets of water. A group of small children were dancing and playing there, singing a song that was both peculiar and familiar to Ryan. Most of the lyrics were hard to make out; however, a repeated refrain of 'We're running through the rainbows, running through the rainbows, running through the rainbows,' hit Ryan hard. His thoughts were transported back to the vision from the night before.

The children's singing grew louder and faster, speeding in time with the recollections from his vision. The world around Ryan began to spiral while the sound of the spring breeze appeared to fold in on itself to become a discordant and piercing squeal. Ryan started to mumble when he felt a comforting hand on his shoulder. He looked up and declared, 'I'm searching for a spark!'

Instantly Ryan composed himself and saw that it was Callie who had placed her hand on his shoulder.

'Are you ok? You looked like you were going to faint or something,' she asked. Her initial concern soon turned to a state of nervous confusion. 'Did you say you were looking for a spark?'

Ryan's mouth ran dry, and the first sound to leave his lips

was a dusty 'pah'. He didn't have a clue what to say; he didn't even know what had just happened. He then got lost in a series of internal questions attempting to determine how acquainted he and Callie were and what the right level of conversation should be in such an instance.

Suddenly, Ryan remembered being spotted at the market by Royal Guards, and a greater fear barged past all other thoughts and took the form of a desperate plea that sprung from Ryan's lips. 'You're not going to arrest me, are you?'

'For what? Searching for a spark?' Callie asked, bemused.

'No, for this.' Ryan opened his bag and gestured to his newly acquired Flex-izdat.

Callie laughed and revealed her own purchases from D'Rekk Creel's market stall. 'I'm a fan of the secret echoes too.'

Ryan's awkward manner disappeared as he leant forward to see which ones she had. He read the labels out loud, his voice rising in excitement as he did so.

'LDN92-99, that's a pretty good one - lots of rawkenrawl on that and some interesting vids too. PO-8oP is a bit strange, but there's some good stuff on there that not many other collectors have access to. Oh, and LV-29 – you're going to love that one. There's a certain magic in the way that one's compiled. I swear, there's a sound file on there labelled o4 that will make your heart burst! In a good way, that is.'

Callie smiled. She'd never heard anyone talk of the secret echoes with so much pure excitement or joy before. She'd met some dreadfully pretentious Flex-izdat collectors who were just that – collectors, not enjoyers. They always seemed much more concerned with what they did or didn't have and the rarity attached to them rather than savouring their contents. She had also met people who claimed to be into the secret echoes, yet she could tell that they didn't get the same kind of inspiration or giddy feeling from the content as she did.

'I look forward to exploring it later this afternoon,' Callie beamed. She was about to ask Ryan what his 'spark' comment was about but suddenly realised that this was the first time she had seen him appear relaxed and confident. 'So what's brought you to the gardens this afternoon?'

Ryan had hoped that the conversion would stay on Flex-izdats but realised that he should make an effort to continue chatting. After all, it was rare that a girl as attractive as Callie would strike up a conversation with him. In all honesty, it was rare that any female would strike up a conversation with him.

'Oh, you know how it is. I was out at the market, and the weather was so nice I decided to take the long way home.' Ryan felt stiff and strained as he attempted to make small talk and almost immediately changed course and began to rant candidly. 'Ok, that's not really how it was. I was daydreaming and trying to work out how I get into certain situations. I mean, there can't truly be such a thing as bad luck, can there? It must be a constant failing on my part. I was trying to work it all out, and maybe I got close. But then I got distracted by those children over there and remembered a strange dream I had last night. So anyhow, to answer your question, I really haven't got a clue why I ended up here.'

Ryan stopped and glanced at Callie, expecting the look of blank confusion that he seemed to encounter so often from people. Callie, however, giggled.

'You certainly are a strange one,' she smiled. 'I'm off to the north gate. Do you fancy walking with me?'

'I live near the east gate, but I'll walk with you to the centre.'

As they walked, there was a brief period of uncomfortable silence that was occasionally punctuated with coy smiles and nervous looks. Both of them knew someone would have to speak, and it was Callie who went first. 'So your name's Ryan, right? I was there when you saved that boy in the Grid. You had some extraordinary moves in there. Where did you learn them?'

Ryan realised that he didn't know her name, but he felt too awkward to ask for it. 'Well, like my wandering into the gardens this afternoon, sometimes stuff just seems to happen. It's been happening more frequently lately. And then there are the recurring dreams....'

'Me too!' Callie leapt in. 'The recurring dreams bit, that is. I keep having the weirdest dreams. Something about an ancient tower, a hoard of Synistrails and a shadowed figure with glowing eyes standing in the Freedom Arch. The Shadox Corporation must be putting something in our water.'

'Have you ever actually seen a Synistrail?' Ryan asked. 'In real life, I mean.'

'Yes. Twice. Both times when I was out on a tour of the outer woodlands with the guards. They're pretty disturbing. I think it's the way they move towards you; it's very methodical.' Callie shook her head as if to shoo the thought. 'Let's talk about something even more hideous – have you also been nagged into attending the ball tonight?'

Ryan let out a hearty laugh. 'Yes, I'm afraid so.'

'There's no need to be afraid,' Callie said, smiling. 'At least we now both have someone we can talk to.'

At that moment, a soft spring breeze blew towards them and shook the branches of the old cherry blossom trees that stood beside the pathway. The blossom from the tree engulfed both Ryan and Callie. As Callie opened her mouth to speak, some of the petals blew into her face. She coughed a little and swatted the pieces away from her mouth. 'This stuff is all over us, just like confetti,' she laughed.

Callie blushed a little, suddenly fearing that Ryan may think that she was proposing marriage. Instead, he just laughed it off as a quip, yet he did notice her blush which in turn brought a shy smile to his face.

As they walked towards the fountain in the centre of the gardens, Callie brushed out the remaining blossom from her hair. As she did so, Ryan noticed an old fashioned Cuff-Linq data storage and receiving device on her arm. 'Wow, that's quite the artefact you have there.'

'It was my dad's. It's very special to me, he gave it to me when I was young to keep me safe. It's been hacked, should I ever get bothered by a wrong-un and there's no way out, it's got a tiny spring loaded tranq stored inside. Plus, I've yet to find a modern Cuff-Linq that gives you as much control over catchment flows and storage.'

At that moment, some children who had been playing in the fountain ran past, flicking water at each other. An older child emerged with a cup full of water and launched it into the air.

As the water hit Callie's arm, the Cuff-Linq began to make a crackling noise. Ryan looked concerned. 'Oh don't worry, it's seen worse,' Callie said, pulling a small handkerchief from her pocket and dabbing away the water. As she held her wrist up to check for any remaining droplets, a bright spark shot from the front of the bracelet.

'Whoah! You said earlier that you were looking for a spark. It looks like you found it!' Callie laughed, patting her bracelet to ensure it wasn't going to catch on fire.

The pair strolled on, and a few hundred metres later, Callie stuck her hands into her pockets and swayed, motioning towards the path leading to the North Gate. 'So anyhow, this is me.'

Ryan smiled and stuck his hands into his pockets, motioning with a sway of his own towards the East Gate. 'And this is me.'

'So it is, Ryan – ' Callie said, leaving a space to find out his surname.

'Tyler,' Ryan replied, in a manner that may have been a little too keen and excitable.

'So it is, Ryan Tyler. I'll see you tonight at the ball. If you can't find me, you should leave a message at the Melodium.' Callie smiled and walked towards the North Gate.

Ryan turned down the path towards the East Gate, stopping only for a moment to let the fresh springtime sunshine hit his face. He had felt so tired during the past few weeks, but now he felt more awake than ever before. Ryan now had a reason to go to the Debutante Ball, and although he knew he'd be nervous to the point of vomiting when he got there, he felt for this one rapturous moment that anything was possible. Plus, if shyness overtook him as it often did, he could simply leave a message at the Melodium so, should she be interested, then she could find him and re-break any ice.

Suddenly the satisfied smile on Ryan's face turned to a frown. 'Oh no, how am I going to leave a message on the Melodium?' he thought to himself. 'I haven't got a clue what her name is!'

Chapter Twelve

TABLE 13

Ryan arrived at the Debutante Ball, weary from the anxiety and excitement crashing against each other in his heart. The ball was held at the Royal Hall, a lavish building situated in the grounds to the east of the Vastridian Royal Palace. Walking through the entrance of the Royal Hall into the first of several foyers leading to the main function room, he was almost immediately seized upon by his cousin Jayden.

'You made it! I really thought that you were going to back out.'

'No, I'm here.' Ryan eyed his surroundings; exquisitely moulded golden pillars, smooth marble floors, floor-length velvet drapes. The décor was undoubtedly expensive, and yet it held no worth in Ryan's eyes. 'Don't expect me to stay too long though.'

'No, no, of course,' said Jayden, brushing his moodiness aside as they began to stroll through the hall. 'So then, who have you got your eye on tonight?'

Ryan shrugged. 'No one.'

'Oh, there must be *someone* you like. How about Tricia Dempsey from your Grid training courses?'

'No, not really. I mean, I hardly know her.'

'How about Hylen Spencer-Jones?'

'Who? What? No.'

'Hmmm, what other nice, single girls will be here tonight?' Jayden tapped her fingers together as she thought. 'I know, Callie Haywood.'

Ryan stuttered and, for a second, wondered if Callie was the girl he'd been talking to earlier in Cardea Gardens. This moment's pause was all that Jayden needed.

'Ooooh,' she grinned, 'so there *is* a girl in the guards who has captured your attention.'

Ryan tried to escape any further questioning by staring at his feet. 'Oh come on, I'm not even sure if I know who that is.'

'Oh but I believe you *do,* my dear cousin,' Jayden smirked. 'Dark, choppy hair, about your height, wears an old broke-looking Cuff-Linq, skulks about the marketplace like you, a bit *distant,* like you.'

'What do you mean *distant?*' Ryan asked, mildly offended at what may or may not have been a criticism of a girl who may or may not have been the girl he was talking to this afternoon.

'Whoa, stand down, Private Tyler! I don't mean anything by it. I just mean that Callie Haywood sort of stands apart from the cliquishness of the guards. She's not rude or anything. She's her own person, y'know?'

Jayden hoped her rambling had made enough sense to defuse the situation and not snuff out Ryan's possible interest in Callie. She worried about her cousin's solitary ways, and the fact he hadn't immediately shut her questioning down was encouraging.

'Plus,' she added, 'Callie's probably the best pilot in the guards. Which will come in handy, as let's face it, you're a bit of a disaster controlling any kind of vehicle.'

Ryan felt a little sick. Jayden was right; Ryan wasn't very good at being a pilot, or being a driver or being much of anything at all. He had a sudden, overwhelming feeling that the girl he spoke to this afternoon outclassed him not only in rank but in all areas.

Even if he could hide his failings tonight, he knew he'd eventually be exposed as a fraud. Ryan's thoughts drifted to a potential future event. He pictured a room full of high society people looking at him, shaking their heads in disapproval. At the very front stood Callie, scowling. This was why he preferred to stay safe and alone in his bedroom.

'Are you ok?' Jayden asked, staring at Ryan. 'You look like you're going to throw up.'

'You might be right. The thing is, I got talking to a girl this afternoon –'

Jayden's eyes lit up. 'Where?'

'If you'd let me finish, I'll tell you,' Ryan replied, taking a deep gulp of air. 'This girl, who I think may be Callie Haywood, started talking to me in Cardea Gardens, and she mentioned she might see me here tonight. I've seen her hanging out with Prince Alistair a few times as well. Does that sound like her?'

'Yeah, Callie does seem to be close to His Highness, but she's not part of *that* crowd.'

'What crowd?' Ryan asked, slightly alarmed. He was already nervous with thoughts and concerns about this new acquaintance he'd made. Now it seemed there was a crowd to consider as well. Ryan sighed with a sense of inevitability. 'I bet those are the people who'll look at me disappointedly in the future.'

'You know which crowd; the rich kids, the sporty types, the kind of people who'd talk down and then all over the likes of you and me. To be honest, I'm not sure how the Prince and Callie know each other or what their relationship is.'

'I bet they're courting,' Ryan sighed, hoping that Jayden would dismiss the idea instantly.

Unfortunately for Ryan, his cousin pondered for a good few seconds before answering. 'Nah, I don't think so. At least, I haven't heard anything along those lines.'

The cousins found themselves at the doorway to the main function room, where an usher waited to check invites and escort them in. Jayden handed over her invitation and smiled, then turned to Ryan and asked, 'So what did you and this girl talk about, then?'

'Well, we had both picked up some Flex-izdats from the market – '

'Oh really, Ryan, Flex-izdats? Still? At your age?'

'You don't understand. There's lots of interesting stuff on them,' Ryan protested as he handed his invite to a second usher.

'Oh, the 'secret echoes'. Oh, the 'stolen past'. I can't believe that you believe in that stuff,' Jayden mocked. 'You'll be running about in a rain cloak saying that you're a member of the Sentry and twirling a great big stick next.'

Jayden's usher returned her invite. 'Ok, corporal, you're clear to enter. Have a good evening.'

'You too, many thanks,' Jayden said, stepping through the curtain into the main room.

Ryan also went to step forward but was stopped by his usher's outstretched palm. 'Sorry sir, we're still awaiting clearance on your status.'

Ryan heard a whistle and looked up to see Jayden poke her head back through the curtain. 'Hey, Sentry Boy!' She laughed and drew a circle in the air mocking the way the Sentry would greet each other. 'Blessing you! See you in there.'

Inside the main hall, Prince Alistair was getting the unwanted introductions and interactions that his position required out of the way. He had brought Probot along to handle any unexpected errands that may need attending to.

Alistair was talking to a retired General named Helms when he noticed Callie and Tanya at the Melodium. Helms had been as tough and rugged as they came when he was a young soldier, but as the decades had passed, he had grown into a kind old soul who liked nothing more than a good long chat.

The Prince had made several attempts to excuse himself, but Helms just seemed to natter on obliviously. 'You're shaping up to be a fine young man. Just like your father. And that's not to mention your heroic efforts at the games.'

Using a tone that conveyed both modesty and gratitude, the young Prince attempted to close the conversation once more. 'You're very kind, General Helms. My sporting results are purely a result of the time I put into training. Now, if you'd excuse me – '

'Still, you had better watch out for that young McCloud boy. He nearly had you on a couple of the events. A bright young prospect, indeed. How many years younger than you is he?'

Alistair's pride was immediately bruised, and the etiquette training from his youth vanished. 'The day the spoilt son of two newscasters beats me is the day the whole of Vastrid falls into the sea. Now unless there's anything else, please excuse me.'

General Helms swirled the whiskey in his tumbler as he watched Alistair march away with Probot following behind. 'That apple has fallen very far from the tree. His father always had time to chat.'

Alistair strode towards Callie and Tanya. The Melodium in the Great Hall was a magnificent creation, a circular raised platform base with four robotic figurines known as Meloquins acting as musicians. The Meloquins had blank, silver faces and were dressed in fancy and frilly costumes based on fashions found in recovered paintings from centuries ago. Each Meloquin had its own instrument, fashioned after ancient pieces such as violins or cellos.

Despite having the appearance of musicians, the Meloquins merely acted out the sounds that were produced by a computer program within the base of the Melodium. The sounds were created by a series of tonal selections manufactured by the Shadox Corporation. The pitch and speed of these tonal selections were determined by the biological data of those on the dance floor, detected by strategically placed data capture panels.

As Alistair approached, he asked, 'What is it with you girls and Melodiums? For me, the novelty of them wore off by the time of my eighth birthday.'

'Along with any sense of wonder or romance,' Callie shot back with a grin.

Tanya could become over-excitable at even the most mundane of times, so when confronted by the flashing lights and noise coming from Melodium, she was just short of hysterical.

'Oh, come on Ali, they're great. And so pretty! Look at this,' Tanya said, dragging the Prince by the hand to the base of the Melodium. She put her hand on top of his and placed them both onto one of the flashing neon panels. The panel began to shine brighter as the pitch of the music slowly increased, and the sound of a synthesised choir sang out four notes in a loop as if they were heartbeats.

As this new sound filled the main hall, Alistair could feel all eyes upon him. He had accidentally ended up taking Tanya to the ball and had shrugged off any gossip about this decision as if he was simply doing a girl a favour. But this public display of affection made him take a long, hard look at Tanya. From her never-ending excitable ranting and squealing to the garish ballgown she had chosen to wear that evening, Alistair suddenly felt embarrassed to be associated with her. Tanya gazed adoringly at him, and Alistair immediately realised that unless he nipped this situation in the bud, people would assume that he was officially courting this girl.

Alistair pulled his hand away. The newly created sound stopped suddenly and slipped back into a generic tonal selection.

Tanya's smile fell immediately, and Alistair shook his head. 'I'm sorry Tanya, I'm just not into this.'

He hoped that she saw the bigger picture from his declaration, but he needed only to glance at her to know this wasn't so. Alistair looked over at Callie and wondered just what it would take to get her to look at him the same way Tanya did.

Callie mustered a huge smile and gestured towards the tables, keen to break the awkward moment. 'We should get something to eat before it gets too crowded.'

Alistair seized the opportunity to dine with Callie. 'I totally agree. You two ladies are to join me at the Prince's table. I have a space either side of me reserved for you.'

'Oh, I had agreed to meet my old friend Jesse for dinner here,' Callie frowned. Would there be space for him too?'

The word 'him' sparked a disappointment and concern in Alistair that couldn't be disguised. 'Sorry, who is this old friend? Is he a member of the guards?'

Callie nodded, 'Oh yes, Well, only just. He completed training just a few weeks ago. I thought that sitting with a familiar face might make the ball less intimidating for him.'

Alistair didn't want a young nobody at his table and certainly one that Callie seemed so enthusiastic about, but he knew if he disagreed that she could be out of his sights for the whole evening. Maybe another of the Vastrid cliques would take her in. She may even dance with some other boy. Then she'd be lost to him forever.

'Very well,' Alistair said, clasping his hands together and forcing a smile. 'I do have one spare seat that this young friend of yours can have. It's at the end of the table, though.'

Probot, who had been awarded the privilege of sitting at the table to deal with any unwanted queries for the Prince, was computing the conversation and had already deduced that it would be his seat sacrificed for Jesse. He had the response of 'Very well, I will await further instructions,' ready even before Alistair muttered, 'Probot, I've given up your chair to a friend of Callie's.'

On the other side of the hall, Ryan had finally managed to gain admission. He surveyed the marble columns and delicate crystal features complementing each other and providing the ultimate herding pen for those who weren't like him. The fine quality of everything there, from silk napkins on the table to the gigantic chandelier hanging above the centre of the dance floor, seemed to taunt him and make him feel unwelcome.

Ryan scanned the hall, telling himself he was looking for Jayden and trying to ignore the flutter of anticipation in his stomach. Much to his disappointment, Ryan saw Callie almost immediately; she was guiding someone to the Prince's table with a welcoming smile on her face. Callie's guest was around the same height and build as Ryan but seemed somehow more comfortable in himself. Her friend had dark, messy hair and two day's worth of patchy stubble gracing his face. It would make most young men look unkempt, but this friend of Callie's managed to wear it well.

Ryan sighed. *Oh great, so that's now the Prince and some other guy I have to compete with.*

Before he could contemplate his position in this fictional pecking order, a loud gong sounded, and Ryan found himself being ushered into another queue by the waiting staff.

A large, matriarchal woman was walking down the queue asking in a brisk voice, 'Reservation code and party number?'

Alarmingly, everyone ahead of him seemed to know what she was talking about and dutifully replied before being led to a table by one of her assistants. Eventually, the woman reached Ryan and eyed him with disdain.

'Reservation code and party number? I suppose you've forgotten them,' she sighed. 'I can tell by the sheepish look on your face.'

Ryan went to speak, but his mouth became dry. Before he could muster his response, she continued. 'There's a space at the table over there to the right. Table number thirteen.'

She pointed to a corner next to the bathrooms. The table itself was much lower than the others in the hall and had the distinct look of two slightly mismatched items that had been hastily pushed together. Ryan eyed the guests suspiciously. The first was a strange-looking girl with greasy hair in pigtails. She was wearing glasses with huge lenses, and as she looked around the hall, she chomped and chewed her food with her mouth wide open.

Next to her, with arms crossed and shoulders slumped, sat the most sullen-faced boy Ryan had ever seen. Ryan wondered for a moment whether they might strike up a bond and take solace in their shared dislike of social events, but the boy glared into the distance and refused to make eye contact.

The third person at the table was a tall young man with glasses and a severely shaved head. He sat solemnly staring at his food, occasionally raising his head to speak to the other two before silently retreating back into himself. Ryan didn't like to think of himself as the kind of person who judged others, but as he looked over at his would-be dining companions, he couldn't help but mutter a disappointed, 'Really?'

As Ryan strolled towards Table Thirteen, the girl with the pigtails looked straight at him and mouthed a friendly, 'Hello.'

As she did so, semi-masticated pieces of food dropped from her mouth onto her gingham dress.

Ryan glanced over towards the Prince's table and looked at Callie. She was leaning across the table, laughing with the mysterious messy-haired boy. Ryan was confused; going by all the signs at Cardea Gardens yesterday, Callie should surely be joking around with him, not some carefree, chortling vagrant type. Who was this boy, anyhow? Ryan could accept Prince Alistair's closeness to Callie as one of the first times he had seen her, they had been walking together. Prince Alistair had always been a consideration and potential rival for Callie's affections. Ryan had thought that since their moment in the Gardens yesterday, he may now be in the race but watching Callie and the new boy flicking peanuts at each other, he wondered if there even was a race anymore.

His disappointment attempted to sell his heart a lie. 'It doesn't matter,' he muttered to himself, 'there are other single girls here tonight.'

He scanned the room but could only seem to see girls who were clearly there with a partner. Ryan realised that the only single girl he could see around was the one with the greasy pigtails eating with her mouth open. He hated how he was judging her on such superficial terms, but his heart sank.

Deciding to try and make the best of the situation, Ryan took his seat at Table Thirteen and smiled at his fellow diners. 'Hi there.'

The others at the table muttered hello as a waitress appeared with Ryan's first course. The few short moments that it took for Ryan's plate to be placed in front of him were enough to plunge the table back into the strangeness he'd witnessed on his way there.

After a few spoonfuls of their meals in uneasy silence, the boy with the shaved head turned to Ryan and blurted out,

'They usually take ages to bring the food. You got yours quick enough though,' before looking away again.

Ryan had noticed how difficult the boy found it to talk to people and recognised some of his own social anxieties in this. 'Maybe I got lucky,' Ryan smiled.

The Boy with the shaved head answered quickly. 'Yes, yes you did!' before looking away again.

Ryan wasn't sure how long he'd have to sit at this table enduring this uneasy silence that so far had only been interrupted by brief, nervy statements and the sound of chomping.

Ryan despised small talk, especially at social gatherings like this. In fact, on one occasion, when he had caught a dust virus, he had stopped taking his medicine so as to ensure the symptoms lasted an additional four days, which was long enough to miss his cousin Matthew's wedding. Ryan looked over at his dining companions and their strange ways and thought to himself; *I need a distraction. I'll settle for anything right about now; a comment on the weather, a discussion about the decorations. Heck, I'd even be prepared to try and bluff my way through a chat about the Ocean Games.*

Ryan glanced down at the place settings around him and realised that one seat had yet to be taken. This lit a spark of hope for Ryan; he glanced over towards the dining queue to assess the late arrivals. Typically all Ryan could see was staff loitering around the stern woman, sharing gossip and cracking in-jokes. He was about to sigh when a beautiful blonde-haired girl came running into the hall. She was wearing an expensive-looking silver dress, and despite her initial panic, a graceful smile spread across her face as she walked towards the stern woman and the waiting staff.

Unlike the cold reception Ryan received, the staff all seemed to rejoice as the girl approached them. Through animated gestures, it appeared that she was explaining her lateness, and soon a small group of other late arrivals emerged behind her.

With friendly smiles, the staff ushered her forward towards the dining tables. To Ryan's surprise, the girl started walking directly towards Table Thirteen. The girl's eyes darted around the hall, trying to find her allocated table, and she locked eyes with Ryan. He flashed a nervous smile which the girl returned as she continued to walk towards Table Thirteen.

'Could it be?' Ryan whispered to himself.

The girl surveyed the number on each table she passed, shaking her head and drawing closer to Table Thirteen.

'Could it be?' he asked again. The girl stepped closer and once again smiled at him.

Suddenly a cry of 'Madeline! We're over here,' bellowed across the hall. The voice belonged to Prince Alistair, who was beckoning her towards his table.

'No, of course not,' Ryan sighed as the girl spun around and skipped towards the Prince's table. Ryan watched her leave and turned back to his table, only to find that the fifth seat was now occupied. To his right sat a short, paunchy, middle-aged man. He was clearly going very bald, but what little hair he had left was slicked back across his scalp. He turned and looked at Ryan with a terrifyingly keen grin. The man thrust out his hand in friendship. 'All righty there, young man. Private Ambrose at your service, but feel free to call me Rex.'

'Hi, my name's Ryan. I'm still not used to being Private Tyler.' Ryan shook Rex's hand, pondering how a gentleman of Rex Ambrose's age had never managed to get further than the rank of Private or make enough money to retire. Ryan suddenly felt a sense of trepidation about his future with the Guards.

'Ryan. Ryan. Ryan. Do you know what your name means, young man?' Rex asked, staring intently at Ryan's face.

'Well, I think it means – '

'That's right! It means the Little King. So then, young man, you're a new recruit?' Rex was now grinning so hard it threatened to become a gurn.

Ryan nodded while he chewed his food. 'Yeah, I passed the Grid just last week.'

Rex grinned even harder and scooped a large portion of food onto his fork before turning to stare at Ryan again. 'Good-good young man, good-good. And tell me, what game were you in before the uniform came a-calling?'

'Oh, I used to work in the library. Mainly dealing with archives, pulling out maps and documents – that sort of thing.'

Rex's eyes lit up, and he patted his hand on Ryan's shoulder in delight. 'Say no more young man, say no more. I know all about the library. My first job was there too.'

Rex winked slowly and gave a thumb's up gesture. 'It seems, young man, we've lots in common and thusly, lots to talk about.'

Ryan sank back in his seat and began to long for the uneasy silence he'd wished away just five minutes earlier.

Chapter Thirteen

ENTER THE MOLINE

At the Prince's table, Alistair's attempts to woo Callie were failing miserably. Quip after quip followed anecdote after anecdote, but Callie remained focused on catching up with her friend at the other end of the table. If not for the fawning and applauding of the other guests, the Prince would have been concerned that his famous charisma was beginning to fade.

When Prince Alistair saw the respected and socially desirable debutante Madeline Chambers approaching the table, he'd hoped for a second that it might stir some feelings of jealousy in Callie. However, that tactic hadn't worked when he chose to take Tanya to the ball, and it wasn't working now.

The prince had one more trick up his sleeve; his eyes scanned the room until they made contact with the headwaiter. The headwaiter indicated his eagerness to serve with a nod, and the prince ushered him forward accordingly. As the waiter approached, Alistair leant forward and, behind a cupped hand, whispered, 'For the next course, bring out the moline.'

A look of concern flooded the waiter's face. 'Forgive me, Your Highness, but I don't think that would be wise.'

The prince raised an eyebrow. 'I would like to be served by the moline.'

'But Your Highness,' the waiter continued, 'the next course is the Potage aux Légumes et Poulet.'

'Before you say another word, just consider who I am and what could happen to your career should I receive bad service. So I'll ask again; I want to see the moline. Now, please.'

The headwaiter swallowed hard and replied in a near whisper, 'Very well.'

In the kitchen, a rotund and heavyset chef named Gustav was barking orders at his assistants while running between ovens, grills and hobs to check on the various dishes cooking.

The headwaiter ran in and shakily relayed the prince's request. 'He wants the Moline to serve the next course.'

Gustav stopped in his tracks and spun around. 'Is he crazy? Does he know what the next course is? Not a chance! Maybe if the next course was the coffee, or if the moline was to stroll around with the breadbasket, it would be ok. But that moline, going out there with the Potage aux Légumes et Poulet!?! Not a chance.'

The head waiter composed himself and shook his head. 'The prince is well aware of what course is next and is demanding that the moline serves it. He is most insistent.'

'Dear mercy!' Gustav threw down his ladle in protest. 'It will be the end of our careers if we send the moline out with that course!'

'It'll be the end of our careers if we *don't*.' The waiter ran his hand over his face and sighed. 'If luck is on our side, maybe the serving will go without a hitch.'

The uncertainty could be heard in the waiter's voice as both he and Gustav looked down at a little wicker basket on the floor. The basket had a sturdy black iron cage door on the front of it. The kitchen lighting made it hard to see what exactly was in there, but the slight movements of the basket and humming sound of a purr made it clear that something very alive and very unique was lurking within.

Nearby the Potage aux Légumes et Poulet had nearly finished cooking, and the aromas of chicken, vegetables, herbs and cream started to fill the room. As the scent's potency increased, so did the volume of the purr within the basket. As this noise reached its peak volume, two bright yellow eyes with large pupils as black as midnight appeared from the darkness within the basket and peered out.

Madeline Chambers was talking, at a significant volume, about her family's recent trip to the Outer Islands and advising everyone that they 'really must go at some point'. Coming from an extremely wealthy family and with minimal real-life experience, it didn't cross her mind that, apart from the prince, no one else at the table could afford the wages of the security team required to survive a day there.

Just as Madeline was about to begin another story about 'annoying little beggars' and the various ways 'Daddy's men taught them a lesson,' Prince Alistair became distracted by Callie's male friend looking at his watch. The boy then made his excuses and left.

Alistair shook his head in disbelief. 'Do we bore your friend?' he called across the table to Callie.

Callie leant forward. 'Jesse makes his apologies, but he is due to administer medication to his father in an hour. He'll be back later.'

'Just in time to join you for the slow dance, I imagine.' The prince's jealousy tainted his voice as he spoke.

Callie was shocked. 'Slow dance? That was Jesse! We grew

up together – he's like a brother to me. I've told you stories about our summers on the farm. I can't believe you don't remember me telling you about him.'

By the expression on her face, the prince could tell Callie was annoyed. Maybe she had mentioned this boy Jesse before, but, as Alistair often had to admit to himself, he was prone to tuning out other people's comparatively ordinary anecdotes.

Even so, he racked his brain, trying to establish when Callie may have told him about Jesse. He experienced a vague flashback to an evening where Callie was crying; she was talking about a farm and the cost of medicine. She had then shown him some holographs of when she was young. All of a sudden, it clicked into place, and as if he was about to win a competition, the prince excitedly blurted out, 'Oh yes, I remember now! That was the night you were sobbing on the Montague Steps because he'd found out his father was dying.'

Everyone at the table stopped talking and looked at him with shocked expressions. Alistair immediately began trying to dig himself out of the hole he made for himself and adopted a more sombre tone. 'A terrible, terrible situation. If there's anything my family can do to help, please let me know.'

The Prince looked around the hall for a discussion point so he could change the topic. Luckily he saw the headwaiter nervously scuttle towards the table, and his face broke into a huge smile. 'Everyone! Everyone! You have to pay attention to this next course. It'll be like nothing you've seen before!'

As the waiter reached the table, he cleared his throat and spoke. 'Ladies and gentlemen, I present the next course, Potage aux Légumes et Poulet. Served, for your entertainment, by a moline.'

At the mention of the word 'moline', a murmur of excitement rippled around the table. Tanya squealed with joy while Madeline clasped her hands together in delight. The prince glanced around to gauge the reactions and was disappointed to see that Callie looked concerned.

'You're worried?' Alistair asked.

'Not worried as such, I'm just confused. I thought molines were extinct.'

'Not quite. There is still a tiny handful of molines out there. They're a rare commodity, though. They cost far too much for the Shadox Corporation to make, so they stopped production. The biggest problem with all the wildlife they attempted to produce genetically was that it couldn't breed. Ah, here it comes now.'

Everyone turned, excited to see what a moline looked like with their own eyes, and the diners fell silent as the door creaked ajar. The moline was covered in rich, black fur and stood on its two back legs, about two and a half feet tall. It held itself in a slightly slouched manner, and behind it, a long tail swayed. It was dressed in a little red waistcoat with a golden pattern sewn in the seams. A long chain that led all the way back to the kitchen was attached to the moline's left foot. Two beaming yellow eyes shone brightly but sadly from the creature's furry, round head as it struggled to the prince's table with the large serving bowl.

Using some steps provided by the headwaiter, the moline hopped up onto the table and placed the heavy bowl down with a sigh of relief. The headwaiter looked at the moline and motioned to bow.

The moline gurgled, 'Oh chess. Sorry,' and lowered its head. 'Chour dinner is served.'

The delighted table erupted in cheers and applause, and the moline raised its head. The faint expression of sadness melted into a glow of pride, and the dark pupils in its yellow eyes widened as it gazed at the approving faces. 'Chess,' the moline nodded.

'Why does it speak like that?' Madeline laughed.

Alistair chucked in agreement. 'It's funny, isn't it? They all seem to do that – "chess" instead of "yes", and what have you. It's a wonder they can speak at all, really; they're mainly a mix of cat and monkey, of course.' He gazed at the moline for a moment. 'Some physiological limitation, I suppose.'

From the other side of the hall, a harried-looking chef was beckoning the headwaiter, who leant down to the moline and whispered, 'I have to go. While I'm away, you serve these people well and without any trouble. If anyone finds so much as one of your hairs in their food, you'll be in big, big trouble. You'll be locked in the cellar without food tonight, for starters.'

The moline cowered as he spoke but took the advice with a nervous little, 'Oh,' sound and began to stir the dish with a spoon. As the moline stirred, the tempting aromas of the food filled its nostrils.

'No, no,' the moline gurgled to itself, 'I musht be a good one. A very good one.'

Tanya was fascinated by the creature and was watching it intently. 'Oh, it's so adorable.'

The moline looked up and stared at Tanya. 'Oh no, I'm not an it. I am girl, like choo.'

'I had absolutely no idea that there were boy and girl molines,' said Madeline.

The moline continued to stir but was excited to be talking to friendly humans and happy to chat. 'Oh chess blonde lady-woman. There is the boy molines, and there is the girl molines. I am the girl moline.'

The moline stopped stirring and went to stretch her legs out. 'I can prove. Do you want to see?'

The prince held out his hands to shield his dinner companions from a potentially inappropriate view. 'No, no,' he said, laughing, 'we'll take your word for it.'

The moline glanced around with a shocked look of innocence on her face. 'Oh! Ok then,' she purred before turning back to the food.

With great care, the moline began spooning out portions of the dish to each of the guests. As she served, Prince Alistair leant forward and asked Callie, 'So what do you think?'

Callie looked down at the chain attached to the moline's leg. 'I think it's cruel.'

The moline responded to Callie's empathy and rubbed her furry head onto Callie's hand as an act of friendship and respect.

Callie couldn't help but be charmed by this and added, 'While I find the concept of making the Moline serve to be disgusting and cruel, I have to admit the creature itself is adorable.'

Callie flashed a smile at the moline as it bowed respectfully to her.

The moline then walked back across the table, past all of the served dishes. As she passed each one, the rich, flavoursome aroma rising from the plates seemed to tempt and tease her more and more. Thoughts of taking a little taste engulfed her brain. The moline shook her furry head in disapproval.

'I musht be the good one. I musht,' she gurgled to herself, trying to drive the temptation away.

As she reached the end of the table, the moline noticed that Madeline hadn't touched her food. 'Maybe blonde-lady doesn't like it?' she mumbled to herself.

Madeline was far too busy chatting about the wildlife she had seen while visiting the Outer Islands. The moline tried to resist, but the prospect of making use of a leftover dish was too tempting to let pass. While Madeline continued to talk, the moline sat at the end of the table, occasionally peering back over her shoulder to look fondly at the steaming food.

The moline's mouth began to water, and her tiny pale pink tongue darted out from her lips to lick them. Finally, the moline could wait no longer and tugged on Madeline's sleeve. 'Scuse me, lady, but don't choo want the dinder?'

Madeline waved her hand distractedly. 'Yes, yes, I shall eat it in a minute,' but it was all too brief to combat the growing temptation thundering through the moline's body.

Madeline was just about to resume talking about wilde-beests when she heard the gasps of her fellow diners. Prince Alistair let out a low 'ahem' noise and looked down towards Madeline's plate, where the moline was bent down, lapping up the food.

Realising that all eyes were upon her, the moline stopped and slowly looked up at the diners with rich, creamy sauce dripping from her furry face.

Madeline let out a horrified 'Eurgh!' while the rest of the table laughed.

Realising her mistake, the moline began to tug on Madeline's sleeve. 'Sorry, lady'.

As she did so, Madeline pushed her away. The combination of the moline's tugging and Madeline's push caused the sleeve of Madeline's dress to tear right off.

Back in the kitchen, Gustav the chef checked the time on his Cuff-Linq. It had been five minutes since the moline was sent out to serve the dish, and he figured that if anything had gone wrong, he would have heard about it by now. He began to sigh with relief, and as he took a deep lungful of air, he spun around. As he exhaled, he saw the moline standing before him with not only sauce around her mouth but also the torn sleeve from an expensive-looking dress.

The moline padded up to him and purred, 'Sorry sir'.

Gustav's face flushed a furious crimson. 'Sorry? You will be!'

. . .

On the other side of the hall, Ryan had managed to stay long enough to be able to excuse himself. He wasn't one for long meals, and the first two courses were more than enough to satisfy any hunger he had. Looking over at the prince's table, he saw Callie making her apologies to her fellow diners and leaving the table in a manner not dissimilar to his own escape.

Callie edged away from the table and stood for a moment, scanning the hall, before slipping into the corridor towards the kitchen.

'Where is she going?' Ryan wondered to himself as his fascination increased.

Pushing and squeezing himself past the many chairs, tables, diners and staff that filled the hall, Ryan attempted to follow her. His diagonal path through the seating area caused much tutting, sighing and even harsh language as he passed.

With just three tables separating him from the corridor that Callie had disappeared down, Ryan pushed on; suddenly, one of the diners reached out, grabbed his arm and yelled, 'Hey! Where do you think you're going?'

Ryan looked down and saw Jayden. 'Well?' she asked. 'What's the big rush? And where have you been? I had a seat on this table reserved for you.'

Ryan was caught off guard as his mind attempted to process the shock of having his arm grabbed and the realisation that it must have been Jayden's reservation number that the large matriarchal woman was asking for earlier.

'Oh,' he muttered, shaking his head, 'I ended up over on Table Thirteen.' Ryan gestured towards his former dining colleagues.

'Is that creepy old Rex Ambrose?' Jayden asked, squinting at the corner of the room. 'Why did you go and sit there? Are you attracted to failure or something?'

'No! Not at all,' Ryan snapped. 'There was this bossy woman who demanded that I sit there.'

'Ryan!' Jayden thumped her fist on the table. 'She was just some old hag from the catering company, whereas you are now a member of the Royal Guard. You need to stand up for yourself. I would have broken her nose and arrested her if she had spoken to me like that.'

One of Jayden's fellow diners, a baby-faced officer named Isaac, looked up. 'Maybe that's why they won't promote you to captain.'

Jayden spun around in her chair and threw a spoon directly at Issac's head. 'Shut up.'

She turned back to Ryan. 'Carrying yourself like a member of the Guards is the first step. Once you – '

Jayden paused to let Isaac, who was clutching his forehead in flying-spoon-induced agony, finish groaning.

' – start acting like a Guard, then you'll find people treat you like one. Anyhow, none of this answers my initial question; where are you trying to get to in such a hurry?'

'Well,' sighed Ryan, knowing that the only way to silence his cousin was to tell her the truth, no matter how much teasing it may induce, 'You know that Callie girl I was talking to when I was in Cardea Gardens yesterday? She got up and left the prince's table and took off down that corridor.'

Jayden frowned and shrugged her shoulders. 'So?'

'Well,' Ryan replied, offering a half-shrug back, 'I guess I just wanted to see if she was alright.'

'Oh, my cousin, you certainly are a strange one. She's fine. There was some kind of cat-monkey-waiter-thing dancing about on their table, and that silly bint Maddie Chambers started making a fuss, as she always does. So I should imagine your girlfriend is making sure that they don't put the little cat-monkey-waiter-thing down.' Jayden paused and took a sip of her drink. 'She strikes me as being an animal-lover type.'

'She's not my girlfriend,' Ryan protested.

'Oh, please! You spoke to her for more than a minute. By your standards, you're practically married to her,' Jayden rolled her eyes and waved Ryan onwards. With a sly smile, she added, 'Go on then, run to the corridor and loiter nervously.'

Ryan blushed but couldn't think of a comeback, so he muttered, 'Thanks' and raced off.

From the kitchen, there was the sound of crashing and clanging. Callie neared the end of the corridor and peeked through the glass in the kitchen's door. She saw the head waiter pacing around, holding an open basket at a tilted angle while Gustav the chef crept towards the rear of the kitchen brandishing a large, brass ladle.

Suddenly the headwaiter yelled, 'There!' pointing behind one of the large stoves.

Gustav threw his ladle at the spot only for the moline to leap over it like a black, furry bolt of lightning.

Gustav screamed in frustration as the moline uneasily landed on a work surface, knocking plates, pots and pans to the floor. As she sped along the long countertop, the moline was so busy glancing back to check where Gustav was that she didn't notice the headwaiter approaching from the other end of the kitchen. When she finally caught sight of him, the moline attempted to change direction. However, her little pelted legs gave in, and she fell backwards onto the work surface. As she did, she was struck on the back of her head by Gustav's ladle.

'I've got you now. No more stealing for you, little bandit!' Gustav cackled as he grabbed the dazed moline by her legs and began to lower her into the basket.

The moline was groggy, and Gustav's words seemed to echo through the ringing sound in her head.

'I am little bandit moline?' she asked through a gurgle to no one in particular. As her large yellow eyes began to focus, she saw the basket below her. 'No more for bandit moline?' she asked, 'Bandit will want more if I am hungee!'

The moline stretched out her arms and pushed with all of her strength against the edges.

'Come on, push her in quickly,' urged the head waiter. 'If we decide to sell her, we won't get as good a price for her if she's damaged. They can't experiment on 'em properly unless they're healthy.

'I'm trying, but she's really strong!' Gustav grunted, trying to coax her arms inside the basket.

The moline's face was full of steely determination as she pushed away. 'No! Bandit will not go in the cage and have no more food.'

At this point, Callie had seen enough and burst through the door. 'What do you think you're doing?' She flashed her Royal Guard identity badge and glared at the men.

Taken by surprise, the headwaiter and Gustav dropped both the basket and the moline and held up their hands to show they were no threat.

'How can we be of assistance?' the head waiter smiled thinly at Callie, adjusting his voice back to a hushed, hospitality tone.

Gustav was appalled by his colleague's cowardice and stepped in front of him. 'We've done nothing wrong. You've got no right to throw your weight around in my kitchen.'

Callie looked around the kitchen before answering. 'I do when you're using animals as servants.'

Gustav snorted. 'Well, as a member of the Royal Guards, you'll be aware that it's not against the law to use artificially created life forms for work purposes.'

'Yes, that's true, but also as a member of the Royal Guard,

I'm aware that you'd need all the authorised permittance paperwork to be able to do so.'

Her tone shifted. 'I'd like to see it. Now.'

As Gustav and the waiter frantically searched the kitchen for all seventeen pieces of paper needed to allow them to use a moline, Callie glanced down towards a small gap between two of the stoves. She had noticed the moline scurrying there after being dropped.

Callie smiled at the gap and whispered, 'It's ok,' before motioning with her head towards the open kitchen door.

A warm purr emerged from the gap, and the moline darted from the kitchen and into the corridor.

As predicted by his cousin, Ryan was indeed loitering nervously about halfway down the corridor, overseeing the whole event. He watched the moline scamper away from the kitchen towards the large windows at the end of the hallway. The moline desperately attempted to work the window's latch, but it was far too intricate for her tiny paws.

'Come on, Bandit paws, come on,' she gurgled to herself as she tried and failed again.

Ryan noticed Callie glancing over her shoulder at the moline's failed escape attempts. He caught Callie's eye, and she gave him a nod to help the creature. Ryan sprinted to the window and opened it up wide. The moline poked her head out and breathed in the fresh breeze emerging from the sea below.

The moline turned to Ryan and bowed her head in gratitude. 'Thank you, sir,' she gurgled before leaping from the window onto a couple of storage hut roofs and then finally landing on a cargo barge that was passing through the harbour.

Ryan looked back at Callie, who mouthed, 'Thanks,' before motioning that he should leave before he was caught.

Ryan walked back to the main hall, trying to work out if and how he'd attempt to romance Callie later that night. His train of thought was, however, interrupted by the angry, piercing scream of a chef realising that his extremely rare and very expensive moline had escaped.

Chapter Fourteen

MISSILES. MED-STICKS AND SHOOTING STARS

Far away from the drama with the Moline in the kitchen, the social interactions of the debutante ball and even Vastrid itself, Rachel Stone was in her chamber aboard Shadox VI. She lay sprawled out on her favourite chez-lounge, being pampered by her personal assistant, Private Holmes. She took a sip of her cocktail and sighed a weary sigh.

'Is something troubling you, ma'am?' Private Holmes asked as he massaged her left foot.

'Oh, you wouldn't understand,' she answered, closing her eyes and throwing her head back in a frustrated attempt to relax. 'Getting what you want can be such a tedious process.'

'I'm sure it is, ma'am.'

Rachel fidgeted and tutted. 'No, get off. This isn't working.' She kicked her foot away from Private Holmes' massaging fingers and shooed towards the door. 'Leave.'

Walking to her video intercom, she adjusted her hair fussily before keying in the priority code to Colonel Bron's troop carrier, which entering Earth's atmosphere and heading towards Vastrid. Rachel's direct line ensured that she could connect to any video telecom screen supplied by the

Corporation, and on this occasion, she caught Bron's troops playing cards at the other end of the ship's deck.

Rachel coughed loudly to get their attention, and eventually, one of the troops hollered to the rest of his squad, 'Hang on, there's some bit of skirt on the Vid-Screen. I'll check it out.'

As the trooper turned his full attention to the screen, the colour drained from his face. 'Bloody hell, it's Rachel Stone'. His comrades did their best to mute their laughter at their friend's faux pas.

He approached the screen and stood to attention. 'Ms. Stone, I'm honoured. How can I help?'

'Thank you, trooper. Can you ask Colonel Bron to come to the telecom, please?' Rachel asked, smiling brightly.

The trooper breathed a sigh of relief as he turned to leave. Maybe Rachel Stone hadn't caught them gambling, and perhaps the microphone was far enough away to have not picked up the moment he referred to the most powerful woman in the galaxy as 'some bit of skirt'.

Within five minutes, Bron had made his way from the control pod of the ship to the Vid-Screen in the communications room.

'Ms. Stone,' he said, standing to attention. 'How may I be of assistance?'

Rachel's smile fell away. 'Firstly, what was the name of the trooper who fetched you?'

'His name is Private Matthews. Why? Has he caused offence?'

'The details are not important,' Rachel declared, calmly turning her nose up, 'but I do insist that you place him in a position where he'll most likely be shot.'

'Very well. Was there anything else, or can I get on with invading Vastrid for you?' Bron sniped.

'There's no need to take that tone with me, colonel – I only called to help.'

The annoyance in her tone mellowed as she focused on her reason for calling. 'How close are you to Caspian City? Is everything going to plan?'

'We're about twenty minutes away. My lads have been instructed as per our plan and are ready to carry out orders. Nox may be a problem, though.'

'Oh?' said Rachel, leaning forward. 'How so?'

'Well,' said Bron rubbing his hand over his face, 'he wants us to straight-out assassinate the Hawthornes and then withdraw. He seems to regard tonight as a hit and run rather than a repossession. Like I've always said, he ain't anything but a glorified bodyguard.'

Rachel fell back in her chair. 'Oh no, that really won't do. If the Hawthornes die too soon, everyone from the Royal Guards to the scum in Baker's End will be thrown into a state of panic. It will be uncontrollable. This news worries me; Mr Nox knows something that we do not.'

Rachel stood from her chair and paced for a moment or two before turning to face the screen. 'The only way we can gain any level of control from this situation is to create our own chaos first.'

Bron looked perplexed. 'Explain?'

Rachel smirked. 'Tell me, good Colonel, is your troop carrier suitably armed to create heavy-duty structural damage?'

Bron nodded. 'Of course, we have enough SX-5 missiles to tear apart a large building – even the palace itself.'

'Are you familiar with the Great Hall in Caspian City? The Hawthornes are throwing their annual Debutante Ball there tonight. Not only will it attract Vastrid's most important and privileged brats but also members of the Royal Guard, who receive invites as a perk. Prince Alistair will certainly be there. I'd suggest that you tear a hole through the crystal ceiling and send a squad of your very best men to pluck the prince out of the chaos and bring him to me alive.'

'And what about the rest of them?' Bron enquired.

'Well, the prince's mother is dead, and my spies have informed me that his sister has already been removed from her finishing school and sent into hiding. We can bring her in later. My sources have also indicated that King Willie is on his way to the ball as we speak, so hopefully, you'll be able to pick him up there.' Rachel paused for a second before continuing. 'Just to be sure, though, send a squad or two to the palace. Seize any of his advisors, staff or personages of power and influence.'

Bron was lost in Rachel's words, gleefully imagining the brutal carnage that this mission would bring. A sinister smile spread across his ragged face. 'As you command.'

Rachel's heart was racing with excitement. 'Good luck, Colonel. I know that neither of us are ones for sentiment, but please come back in one piece. I would certainly prefer to celebrate the fall of the Hawthornes together.'

Bron smirked. 'I've survived a lot worse than Hawthorne's silver spoon brigade. One last thought, though – if the Guards spill onto the streets and scatter, I won't have enough troops to hunt them down.'

'That's a good point.' Rachel pondered for a while. 'We'll get the scum and the scoundrels to take care of them. They will have been aching to lay their hands on their oppressors for years now, and we will make it not only legal but encouraged. I will send out a bulletin offering to reduce any outstanding service for each member of the Guards they bring us alive.'

Bron laughed. 'You truly are a brutal woman. I fear the day I get on the wrong side of you.'

'Well, Colonel Bron, you had better not let me down then

– it's safer that way.' Rachel may have said the line as a light-hearted parting remark, but it was savagely true of her nature.

Bron switched off the Vid-Screen and walked through the carrier. As he reached the cargo bay, he noticed Nox and three troops he didn't recognise entering one of the smaller dispatch ships.

'Where do you think you're off to?' hollered Bron.

Wearing a sharp suit made from some of the universe's most expensive materials, Nox was hardly dressed for a military operation; however, with his custom-built katana sword harnessed on his back, only an idiot would have dared to raise this point.

He looked over his shoulder and smirked at the colonel. 'Ah Bron, no need to get all hot and bothered. I have left a message with your second-in-command. You'd know all about it if you weren't too busy gossiping with, what is it you have to call her – Ms Stone?'

Nox always knew how to get Bron's temper flaring, and it could not be hidden in his voice. 'Well, tell me then, what is it I would've known all about?'

'— if you hadn't been gossiping?' Nox asked with a poker face, further angering the colonel.

Bron stepped up to Nox and stared him straight in the eyes. 'Just answer the question, where are you going?'

Nox refused to break eye contact with Bron. He cracked his knuckles and spoke calmly, 'No need for hostility, Colonel. We are both working for the good of the Corporation, are we not?'

Nox motioned to his troops to board the dispatch ship before responding. 'To answer your question, it has been decided by Professor Shadox that I'll go to Caspian City first with a smaller squad to ensure the Hawthornes are dealt with quickly and cleanly.'

'And what are the rest of the squad and I supposed to do?' Bron asked.

Nox smirked and answered as the hatch on the dispatch ship began to rise. 'You can come down once we are successful and pick up the pieces.'

A protective, metallic gravity door closed in front of Nox, and the dispatch ship took off towards Caspian City.

Bron was still fuming but turned to look at the giant cylinders used to launch the powerful SX-5 missiles from the troop carrier. 'Oh Mr Nox, when I come down and pick up the pieces,' he muttered to himself, 'I do hope they're pieces of your dead body.'

As Nox's dispatch ship began its journey to Vastrid, a larger and grubbier ship was being prepared to leave Earth's atmosphere. The ship belonged to a tall, rugged man named Marcus Hagen and a group of vicious thugs who worked for him. Hagen had spent most of his life selling the accomplished combat skills of his crew to the highest bidder.

For a while, this path had brought him riches and a sense of personal pride, but a recent job had gone badly wrong. Now he found himself tagged and tracked by the Corporation, desperately trying to round up fugitives for the Shadox Corporation to reduce the Outstanding Service he and his crew owed them.

Usually, this situation made Hagen feel like a trapped man; however, on this occasion, he was in high spirits. A few hours earlier, he had managed to capture one of Shadox Corporation's most wanted fugitives, and the reduction in outstanding service would be ample. On top of that, the fugitive in question was someone Hagen held a longstanding grudge against.

With his crew preparing the ship to take their prisoner to

Shadox VI, Hagen walked towards the holding cells. The fugitive was in his mid-twenties, and his wrists were cuffed to his chair. Wearing an oversized black trenchcoat, he sat slouched, with his dark eyes staring sullenly at the floor. He had grown up on Terra-Cylus, an off-planet colony created by the Shadox Corporation when they first rose to power.

As Shadox began to tighten its stranglehold, the colonists started forming armies in an attempt to gain their independence. To curb these rebellious acts, the Corporation reduced the quality of the artificial oxygen substitute pumped into large domes that surrounded the colonies and created their atmosphere.

As a result of breathing in this artificial air as a child, the captured fugitive's skin was tinged light blue, and his hair was a mop of silver. His lungs were also weaker than those of humans who had been raised on Earth, and as he sat confined in the chair, the sound of his wheezing matched the sound of Hagen's footsteps.

'What's the matter, my friend?' Hagen asked, pulling a thin white tube out of his pocket. 'Would you like this? I believe it's your Med-Stick. It would appear that it fell to the floor during the scuffle we had earlier today. I'll let you have it. All you have to do is plead for it.'

The prisoner looked up at Hagen and scowled. Hagen knew his captive well enough to know he'd never plead for anything, even if his life depended on it. Hagen reached through the cell bars and placed the Med-Stick in the prisoner's mouth, allowing him to take a deep inhalation. It was far from an act of mercy; Hagen felt a sense of victory and smirked as the vapours from the Med-Stick filled the prisoner's lungs, causing the wheezing to fade.

'See? I'm not so bad, my friend. I know we'll never agree on the decision I made all those years ago on Terra-Cylus, and I know how much hatred we harbour for each other. But despite all of that, I wouldn't dream of letting you sit in agony as we ship you off to the Corporation, most probably to a death penalty.'

The prisoner continued to sit in silence as Hagen mocked him again. 'Come on, my friend! Don't you have one of your spiteful barbed comments to throw at me? I can't believe that you've changed that much since we last met. It's even more unlikely that your capture has humbled you.'

The prisoner remained silent, but before Hagen could continue his taunting, he was interrupted by one of his crew. 'Hey, 'scuse me Marcus, but you need to hear the deal that's just been posted on the Corporation worklist.'

The voice belonged to Rico Akabusi, the youngest yet longest-serving of Hagen's current crew.

Hagen rubbed his stubbly chin and looked back at his prisoner. 'Well, it appears that I have some business to attend to with Mr Akabusi. But fear not, my friend, I will return later to check you're still comfortable.'

As they walked through the ship towards the control deck, Rico asked, 'Just what is the deal with you and our latest bounty?'

'It's a long story,' Hagen answered. 'Like all long stories, it involves a girl. In this case, his sister.' He paused for a moment to push back an emerging sadness in his eyes. 'It doesn't matter much now – he's on the way to a death sentence. So what's this new deal that's got you so excited? '

'It's from Rachel Stone herself! I don't know what they have planned, but they're offering six months deducted from any outstanding service for each member of the Vastridian Royal Guard brought to them from midnight. We snatch up a bunch of them, and we could be out of the Corporation's bad books.'

This news pleased Hagen immensely. 'Now that is a very interesting development. As much as I'd like to take our blue-skinned guest straight to the Corporation, I don't think we can afford to miss this opportunity. Tell the boys to halt all current preparations. We're changing course.'

Back at the debutante ball, all of the courses had been served, and the tables were being cleared away to leave more room for dancing and mingling. Having issued a court summons to Gustav the Chef for illegally using a Moline as a servant, Callie worked her way back through the crowd. She looked around the great hall, eager to find people she knew before she was forced to make awkward chit chat with a stranger.

Glancing over at the table where she had been sat, she could see that Alistair was still there but appeared to be locked in a conversation with Madeline Chambers and some of her unpleasantly vain friends. Callie had absolutely no desire to stand around like a spare part while they squawked and bragged about their social standing.

Callie saw that Tanya was standing with them and still trying to play the part of Prince Alistair's date. A forced smile remained on Tanya's face, but her sad eyes betrayed it. Tanya was coming to the realisation that no matter how she acted or looked, the Prince would never see her as a potential girl-friend, or indeed, as an actual friend. Watching the natural connection he had with Madeline and her friends, she knew that she'd only ever be an acquaintance.

Callie felt bad for her friend but had no desire to get caught in the melodrama that would inevitably unfold between Tanya and the Prince; instead, she looked around the room and saw Ryan ordering a drink from the refreshment table. As the waitress poured the bright beverage into a glass, Callie noticed Ryan nervously fussing with his hair and then break into a shy smile as he received his drink. She couldn't explain why but that smile charmed Callie in a way that she had never been charmed before. Her thoughts raced back to her unexpected encounter with Ryan at Cardea Gardens. Suddenly the smell of the garden's bloom and the warm sun-kissed air of that afternoon seemed to surround her. Hoping for that feeling to return, she slowly walked towards Ryan.

He hadn't noticed her and turned to look out of one of the hall's huge bay windows. Ryan was taking a look at the sprawling moonlit gardens that surrounded the hall when he suddenly felt a playful yet forceful whack on his shoulder. He spun around expecting to find some hooligan looking for a fight or even Prince Alistair having a jape at his expense but instead, he saw Callie.

Callie was hoping for Ryan to say hello and break the ice, but he just stood there looking surprised.

'I just thought that I'd say thanks for helping me with the Moline.'

'Oh, it was no trouble,' Ryan answered shyly, adjusting his hair again. 'I hope 1 did the right thing by letting it escape. I'd hate to think of it starving to death or something.'

'She'll be fine, at least for tonight. I shouldn't imagine she went far,' Callie replied, even though she hadn't actually considered what would happen to the Moline once set free. 'I'll take a look for her tomorrow during my patrol. So, who are you here with tonight?'

Ryan wasn't sure how to answer that question. From their brief chat earlier at Cardea Gardens, there had been the indication that he'd be hanging out with Callie this evening. Ryan suddenly feared that he had read too much into her friendliness towards him and decided to play it cool in case he had misread the signals.

'Oh well, my cousin Jayden's around and about. To be honest, I'm not sure what I'm doing here. I'm thinking of leaving soon if I can.'

Callie looked disappointed. She had thought that they

might have some common interests and could have a fun evening together at the ball. Callie was beginning to realise that she found his kind face and shy manner somehow attractive.

She decided to make an effort and attempt to keep their conversation going. 'I saw that you were looking at the Great Hall's garden earlier. They look really beautiful at night, don't they? I'm thinking of going for a walk through them; would you like to join me?'

Truthfully, Ryan wasn't all that interested in the garden and had only been looking out of the window for something to do, but he was elated at Callie's offer. 'I'd love to,' he answered before pausing to consider the words he had used.

The word 'love' hung in the air like an awkward declaration. Despite registering this and blushing, Callie coolly smiled as if it was nothing. 'Ok, let's shake this place and get out of here.'

Ryan realised that he had no idea where the exits to the garden were. In a moment born out of awkwardness rather than rebellious spontaneity, he pushed the bay window next to him open and hopped out of it.

Callie chuckled. 'You certainly know how to keep a girl guessing, don't you?'

'Guessing?' Ryan asked.

'What you'll do next?' Callie answered, countering Ryan's puzzled expression with an arch of her eyebrows.

'Oh, sorry about that, I just thought it would be quicker.'

'It's not a problem,' Callie smiled, although, in the ball gown she was wearing, it *was* a problem. She cursed to herself as she attempted to lift her legs onto the window ledge with her skirt either getting in the way or lifting revealingly. Callie eventually managed to get up on the ledge and felt Ryan's hands on her waist as he helped to lift her down. In any other similar instance, she would have refused the help of a boy;

and in any other similar instance, Ryan would have been too shy to suddenly reach out and put his hands around a girl's waist. There was, however, a certain magic about the moment that pushed the two of them beyond the boundaries of character.

As Ryan's hands held her, Callie felt a strange yet welcome glow rush through her body. The sensation escalated as he lowered her to the ground below. As her feet touched the floor and Ryan removed his grasp, the feeling died away. For a second, she considered telling Ryan about this but realised how crazy it would make her sound and decided against it.

Ryan and Callie smiled at each other and began to walk through the garden outside, unaware that Prince Alistair had been watching them the whole time from inside the hall. Madeline and her crowd had left to mingle elsewhere, leaving Tanya to stand awkwardly beside her supposed date as he worked himself up into a temper over Callie's interest in another boy. Alistair was used to getting what he wanted and had little experience of things going awry. This new feeling of failure confused him, and, willingly or not, he decided to channel it through anger.

'Where does she think she's going?' Alistair fumed. 'With a cadet – a cadet on secondment no less. That boy from the library? What does he have to offer? An ill-fitting jacket and conversation flavoured with stutters?'

Tanya attempted to cool him down. 'She's just going for a walk.'

Alistair continued to stare at the bay window. 'She is supposed to be on duty. That's what we agreed.'

Tanya forced a laugh, attempting to lighten the mood and snap the prince out of his pettiness. 'When was that agreed? This is the ball, the one time of the year when we can let our hair down. No one's really on duty, are they?'

Alistair turned to Tanya and glared at her. 'It was agreed

when she refused to come to the ball with me. You should remember, you were there.'

Tanya knew where this was going, and as tears welled in her eyes, her voice began to break. 'Alistair, please stop this; you're being ridiculous and embarrassing me.'

'I'm being ridiculous? I'm being embarrassing?' Alistair yelled. 'Look at you! How many times do I have to make it clear that I'm not interested in you?'

With tears streaming down her cheeks, Tanya managed to whisper, 'Ali, please?'

'See what I mean? You're still here! Still following me around like a stray dog in that stupid ball gown.' Alistair continued to rant. 'What is it? What exactly do you think will happen if you keep following me around?'

Tanya started sobbing. 'I don't know why you have to be so mean. I'm going home. I – I can't deal with this anymore.'

She dried her makeup-smeared eyes with one of her evening gloves and walked out of the hall.

Alistair muttered to himself, 'Good riddance' before taking a sip of his drink and turning to present the bay window with his angry scowl.

In the garden, Ryan and Callie were talking about Flex-izdats. They were both glad to have moved on to a topic they could speak passionately and freely about. The moon beamed brightly in the night sky, illuminating the garden in a pale blue glow.

Spotting a clutch of buttercups growing on the lawn, Callie ran to them and plucked one from the ground.

'Wait there,'she cried out to Ryan with a smile on her face before racing back with the small, golden flower in her hand. 'Hey Ryan,' she asked, reaching out to hold the buttercup under his chin.'Do you like butter?'

Ryan recognised that Callie was mimicking the first-ever vid-clip to be distributed on a Flex-izdat. It was from a distant age and showed a young lady placing a buttercup under the chin of a young man and asking that same question. As she did so, the man would smile shyly before the footage paused and then softly dissolved. Amongst collectors of secret echoes, it was considered one of the most important and artistically beautiful pieces ever found. Ryan laughed at the reference. 'That's really impressive. I wonder who those people were?'

'I don't know,' Callie answered, 'but I adore that clip. The way the sun shines through their hair, the way they look at each, the bittersweet music that plays in the background.'

Ryan knew exactly what she meant. There was a certain sense of romance in that footage that he, along with every other fan of the secret echoes, could live vicariously through. The romantic nature of the clip went beyond indications of courtship and touched on something more universal. Watching it always made Ryan feel that magic could arrive at any moment and that maybe the bigger moments in life only arrive due to the smaller ones. Having lived a life consisting only of small moments, he found this extremely reassuring.

Callie was still talking about the clip, but Ryan felt his mind begin to wander. He found himself staring into the night sky. He focused his sight on individual stars and thought about how their light could bewitch and inspire for many years after they expired, the same way that the moments from the past lived on through Flex-izdats.

'The stars are pretty tonight, aren't they?' Callie said, noticing Ryan's distraction. In any other instance, she may have been offended if a boy decided to stare off into the sky while she was speaking. However, something was enticing about the sky that night, and she found herself also looking deep into the cluster of stars that shone above them.

Standing side by side with Callie, Ryan felt a sense of calm and happiness that he hadn't felt before. It felt like a fresh start or a sudden sense of approval. He quickly glanced over at Callie, who was still looking at the stars. 'Everything is pretty tonight,' he said.

Callie softly bit her bottom lip and continued looking at the sky. 'I think,' she said, 'you should hold my hand.'

Slowly, Ryan and Callie stretched out their arms until their fingertips met, their fingers entwined, and eventually, their palms were resting against each other. As they held hands, they both felt a glowing energy flow through their bodies. Callie had felt something similar when Ryan helped her down from the ledge, but this time it felt not only stronger but also more controllable. The feeling reminded Ryan of the strange sensations he had experienced at the Grid and during his altercation with the Wise Guys at Craydon's Corner. This time the surge of energy flowing around his body felt calmer and less volatile.

As the feeling continued to surge within them, they found the way that they looked at the stars began to change. They were no longer looking *at* the sky; they were now looking *into* it.

Just as Callie and Ryan were beginning to grow aware that there might be something more to the sensations running through their bodies, a travelling light in the sky distracted them.

Breaking contact with Ryan's hand, Callie pointed to the sky. 'Look!' she cried, 'A shooting star!'

Ryan went to speak but was distracted by the sound of a twig snapping. 'What was that?'

They both looked around but were unable to see anything unusual. 'It's probably just an owl or a squirrel, or maybe that Moline from earlier,' Callie joked.

However, it wasn't an owl or a squirrel or even the Moline.

Hidden in the branches of one of the garden's largest blossom trees, Ryan and Callie were being observed with keen interest by Kendra Lomax.

'A shooting star?' Kendra grumbled to herself quietly. 'That's a security satellite that's been blasted out of the sky if ever I've seen one. They're on their way. It's all about to begin.'

As Kendra pondered over the events that were sure to unfold, old wounds that would be reopened and an inevitable meeting she'd always hoped she would manage to avoid, she added, 'Or more likely, end.'

Chapter Fifteen

BANDIT AND THE BARGE

Across a stretch of water that separated the Great Hall and a nearby harbour, an altercation between a small furry creature and a fisherman was about to come to a head. The Moline who had caused a commotion earlier at the Great Hall was now being flung from a fishing boat with great force and little sympathy by a furious crew member.

The Moline landed on the sandy shore with a dull thud. The force of the crewmember's throw made the Moline's small, furry body bounce several times before she crashed softly into the wreckage of a disused barge.

Sitting amongst the splinters and rust of the old boat, the Moline shook her fluffy head to clear the cobwebs away. Looking around, her bright yellow eyes caught a glimpse of her reflection in one of the broken mirrors lying on the floor. The sight of her own image took her by surprise. 'Oh!' she declared.

She approached the mirror with both trepidation and fascination. As she slowly lowered her head closer to the mirror, memories of her final encounter with Gustav the Chef echoed around her head. Gustav's cackle of 'little bandit' repeated in the Moline's dazed mind with such intensity that as she stared at her reflection, she found herself matching the name with her image. 'I'm little bandit? Chess, I am Bandit,' she gurgled to herself, eventually nodding in approval.

Just as the newly self-named Bandit had begun to feel calm and relaxed, she heard someone approaching. As the footsteps became louder, she scampered into a dark corner of the barge. Sitting in the darkness, Banditobserved as a figure entered, clutching a large bundle of wooden planks and blankets. The footsteps belonged to Caleb Scudder, who, having been cast out by his family, had made his way to the harbour. He had hidden there several times in the past and figured that it would be as good a place as any to stay for a night or two. Caleb struggled to clear the small inner door frame of the barge with his large bundle of materials and ended up dropping the top layer of planks.

'BLEAK!' Caleb cried out in frustration as they noisily bounced off the floor of the barge. The noise of the planks dropping startled Bandit, who quickly scurried to another dark corner. The frame of the Moline's body caught Caleb's eye.

Fearing the worst, he grabbed one of the planks and held it like a weapon. 'Oh great, there's some dirty wildlife in here,' he murmured to himself.

Creeping towards the corner where the Moline was hiding, he attempted to entice the creature out by making some soft animal noises. However, his mimicry skills were minimal at best and, if anything, only confused the Moline, causing her to ask, 'Wha'?'

Caleb jumped back in fright. 'Bleakin' 'eck! You can talk?'

Having grown up in Baker's End, Caleb's experience and knowledge of the animal kingdom was limited to snarling dogs, gutter foxes, diseased rats and stray cats.

From the shadows, Bandit proudly declared, 'Chess. I can

do talk. I am the Moline, after all. Who are choo? Choo are – a man?'

Caleb was still somewhat shocked. 'Yes, I am a man.'

He had remembered Molines being mentioned on the news as a child but couldn't recall if they were dangerous or not. He tightened his grasp of the plank of wood.

'Are choo the chef?' Bandit asked, her eyes narrowing.

'No, no – I'm a locksmith.'

'Oh.' replied Bandit, flatly. A moment of uneasy silence filled the barge before she spoke again. 'Choo have food, though?'

Caleb didn't know how to answer for the best, so he decided to go for the truth.

'Yes. Well, sort of. I mean, I have some tins and – '

Before he could finish his sentence, the Moline emerged from the corner and began softly rubbing her head on his leg.

'Bandit Moline stay for a while, please, sir?' Bandit asked.

Caleb hadn't planned on rebuilding his life with a rare animal by his side, but to be honest, his current plan consisted of nothing more than sitting in the wreck of a barge and eating tinned food.

He looked down at Bandit's eager and expectant face and replied, 'Oh go on then, why not?' while giving her head a soft stroke.

Caleb went to turn away, and a look of alarm suddenly appeared on Bandit's face. Tugging at Caleb's trouser leg, Bandit frantically begged, 'But sir, we mustn't go back to the important job! We can not go back to the important job!'

'What are you on about?' Caleb asked. 'What important job?'

Bandit pointed in the direction of the Great Hall. 'The important job! Across the waters, where all the ladies and the mans are dancing tonight. Bandit did the serving wrong – all wrong, and now the chef wants to put me in the cage. Pretty lady and friendly man helped me run away.'

Caleb's eyes lit up. 'The debutante ball? Is it the debutante ball tonight?'

Bandit nodded sadly.

'Don't you worry, my little furry friend; we won't be going there. For starters, I'm sure they'd shoot me down with tranq darts if I so much as stepped foot in the Great Hall,' Caleb answered.

'But,' he continued, racing up a ladder towards the roof of the barge, 'that's not going to stop me having a gander at how the other half lives. I hope there are peachy rich girls there tonight!'

At the top of the ladder, there was a powerful golden telescope. Caleb pushed his eye against it and started feverishly adjusting the focus and distance dials.

'No! You mustn't spy,' moaned Bandit at the bottom of the ladder.

'Oh, don't be so beige,' Caleb snapped back, still twisting and turning the dials of the telescope.

'Bandit is not beige. I have a black pelt.'

'No, no, I have a chip in my head. It makes me say stuff like beige and bleak. Anyhow, stop distracting me; I'm just about to focus in on a girl. Nothing seedy or untoward. I just need to know there's some beauty and class existing beyond my daily run-ins.'

Much to Caleb's displeasure, the girl he had managed to focus on was Tanya Masters, who, although would usually be described as attractive, was currently storming out of the Great Hall sobbing uncontrollably. A slushy combination of tears and mascara streamed down her face, eventually reaching her lower lip which had become sore and puffy from her nervously biting at it.

'Crikey! I don't fancy yours much,' Caleb grumbled, glancing down at Bandit. 'Let's try a bit further along.'

Caleb twisted the dials once more and was about to focus on a couple of girls frolicking on the roof terrace when something above them caught his eye – a bright glowing sphere was shooting across the sky. It looked like a fireball or a comet. He eased the telescope upwards and focused his lens on it, only to find that the glowing orb was, in fact, a satellite, or more accurately, the burning remains of a satellite.

'What the bleak?' Caleb muttered to himself as he slowly panned the telescope to the left. Following the blazing satellite, he saw the dispatch ship containing Nox racing towards the Great Hall. Behind itwas Bron's troop carrier travelling to the same destination at a much slower pace. Caleb took a deep breath and stepped away from the telescope.

Making his way down the stairs, he mumbled to himself, 'Looks like there's trouble afoot tonight.' Drops of rain began to fall through a large gap in the barge's roof onto his head. 'And grim weather too,' he grumbled. 'Just as well I managed to swipe those blankets.'

However, as Caleb turned around, he found that his blankets had been occupied by a certain Moline who had grown tired of her evening's adventures and now just wanted somewhere soft and comfortable to snuggle down and sleep.

Caleb looked down at Bandit snoring away on the pile of blankets he had spent all evening securing and sighed. 'Well, that's just bleakin' great, isn't it?'

Chapter Sixteen

HEARTBEATS

Back at the ball, Prince Alistair continued to stare through the open window into the garden with a jealous fury building inside of him. The sound of Callie and Ryan's high spirits spilt into the hall as they approached from the outside. As their joviality escalated in volume, it doubled as a countdown to Alistair losing control of his temper.

Ryan leapt back into the hall through the window before turning to help lift Callie through. As the pair prepared the re-join the party inside, Alistair marched towards them.

'Officer Haywood,' he barked at Callie, 'where have you been?'

'I was just taking a walk through the gardens, not that it's any of your business,' Callie replied, offended at the prince's ire.

She read the moment for what it was - a rich, handsome boy realising that, for once, he wasn't going to get what he wanted. She already felt awkward about Alistair's interest in her but had hoped that his fickle nature would have led him to another pursuit before this moment arrived. Callie went to march off but felt the prince grab her arm with malicious strength.

Ryan immediately stepped up to the prince and let out an angry, 'Hey –'

With his free hand, the prince pointed at Ryan. 'If you know what's good for you and your family, you will walk away. Now.'

With the prince's firm grip still on her arm, Callie looked at Ryan and said, 'Ryan, I'm ok, please go. This isn't your problem. We'll talk later.'

Ryan didn't know what to do for the best, but as Callie mouthed the word 'thanks,' he realised that she had matters in hand, and his presence was probably causing more harm than good. As he walked away, glancing back occasionally, he wondered whether his initial perception that the Prince and Callie were more than friends was indeed correct. And even if that wasn't the case, Ryan feared that his retreat from the incident might have severely damaged any positive feelings that Callie may have begun to develop for him. Ryan's heart sank a little further with every step that he took.

'Good, now that he's gone, you can explain yourself,' the prince ordered.

'Explain myself? Like I said,' Callie shook her arm free from Prince Alistair's grip, 'it's none of your business.'

'It is my business, though,' Alistair snapped. 'You're supposed to be on duty tonight as my bodyguard.'

'What? You can't be serious! You were surely joking when you said that,' Callie replied. 'If you wanted me here to protect your safety, you wouldn't have bought me this gown!' She held the long sides of her skirt toemphasise to the Prince how impractical the garment would be in combat.

'Well, I certainly didn't buy you a dress so you could go running off with some cadet and ruin it with grass stains,' Alistair retorted.

Callie knew this conversation could go round in circles for hours with no beneficial outcome. She inwardly cursed her politeness for getting herself into this confrontational cul-de-sac in the first place.

'So, as your bodyguard, what would you like me to do?' Callie asked.

The question caught Prince Alistair off guard. 'Well, I don't know – just walk around and make sure that there's nothing untoward going on.'

'Fine,' Callie turned on her heel and left, allowing herself a secret smirk as she did so. She felt a great deal of satisfaction from talking the Prince into suggesting she should roam the hall freely, if only for the next twenty minutes or so.

As he watched Callie walk away, the Prince's temper began to fade and in its place grew a cold feeling of shame. He turned to leave and saw his father, King William Hawthorne, marching towards him, backed with a squadron of his guards.

The King's face was full of purpose, while his troops marched with such concentrated expressions that could only indicate they were masking fear.

'Father! I wasn't expecting to see you here tonight,' Alistair smiled. 'Have the charms of the Melodium finally conquered your old heart?'

'No, my dear son, I'm here with grave news.' The King wrapped his arm around his son's shoulders and whispered, 'Do you remember our recent discussion in my study? It would seem that the Corporation are ready to take Vastrid. All of our key satellites and decoding capabilities have been destroyed. An attack is imminent.'

Alistair's initial shock and concern dissipated as the sense of duty he'd been instilled with since birth took charge of his emotions. 'Do not worry, father, I will prepare the troops. The Corporation will not make a mockery of Vastrid.'

'Son, I admire your bravery, but this is a fight we won't win. We must consider the bigger picture. We will fight, but only to protect our people. No matter what happens in this battle, you must survive. We have the resources to fight off the growing control of the Shadox Corporation, but you're the only one who can access it. Do you understand? You must survive.'

'What about Darla?' Alistair surveyed the area, trying to predict the chaos that would soon ensue.

'Don't worry, son; your sister is safe. I have taken the precaution of removing her from her school and hiding her with the McCloud family.'

Alistair frowned, confused. 'The newscasters?'

'Yes indeed,you have much to learn about the way Vastrid is being run. Now go and prepare. I doubt we have more than fifteen minutes until they arrive,' advised King William. 'And remember, no heroics!'

Alistair walked towards the side of the hall, where Probot was waiting for his next instruction. 'Probot, please go to the cloakroom and fetch my pistol and my sword from the locker.'

The Prince pressed a key-fob into the robot's hand and motioned in the direction of the lockers.

'Certainly, your highness,' Probot replied.

Alistair looked around. He wished that either Callie or even Tanya were there for support, but thanks to his arrogance and pride, they had gone. Despite his strong bond with his father, Alistair's duty as heir meant that he could never truly be candid with the King. Even though he was standing in a hall surrounded by people, he realised, for the first time in his life, that he was alone.

On the other side of the hall, Ryan caught up with Jayden, who greeted him with a disapproving shake of her head. 'Well, even by your standards, that didn't last long.'

'Sorry?' Ryan sighed, kicking a discarded cup across the floor.

'Well, I saw you leap through the window with a certain Miss Haywood to go a-tiptoeing through the tulips,' Jayden answered with a smirk, 'or so to speak.'

'Oh, you saw that?'

'Everyone saw it,' Jayden answered excitedly, 'or if they didn't actually see it, they heard about it. The girl known as 'Callie Hay-wouldn't going for a frolic in the garden with a boy, a seconded cadet at that, well – that's going to turn heads, isn't it? Especially on a night as dull as this one has been. Although, it doesn't appear there's much to gossip about judging by the amount of time you spent together.'

'Try telling that to Prince Alistair. He seems to think something happened that didn't.'

'Ooooh, my little cousin – involved in a royal love triangle,' Jayden laughed. 'What next? I expect you'll be interviewed by one of the McClouds soon.'

'It's not funny,' Ryan groaned, suddenly picking up on something that Jayden had just said. 'Anyway, how do you know the song "Tiptoe Through The Tulips"?'

'Listen up, cousin,' Jayden answered, 'do you really think that you and your scruffy friends from the market are the only ones to have owned a Flex-izdat or two in their time? It's just that most of us don't get all demented over them.'

'Demented? That's a bit strong,' Ryan protested.

'Indeed, but not as strong as the unshakable odour of a musty Flex-izdat stall,' Jayden answered, 'so you better start showering more often now you've got a girlfriend and everything.'

Across the hall, Callie was still feeling fired up from her argument with the Prince. She glanced at her reflection in a silver ornament and adjusted her hair before attempting to scratch a sudden and barely reachable itch on her back. Callie had felt this itch before, travelling just below her shoulder blades and along her spine. The itches usually occurred after experiencing a distraction, but they were starting to happen at other times, too, growing not only in frequency but intensity as well. After a brief period of attempted scratching, the itch began to fade.

'I could do with a drink,' she thought to herself, seeking a way to ease back into the night.

Callie looked around and realised that she would either have to walk back past where she had just argued with the prince or cross the Melodium's dance floor to reach one of the two refreshment stalls.

The party was in its early stages, and the dance floor was nearly empty. The typical selection of nervous singletons standing in their gangs at the back, bobbing their heads to the music. A handful of overly-confident socialites danced in separate clutches on the dance floor's inner fringes. Callie observed how they danced, chuckling to herself with the realisation that the effort they'd made to get ready seemed to match the effort they were putting into being seen on the dance floor. Being seen was the very last thing Callie wanted. Whether it involved being harassed by drunkards, having drinks spilt all over her or slipping over and breaking her collarbone, dance floors had never been kind to her. But all of these dangers seemed a much more attractive gambit than having to endure another second of the prince's temper tantrum.

Callie made her way to the edge of the dance floor as its panels shone brightly, alternating between hot neon pinks, purples, whites and blues, depending on who was dancing over them at the time. It was like a chessboard with rules based on attraction and courtship, and tonight it placed a strange shiver into Callie Haywood's young and relatively inexperienced heart. She didn't need to do much soul searching to realise why.

'This is all because of that damn Ryan Tyler boy, isn't it?' she said, addressing her thumping heart.

Callie took a step forward and slowly began to weave through the people dancing. She caught the eye of a few acquaintances but managed to brush past them with a polite nod of the head and mouthed greeting. She could see the refreshment stall just ahead and decided to push through the crowd as subtly as she could to avoid being noticed.

Walking across the dance floor, she glanced to her left and looked at the Meloquins elegantly pretending to create the sounds coming from the Melodium. As she did so, the violinist Meloquin broke from its programming and lent forward slightly, as if to look Callie straight in the eye. She almost couldn't believe what she had seen. Even the most expensive Meloquins moved in a very preset way; to see one suddenly break from this was both fascinating and terrifying, especially as it seemed to be aware of her presence.

This motion stopped Callie dead in her tracks and, as she stood still, all of the lights on the dance floor left their positions and raced onto the square beneath her feet. Bathed in the soft light emerging from the floor, Callie stood perplexed as the violinist Meloquin gracefully waved a mechanical hand in the air in a gesture to its fellow Meloquins that the current tonal selection was coming to an end.

As the final note of music faded, all of the Meloquins politely bowed and curtsied to the crowd of dancers who, although surprised that the music had finished somewhat suddenly, applauded gratefully.

The violinist Meloquin lent forward in a non-threatening manner and motioned to Callie to place her hand on a panel resting at the very front of the podium. An electronic voice echoed from the Melodium's speakers, 'We welcome Officer Callie Haywood to influence the basis of the next tonal selection.'

Callie pondered just how the Melodium knew her name, but with the spotlight on her and a strong desire to get away from it, she decided to comply with the machine's request as quickly as she could.

'So much for not drawing attention to myself,' Callie muttered to herself as she walked towards the panel and placed her hand down.

She heard mocking chants of, 'Go Callie! Go Callie!' from the back of the dance floor. The voices belonged to her patrol partner Dev and some of the rowdier members of her squad. She worried about what kind of noise was going to emerge from the Melodium as the panel lit up around her palm and began to construct a tonal selection from the data it received from her.

After a few seconds, the light from the panel dimmed, and once again, the voice emerged from the speakers. 'Thank you for your data Officer Haywood. Ladies and gentlemen, please take your places on the dance floor for this evening's signature dance.'

Callie began to walk away from the base of the Melodium. As she did so, not only did the floor illuminate wherever she stepped, but the cellist Meloquin also matched each of her footsteps with a bow stroke, producing a deep, pulsating note. The long and slow synthesised notes that soundtracked her steps became almost hypnotic, and she found her nervous heartbeats beginning to slow in time with the strikes of the cello. A new tone joined the cello note. Sounding like a robotic clap drenched in reverb, it matched Callie's heartbeat and produced a steady rhythm that began to herald in the other instruments. The dance floor started to fill as those nodding along to the beat were drawn to the sound and rhythm of the Melodium's tonal selection.

Callie stepped away from the dance floor and noticed that the combined sounds of the Melodium were producing a melody that was strangely familiar to her. It was definitely based on a secret echo but not one she was overly familiar with.

Her mind raced back a few hours, to that afternoon. She had been relaxing in her room while the springtime sun shone through her balcony window. Lying on the bed, she had been attempting to immerse herself in the rare delights that were being projected from the Flex-izdat she'd just purchased. Despite all of the intriguing sights, sounds and wonders offered up by the disc, Callie's thoughts were preoccupied with the time she had spent in the park with Ryan and her eagerness to see him that night at the ball. It struck her as odd, as she usually found herself pondering how she could best avoid the company of boys rather than hoping to spend more time with one.

As the Melodium's tonal selection emerged in its full arrangement, Callie realised two things; one was that this was the song that she'd heard that afternoon, and the other was that this was the moment she had to dance with Ryan. It no longer mattered about the heckling she'd receive from her squad members or the inevitable fallout from the Prince's jealousy. Callie had to take a gamble on romance while the song lasted. It was a rare moment when her heart fully controlled her actions; she realised it would be a shame to waste it.

Usually, Callie was guided by the sensible head on her shoulders. It kept her safe, and it kept her out of danger. This was all well and good, but she questioned whether or not it had sometimes restricted her from fully living.

Callie raced through the Great Hall, looking for Ryan. She

sprinted past her squad, not stopping to hear the banter and mockery they were hoping to send her way. She eventually leapt up onto one of the marble statues to survey the room. Callie searched around for Ryan, scanning clusters of people that she didn't recognise. With each bar of the tonal selection passing, she realised that she was running out of time. Finally, she saw him – standing at the back of the hall with Jayden. Taking advantage of her high position on the statue, Callie jumped onto a motorised linen cart travelling with its cargo of soiled tablecloths to the laundry room. As the cart reached Ryan and Jayden, Callie slid from the vehicle and landed in front of Ryan, greeting him excitedly. 'Listen! Do you know what this song is?'

The music drifting from the other end of the hall caught Ryan's ear, and it was indeed familiar to him.

'Is that selection 4 from – '

'LV-29!' Callie finished his sentence and grabbed his hand. 'Come on; we HAVE to dance!'

The invitation came too fast for Ryan to blush or manage to talk himself out of the moment. As Callie dragged him away, Ryan looked back at Jayden and said, 'I'm just going to dance.'

'I gathered as much,' Jayden smirked, taking a sip of the drink she was holding. She had to admit to herself that she was more than a little shocked at the speed of her bashful cousin's new romantic association.

'There'll be wedding bells next,' she muttered to herself before turning to a nearby debutante sporting an extravagant and ridiculous fascinator. 'You'll have to tell me where you got that hat.'

As Jayden watched her cousin and his new acquaintance, something caught her eye in the rigging above the Melodium. Questioning herself, she squinted at what looked like armed figures moving in the darkness.

Jayden had been to enough of these debutante balls to know that they were never exciting enough to warrant people lurking about in the rigging, let alone ones armed with rifles. She considered reporting it but feared the panic that may cause. She knocked back the rest of her drink and reached inside her boot to pull out a knife. 'It looks like I'm back on duty,' she said, heading towards the Armoury.

Callie raced back to the dance floor with Ryan's hand held tightly in hers. Ryan was too busy savouring the softness and comfort of his hand nestling against Callie's to feel shy about this sudden turn of events. As they both reached the edge of the dance floor, he felt his heart begin to glow, and the nagging fears that had held his mind hostage since childhood faded.

As they stepped onto the dance floor, Ryan suddenly realised that he had no idea how to dance with a girl. Should he just sway next to her, or would he have to formally dance with arms and elbows at certain positions and rigid step procedures for his feet to adhere to? Luckily for Ryan, Callie took the lead. She smiled at him as she placed his left hand in her right hand and wrapped his right arm around her waist. Together they began to sway, and as the middle section of the song unveiled itself, Ryan and Callie found their bodies brushing against each other.

With each beat of the song, their physical closeness intensified until their bodies were locked together, swaying in a single motion. Ryan brushed Callie's back with his right hand and could feel the bones of her back through the soft material of her ball gown. He ran his fingers down her spine and rested his hand a little lower than it had been; as he did so, he felt Callie pull him even closer to her.

Whether out of shyness or pleasure, Ryan had initially

closed his eyes as they danced. He opened them a little to catch a glimpse of Callie's face and noticed that she had her eyes closed too. Ryan removed his hand from Callie's and softly brushed her cheek; she opened her eyes and smiled. Ryan was suddenly struck by the realisation that he was about to kiss her.

As he leaned towards her, the final repeat of the chorus blasted out from the Melodium, and with it, balloons and streamersfell from the ceiling. Ryan and Callie's bodies separated slightly from the shock of this, but they laughed, and Callie's giggling body collapsed back into Ryan's arms as the dancers around them chimed in with ad-libbed, 'Yeah yeahs' and, 'Whoah whoahs' that seemed to complement the arrangement of the song.

As the song came to its close, Callie looked up and smiled at Ryan. They held each other close again, and both closed their eyes. They knew in that moment that they were about to kiss. It was a certainty; it was a cosmically charged moment that was destined to happen.

Except, it didn't.

Ryan and Callie's lips were about to touch when a thunderous explosion drowned the sound of the Melodium out. The seconds that followed were hazily recorded in Ryan's mind, and he was only able to understand them after they had happened. Ryan's body landed with a thump several meters away from the dance floor. Tiny shards of glass left small cuts on his skin as they scattered around him. As they pierced his skin, he recalled being flung from the dance floor and the desperation to keep hold of Callie's hand. The softness and comfort he had felt when she had taken his hand just minutes earlier were taken from him as, finger by finger, her hand slipped out of his.

Ryan lay in shock, trying to understand what had just happened. He glanced to the left and saw a gaping crater in the floor; looking directly above it, he saw that the painted dome ceiling of the Great Hall had been blown apart. A vast troop carrier with the Shadox Corporation logo hovered above the destroyed roof. Ropes dropped from the ship with speed and efficiency, accompanied by fully-armed Shadox troops abseiling down them.

Ryan felt someone checking his body for injuries before grabbing him by the jacket and dragging him to his feet. His vision was blurry, and his hearing was still impacted by the explosion. The person who had hoisted Ryan up appeared to be a high-ranking member of the Royal Guard. Ryan glanced around, hoping to locate Callie, but she was nowhere to be seen. The Guardsman yelled something at Ryan that he was too disorientated to understand before shoving him towards several other Vastridians in uniform, making their way towards a side entrance. Without warning or debate, former librarian Ryan Tyler had become a soldier in the blink of an eye.

Chapter Seventeen

MASSACRE

The shock and panic of the explosion were not restricted to the dance floor. Up in the rigging, Nox and his strike team had been knocked from their feet. Their minds were thrown into a state of frenzy as they struggled to regain footing amongst the dust and debris. One by one, the team dusted themselves off and looked up at the troop carrier through the crumbling hole in the ceiling.

'What in the name of Vastrid do they think they're doing?' shouted one of the men.

Nox rose to his feet. He brushed down his expensive suit and stared venomously at Colonel Bron's troopers descending through the destroyed ceiling.

As they landed in formation onto the floor of the Great Hall, Nox hissed, 'It would appear that Colonel Bron wants me to slaughter him.'

On a rope ladder leading up to the first section of the rigging, Jayden Tyler found herself trying to make sense of what had just happened. The last thing she recalled was climbing up to investigate the group of silhouetted figures she had seen before the explosion hit.

She could tell by the blood rushing to her head and the feeling of the rope ladder twisting around her knee that she was not upright. She slowly opened her eyes, which, as they focused, confirmed she was dangling upside-down nearly thirty feet above the ground.

Taking a deep breath, she managed to pull herself up and grab hold of the ladder with both hands. As the rope unwound from her legs, she grabbed a higher rung and continued to climb.

Meanwhile, up in the rigging, Nox continued to fume at Bron's change of plan. He vowed to ensure that the Colonel paid for this treachery.

Nox ran his fingers through his long hair, slicking it back across his scalp, and took a long, slow breath.

'Unfortunately, Bron will have to wait. Time is of the essence.'

Peeking over the top of the rigging, Nox scanned the floor beneath him until he found what he was looking for. Deep amongst the staggering, injured debutantes and Royal Guards, Prince Alistair, with Probot by his side, frantically searched for both Callie and his father. With a blaster pistol in his hand and a sheathed duelling sword by his waist, his eyes darted around the hall, trying to make sense of the situation. Despite being fully armed, he looked far from ready for battle. His usually tanned complexion had drained to a pale tone, and his eyes were consumed by fear.

Nox grabbed the only prepared member of his team and thrust him against the barrier. 'Come on, quickly! Your target is down there,' Nox pointed out the Prince as the trooper prepared the sight on his rifle.

Keeping his eyes on the activity on the floor, Nox scolded the troopers who were still regaining their composure from the explosion. 'I would appreciate a little more efficiency from those of you loitering back there.'

The trooper at the bannister spoke. 'Sir, I have the target in my sight.'

The trooper tightened the focus on his rifle's optics with the Prince directly in the middle of the crosshairs. A sinister grin spread across Nox's face; rubbing his hands together, he gave the command. 'Fire!'

Just as the trooper's finger began to squeeze the trigger, a long wooden object came whistling through the air. It collided square-on with the trooper's jaw, shattering the bone and causing him to shoot off-target before landing on the floor of the rigging with a thud. As Nox's eyes followed the object's trajectory, he realised that it was a bo-staff. Nox and his troops stood transfixed as the staff began to glow and quiver. Nox bent down and reached out to pick the bo-staff up but, as his hand was about to make contact, it shot through the air, back to a section of rigging on the other side of the hall.

'LOMAX!' snarled Nox as he watched a cloaked figure step from the shadows.

Catching her bo-staff gracefully, the woman in the cloak pulled down her hood and made eye contact with Nox.

With a smirk on her face, Lomax held up her hand and traced a circle in the air before launching herself from the rigging to the floor below. Upon Nox's order, his troops opened fire. Lomax darted through an emergency exit, avoiding the shots. Enraged, Nox grabbed a nearby cable and slid down onto the ballroom floor. For years the legacy of Kendra Lomax had taunted him; it was one of the few things in his life that he hadn't been able to control, and he was determined to remove this source of vexation once and for all.

With his eyes focused on the door that Lomax had escaped through, Nox strode across the hall, impervious to the chaos and panic surrounding him. Shadox Corporation troops had begun their assault on the Royal Guard, shooting them unarmed and without warning or mercy. With her gown now torn and covered in ash, Madeline Chambers searched frantically for someone to help her escape. In all the noise and violence, she had missed the evacuation of civilians led by Captain Dunnell.

Madeline noticed Mr Nox across the hall and recognised his face from various news broadcasts she had seen. She wasn't sure what he did but knew it was something to do with the Shadox Corporation. 'He must be here to help us,' she thought to herself, failing to notice the logo on the troop's uniforms.

'Excuse me – ' Madeline began to shout, running towards Nox.

Without removing his focus from the exit ahead, he grabbed Madeline by the throat and threw her like a rag doll across the hall, then drew his sword and casually tore through several approaching Guardsmen.

Nox barged through the door and found himself in a small room with nothing but a narrow corridor to his left. As he glanced around, looking for Lomax, he heard a series of short beeps and realised he had been tricked. Following the sound, he looked up and saw a dozen crudely-made timebombs on the ceiling. He spun around to escape back through the emergency exit door only to see it slam shut. A homemade magnetic locking device had been screwed into the door, and a Sentry blessing circle had been drawn in chalk beside it, serving as both a taunt and a message. With the beeping sounds on the explosives now quickening, Nox had no option but to run as fast as he could down the corridor. Within seconds the bombs began to detonate, causing the ceiling to collapse.

Fleeing the falling rubble, Nox made his way out of the Great Hall's escape route and found himself in an empty courtyard. Sealed off and separated from the battle in the Great Hall, Nox screamed Lomax's name into the darkness of the night sky.

Back on the platform by the rigging, Nox's troops had regained their composure after Lomax's interruption. With their mission now in tatters and Nox gone, they had no option but to join the rest of their fellow troopers and aid in the attack against the Royal Guard.

Still crouched high up on the rope ladder, Jayden was trying to work out what her next move should be. She couldn't go back down without being spotted and shot by a trooper on the ground. The only other option would be to climb onto the platform and go hand-to-hand against Nox's squad. She had her knife, but, realistically, she'd only be able to take down one or two of them before being shot. Suddenly fate made her decision for her, as a stray bullet tore through the top right-hand corner of the rope ladder, causing an audible snap. The trooper nearest to Jayden heard this and motioned for his squad to stop shooting. 'Did you hear that?' he called out.

This was the distraction that Jayden needed. Leaping onto the platform, she slid across its floor, knocked the trooper off his feet and drove her knife into his chest as he fell. Grabbing the fallen trooper's assault rifle, Jayden began to run across the platform, letting out three quick bursts of fire and taking down a further four members of the squad before leaping onto the nearby cable Nox had used minutes earlier.

Using the momentum of her jump, Jayden swung towards a nearby open hatch in the hall's roof as the remaining squad's bullets narrowly missed her. Pulling herself through the hatch, Jayden found herself on the highest part of the Great Hall's roof. Crouching down, Jayden took a minute to control her breathing and steady her heart rate. Running her hand over her face, she considered her next move. Hearing the gunfire and screams emerging from the hall below, she knew that the Royal Guard had no chance of surviving this battle. She had no idea why the Shadox Corporation should be attacking Vastrid, but they were, and she knew the Corporation were far more powerful when it came down to it, despite the style and pageantry of the Royal Guard.

'If only this were based on who's got the best uniforms, not the most weapons,' she muttered, glancing into the sky as more Shadox Corporation ships approached.

Jayden glanced at the Great Hall's balcony to her right – an ideal escape route if not for the fact it was now crawling with Shadox troops. She walked to the edge of the roof and noticed a large freight ship about a quarter of a mile out. The jump into the seawater below would be dangerous, but Jayden knew she had a greater chance of surviving that than attempting to battle her way across the balcony. A plan began to form in her mind; she could swim to the ship, claim that she was a debutante and then pick up whatever pieces of her life were left in the morning.

Jayden placed down the assault rifle that she had seized and inched closer to the edge, but as she closed her eyes, ready to make the jump, she realised that she couldn't. Thoughts of the Guards she had served with filled her mind, and then there was Ryan.

'I can't leave my cousin down there alone,' she thought to herself, 'especially when he hadn't even wanted to come to the damn ball in the first place.'

She picked the assault rifle up from the floor and walked back across the roof, glancing down at the troopers on the balcony. In her mind, she issued the Shadox Corporation a threat. 'You may win the battle tonight but believe me, I'm going to make it far from easy for you.'

Inside the Great Hall, Prince Alistair had managed to

rally a dozen members of the Guard into the concealed armoury. With Probot still beside him, he instructed his father's friend, Captain Dunnell, to hand out assault rifles and body armour.

Callie's patrol partner Dev grabbed a rifle and raised it high in the air. 'Alright! Now we get to waste those Shadox scumbags!'

Prince Alistair motioned for silence. 'NO! I command that all rifles are loaded with tranqs. No member of the Shadox Corporation will die by our hand.'

A groan of disdain began to ripple amongst the gathered Guards, and the battle-weathered Captain Dunnell stepped forward. 'You mind your mouths; this is the Prince of Vastrid addressing you. You'd do well to remember your conduct as I intend to not only survive tonight but also find me some new whipping boys and girls for the clear-up work tomorrow morning.'

The Guards immediately fell back in line. Dunnell was infamous amongst the Royal Guards as a hard taskmaster and stern disciplinarian. Day to day life was distinctly less pleasant should you fall into his bad books.

'Thank you, Captain,' said Alistair before clearing his throat to address the room. 'I know how you feel. For unknown reasons, the Shadox Corporation has decided to wage war on us. They've attacked us without honour, without courage and without mercy. Good Vastridians have died and will die tonight, but we cannot sink to the level of our new enemy. We must remember that the troops out there are human beings following orders, many of whom are Vastridians and some former members of the Guard. Certainly, take them out hard and fast, but we must ensure they survive so we can decide on their punishment with a clear head and a clear conscience in the morning. The King has arranged for a battleship full of reinforcements to arrive in the harbour within the next five minutes. We must push the troops back through the hall and onto the outer balconies to ensure they are trapped between us and the reinforcements.'

Alistair looked at the assembled members of the Guard; he feared that he would see fear or, worse, a lack of belief in his leadership. Instead, he saw a group of soldiers hungry for retribution, nodding eagerly in response.

'Are you ready?' asked the Prince. The Royal Guard roared in approval. Removing his sword from its scabbard, Prince Alistair thrust it into the air and hollered his Father's old battle cry. 'FOR VASTRID!'

The Guards charged back into the hall, immediately taking down squad after squad of Shadox Troops with an unexpected level of fury and intensity.

There was significantly less fury and intensity to be found at the very back of the hall. Underneath table number thirteen, Ryan Tyler's former tablemates were hiding.

'We're all going to die! They're going to kill us.' The formerly sullen boy had now assumed the role of terrified narrator and was peeking at the carnage through a gap in the tablecloth.

'Possibly not, young man,' whispered Private Rex Ambrose, focusing on a bottle cork he was rolling on the floor. 'Almost certainly not, in fact.'

'I thought you said you had a plan,' the boy with the shaved head and glasses answered in a quick and nervy tone.

'Ah, I did, and I do, young man, and it's a very artful plan at that,' said Rex, turning towards the girl with pigtails who was quietly sobbing. 'Now then, my dear, what do they call you when you're at home?'

'My name's Florence,' the girl answered quietly.

Rex took a deep breath and looked away for a moment as a huge grin spread across his face. He spun his head back around and looked deep into the girl's eyes. 'Florence! That's a very charming name. It means "to flower", did you know that?'

Florence nodded nervously, more out of awkwardness than interest in name origins. Rex placed his hand on her shoulder. 'Well, I need you to flower and blossom tonight for us. You've got the slimmest arms; can you please reach up and bring down the spare glasses and knives from the table?'

Florence was more than a little scared but felt a strange sense of pride at being chosen for something for once. She reached up, carefully retrieving the items one by one.

Rex turned to the two boys. 'Now then, what are your names?'

The terrified boy turned from his peephole in the table cloth long enough to answer. 'My name's Leon, and his name is Stephen.'

'Ah, the Lion and the Crown. Two strong names for two strong boys! I'll need your strength in a moment. When I give the signal, I need you to tip the table forward as if it were a giant shield, because that will be the part it plays.'

Rex poked his head from out of the tablecloth and saw a squad of Shadox troopers approaching. 'Young men, if you could turn the table now, please.'

As the boys did this, Rex gathered up the glasses and knives secured earlier. 'We'll be throwing these as weapons in a moment, but not until I give the order. I can't stress that enough, NOT until I give the order'.

As the table crashed over, the approaching squad opened fire in its direction, but the stranded Vastridians remained safe and still behind the strong surface of the table. With bullets ricocheting around them, Florence and the two boys looked nervously at Rex, who was counting with his eyes closed in concentration. 'And eighteen, and nineteen – ' Rex continued to count, 'and twenty! Ok, Table Thirteen, aim for their eyes and throw!'

The four Vastridians poked their heads above the table and launched their cutlery and glassware in a clumsy yet forceful manner.

Most of these makeshift weapons completely missed; however, those that didn't shattered and pierced directly into the faces of the Troopers as they attempted to reload. Out of surprise more than pain, one of the troopers dropped his rifle. The fallen weapon slid across the floor towards Rex, who quickly picked it up, ensured it was loaded and opened fire on the remaining squad members. One by one, the approaching troopers fell, leaving Florence, Leon and Stephen to look at Rex with a silent mixture of shock and respect.

'The dependability of a Vastridian Pure Oak table, the structured attack pattern of a Shadox squadron and the ever-reliable descending gradient of the Great Hall's bedrock. I told you I had a plan, did I not?' Rex declared in a modest yet proud manner.

Stephen noticed that more squads were approaching. 'What now? We can't keep throwing cutlery at them!'

'Very true young man, very true,' answered Rex, 'and that is why we will escape through the washroom behind us.'

Leon stepped forward, 'But... but won't you get in trouble? I mean, we're from the Logistics department, we'll be ok, but you're a member of the Guards. Surely you'll be court-martialed for desertion?'

'Oh, I very much doubt it,' answered Rex. 'Not being missed is one of the perks of being placed on a table like this one; that and a close proximity to the toilet. Which is very handy indeed, when you get to my age.'

While Private Rex Ambrose and his new friends from the Logistics Department escaped, Colonel Bron prowled through the Great Hall, barking orders at his men to find and capture the King and the Prince. Following the charge from the armoury, Prince Alistair had managed to begin pushing the Shadox Corps back towards the balcony. Splitting off into smaller fire teams, the Royal Guard had taken down a couple of Bron's squads, but they were still woefully outnumbered. Bodies of slain or injured Vastridians were scattered throughout the hall, many of them hidden by the smoke and debris of battle. Chandeliers lay in pieces on the floor, the ornate bay windows were shattered, and several of the Meloquins on the battle-bruised Melodium were now missing limbs.

Amongst the wreckage lay a vast velvet curtain, under which Callie Haywood was slowly regaining consciousness. In near darkness, she was attempting to focus her mind and bring some clarity to the situation. She could sense that someone was standing over her and that she was in grave danger.

A muffled voice became clearer. 'Nah, don't waste your bullets; use the knife.'

Callie rolled to her right; a large combat knife pierced through the fabric above her as she did so. She continued to roll, narrowly avoiding each repeated stab. Finally, she felt the edge of the curtain and, flinging it aside, found herself face to face with the knife-wielding trooper.

From her position on the floor, Callie attempted to tackle the oncoming enemy with a leg sweep but realised that her movement was severely hampered by the ball gown she was wearing. Callie let out a frustrated groan and leapt to her feet, narrowly avoiding another stab. As the trooper swung his arm back, ready to attack again, Callie thrust the palm of her right hand out with concentrated force, smashing through his visor and knocking him unconscious. Seizing his knife, Callie slashed through the bottom of her dress, enabling her to kick the rifle out of another approaching trooper's hands before plunging the knife deep into his arm.

She grabbed the rifle and let off a few shots to keep the approaching troops at bay while backing towards a large stone sculpture of the King. With a flurry of enemy fire exploding around her, Callie dived behind the monument for cover. After landing more awkwardly than she would have liked, she tried to focus; however, her head was still foggy from the concussion, and her body was bruised and aching. The pain sent waves of discomfort to interrupt any clear thoughts as soon as they arrived. She tried to comprehend why Shadox Troopers were attacking and what might have happened to Ryan. A combination of shock, fear and panic caused Callie to vomit. It was at this point she heard a familiar chuckle.

'Blimey – stay classy, Haywood.'

'Dev! I've never been so happy to be mocked,' said Callie, standing to slap hands with her patrol partner.

'What's going on? Why are Shadox Troops attacking us? Where's Alistair? Is Ryan OK?'

'Whoah there!' Dev placed a reassuring hand on her shoulder.

'Alright, to answer your questions, nobody knows why they've come down here to pick a fight with us. Princey-Boy is more than well; in fact, I think he's beginning to enjoy himself. He's started taking down troopers with his sword rather than blasting them. Oh yeah, that's the other thing; we have to load with tranqs. The Prince doesn't want any enemy deaths tonight. The foolish – '

Bullets bounced off the statue, interrupting Dev.

'And what about Ryan? Ryan Tyler? Private Ryan Tyler.'

'Ryan who? I don't even know who that is,' Dev was puzzled for a moment. 'Oh, do you mean that skinny boy you were dancing with? Wait a minute! Are you two – you know?' He pulled a face by sticking his chin out and raising his eyebrows, hinting at something a little more romantic than dancing together.

'Are we what?' Callie snapped.

'You know,' said Dev pulling the same expression again in a more exaggerated manner. Callie caught the gist of Dev's accusation and was about to scold him for being so crude when a hail of bullets again hit the statue, narrowly missing them both.

Shaken by the near-miss, Dev and Callie pulled in close to the base of the statue.

'That was too close!' panted Dev. 'Anyhow, your boy Ryan – I think he was led out with a clutch of newer recruits when they blew the roof off this place. It seems the plan is to get to the balcony, where King Willy's gonna save the day in his big boat. We gotta provide cover so Princey-Boy and company can storm the staircase and push these Shadox pigs back up there. Man, no training could ever have prepared us for this!'

Callie was about to reply when she noticed something land by their feet. Instantly she grabbed Dev and yelled, 'Grenade! JUMP!'

The pair of them leapt away from the statue, carried more than a little by the explosion as the grenade detonated. They crashed down into a corner, covered in tiny shards and dust. Callie dragged herself towards Dev, who had landed in a sitting position against the wall, and tugged his sleeve. 'That was another close shave. If we get out of this alive, I say we quit and just go become farmers or something. Dev? DEV?'

Callie shook her friend hard, but there was no response. As she let go of his shoulder, Dev's head slumped to the side, revealing a fragment of the King's statue pierced through his neck.

Callie stood up suddenly as a strange numbness ran through her. She knew death more than most; during her earliest years, it seemed to stalk and steal everyone she loved. As a child, she learned to dilute her distress with theories of fate and honour but witnessing the needless carnage erupting through the Great Hall, this reassurance ebbed from her heart.

She glanced around the hall, looking for something to help inspire a plan. Amongst all the smoke and gunfire, she noticed the corridor leading to the kitchen. With squads now sweeping the area looking for remaining members of the Royal Guard, Callie decided the best course of action was to bolt through the kitchen and form a plan in the courtyard outside.

Callie eased her way through the long corridor with her rifle raised, listening for Shadox troopers.

Kicking open the kitchen door, she took an anxious look around the room but found only Gustav the Chef, cowering by the sinks.

'Please help me! I know we had our differences earlier, but I'm just a Vastridian like you. Please come with me through the fire exit; I'm too scared to go alone.'

Callie wasn't in the mood to talk to the man, so she just nodded solemnly. The pair of them walked towards the exit located at the back of the kitchen.

'Please,' cried Gustav, 'you go first. I can't do it.'

Callie's head felt bruised and weary. She was tired, in pain and needed a minute or so just to shake it all off and make a plan.

'Ok, ok, I'll go first,' she muttered to the chef.

Stepping through the exit, Callie sensed something was wrong. It was pitch black out there; usually, the emergency lighting would go on if a fire escape door were opened. Before she could process what was happening, she heard the sound of a chain whipping through the air and felt something hard smash against her hand, causing her to drop her rifle. She looked around in a panic and saw she was surrounded by a group of men whose features were obscured by the darkness. She felt two hard kicks to the back of her legs and fell forwards onto her knees. Her arms were held down as she did so, and a black sack was placed over her head. As Callie struggled and screamed, she felt a needle going into her arm.

She could sense one of the figures was kneeling in front of her.

'Please do not struggle, my friend,' he said calmly. 'I can assure you that my men won't harm, disfigure or debase you. But I must ask you to remain calm until the tranq takes effect, to ensure no accidents occur.'

Callie heard more footsteps approaching. 'And that's for the fine, you skunk-piece.' Callie recognised Gustav's voice then heard him clear his throat and spit at the sack covering her face.

She then heard the first voice again. 'Rico, please deal with this vile, pathetic man.'

Once again came the sound of a chain tearing through the air, then the sound of Gustav screaming. The chef's cries became fainter and fainter as he was carried away.

The man leaned in close to her and began to mop the saliva off. 'I must apologise for the chef's conduct. Gloating was never part of the deal. My men will deal with him. He will survive, but he will be severely punished. Please believe me; this is nothing personal. I just want to be free, my friend. Please sleep; it'll make things easier for you.'

The words span around in Callie's head as the tranq took effect. She eventually passed out and collapsed, giving Marcus Hagen and his crew their first bounty of what would turn out to be a very eventful day.

On the long and winding staircase leading from the hall to the outer balconies, Prince Alistair cut, thrust and dodged his way through squad after squad of Shadox troopers. Despite the tragedy of the attack, the prince was joyously lost in the moment, beaming with pride at his excellent swordsmanship. The fact that he also had over fifty members of the Royal Guard behind him, firing at the enemy, seemed lost on him. Still, despite the lack of self-awareness, no one could fault the prince's bravery, least of all Probot. Without any further orders since Alistair's original request to follow him, the Man-Droid simply walked unarmed alongside the Prince into battle with the outrageous chances they were taking forming alarmingly low survival statistics in his head.

As they approached the top of the stairs, the Royal Guard noticed the Shadox troopers decrease in number and, true to Alistair's plan, the enemy began to back away through the arched exits to the outer balcony. The prince paused and turned towards his fighters, surveying their faces as they braced themselves. He nodded slowly.

'Guards, on my command. Charge!'

The Royal Guard roared in unity and, with their guns blazing, ran towards the exit. The confidence of their attack was cut short when measured enemy shots from inside of the archways picked off enough of the Royal Guard for Alistair to halt the charge and take cover against the entrance to the balconies. Each attempt to pass through was foiled by enemy fire. Taking stock, the prince came up with a plan. He turned towards Probot, who had already drawn the same inevitable conclusion.

'Probot – ' Alistair began.

'It's ok, sir,' Probot answered. 'I know, and I am ready to proceed.'

Grabbing the lapels of the robot's jacket, the prince looked apologetically at Probot before charging through the archway using him as a shield. Bullets tore through his artificial flesh, causing his circuits to spark and fail. With one huge push, the prince rammed Probot into the small group of troopers. The momentum pushed not only the enemy snipers but also Probot's deactivated frame over the edge of the balcony and into the cold sea below them. To avoid the same fate, Alistair steadied himself and grabbed hold of a nearby serving dish, which he flung with vigour at a group of approaching troopers. Aided by this distraction, he quickly drew his sword, and with a swift leg sweep, he managed to ground two of the soldiers, taking out the third with his sword.

As skilled as he was in combat, the prince knew he couldn't survive this attack without help. He glanced around for sight of his Father returning with reinforcements. Alistair prayed for a battleship with its guns blazing and hoards of Vastridians storming the balcony to take back their country. However, all he saw was a burnt-out husk of a ship beaten and defeated underneath a sky full of Shadox aircraft.

Instantly swarms of Shadox troopers emerged from the corners of the balcony, led by Colonel Bron.

'Well, what are you waiting for?' barked Bron.

With tears of frustration welling in his eyes, Prince Alistair raised his sword and pointed it in the direction of Bron and his men. As he went to charge, the Shadox troopers opened fire on him. The shots pounded hard and fast into Alistair's body, causing him to fall with a graceless thud onto the balcony floor.

Bron signalled to two of his troops. 'Make sure he's still breathing, and then bring him to me.'

The soldiers approached the prince's fallen body with caution; they'd be in for a scolding if just one of their squad had been loaded with live ammunition instead of tranq rounds as ordered.

The first trooper knelt down and saw the prince's chest rising and falling. Letting out a sigh of relief, he motioned to his comrade to begin lifting Alistair's body up.

From the other side of the balcony, the sight of Shadox

soldiers picking up the body of the Prince was being observed by Jayden Tyler. Jayden had fought hard, taking out troopers when and where she could, but now she was low on ammo and looking for salvation.

As the two troopers began to drag Alistair away, Jayden knew she had to do something. With her remaining bullets, she could take down at least two of them. She moved silently, taking cover behind a crate that was closer to her targets. She squeezed the trigger on her rifle and let out two quick, expertly positioned bursts of fire, taking out both troopers and avoiding the prince. Any sense of triumph was dampened when she heard the cold, gravelly voice of Bron barking orders, followed by the sound of the heavily armoured Shadox troops approaching. Emerging from behind the crate, Jayden saw three soldiers pacing towards her with their rifles raised. Without wasting another second, Jayden opened fire, taking down two of them and skimming the third, causing him to stumble briefly. As he steadied himself, Jayden squeezed the trigger once more, only to hear the clicking sound of an empty chamber.

The trooper took aim and was about to fire but was interrupted by Bron, who pushed past him and grabbed Jayden by the throat.

'Stand down, trooper,' Bron snarled. 'I'm going to finish off this grubby little piece of filth by hand.'

Bron tightened his grip around Jayden's throat and stared menacingly into her eyes.

'Do you think you're a hero? Did you think you could save the day? You've already lost! Unfortunately for you, I've had a very stressful day, and I need to let off some steam, so I'm afraid I'm going to hurt you until you scream and cry. After that, I'm going to keep on hurting you until you can no longer scream and cry. Eventually, you'll let out one final pleading gasp, and I'll hurt you for the final time in your miserable life.'

At this point, a group of evacuated cadets made their way up to the balconies. Amongst them was Ryan, who immediately saw his cousin in peril and broke away from the crowd. Grabbing an assault rifle from the hands of a fallen Shadox Trooper, he raised it in the direction of Bron.

'Let her go!' Ryan hollered.

Noticing how unsteady Ryan's hands were, Bron laughed scornfully.

'Son, you ain't got the bottle to fire that.'

Deep down, Ryan knew that Bron was probably right; he had never fired a weapon before.

Bron tightened his grip around Jayden's throat. 'Sorry, sweetheart, it looks like I don't have time to play after all.' Jayden gasped for air as Bron's grasp began to choke her.

Out of desperation and fear for his cousin's safety, Ryan suddenly squeezed off a series of wildly aimed shots, tearing through the skin on Bron's face and shattering the right side of his jaw.

Bron howled in agony as he dropped Jayden and fell to the floor. Ryan had never caused physical pain to another human being to this degree; shock strangled his body, causing him to drop his rifle and begin to shake uncontrollably. Using his right hand to hold together the bloody remains of his face, Bron scrambled about on the floor for a rifle. He staggered to his feet and aimed at Ryan.

Before Bron had time to fire, Jayden leapt at him with a hard body tackle. With all of her strength, she pushed both herself and the colonel through one of the windows of the Great Hall. Falling thirty feet, they both landed with a colossal thud on the dance floor. The fall would have been enough to kill most people; however, Jayden had managed to land on top of Bron, whose advanced armour had absorbed most of the impact. Jayden rolled off of the unconscious body of Bron and staggered to her feet.

She was about to smile at the relief of surviving the fall when she heard a loud rattling bang followed by a sensation of being hit hard in the chest.

In all the confusion of the moment, it briefly felt like someone had played a trick on her. She looked around to see if one of her fellow guardsmen was smirking at her, but all she saw were hoards of Shadox troopers, most of them evacuating the building, but some approaching her. The pain in her chest now felt less like a punch and was beginning to burn with an insidious intensity; she glanced down and noticed blood pouring from three bullet holes. The room around her began to spin, and she found it hard to breathe. She attempted to reach for a rifle but instead fell to the floor, panting for air and wishing desperately for a way to undo this situation. With everything slipping away from her, Jayden found herself sadly asking the inevitable question; 'is this it, is this how I die?'

Noticing a pistol on the dance floor, Jayden crawled across its tiles, illuminated by their neon glow. The Melodium's sensors detected her decreasing heartbeats, triggering the tattered remains of the Meloquins to sombrely react to Jayden's fading movements as the Melodium soundtracked the scene with a mournful series of notes.

Surrounded by the light of the dance floor, Jayden reached for the pistol and fired it directly at one of the approaching troopers. Unable to breathe and fading from blood loss, she knew it didn't make a difference either way but felt a sense of relief that she had managed to win her final tussle.

Jayden's thoughts turned to her cousin. 'I saved him,' she muttered to herself with a smile. The dance floor lights remained as bright as they had ever been, but her view of them began to fade. Jayden's head fell limply to the floor as the final note emerging from the Melodium abruptly ended.

Through the smashed window above her, Ryan stared down at his cousin's lifeless body. He had never experienced death in this form before; it seemed too sudden and too cruel. His heart and mind became consumed by a draining vagueness as he desperately hoped that Jayden's death had been some kind of mistake that would be rectified and undone. Lost in the shock and confusion of the moment, Ryan stepped back across the balcony. Bodies of fallen soldiers from both sides of the conflict lay around his feet, and the escalating fumes from the smoke and fire began to fill his lungs, causing him to choke. As Ryan coughed and covered his mouth, something occurred to him.

'Why is no one firing at me?'

Ryan looked across the balconies and saw squad after squad of Shadox Troopers evacuating the area with great haste. He quickly glanced at the walls and windows leading back into the Great Hall itself and noticed a series of explosive devices set to detonate.

Ryan ran to the edge of the balcony and leapt into the turbulent sea below. As he hit the water, a wave crashed over him, and he found himself dragged deep into the water. Using all the strength he could muster, Ryan kicked and swam back towards the surface. As his head broke through the waves, he heard an explosion. Debris from the Great Hall crashed around him, hitting the water with great force and knocking Ryan back under. As he swam back to the surface once more, a chunk of wood landed hard on his head. The world around him faded from view, and Ryan's body started to go limp.

Instinctively, he flung out his right arm and managed to cling to a large piece of wood panelling floating above the waves. Using the last ounce of strength in his body, he pulled himself up onto this makeshift raft and pierced the jagged edge through his jacket sleeve to attach himself. Ryan sighed and fell unconscious; a combination of the injury to his head, exhaustion and stress had taken their toll on him.

As the raft drifted past the carnage of the battle and into the dark of midnight, Ryan had secured his status as one of the survivors of the night, an event soon to be known as the Debutante Ball Massacre. Four hundred and twelve people had died that night, their stories coming to an end while Ryan Tyler would live to see another day. Rain started to fall as the wind whipped the sea, creating the waves that would carry Ryan through the night towards a new day in a now uncertain world.

SURVIVE THE UNIVERSE #2

THE NEW SENTRY

Chapter Eighteen

THE MORNING

'Bleaking 'eck!'

Caleb was standing on the roof of the barge where he had spent the night.

'Oh!' proclaimed Bandit, beside him. They both stared across the sea as the sun rose, surveying the burnt-out remains of The Great Hall.

The Baker's End locksmith and the furry black-pelted Moline turned to look at each other with their faces frozen in shock. Both exhaled slowly before looking back towards the wreckage, to check their eyes weren't playing tricks on them.

The pair had slept through the carnage of the night before, and only when the smell of smoke and death travelled across the sea did Caleb begin to stir from his slumber.

The thing, however, to truly rouse him was Bandit's snoring, the sound of which made Caleb dream of the Moline using a vacuum cleaner to suck an angry asthmatic ghost out of a tree. The escalating noise and the increasingly surreal creepiness of the dream caused him to wake with fright. Between that nightmare and the scene he was presented with as he stepped onto the barge's roof, the young locksmith was more than ready for the day to end, even though it had only just begun.

The pink sky was peppered with Shadox aircraft. Caleb watched as several armed helicopters hovered at low altitude above the harbour, slowly sweeping their searchlights around for surviving targets. As the lights moved closer, Caleb leapt back down into the barge and began to stuff his possessions into a large burlap backpack.

'I don't know about you,' Caleb hollered up to Bandit on the roof, 'but I don't fancy sticking around here. Last time that lot got hold of me, I ended up with this bleakin' chip in my head.'

Bandit poked her head down through the entrance to the roof. 'Choo have the chip? The fish and chip? Bandit have breakfast now?'

Caleb was in too much of a panic to listen and continued packing up his belongings, muttering to himself.

'Right, that's everything I need. Just got to get a plan formed.'

He booted open the barge's hatch and stepped across the shore. 'What to do? Where to go? This is a beige situation, a really bleakin' beige situation.'

Bandit hopped down from the roof of the barge and followed after him, still under the impression that she'd be getting a fish and chip breakfast.

'Sir! Sir! Where is the breakfast? Choo eat it all? None for Bandit Moline?'

Caleb was too distracted to pay the creature any attention. 'I need to go somewhere safe. Somewhere protected. Somewhere with no affiliation to the Royal Guard. Oh no, there's only one place that's safe for me; Baker's End.'

Caleb's face became pale, remembering how his family had cast him out two nights previously. As he stopped to contemplate how he could get back to Baker's End surreptitiously, the now-furious Bandit caught up to him.

The Moline tugged at his trouser leg and let out an angry tirade. 'Ooooh choo said that Bandit would have the fish and chip breakfast, but choo have eaten it all yourself. Now Bandit is hungee, and there is none left? That is very cheeky of choo.'

'Not now, you little critter, I'm trying to think,' Caleb moaned, softly kicking the Moline aside. 'Mother Scudder said I could go back if I brought back something hard to come by, something of use – hmm?'

Scanning the ground for any valuable artefacts washed up on the shore, Caleb spotted the motionless body of Ryan Tyler draped across the piece of debris he had used as a raft.

Caleb dropped his backpack and grinned. 'Something hard to come by. Something of use. The jacket of a guardsman might just be my ticket back. And the fact he's dead makes getting it even easier.'

Caleb cautiously approached Ryan as Bandit continued to march behind in a temper. Leaning over Ryan's body, Caleb began to remove the jacket. As he pulled the garment's right arm free, Bandit nosily leaned in to take a look. The Moline recognised Ryan's face from the previous evening and tugged on Caleb's sleeve to protest. 'No! Choo leave this Mister Man alone; he helped Bandit last night.'

'Listen here, my furry friend,' Caleb replied, trying to detach the jacket from the raft, 'my need is much greater than his now. In fact, the only thing this poor soul needs is a six-foot-deep ditch, and I'm no gravedigger.'

'No! Choo are the thief!' Bandit shouted, pointing an accusing claw at Caleb.

'I'm not a thief; I'm a locksmith,' Caleb panted as he continued to tug the left sleeve free from both Ryan and the debris as quickly as possible.

'Anyhow, like I said, it doesn't matter if I take this jacket as your friend here is no longer with us.'

With that, Caleb gave the jacket one final tug, unhooking it from the raft while Ryan fell limply from the garment. As his body hit the floor, Ryan let out a muffled and confused groan.

'LIAR!' bellowed Bandit. 'The Mister Man is alive and well. Choo stop being cheeky and give him his jacket back, please.'

'I could've sworn he wasn't breathing. I should have checked his pulse, really,' Caleb answered uneasily. He then noticed that Ryan was still too groggy to realise what was happening.

Caleb held the jacket up by the sleeves to take a good look at it. 'Oh well, finders keepers and all that.'

Bandit could not stand by. She leapt up in the air and sank her tiny fangs into Caleb's left hand, causing him to drop the coat and howl in pain. The commotion stirred Ryan. As his eyes focused, he saw his jacket on the floor in front of him. As Ryan reached out to pick it up, Caleb stamped on his hand and grabbed the coat. Acting more out of instinct than a sense of being wronged, Ryan rolled up onto his feet and unleashed a furious uppercut punch to Caleb, knocking him to the floor. Caleb, however, kept a tight hold of the jacket and attempted to scramble away, only for Ryan to catch him and twist his arm in a lock.

'Let me go,' Caleb whined.

'Drop the jacket, and I'll let you go,' Ryan replied, suddenly realising that his mugger seemed familiar to him. 'Wait, don't I know you from somewhere?'

'I don't think so, chief. Please, just let me go – you're going to break my arm.' Caleb realised that he wasn't going to be allowed the scamper off with the jacket and dropped it in defeat. 'See, you win. Take your bleakin' coat and let me go!'

Ryan glanced down at Caleb's hand and stumbled back in shock. The letters KEY-C, tattooed across Caleb's fingers, triggered a memory that not only placed how Ryan knew the young thief but also caused the previous night's massacre to flash in his mind.

'Murphy's,' Ryan whispered to himself as images of Jayden flooded his thoughts.

As Caleb groaned on the floor, trying to rub the pain from his arm, Ryan picked up his jacket, dusted it off and put it on. He turned to look across the sea, out towards the remains of the Great Hall.

Everything felt unsure and distant to him. Ryan thought about Jayden's death and, although he knew he should be sad, he was numb. He thought about the violence of the night before and knew he should be scared, but again, he felt almost nothing. Just confusion – none of this felt real. It felt like someone would soon be there to reassure Ryan that this was all a mistake and everything would be fixed. And then there was Callie; did she survive? Would he see her again? And if so, how? Was he expected to report for duty? Was there even a Royal Guard of Vastrid anymore? It all seemed too unfair and too cruel; what right did the Shadox Corporation have to ruin his life like that? As the weight of his predicament began to register, Ryan's numbness gave way to anger.

Bandit the Moline, however, was no longer angry at all and had spent the previous minute chuckling at the tussle over the jacket.

'Haha, that will serve choo right,' she chuckled as Caleb got back to his feet.

'This is all your fault, you little critter,' yelled Caleb kicking a clutch of pebbles at the creature, who scampered away to hide behind some large crates further up the shore.

'So then Key-C,' Ryan spun on his heel to face Caleb. 'I guess you decided to rob me because we chased after you at Murphy's.'

'What? Was that you? Alright, listen, there's no need to build this into something more than it is.' Caleb held his opened hands out in front of him to try and calm the situation. 'I only wanted your coat because I need something valuable to get back in with my family in Baker's End. It's not as if you caught me trying to take your wallet or anything, is it? To be honest, I thought you were dead, so no harm done, eh?'

Ryan saw the fear in Caleb's face and realised he was taking his anger out on the wrong person. Ryan had never intimidated anyone like this before, and it made him feel uneasy – as if his current situation was forcing him to change who he was. He took a deep breath and asked calmly, 'Why not just take the Moline?'

Caleb was expecting things to escalate and turn ugly, the way such confrontations would in the slums, and was surprised by Ryan's reply. 'I beg your pardon?' he answered with a perplexed look on his face.

'The Moline you had running around here. Why not just take that back to your family in Baker's End?'

Caleb hadn't even considered that the creature could be of value. 'What? Are they rare?'

Ryan nodded and smiled.

'Are they valuable?'

'Oh yes,' replied Ryan.

Caleb needed to know one last thing. 'Are they of use?'

Ryan cast his mind back to the drama the Moline had created the previous evening and made a so-so gesture with his hand.

'That's good enough for me!' Caleb looked around excitedly and ran in the same direction he had seen Bandit go, but the Moline had vanished. 'Oh, that's just bleakin' great, I've pebble-kicked a fortune away.'

Caleb turned back towards Ryan. 'So then, are we good? Sorry about your jacket; I coulda swore you were dead. I mean, just how in Vastrid did you manage to survive that?' Caleb pointed across the sea towards the wreckage, and Ryan realised he had no idea how he'd escaped; luck and skill had rarely been reliable allies for him.

Thoughts of Jayden's final moments began to stab Ryan hard in the heart, but he refused to show it. 'Yeah, we're good.' Ryan offered a handshake to settle the misunderstanding.

Caleb shook his hand. 'So where are you off to? It's gonna get uber-bleak around here very soon, especially for you in that jacket. If I were you, I'd ditch it; it doesn't fit you right, anyhow.'

Ryan gave his jacket a quick tug, attempting and failing to make the long sleeves and short sides fit a little more conventionally. 'To be honest, I don't know where I am, let alone where I'll be going.'

Caleb was shocked. 'Crikey, for a Guardsman, your bearings aren't up to much, are they? This is Magna Harbour, in the forgotten south.'

'Isn't that about fifteen miles away from Caspian City?'

'More like twenty-five.'

A plan began to form in Caleb's mind. 'If you're hoping to get back to Caspian City by foot, you'll have to go through Baker's End and Kemsley – that is, if you want to avoid the Corporation.'

Ryan pondered for a moment. 'As much as I don't fancy my chances going through the slums, no offence – '

'None taken.'

' – I will be slaughtered on sight by the Corporation. So I

guess I'll be heading towards Baker's End,' Ryan sighed, running his hand through his hair and over his face.

'You know what we should do? We should buddy up. I'm on my way to Baker's End; if you vouch for me on the journey, I'll vouch for you when we get there,' Caleb suggested, filling the tone of his offer with as much kindness as his acting skills would allow.

Ryan communicated his acceptance with a nod, unaware that Caleb's offer was simply a way to ensure not only that the jacket would end up in Baker's End but also that it would arrive with a hostage wearing it.

'Great! Let's go then,' Caleb beamed and attempted to lift his backpack. Groaning in agony, he dropped the bag to the floor and grabbed his arm. 'Either my backpack has become inexplicably heavy all of a sudden, or you have really bleaked my arm up.'

'You were trying to rob me,' reasoned Ryan.

'Well, yeah, fair enough. Wait here a moment, I think I can see a trolley over there,' Caleb said, heading towards a pile of debris and junk that had washed ashore.

As he walked, Caleb began to feel a little guilty about the plan he had hatched. The young guardsman had shown mercy and appeared to be an alright kind of guy. Caleb realised that with all the madness going on around them this morning, the guardsman was in the same situation as he was, just a young man looking for shelter and safety. Could he really betray a fellow victim and hand him over to his wicked family? In the best-case scenario, they'd sell him off to the Shadox Corporation, but in the worst? Caleb didn't want to think about what would happen in the worst-case scenario. He'd seen the sick, violent and occasionally psychopathic sense of humour that his family members harboured, and it had never sat easily with him. Caleb paused for a moment and shook his head.

'No. I won't do it,' he thought to himself. 'I won't sink to their level. I'll – no, we'll get back to the city some other way.' As Caleb felt his burden lift slightly, he glanced deep into the pile of debris and saw something that made his eyes light up.

Moments later, Ryan observed his new acquaintance bounding back towards him pushing a Vastridian battle fleet Medi-trolley with what appeared to be a body in it.

'I've only just gone and hit the jackpot,' Caleb hollered, grabbing hold of the torso on the trolley and hoisting it high in the air. 'Look – a Mandroid!'

Ryan looked at the machine carefully; it was in a bad state. Its left leg had been torn off completely. Broken wires hung limply from the bullet holes in its chest. The artificial skin looked saggy and waterlogged, while its hair has become a tangle of knots.

Despite this damage, Ryan still recognised its face. 'I don't know if this will excite or alarm you, but I've got a strong feeling that it belongs to Prince Alistair.'

'Really? REALLY?' The tone of Caleb's voice confirmed that he was far more excited than alarmed.

Caleb darted around to the front of the Medi-Trolley and rolled Probot onto his chest. He pulled down the Mandroid's trousers and began to rummage around in his own pockets.

'What are you doing?' asked Ryan.

'I want to see how useful he'll be to me – well, I should say to us, really,' Caleb replied as he continued to root around. 'You'll be getting as much benefit out of him as I will if we're going to be travelling together.'

Ryan began to question if travelling with Caleb was going to be the best idea after all.

He was about to make his excuses and leave when Caleb thrust his hand back out of his pocket and cried, 'Here it is!' In his hand was a small electronic device.

Clearly handmade, the item appeared to be two pieces of

plastic welded together, with a small red light on top. It certainly wasn't from the Shadox Corporation.

'What in Vastrid is that?' Ryan sighed.

'Look and learn, my son, look and learn.' Caleb hovered the device over Probot's posterior until he heard a small beeping noise. Caleb motioned to Ryan that he should wait a moment, and within seconds the device's speaker activated.

'Probot Unnamed belongs to Prince Ali. Aged eight and a half.'

'GET IN!' cried Caleb clenching a fist and pulling it backwards in celebration. He turned to Ryan. 'In case you haven't managed to put two and two together, this is an infrared security chip reader. Naturally, they're illegal, but it's totally worth tracking down someone who can knock one up for you. It always pays to know who you're robbing or, in this case, just how valuable the stolen goods might be.'

'So then,' Ryan asked, 'that Mandroid, Probot – whatever it's called, has a security chip in its buttocks?'

Caleb nodded vigorously. 'Oh yes, right in one of the old bum cheeks. All of the Corporation's artificial life does. Best place for them. Loads of cushion to keep it safe, you see?'

'And your device can read the chip using an infrared beam?'

'Yes. I run the chip reader over its bum, and it lets me know who it belongs to,' Caleb frowned. 'It's pretty bleakin' simple, what is it you don't get?'

'Well,' Ryan paused, trying to find the words to explain his confusion, 'if your device uses an infrared beam that's strong enough to get through fake skin and muscle, why was there a need to remove his thin cotton trousers?'

The question stopped Caleb in his tracks. 'Well, erm – no, you're right. I'm not sure why I removed his trousers.'

The young locksmith blushed a little, and Ryan rolled his eyes and shook his head in disbelief.

'Come on, let's get out of here. Those spotlights are getting awfully close to the shore.' Ryan pointed towards a fleet of Shadox helicopters. Caleb nodded and pulled up Probot's trousers, rolling him onto the Medi-Trolly.

'So then, if we're going to be travelling together, what should I call you?' Caleb asked.

'My name's Ryan. Ryan Tyler. And what about you? I'm not going to call you Key-C.'

'Oh alright, you can call me Caleb and the surname's Scudder, if you're that interested. Anyhow seeing as how we're now on first name terms, I don't suppose you'd mind – ' Caleb nodded downwards at his backpack and then bobbed his head towards the Medi-Trolly, 'popping my bag up there. I hate to ask, but you did injure my arm.'

Despite it not hurting as much as he claimed, Caleb gave his arm a tender rub to highlight the fact.

Ryan sighed and hoisted the heavy backpack onto the Medi-Trolly. 'Thanks, mate,' beamed Caleb as he began to push the trolley across the thick, moist sand of the shore.

The duo walked together, shrouded in an awkward silence that Caleb was keen to break. 'So we're totally good, right? I mean, you're not going to hold that jacket situation or the night at Murphy's against me when we get back to the city, are you?'

'No,' Ryan answered. 'I just want to get back to my room, that is, if it still exists and hasn't been blown to smithereens like the Great Hall was. I'm tired, I'm sore, and my clothes are soaked through.'

'Yeah, I noticed that,' Caleb replied. 'As soon as we can get away from the shoreline and the spotlights, we'll find somewhere safe to rest, and while your clothes dry out, you can wear some of my spare threads if you fancy?'

Ryan smiled. 'Thanks, that would be great.'

'So then, I hate to keep bringing it up, but that night at

Murphy's, you were with a pretty damn fine looking female guard. A bit boyish, some might say, but she wore it well,' Caleb continued to probe. 'Who was that? I thought it was weird for just two members of the Guard to be hanging out having a drink together, like you two were. Was she your girlfriend or something?'

Ryan wasn't expecting Jayden to be brought up in conversation, and it shook him hard. 'No. She was my cousin,' he replied, feeling like a huge weight was about to crash down upon him.

Ryan's discomfort went unnoticed by Caleb, who continued to probe. 'I don't suppose we'll be bumping into her at any point on our journey?'

'No. She – ' Ryan paused. 'She died.'

'What?' Caleb asked softly, 'Over there?' He nodded towards the Great Hall.

The enormity of the previous night's events suddenly hit Ryan. As his bottom lip quivered, he managed to murmur, 'Yes,' before tears began to stream from his eyes.

Caleb's face grimaced as he realised that he'd managed to take a moment of awkward silence and make it much worse.

Unsure of what to do next, Caleb sighed, 'Sorry mate,' and hovered his arm around Ryan's shoulder, where it loitered for the next five seconds in an uncertain manner. With both young men buckling under the embarrassment of the moment, Caleb decided to give Ryan a sturdy pat on the back before letting out a cough and declaring, 'We should make a move before we're spotted.'

Ryan wiped his eyes, nodded in agreement, and they continued to walk. Caleb made one last attempt at conversation. 'We'll get back to the city, don't you worry about that. If we can survive last night, we can survive anything; and now we've got each other's backs, we're doubly safe. It's you and me against the world, Ryan Tyler, you and me against the world.'

Little did Caleb know, it wasn't just him and Ryan against the world, as deep in the darkness of the large burlap back-pack, the two bright yellow eyes of Bandit the Moline stared hungrily out of the bag's opening.

Chapter Nineteen

THE CHAIN

The first thing Colonel Bron sensed as he regained consciousness was the smell of antiseptic. His heart sank as the heavy stench of antimicrobial substances consumed his nostrils. As a man of combat, the smell could only represent one thing, and that was failure.

His mind was foggy, and his vision was blurred. As he attempted to focus his eyes, he experienced an excruciating pain travelling through his right retina. A scream tried to leave his throat without success. His mouth felt more than numb; it felt non-existent. He tried once more to open his eyes and focus, on this occasion using his left eye more than his right.

Managing to push his focus beyond the blur, he saw a sharp surgical instrument hover over his eye before moving diagonally downwards towards his cheek. Bron's left eye followed the blade downwards and witnessed it pierce through a loose flap of his skin and begin to drag it sideways.

The colonel felt vulnerable and compromised; he didn't like it. He attempted to move his arms but felt almost nothing. He tried his legs, but once again, they felt numb and life-less. He realised that he had been tranquillised, but by who?

As his one good eye watched cold metallic devices and instruments pluck and pull at his face, he searched his mind for his last memory. Images of gunfire, smoke, explosions and carnage fell through his thoughts like confetti, escalating in pace as the sterile apparatus rapidly clutched and tugged his skin. Bron tensed his body as both the surgical work on his face and his feverish recollections of bloodshed became too frenzied for him to withstand.

As his muscles tightened, Bron managed to clench his right fist just as a surgical staple was punched into his face. Suddenly a clear memory from the night before emerged before his eyes; it was of a frail boy nervously raising and aiming an assault rifle at him. The boy squeezed the trigger, and another staple entered his skin forcefully as the memory repeated. This time it was faster; the boy aiming the rifle and then squeezing the trigger; crack, another staple. The image repeated over and over again in Bron's mind as each staple pierced his skin. Incensed and alarmed, Bron bolted upright and attempted to scream with anger, but little more than a pained groan emerged from his mouth.

He glanced to his right and caught his reflection in a long piece of mirrored glass that ran alongside a white work surface. The right side of his face was destroyed; bloody, red and swollen, barely covered by flaps of skin loosely held together by staples. Below the flaps of skin, half of his jaw was almost completely missing and had been replaced by steel and wires. Above the staples, his eye was a bloodshot mess glancing out through inflamed and infected skin.

Using his right hand, Bron began to tear the surgical devices buzzing around his face from their computer termi-nal. With one of the mechanical arms still hanging from a loose flap of skin on his cheek, Bron slid off the operating table while steadying himself with his right hand. He clenched and relaxed his leg muscles three times to attempt to wake them. He noticed a slight improvement, but it wouldn't be enough to enable his escape.

Bron collapsed over the operating table and dragged his torso across it until he was within reach of a surgical tray. He stretched out and began to rummage around, eventually retrieving a large syringe full of Methylphenidoxy-Sterane. Created by the Shadox Corporation, M-Sterane was a powerful drug used in emergencies to counteract the effects of an anaesthetic quickly.

Bron plunged the needle into his leg and glanced towards the door, behind which muffled, panicked shouts were emerging. As the drug began to travel around his body, Bron focused on the voices to try and understand what they were saying.

'What do you mean, "he's woken up"?'

A collection of nervous voices attempted to explain as Bron continued to tense his leg muscles and clench his fists, hoping to speed up the effect of the M-Sterane.

'C'mon, c'mon,' Bron grunted to himself, frustrated at the numbness that still lingered in his limbs.

'I want this door open,' a voice outside was ordering. Leaning against the operating table for support, Bron glanced at the door briefly before returning his focus to his body. Again he clenched and tensed, although this time faster and with more determination. Bron groaned in frustration at the lack of progress he was making until suddenly, the numbness in his left hand began to fade as he stretched his fingers out.

He slowly curled his fingers back inwards, and the left side of his face smirked as he felt his left hand become a good, strong fist.

'Now just the legs,' his mind urged as he glanced down at

his thighs which he continued to tense, before returning his focus towards the door.

'Right, when I give the signal, you two run in with me. We'll hold him, you jab him,' the voice outside instructed. 'Ready? One...'

Bron gave his leg muscles one last strong tense and was relieved to feel some sensitivity returning to his thighs. With an eye on the door in front of him, Bron began to warm his body up, shaking and stretching his arms and legs before stiffly stepping away from the operating table.

The voice outside the door continued, '...Two...' as Bron began to feel the last of the numbness fade from his legs.

'C'mon then,' Bron thought to himself, clenching both fists and staring at the door, 'I'm ready.'

'...Three!'

The door burst open, and a hefty security guard charged towards Bron with two colleagues and a young junior doctor following close behind.

The tattered remains of Bron's face scowled as the security guard reached out to grab him. Ducking under the guard's arms, Bron thrust his knee into his attacker's stomach before quickly smashing the guard's head against the hard surface of the operating table. The guard's head bounced off the bed sharply, causing the surgical tray and all of its contents to fly into the air. The guard stumbled backwards, falling to the floor as the contents of the tray crashed to the floor around him.

As this happened, the second security guard had managed to run behind Bron and restrain him with a double shoulder lock. Bron wriggled and attempted to fight his way free as the third security guard battled to lock his legs.

With the colonel almost restrained, the junior doctor approached with a metallic syringe in his trembling hand. Bron continued to wriggle and fight, eventually kicking the third guard away from his feet and then launching the second guard over his shoulders into a surgical light hanging over the operating table.

Stamping down hard, Bron shattered the rib cage of the guard that lay by his feet and then turned his attention to the junior doctor, who had begun to back away.

Illuminated only by the flickering bulbs of the emergency lighting, Bron paced towards the cowering young doctor, seizing him as if he was prey. Bron slowly wrapped his fingers around the doctor's throat and lifted him off his feet. Lost in the moment, Bron choked the doctor with a practised, precise force, allowing him to savour this kill for as long as possible. The horrific strobing image of Bron's tattered face emerged and faded before the doctor's eyes as Bron loosened and tightened his grip accordingly.

Bron hadn't enjoyed a kill this much in years. His rank and the Corporation's advanced weaponry had provided him with ample opportunities to take life, but it had also reduced the physicality and intimacy of the moment. As the doctor's facial expression changed from one of terror to one of pleading surrender, Bron heard something whistling through the air. Instantly his arm became numb, and the young doctor fell from Bron's grasp, landing gasping and wheezing on the floor. Bron glanced at his arm and noticed a tranq-dart sticking out of his bicep. More whistling noises followed as a flurry of tranq-darts flew through the air and pierced Bron's body. Everything became hazy for the colonel; he looked towards the door and blearily saw a squadron of Shadox troopers firing.

'But they're my men,' Bron thought to himself angrily, 'my own men!' The colonel stumbled back a little. The looped chain of memories from earlier returned to consume his mind; the boy aiming the rifle and then squeezing the trigger, followed by a staple being pounded into his face. As his troops opened fire on him, images of this act joined the chain, driving the speed of the recollections to escalate in his mind. With the colonel distracted by the circular memories playing in his mind, the young doctor scrambled back onto his feet and plunged the large metallic syringe he was carrying into Bron's leg.

Bron took one weak step backwards and collapsed. As he laid flat on his back, the pattern in his mind continued at greater and greater speeds until it stopped abruptly, and Bron fell into a heavily anaesthetised sleep.

Bron woke hours later. Although conscious, his mind seemed to dwell for a moment in the darkness and silence of sleep. Eventually, the sound of voices pierced through and slowly began to pull the colonel's senses back into the room.

The first thing Bron was aware of was a strange sensation of weight on his face. As it was, his face felt puffy and sore, but he jiggled his jaw about a little and realised that his whole face was very heavily bandaged.

The colonel attempted to focus on the conversation. One of the voices sounded familiar, but he couldn't place the owner through the fog of anaesthesia. He arched his neck a little to the side and squinted his tired eyes, hoping to catch a glimpse of the people talking by his bed.

As his eyes focused, he realised that the familiar voice belonged to Rachel Stone. She was talking to two doctors who looked more than a little beaten down by her questioning. Despite his cold-hearted nature, Bron's spirits rose. Following the previous night's carnage and the brawl in the operating theatre, it was a welcome relief to have a friend by his side.

Bron listened carefully to the voices, understanding fragments of the conversation. He heard the doctors explain how the interruption to his facial reconstruction surgery had impacted its success and left his wounds open to bacteria.

These factors and, most critically, the colonel's own decision to inject himself with M-Sterane, had caused immense complications to the medical procedure. Bron watched as Rachel ran her hand over her face before wearily asking, 'What kind of complications?'

The doctors glanced at each other before beginning the list of disfigurements and disabilities that would now define the colonel. His face was unrepairable; it would be impossible to mould or recreate it to anywhere near its original state. What remained of his face was a frail tapestry of skin stretched and stitched to the best of the Shadox Corporation's top surgeon's ability. To protect his new face from damage or infection, the colonel would need to wear a clear protective mask made from polycarbonates at all times. His spine had suffered trauma from the fall through the balcony window, and a stray piece of shrapnel had severely damaged his left thigh muscle as the Great Hall exploded. These factors would impair his mobility and inevitably threaten his status as the Corporation's deadliest soldier.

The colonel closed his eyes, feigning unconsciousness just before Rachel Stone glanced briefly at his bandaged face. 'And what about his mind? Will he have any mental deficiencies from all this?'

'We have various therapies we can implement for these types of trauma,' the youngest doctor advised, stepping forward. 'There shouldn't be lasting mental issues – well, I mean apart from his usual ones, that is.' The other doctor beside him let out a nervous chuckle while Rachel smiled politely, forcing out a thin, clipped laugh if only to show that the doctor would not be punished for his flippant comment.

Rachel turned once again to glance at Bron, who lay with his face wrapped in bloodied bandages, hooked up to machines, wheezing through breathing apparatus. The colonel was no longer the fearsome warrior he once was.

Rachel pondered how best to rid both her personal life and the Corporation of this sad remnant of a once-formidable man. She could easily have him murdered as he lay defenceless in his hospital bed, but with his mind intact, he could still be of use. By the time Rachel had begun to work for her Uncle Maxwell, Bron had served with Vastridian Royal Guard and the Shadox Corporation for several years. He knew about missions that most had long forgotten and, more importantly, had taken on Kendra Lomax in battle and lived to tell the tale. Rachel knew that she would almost certainly need his knowledge and experience to obtain her ultimate ambition of overthrowing her uncle.

Bron opened his eyes and attempted to make contact with Rachel and the doctors as they talked, willing her to walk up to his bed and assure him that she'd be getting him released as soon as possible. However, the colonel's hopes crashed, and the agony of rejection bludgeoned his heart as he saw Rachel exchange farewells with the doctors and walk away without even glancing in his direction.

Each footstep she took as she left triggered the chain of memories in Bron's mind; the boy with the rifle, the staples, the betrayal by his own men and now his only friend walking away from him. Pushing through the madness of the memories playing out in his mind and the wretched sense of abandonment in his heart, Bron reached out and pleaded, 'Rachel.' But it was too late. She was gone.

Chapter Twenty

SILENCE

'All you have to do is confess. Just look towards the screen and confess,' were the first words Prince Alistair heard as he regained consciousness. The voice was calm and measured yet laced with threat. The young prince realised he wasn't being addressed, and even though his hands were bound, he felt a small sense of relief.

As his eyes focused, he lifted his head to see his father bound in a chair, staring sadly at a large Vid-Screen that was broadcasting his image back at him. The King's face and shoulders looked fine; however, the lower part of his torso was barely concealed by torn clothing, revealing battered and bruised skin beneath. It was a relief to Alistair to know that his father had survived the massacre of the previous night, but the situation they were both in filled his heart with dread.

The man addressing his father was familiar to the prince. 'Nox?' he groaned, recognising him from Newscasts and several high-profile meetings at the palace. Alistair glanced around the room and realised that a number of the Shadox Troopers were familiar to him, mainly from their days serving in the Royal Guard. One in particular, however, caught his eye. His name was Jon Bradlock, and he was one of the nastiest and most brutal men ever to disgrace the Royal Guard uniform. After allegations emerged that Bradlock had shot an unarmed Baker's End family dead in their sleep, he had disappeared.

'So he ended up working for The Corporation,' Prince Alistair thought to himself, noticing the Captain's Insignia on Bradlock's uniform. Bradlock caught Alistair looking at him and flashed the prince a malicious little smirk in return.

It suddenly dawned on Alistair that a small group of captured Royal Guards were also in the room, and Captain Dunnell was amongst them. The Captain's eyes stared down at the floor, seemingly lost in thought.

Nox unbuttoned and rolled up the sleeves of his expensive shirt, circling the bound King as he addressed him. 'Mr. Hawthorne – I hope you don't take offence at me calling you that, but you're not *King* William anymore, are you? I mean, it's not like you rule anything anymore. We've taken away Vastrid. We've taken away your home. Do you also want us to take away your life?'

Nox crouched down and met King William eye to eye. 'Just confess, William,' he suggested softly. 'Just play the game this one last time, and we'll let you and your family retire peacefully.' Nox's voice was quiet yet insistent, and the words within it hypnotically flew into the former monarch's ear and rested welcomingly in his mind.

For a moment, King William's tired face lit up, and a sense of calm and tranquillity soothed his defeated heart. He was about to relent and give Nox and the Corporation every-thing they requested when a feeling of dread hit his stomach like a thunderbolt; he knew that by doing this, he would be repeating the mistakes that had led his kingdom to this sorry situation.

Realising the time for diplomacy and tact had long since

passed, William looked straight into Nox's cold dark eyes and spat his refusal into his captor's face.

Nox stepped back in shock, wiping the saliva from his eyes before bounding forward furiously and clutching the King's jaw in his left hand. 'Just confess!' Nox demanded while striking King William's face hard with his right fist.

The King's head jolted back, and two teeth flew from his mouth as Nox mounted the chair, striking William's head once again.

'Just confess. Just confess. Just confess.' The anger in his tone gradually morphed into maniacal vicious glee as Nox continued to beat on the King of Vastrid.

Alistair jostled around in his chair, attempting to free himself. Eventually, he managed to force his right hand out of its binding, splitting the skin and spraining his wrist in the process. Despite his pain, the young prince gritted his teeth and dashed towards Nox to rescue his father.

The chair the King was bound to had tipped over backwards, and Nox stood over it, continuing his assault on the monarch. With both hands clutching King William by his shirt, Nox turned towards the approaching prince, causing him to stop in his tracks. As Nox smiled, his eyes glowed a sinister shade of crimson and cold terror coursed through Alistair, freezing him to the spot.

Captain Bradlock seized the moment, pouncing at Alistair and knocking him to the floor with the electroshock device in the butt of his service pistol. Although the muscles in his body began to spasm and jolt, Alistair attempted to get back onto his feet, only to feel the sole of Bradlock's military boot stamp down on his head. 'You ain't going anywhere, your majesty,' Bradlock mocked, as the Prince desperately attempted to turn his head to at least try and see his Father.

Although his view was restricted, the sounds of Nox's brutal attack on his father painted the picture clearly enough.

He heard knuckles piercing the skin, breaking bones, squelching blood and tissue. He heard the sound of his father, once a proud and strong warrior, reduced to a wheezing and gasping victim. And even though he couldn't see them, Alistair could still feel the stare of Nox's venomous red eyes.

Amongst the sounds of violence, Alistair heard one final, pleading gasp of air from his father and knew it was over. Alistair closed his eyes, attempting to shut out the situation until the growing weight of the tears building behind his eyelids forced him to open them. With the red glow fading from his eyes, Nox strolled towards the prince, covered in the King's blood.

'Well, that was fun,' Nox declared, cleaning his hands with a towel. 'Messy, ineffective,' he leant down to face the prince, 'but fun nonetheless. Don't worry, young Alistair; this is a good day. If I had my way, you would have been killed yesterday, but a certain colonel decided to turn an assassination into a massacre, so we need *you* to do what your father was too pig-headed to do. Confess. That's all, just confess.'

Nox looked at the prince's exhausted and distraught face. 'You will confess, but not today. We need you to be convincing and healthy. You should rest and think about what happened here today. I allowed your father to live free and well, but he chose silence.' Nox glanced at the bloody corpse of King William Hawthorne. 'And now, that silence is all he will ever have.'

Nox strolled past the prince as Bradlock removed his boot from his head. Alistair rolled onto his back, wearing a face that was full of frustration and rage. He began to think of various ways to attack Nox, but as he did, he noticed Captain Dunnell slowly lift his head and make eye contact with him. As if he knew what the prince was thinking, Dunnell looked him straight in the eye, gently shook his head and mouthed the words, 'Stay down.'

The prince nodded before Bradlock grabbed hold of him and placed him back with the rest of the Royal Guard. Alistair looked towards Dunnell and whispered, 'How did you know what I was going to do?'

'I know what it's like to be a young soldier compromised in battle,' Dunnell answered, 'and I know what loss feels like. Now is not the time for vengeance. We're trapped on a shuttle taking us to who knows where, we don't know what the state of Vastrid is, and, more importantly than that, the Royal Guard need their leader to survive more than ever, King Alistair.'

The words "King Alistair" felt like heavy shackles to the young prince. Growing up, he would daydream about his coronation; he always presumed it would be a joyful occasion, full of people from all walks of life singing his praises while his retired father looked on proudly. But here it was, in its tragic reality; his ascension to the throne unofficially bestowed to him by a captured soldier, surrounded by his captors and witnessed by his father's corpse. For all the training he had received as a boy, Alistair feared he had no idea how to come out of this situation as a hero. He closed his eyes and attempted to focus his mind; however, the image of Nox's smile and his red glowing eyes kept appearing between each thought. Alistair sank down, sorrowful over the loss of his father and, for the first time in his life, truly afraid.

Like the prince, Callie Haywood was also a bound prisoner but held by a different captor on a different vessel.

She had been awake for a while; the watered-down, black market tranqs used by Marcus Hagen and his crew had only kept her unconscious for an hour or so. She'd spent the rest of the night drifting in and out of sleep and was now attempting to attract the attention of a sullen, blue-skinned prisoner opposite her. Callie had no idea who'd managed to capture her but, having dealt with more than her fair share of challenges in life, there was no way she was going to be whisked away to an unknown destination without a fight. She also knew that to escape, she'd need a team, and the only other prisoner on the ship who was currently alert and awake was the grumpy-looking off-worlder with a Med-Stick hanging casually from his mouth.

Callie had spent the best part of two hours throwing nods and 'Pssst' noises in his direction whenever the crew guarding them had been distracted. The colonist prisoner met each gesture by either scowling disdainfully back at her or turning his gaze towards the floor. Despite usually being appalled at such an approach, Callie had even tried to use some of the 'tactical flirting' skills from her Guards training to try and entice some interest. She leaned back in her chair as seductively as she could stomach and attempted to make eye contact, only for the prisoner to look as disgusted as she felt for stooping to such behaviour.

Just as Callie was about to give up, fate gave her what appeared to be a helping hand. The intercom at the other end of the ship began to sound with an urgent message, calling for all members of Hagen's crew to proceed to the cargo area. As they did so, one of the crew members clumsily barged past the blue-skinned prisoner and knocked the Med-Stick from his lips, causing it to bounce off the floor and rattle towards Callie.

Callie smiled; she knew exactly how to win over the prisoner and gain his trust. Callie stretched her legs out as far as they would go and plucked the Med Stick between her two feet. She softly whistled in the direction of the prisoner. 'Hey, you in the trench coat. Looking for this?'

Callie kicked both legs into the air and managed to flip the Med-Stick over towards the prisoner. It landed just above his collarbone, which allowed him to nudge the device back into his mouth. Once again, he slumped back into his chair and looked down at the floor disdainfully.

'You're welcome,' said Callie sarcastically. 'You know something, Boy Blue? A simple "thank you" wouldn't have killed you.'

'Calling him Boy Blue won't endear you to him now, will it?' A voice behind her croaked. Callie arched around and noticed that a fellow member of the Guards named Kurtis Lackner had woken up. Callie tensed up; she had never had any direct dealings with Lackner, but he was well known amongst the Guards. A dark cloud of rumours had followed his career of seventeen years, with most of those daring to challenge him coming away worse for doing so.

'No, I suppose not,' Callie stammered.

'We're the reason why his skin is blue. We're the reason why he needs to puff away on that piece of plastic. Oh, the brave and just Royal Guard of Vastrid, what a joke we are,' cackled Lackner softly. 'We sat back and watched as The Corporation ravaged those free-thinking off-world colonist fools, and when Shadox got bored of tormenting them, he handed them over to King William to finish off. Believe me, girly; you'll get no help from him.'

Callie frowned. 'The Colony Wars ended over a decade ago. I wasn't even born when they started; how can he hold that situation against me?'

'You've never actually met an off-worlder before, have you? They're a proud and stubborn bunch. Not that there are many left after what we did to them.' Lackner heard the colonist prisoner's breathing intensify, building to a seething series of inhalations and exhalations. 'They're an arrogant bunch too. Especially that one sat in front of you. He really rates himself. You may have heard of him; his name's Alex Navin – yeah, that's right, pal, I know you,' he raised an eyebrow at Navin, then turned back to Callie. 'I'm not surprised if you don't, though – he's nowhere near as infamous as he likes to think.'

Callie looked at the prisoner and tried to think if the name rang any bells, but it didn't. She still couldn't see, despite the previous bad blood between his people and the country she served, why he wouldn't want to join forces and escape.

'That's all very well, but surely he wants to escape. I mean, where the heck are we anyhow?' Callie whispered.

'We're on Marcus Hagen's ship. Hovering somewhere above Vastrid while his men gather more prisoners,' Lackner answered in a dour tone. 'Hagen's a bounty hunter, in case you haven't guessed. Not one of the best, but he's got lots of experience and always captains a skilled crew. He also has a very annoying habit of peppering his speech with the term 'my friend', even when he's stabbing you in the back.'

Callie thought back to her capture outside of the Great Hall. 'Oh yeah,' she sighed, 'I've met him. So where are they taking us?'

'I should imagine they're planning to round up enough Guards to fill up this vessel and then whisk us all off to the Corporation. What *they'll* do to us is anyone's guess: prison, firing squad or even worse than that, experimentation,' Lackner scowled. 'But I tell you what; I'll be damned if I let that happen. We'll wait until this ship is full of our own, and then we'll take it.'

Callie felt a renewed sense of hope. Maybe Lackner wasn't as bad as people had said, or perhaps the situation they had been thrust into had changed him. Admittedly, she could do without being called 'girly', but at least, unlike Alex Navin's stroppy silence, it came attached to something resembling a plan.

Callie smiled to herself as the crew began to filter back past the prisoners.

'Like I said,' Lackner whispered, 'we will take this ship but not yet. You'll need your rest, so get some sleep. I'll keep guard in the meantime. Remember what I said about Navin; he is not our friend. He will not aid us. He will betray us. When we get free of these chairs, make sure you take him down first. He cannot be trusted.'

Throughout all of his years of shady negotiations and scams, Lackner had become an expert at quietly directing speech to one set of ears only. Somewhat arrogantly, Lackner had presumed that his whispers would be inaudible to anyone other than Callie. However, sitting calm and focused in his chair, Alex Navin had read Lackner's lips and picked up every word. It didn't surprise him that he was to be targeted as a threat, but it was an unexpected development that they intended to attack him first. Alex felt unthreatened by this. There was plenty of time to account for this new hazard and to add another contingency step to his own thoughts of escape. As Callie drifted off to sleep and Lackner focused on the comings and goings of Marcus Hagen's men, Alex Navin looked down at the floor and once again began to plan in silence.

Chapter Twenty-One

CUL-DE-SAC

'I thought you said we were going to stop somewhere so I could get dry,' Ryan moaned to his new acquaintance.

'Yes. I know I did, and we will. When it's safe,' Caleb answered, pushing his recently obtained Medi-Trolley. The device carried not only the deactivated body of Probot but also Bandit the Moline, who had secretly hidden away in the locksmith's backpack.

Following the traumatic events of the previous night, Ryan was tired and irritable. 'Well, can you find somewhere safe soon because – '

'Yes. Yes. I know, your clothes are soaked through. You've told me. In fact, you've been whinging about your wet clothes every five minutes since we left the harbour. I bleakin' get it. As soon as I find somewhere safe, we'll rest up, and you can get into some dry clothes,' Caleb replied. 'And then maybe, just maybe, I'll finally get some bleakin' peace and quiet.'

The duo had been walking for nearly four hours as the plethora of Corporation patrols, checkpoints and overhead scouting helicopters had forced them to deviate substantially from their planned route back to Caspian City. They had escaped detection by travelling through the rugged, untamed terrain of Sleaterstone Quarry and were now making their way through the industrial sector of Barneston.

As Ryan and Caleb walked past a disused Vid-Screen factory, a battered, white van that had seen better days sped towards them.

'What the bleakin' heck?' Caleb yelled as he pulled both his trolley and a weary Ryan Tyler off the road, bringing them in tight and close to the factory's steel fence.

Caleb spun around to watch where the van was going, only to see it come to a screeching halt and then begin reversing back towards them.

'Oh, I don't like this. I don't like this one bit,' Caleb cried.

Ryan looked at Caleb. 'I agree. RUN.'

The duo turned and began to sprint back past the factory they had just passed. Ryan was the quicker of the two and darted down a sideroad, hoping that it would prove too narrow for the van. Caleb soon followed, puffing and panting with the Medi-Trolley.

Their hearts sank as they looked around and discovered that the sideroad was, in fact, a cul-de-sac surrounded by a twenty-foot steel fence. Ryan and Caleb turned back towards the main road, only to see the white van halt in front of their exit.

The sound of the van front doors being slammed shut echoed around the cul-de-sac like an unwelcome indication of what was about to come.

'That doesn't look like a Corporation vehicle. Who have you narked off this time?' Ryan asked Caleb. 'Is this something to do with that night at Murphy's or one of your other failed scams?'

'Oh, that's right, blame the boy from Baker's End, why don't you?' Caleb snapped before stopping to think. 'Although, theoretically, if I had upset someone because a scam had gone a bit beige, then they would almost certainly be driving a van looking like that.'

Three Wiseguys clutching hockey sticks had hopped down from the van and were now marching towards the duo.

'OK, Ryan, you're a member of the Royal Guard, right? You should be able to take care of this, yeah?' Caleb gulped.

'I'm just a librarian, not a full member of the Guards. I'm only on a secondment,' Ryan replied. 'What about you? You're from Baker's End; you must be able to hold your own in a street fight.'

'Nah, I'm just a locksmith.'

'I guess we're out of luck then,' Ryan said, taking a deep breath to prepare for the oncoming trouble.

As the Wiseguys approached, they seemed familiar to both Ryan and Caleb, although neither could place where they recognised them from.

The largest of the Wiseguys, known amongst his peers as Slider, held out his hockey stick and bellowed, 'YOU! We've got unfinished business with you.'

Caleb stepped forward. 'I don't recall who you are, but I'm sure if I did anything to offend you, it was an honest mistake.'

'No, not you, slum rat. I mean him,' spat Slider, pointing his hockey stick straight towards Ryan.

'Me? How in Vastrid have I managed to upset you?' Ryan asked in a tone that juggled anger with nerves.

Pounding his hockey stick into his open palm, Slider continued to walk towards Ryan. 'Oh, you don't remember us, Soldier-Soldier? Well, we remember what you did to our Tone two nights ago at Craydon's Corner.'

A chill ran down Ryan's spine as he remembered not only the scuffle he'd been involved in but also how he had lost control of the situation.

'If my memory's correct, I only finished what he started,' Ryan replied.

Slider shook his head dismissively. 'Yeah, but it's *how* you finished it, Shiny-Eyes.'

Caleb arched his eyebrows. *Shiny-Eyes?* he thought to himself, wondering whether it was a nickname, a piece of slang he was unaware of or something more involved.

Holding his index finger in the air, Caleb stepped forward to interject. 'If I may, can I just state that I've only just met this guy. I have literally no idea what all this shiny-eyes stuff is about, but I'm oh-so-very sure you're in the right.'

Slider laughed and shook his head. 'Nah, slum rat, that was a good try, but you ain't getting out of this. You see, the boys and me have to get our Tone some medical care, and what with your Soldier-Soldier mate breaking both his legs, we're tired of carrying him around. So we're going to beat you down hard. Then we're taking your sweet Medi-Trolley and that broke-up Mandroid you've got.'

For a moment, Caleb considered simply offering the Wiseguys his bounty in order to escape a beating but almost instantly remembered that he needed it to win favour in Baker's End.

So distracted was the young locksmith with thoughts of bargaining that it took a second or two for the full contents of the Slider's speech to register in his brain. 'Wait a minute,' Caleb said in shock as he turned to face Ryan, 'you broke both of someone's legs in a fight?'

Ryan looked even more shocked. 'I didn't. I swear that I didn't. I only bust his head open.'

'Oh is *that* bleakin' all,' Caleb snapped as the Wiseguys closed in on them. 'And to think you were blaming this on me. I'm going to have a good think about us pairing up – '

Caleb's rant was interrupted as his right arm was struck hard by Slider. The other two Wiseguys, Garrett and Jonesy, attacked Ryan, beating him with their hockey sticks, eventually pushing him to the floor. Slider appeared above him, grinning as he shoved his hockey stick against Ryan's throat, pinning him to the floor.

Garrett and Jonesy made their way over to Caleb, who was struck once more and fell to his knees. He felt a swift kick to his jaw and collapsed backwards. He watched Ryan being beaten some more by Slider and concluded his earlier rant in a mutter, ' – if we both survive this.'

A loud thudding sound suddenly echoed throughout the cul-de-sac, cutting the Wiseguys' assault on Ryan and Caleb short.

'Boys? Did you hear that?' Slider asked, glancing around.

Garrett and Jonesy began to survey the area. Caleb caught Ryan's eye, and they jumped at their chance to escape, scrabbling towards the back of the alleyway.

Garrett was uneasy. 'What do you think that was?'

A louder thumping sound. 'I think it's coming from the van,' said Jonesy.

The three Wiseguys turned to focus on the van, and sure enough, three further thuds emerged from that direction. Each one sounded increasingly frantic and angry, like something was attempting to escape. After the third thud, there was a short pause before a teeth-peeling sound of slow scratching against the metallic wall of the van.

'Could it be Tone?' Garrett asked.

'I don't know,' Slider replied, turning to Ryan. 'Just what did you do to our Tone?'

Ryan looked back, perplexed as another quick three thuds sounded followed by more scratching.

Slider approached the van cautiously. 'Tone? Mate, are you OK?'

A crashing sound thundered through the alley. It was accompanied by the shape of a contorted torso hammering itself into the side of the van's bodywork, leaving a twisted and eerie indentation of its form.

Slider dropped his hockey stick in fright and slowly paced closer towards the van as the colour drained from his face.

'I told you,' Jonesy said, 'Tone's a damn Synistrail now. I told you there's no point taking him to a hospital. That soldier boy's done something shady to him. We should just get out of here.'

The van began to shake and rattle as the body inside of it frantically rammed and smashed into the walls, trying to escape.

At the end of the cul-de-sac, Caleb looked over at Ryan and mouthed, 'Synistrail?'

He was hoping that his new acquaintance could give him some sort of gesture or reassuring nod that this strange development was all part of some Royal Guard inspired escape plan but, as Ryan looked back offering little more than a fearful expression, it was clear that this wasn't the case.

'Alright boys,' Slider ordered as his mouth began to run dry, 'forget Tone, forget the van, let's just get out of here.'

The three Wiseguys fled through the alley, running past their clattering van and off into the distance. Ryan walked over to Caleb and helped his new friend to his feet. 'You OK? You took quite a beating. I swear I don't know half of what they were talking about. I didn't break that guy's legs, and I sure as heck didn't turn him in a Synistrail.'

Caleb looked concerned. '*Can* you turn people in Synistrails?'

'Of course not,' Ryan snapped back. 'I don't think anyone can turn other people into Synistrails. I'm not even sure Synistrails actually exist.'

'Alright. Alright. Just checking, it's been a rather eventful day. At this stage of the game, I doubt anything would surprise me.'

There was suddenly an almighty crash at the foot of the alley as the van tipped over onto its side, causing Caleb to jump back in fright. As the van landed, its back doors flew open, and the crumpled-up figure of a young man began to emerge from the rear of the vehicle, using his long muscular arms to pull himself out. When the majority of his body was free, the figure slowly stretched its neck and turned towards the end of the cul-de-sac. The platinum blonde hair and deep stitches on his forehead confirmed to Ryan that this was indeed the Wiseguy he'd previously encountered.

'Caleb, I did get into a fight with this guy, but there's nothing to suggest that he's an actual real-life scary monster Synistrail.'

'Great,' Caleb added dryly. 'Let's just hope his legs are still broken. That way, we may actually stand a chance.'

Tone's pupils began to glow a luminous shade of emerald as he looked directly at Ryan and smirked, his head twitching and nodding gently yet without control. With one final push, Tone freed himself and landed uneasily, then began to drag himself in the direction of Caleb and Ryan. He kept his gaze focused on Ryan and crawled with increasing speed, dragging his two shattered legs behind him. The colour in his eyes intensified, and a poisonous smile spread across his face. Once more, his body movements began to jolt and judder in short spasms.

'Well, Ryan,' Caleb's voice began to crack, 'I don't know about you, but I think I've seen enough to believe that Synistrails exist. I think we should try and climb that impossible fence behind us.'

'Agreed,' answered Ryan, and they both turned and ran towards the fence. As they started climbing, Tone suddenly stopped, arched his back, and howled before dropping his head for a moment. When he looked up, his skin had become a faded tone of strangulated mauve, and all trace of life had drained from his eyes. A caustic hiss emanated from his mouth while the nails on his right hand creaked and screeched, growing over and grinding against existing bone and tissue before piercing through his skin as they extended.

The last ounces of strength were fading from Caleb's right arm, and he fell from the fence, landing on some trash bags below. As he rolled back onto the ground, Caleb glanced up to see Tone in his new Synistrail form, hungrily scuttling on all fours towards him.

'Oh, bleak this,' Caleb cried out, darting across the alley and pushing his Medi-Trolley towards the Synistrail with as much force as he could muster. Using its left arm to prop itself up, the Synistrail punched the trolley away, sending Caleb's backpack and Probot into the air and causing all three items to crash down behind him.

Ryan was about halfway up the fence when he glanced down to see the Synistrail extend its toxic nails and clamber towards Caleb. His survival instinct told him to keep climbing, but Ryan knew he couldn't leave his new ally to perish due to a situation he had unwittingly created. Ryan climbed down as far as he could and then leapt to the floor. Running towards the Synistrail, Ryan grabbed a trash can lid and used it as a shield to push away the creature's clawed hand.

The Synistrail swatted down towards Caleb and Ryan, only to find its attack blocked by Ryan's trash can defence. A pained scream left the Synistrail's mouth as it began thrashing wildly towards Ryan and Caleb. The strength of its attack began to dent and damage the trash can lid, pushing Caleb and Ryan back against the fence as far as they could go.

'I can't hold it off much longer,' Ryan cried out, shielding the pair of them from the Synistrail's onslaught.

Suddenly, a cloaked figure vaulted over the fence behind them and landed behind the Synistrail, hitting the side of the creature with one smooth strike of a bo-staff and creating a graceful arc of light as the weapon swung through the air.

The force of the blow caused the Synistrail to crash into a pile of rubbish at the side of the alleyway. Caleb and Ryan's rescuer pulled down the hood of her rain cloak to reveal she was Kendra Lomax. She looked older and with much shorter hair than the public perception of her image; however, both Caleb and Ryan recognised her face from a lifetime of Newscasts. They were certain of who had arrived to save them, but both were unsure why.

Lomax walked towards the Synistrail, who was frantically attempting to reposition itself amongst the trash bags and cans it had fallen into. Looking into the creature's cold, hungry eyes, Lomax realised that this Synistrail had been the Wiseguy she had met two nights previously.

The creature fumbled and flailed, jerking its head up to hiss at its attacker.

'I am so sorry,' Lomax said softly, looking into the creature's eyes. Raising her bo-staff high in the air, Lomax spun the weapon over her head until it began to glow. With a pure and unworldly light beaming through her eyes and a luminous aura surrounding her body, Lomax brought her bo-staff crashing down, striking the Synistrail hard. As the weapon connected, it instantly shattered the creature into a pile of dust and ash. The remains crumbled and separated, following the last traces of the light flowing from Lomax into the evening's breeze.

Ryan dropped the lid of the trashcan and stepped forward. 'Was that... a real-life Synistrail?' he asked.

Lomax turned to him. 'Sure was. You can't tell me that you've never seen one before?'

'I haven't,' Ryan answered. 'I wasn't convinced they even existed. I met a girl in the Guards a few days ago that said she had. I believe her, but I'm the sort of person who only puts stock in things I've seen myself.'

'Very wise,' Lomax replied, spinning the bo-staff over her shoulder, back into its leather holder. 'Let me guess, this girl's name was Callie Haywood, right?'

Ryan was suddenly struck with the fear that the infamous terrorist Kendra Lomax was the mother of the girl he had his eye on; after all, they hadn't spoken about their families yet, and with all the drama and chaos of the past twenty-four hours, a development such as this wouldn't be out of place.

'H—how do you know Callie?'

'I know lots of things, kid,' Lomax replied with a warm smile. 'I'm the last member of the Sentry, in case all that bo-staff and glowing eyes stuff didn't clue you in.'

'Kendra Lomax?' Ryan asked softly.

'Yep, that's right. You don't need to be impressed or afraid; my legend is far more sensational than the dreary truth of who I really am,' Lomax stepped forward and placed her hand on Ryan's shoulder. 'The big question is, do you know who you are? Who you truly are? I do. I know *you* arguably better than you know yourself, Ryan Tyler.'

Ryan was shocked to hear the last survivor of the Sentry say his name; he wondered how Kendra Lomax could possibly know who he was. Before he could speak, Caleb's voice cut in.

'How the bleakin' heck do you know his name? What are you doing here? What's going on?'

Lomax rubbed her hand over her face and grinned. 'I know lots of things, pal. I know important things like he's Ryan Tyler, a well-meaning but unfulfilled librarian who has just been seconded to the Royal Guard of Vastrid. I also know less important things, like your name, for instance, Caleb Scudder, the least talented thief in Baker's End.'

'Hey,' Caleb protested, 'I'm not a thief, I'm a locksm—'

Before Caleb could finish interrupting, Lomax gave him a

measured smack on the back of his head before placing her index finger to her lips to 'Ssh.'

Lomax strolled towards the overturned Medi-Trolley and pointed to the deactivated Mandroid trapped underneath it. 'And this poor neglected toy belongs to his Royal Buffooness Prince Alistair and is still called Probot because nobody ever learnt how to program it.'

At this point, something distracted Lomax. 'I don't, however, know who this is,' she said, crouching down and pulling Bandit the Moline from Caleb's backpack by the scruff of her neck.

After somehow managing to snooze through the confrontation with the Synistrail, the Moline was shocked to be held aloft in front of everyone and could do little more than utter a confused and apologetic, 'Oh!'

Before anyone could explain just why a Moline was sleeping in a backpack, red targeting dots from unseen sniper rifles peppered the three humans in the alleyway.

A bellowing voice emerged from a speaker system some-where above them. 'FREEZE AND PUT THOSE HANDS HIGH IN THE AIR, OR WE WILL SHOOT. AND YOU IN THE RAIN CLOAK, PUT THAT BIG OLD STICK OF YOURS ON THE FLOOR.'

Caleb immediately threw his hands in the air, whimper-ing, 'Oh bleak!' as Ryan slowly raised his arms in surrender.

Lomax dropped Bandit and placed her bo-staff on the floor. She glanced down at the furry creature and muttered, 'Oh! Indeed.'

With her arms in the air, Lomax glanced around and observed the distant silhouettes of snipers on nearby rooftops. She realised that this wasn't the work of the Corpo-ration; they wouldn't have attempted to keep control with targeting lasers. If Corporation troops knew of Kendra Lomax's location, they would have called it in, and the cul-de-sac would have been blown sky-high without warning. Lomax realised that they were being held hostage by mercenaries. Plans of attack ran through her mind, but they were all too risky; all it would take would be for one stray bullet to strike Ryan, and everything would be lost. As much as it pained her to admit it, her attackers had the upper hand.

High on a nearby rooftop, Rico Akabusi once more spoke down to the cul-de-sac. 'THAT'S GOOD. NOW KEEP STILL AND KEEP THOSE HANDS IN THE AIR. DON'T TRY ANY FUNNY BUSINESS, AND I SWEAR THAT MY MEN WON'T HURT YOU. WE'LL BE THERE SOON TO TAKE YOU ON A LITTLE TRIP.'

Rico stepped away from the speaker system and switched on his Cuff-Linq communicator. 'Marcus? Yeah, it's Rico. We're in Barneston. Listen, boss, we're going to need serious backup. You're never going to guess who we've just picked up. We've hit the damn motherlode, sir. We've got Kendra Lomax, and we've got her alive. You want me to shoot her in the arm or leg or something? Y'know, lame her up in case she becomes a bit of a handful?'

There was an uneasy moment of silence as the young mercenary waited for his boss' response.

Eventually, it came, 'Good work, my friend. Please don't open fire on her. Just keep them held at a distance. Don't do anything too risky. Sometimes the bigger prizes are best left for others to try for and fail for. I'll bring the ship there. Expect us in the next ten minutes or so.'

'Thanks, Marcus. See you soon,' Rico turned off his Cuff-Linq and looked over the rooftop edge and down towards the cul-de-sac. There was something about the trepidation in Marcus' voice that alarmed him. He hoped that he hadn't bitten off more than his team could chew by seizing such a high-profile target. Rico wanted out of the Corporation's system once and for all, but as he stood looking into the clear night sky, he started to wonder what the benefit would be to bring in a prize as big as Lomax to the Corporation. Mercenaries and bounty hunters don't get medals; there'd be no public recognition for their actions. Rico also doubted that they'd get paid in money for their deed as the Corporation only paid off Outstanding Service. Lomax seemed too high a risk for too little a reward – Rico was young and only had another five years or so Outstanding Service to work off. Even after that he knew he wouldn't have enough wealth to retire, and he'd probably still need to work for the Corporation in some capacity anyhow. The whole thing was beginning to feel like a con to him.

'Damned if you do. Damned if you don't,' Rico muttered to himself. 'Got a squadron of rifles aimed at the most wanted woman in Vastrid, and I'm just as stuck in this cul-de-sac as she is.'

And so for the next seven minutes and twenty-two seconds, everyone waited, anxiously and silently lost in thoughts of their fate.

Chapter Twenty-Two

ALL ABOARD THE SALVATORE

Yawning more loudly than she would have liked, Callie woke to find herself still bound in a chair aboard Marcus Hagen's ship. As her eyes focused, she glanced across and noticed Kurtis Lackner finishing a conversation with one of Hagen's men. Lackner was swiftly led back and cuffed to his chair.

As the guard left, Callie threw a whisper laced with accusation over her shoulder towards Lackner. 'What were you talking about with that guard?'

Lackner leant forward. 'Don't you worry about a thing girlie, it's all part of the plan.'

Callie didn't trust a word of this. She knew something was afoot but was unsure what game Lackner intended to play. Looking ahead, Callie noticed the disdainful glare from Alex Navin, opposite her. She attempted to obtain some kind of affirmation of her fears using eye contact, to which Navin scowled and threw his glance to the floor.

'Fine,' Callie huffed under her breath, lamenting the lack of any help from her fellow prisoners. As if to prove her point, the rest of the captured Guards looked unable or unwilling to be of any assistance as they sat ashen and trembling in their seats. Callie arched her neck and realised that Hagen's ship was no longer hovering above Vastrid and had finally landed.

She noticed that a cargo door was open, and more captives were about to be led aboard. Callie imagined that these new prisoners would be fellow members of the Royal Guard who were strong, cunning and tenacious. Maybe even Prince Alistair would be among their number. For a second or two, she entertained the thought that perhaps these new bounties had allowed themselves to be captured as part of an artful rescue mission. She would never have guessed that instead of her imagined saviours, she was about to be joined by the tattered remains of Prince Alistair's Mandroid; the boy she had danced with at the Ball; the Moline she had recently freed; the last living member of the Sentry and a locksmith from Baker's End.

Hagen's second-in-command, Rico Akabusi, monitored the boarding process from the cargo door ramp but noticed two newer members of the crew patting down Kendra Lomax to check she wasn't armed.

'Damn amateurs,' Rico cursed, spitting out a toothpick he'd been toying with and darting down towards the foot of the ramp to scold the pair.

'What the heck do you pair of clowns think you're doing?' Rico hollered at the two bounty hunters, pushing them away from the prisoner. 'This one could have all manner of explosives or self-sacrificial nonsense strapped about her being. How many times do I have to tell you to use the Scanner-Tech?'

'But boss,' one of the bounty hunters moaned, 'the Scanner-Tech you gave us is slow as bones. It'll take ages to scan that broke-up Mandroid alone.'

Rico wasn't in the mood for listening and ranted over the end of the bounty hunter's complaint. 'But boss-nothing! I don't want a tirade of nasty shrapnel splicing up my pretty young face because two lazy-butt amateurs wouldn't do their job properly. Now, you scan these bounties in, using the tech. Otherwise, y'all be joining them.'

Rico went to storm back up the ramp until he heard one of the bounty hunters wearily sigh. 'Oh, and another thing,' Rico continued, 'If you two think the Scanner-Tech takes a long time, you wait until I make you clean the whole ship tonight.'

Rico shook his head. 'Man-oh-man! You just cannot get the staff these days,' he said before smirking and throwing a wink at Lomax. 'You'd know all about that, wouldn't you, toots?'

Lomax frowned and looked up into the ship where she could see her confiscated bo-staff. She was desperate to summon it but knew it would be too reckless a gamble. She had to ensure Ryan survived, at least until he was fully blessed by the Tide. If Ryan were to fall before the first hurdle, then everything would be lost.

Eventually, Lomax, Ryan, Caleb, Bandit and the remains of Probot were scanned and cleared of carrying any weaponry or disease, then led aboard the ship one by one.

'Yo! Wait a minute! We've nearly run out of restraint chairs,' Rico shouted to the two bounty hunters escorting Ryan and Caleb. 'Stick these two low priorities on the back benches with their hands cuffed behind their backs. Lomax can go in a cuff chair. Send the Mandroid and the monkey to the storeroom.'

'I AM NOT THE MONKEY! I AM THE BANDIT MOLINE!' Bandit hollered as she was dumped unceremoniously onto the Medi-Trolley carrying Probot and carted off.

Callie couldn't believe her eyes as she watched this scene unfold.

'Ryan survived. Thank the stars he survived,' she sighed to

herself. Ryan hadn't noticed her, and she felt a strange trepidation over when he would. She bit her bottom lip and sat back straight in her chair, readying herself for some form of greeting.

Alex Navin noticed this change in her behaviour and furrowed his brow in puzzlement. He glanced over his shoulder and silently observed the new passengers. To Alex, they represented a new set of opportunities; toys, threats and liabilities all of potential use, depending on how the next few hours played out. Starting with his pinkie, he drummed each finger on his right hand on the armrest of his chair in a short, solid motion and looked at Callie for a reaction. She remained distracted by the new prisoners. Alex sat back and smiled; his plan was already beginning to work.

With his hands cuffed behind his back, Ryan found himself being jostled down the aisle, past a series of bound and anxious guardsmen, towards some uncomfortable looking benches at the back. He felt dreadful inside; he was too tired to fear his uncertain fate and too shocked to consider how, or indeed if, he would be able to escape it. His heart was pounding, and his head felt as if a storm of bees were laying siege to his brain, sabotaging each thought. Ryan passed unfamiliar face after unfamiliar face until eventually, his eyes met with a pair of eyes he knew. The distractions and discomfort in his head and heart faded as his realisation reassured him, 'Callie Haywood is alive and here.'

With their eyes still locked, Ryan and Callie shared a shy 'Hello,' as he was led past her chair towards the benches at the back. Callie sat back in her chair and tried to fathom what the next few hours would mean now that Ryan Tyler was back in her life.

'I was a second away from kissing him,' Callie thought to herself, 'do I still want to? I mean, the moment has sort of been and passed. Maybe he's a bad kisser. If the Great Hall hadn't been invaded, maybe I'd be desperately trying to avoid him like I end up doing with most boys.'

Callie glanced over her shoulder and saw Ryan slumped in his chair wearing his ill-fitting jacket and browbeaten facial expression that blossomed into a warm, boyish smile when he caught her looking at him. Her thoughts raced through the moments they had spent together: their first chance meetings, the afternoon spent chatting about Flex-izdats in Cardea Gardens, the Moline rescue, spotting a shooting star, some electrifyingly close dancing and, finally, a potential first kiss foiled by The Debutante Ball Massacre.

'He's not like most boys, though, is he?' Callie thought to herself. She was intrigued that, after years of indifference, someone had captured her imagination romantically. Yet, she was also slightly resentful of the emotional compromises that this may bring to the dangerous situation they were in. Ryan appeared to have a good heart and an inner strength, but he wasn't a soldier; she'd be sick to death with worry if he got into a street fight, let alone battling his way out of this situation. She grimaced and cursed herself for worrying so possessively about a boy she hardly knew. Callie looked down at the tattered ball gown she was still wearing from the previous night. 'This is all *your* fault,' she said, addressing the garment. 'I never had these problems when I wore a vest and terrain boots to the Ball.'

Likewise, Ryan was also lost in thoughts about him and Callie being thrown together by fate once more. These contemplations were interrupted by the sound of Caleb Scudder being dumped rather harshly on the bench in front of him.

Unlike Ryan, Caleb hadn't accepted his imprisonment quietly. His objections had started with a loud and angry tirade about being considered a low priority captive. The seriousness of his predicament then sank in and fuelled a panicked plea as he insisted that they had made a mistake and should let him go. He then, in short order, tried to bribe them (with money he didn't have), offered to join them (they weren't interested) and finally turned the content of his vocal tirade back around to anger and idle threats.

'Oh, next time you've found yourself in Baker's End, you're gonna bleakin' get it,' Caleb hollered to the two guards walking away, unbothered by his bluff.

Caleb threw his head back at a tilted angle to further interrupt Ryan's thoughts of Callie. 'What a bunch of swine heads. Still, these benches aren't too bad, are they? Plenty of space to stretch out.' To highlight his point, Caleb spread his thighs out as far as they would go and began to swing them inwards and outwards in a carefree, rhythmic manner.

Ryan was in no mood to observe Caleb's spread-legged, seated dance and looked away to the side, muttering, 'Well, I'm glad you're comfortable.' Ryan attempted to return to his thoughts, only to hear the sound of a bench creaking as Caleb leant even further back to continue chatting.

'So,' Caleb asked in a tone that was uncharacteristically hushed for him,

'Who is she then?'

'What? Who do you mean?' Ryan answered.

'You know who! That girl. The one you said hello to. Wearing a ball gown. Dark hair,' Caleb asked. 'Do you know her properly? Like, her name and everything? Please tell me she's single. She's hot but not obviously hot, and she looks unaware of her unobvious hotness, so I'm sure that's unlikely. Girls that don't know their own worth always end up being all true-blue shackled to some fool.'

Ryan didn't know how to answer Caleb's question. He wasn't sure he could call Callie his girlfriend. He wasn't even sure if he could call her his friend. Ryan then became briefly distracted by an internal wrangle over whether a girl who is a girlfriend would automatically qualify as a friend. The debate was short and swift when Ryan drew upon his difficult relationship with Bernadette Bleasedale and realised the two terms were not necessarily mutually inclusive.

'So,' Caleb asked again, 'do you know her or don't you? Is she single or what?"

'Well,' Ryan answered, 'I danced with her at the Ball the other night. We nearly kissed.'

Caleb stifled a laugh and patronisingly sucked in an inhalation of air.

'Ooooh. You want to step back a bit, son. She's out of your league, if you don't mind me saying. No offence, you're a nice guy. I'm only warning you before you mug yourself right off.'

Ryan wondered which part of his statement held no weight within Caleb's criteria for courtship and then began to feel somewhat offended by the suggestion that a scruffy locksmith from Baker's End would stand a better chance with Callie than he would. Ryan contemplated challenging this point, but when he considered that his only real experience in this area was with a girl nicknamed 'Sour Bernie' who dumped him after just six troubled weeks together, he decided to let sleeping dogs lie.

'Stop zoning out on me, Ry!' Caleb chattered on. 'What's her name? Is she rich? How comes you know a Debutante?'

'Her name's Callie,' Ryan answered. 'She's not a debutante; she's in the Royal Guards – '

Caleb's excitement faded instantly. 'Oh, don't worry about it then. Not interested, thanks.' He sank back down onto the bench.

'What's wrong? A second ago, you were poised to make a move.'

'No. Not with a member of Royal Guards,' Caleb frowned. 'More bleakin' trouble than it's worth. She'd make me go and get a proper beige job, for starters. Nah, not for me, I'm afraid. You seem keen, though? Shame she's out of your league and wouldn't be interested. I'm sure there's somebody out there for her, though.'

'Great,' muttered Ryan, attempting to heal his bruised ego with a heavy sigh.

'Still,' Caleb beamed, 'life's not all that bad. I'm loving the fact I've got this nice two-seater bench all to myself.'

As if on cue, their conversation was interrupted by the sound of Rico's voice calling out, 'Hang on a moment; Bad Boy Stevie's just turned up with five more.'

From his time hanging around in Murphy's, Caleb had heard of Bad Boy Stevie. He was a large, bawdy scoundrel in his late thirties. Most of his youthful muscle had since turned to fat, but he was still an intimidating presence. Caleb wondered what Bad Boy Stevie was doing working with bounty hunters but wasn't concerned about his arrival. Caleb was, however, anxious about the 'five more' part of Rico's announcement.

'Ry! Ry!' Caleb whispered over his shoulder.

'What now?'

Caleb's hushed answer was full of urgency. 'Did you hear that? There's going to be five more prisoners brought on board!'

'So?'

Caleb couldn't believe his friend wasn't alarmed at this new development.

'Ryan! It means we're going to have to share our benches!'

Caleb's comfy, double-spaced bench dream was further shattered when he observed a huge mountain of a man amongst the clutch of new captives. Standing high and wide at just over seven feet tall, he carried four hundred and forty pounds of pure muscle on his body.

'Oh, that's just bleakin' great!' Caleb whimpered to no one in particular.

'Look at the size of him! He's bound to be crammed in next to me.'

Caleb counted the number of bench spaces around him and matched them against the number of prisoners coming their way. He deduced that two smaller prisoners should reach his bench first, ahead of the giant captive.

Unluckily for Caleb, the two smaller prisoners foolishly attempted to escape and were dragged off to the side after being knocked out by Hagen's men.

The large prisoner paused for a moment and looked down sadly at the two unconscious captives being further shackled and tranquillised. From back at the hatch, Rico observed this and hollered, 'Hey beefcake! Unless you want some more chains wrapped around you and a tranq drip in your arm, you best keep moving.'

The prisoner did as instructed and squeezed in next to Caleb, his sheer body mass and physical girth pushing the young locksmith hard and tight against the ship's wall.

'I am sorry,' he softly apologised, noticing not only Caleb's discomfort but also his annoyance at the situation. The prisoner's face was at odds with his intimidating body; his mouth formed a nervous yet friendly smile, and his kind eyes were a unique shade of deep blue that beamed out brightly.

'Back on the ranch, they'd call me Big Joe,' the prisoner said, by way of an introduction.

'Really? I can't imagine why,' Caleb replied, motioning at the lack of bench space he'd been left with.

Big Joe smiled. 'You're funny, man. If we get out of this alive, I'll let you take the aisle seat on the way back.'

With all the prisoners now on board, the cargo ramp thudded closed, and the ship's engines began to rumble. Marcus Hagen stepped into the prison bay to greet the captives. He had always taken a theatrical approach to his work, and on this occasion, he felt even more inclined than usual to address his new bounties personally.

'My friends, I'm sure most of you are either confused, scared, angry or all three of those things. These states of mind can be such wonderfully useful distractions should a *captor* wish to control his *captive*. Most other bounty hunters would use this to their advantage. Luckily for you, I have a strange sense of morality over such matters. I think it is only fair and right that I tell you the truth and keep you informed to the best of my abilities. For starters, my name is Marcus Hagen, and this is my ship, The Salvator. I have no idea why this ship is named that or what it even means. And neither did the man I stole it from after I turned him in. Or maybe he did but just wouldn't tell me. Some folk struggle to face their fate graciously, which in turn leads me to you. We have probably the most diverse group of misfits this ship has ever carried. We have a clutch of two-a-penny thieves, a ranch warrior with emotional issues, a colonial troublemaker with an inflated sense of ego, and a famous terrorist. Most surprisingly of all, we have several members of the Royal Guard of Vastrid. If you had told me as little as two days ago that the Guards would be on my ship, I would have supposed that it was I who was the one in trouble, but it appears your charming little kingdom has really, really managed to nark off the Shadox Corporation.'

With that, Marcus used his Cuff-Linq to flick on several overhead Vid-Screens remotely. The group watched as a recorded message of Rachel Stone played on a loop, in which she stated that The Corporation was taking over the Kingdom of Vastrid due to King William's harbouring of wanted fanatic Kendra Lomax.

Footage from the previous night's massacre had been manipulated to give the impression that the Royal Guards were protecting Lomax from the Shadox troopers. Rachel was keen to reassure residents of Vastrid that no matter the outcome of this dispute, the Corporation would continue to serve and protect them. In closing, she also revealed some news that nobody on the ship expected.

'Before I go, it saddens me to report that during the battle at the Great Hall, your sovereign King William Hawthorne died attempting to protect Kendra Lomax. We are currently searching for the Prince and Princess of Vastrid to discuss how the fair Kingdom of Vastrid moves forward into an era of peace and mutual prosperity. Until we are able to have this conversation, please consider us your friends. Together we may bring calm and reason back to this land.'

A strange, unnerving silence fell amongst both the prisoners and Hagen's crew. No matter what political views they held, King William had been a big part of all of their lives. In place of the figurehead they'd all known since childhood stood an anxious mist of uncertainty and doubt.

Marcus Hagen stepped forward once more. 'So, as you can see, the world we're about to leave behind has become an undetermined landscape. The only thing I know for certain is that we are taking you all to the Shadox Corporation as bounties. I cannot guarantee your wellbeing after we hand you over to them, but I can guarantee your safety until we do. My crew is dangerous. My crew are skilled, but more importantly, my crew are professionals. My friends, you shall not be robbed, abused or damaged as long as you remain safely shackled in your seats. I thank you for your time, and I wish you all a very safe journey.'

As Marcus walked away and his crew began the final stages before takeoff, Caleb stifled a laugh and whispered over his shoulder, 'Bleak! He's a bit full of himself, ain't he? So c'mon, when are you lot going to do your thing?'

'What thing?' Ryan asked, perplexed.

Caleb rolled his eyes and waited until one of the crew had passed. 'You and your Royal Guard mates. When are you going to bust us all out of here? Surely there's a plan?'

Ryan shook his head in disbelief at his new friend's presumption. 'No. No, I don't think there is a plan.'

Caleb started to panic. 'So, you mean we really are going to the Corporation as prisoners?'

'Yes. It looks that way.'

Caleb's mouth ran dry. He quickly looked to Big Joe for a different response only to find him nodding as well.

As The Salvator rose into the smoky sky of the industrial estate, Caleb swallowed and muttered, 'Oh Bleak'.

Chapter Twenty-Three

THE ABSOLUTE ESSENCE OF NOTHINGNESS

Aboard Shadox VI, the charcoal-coloured remnants of Professor Maxwell Shadox's physical body were encased within a dark cloud, channelling the nihilistic urge of the Dark Lethe. With a face flickering between that of an old man and a pained distortion a human skull, he groaned and laughed maniacally to himself while his eyes steadily burned a deep hypnotic shade of red.

Distracted by the sound of footsteps, Shadox suddenly turned to face the door to his chambers.

'Mr Nox. Such a pleasure to see you,' he hissed.

'I take it you know what happened in Vastrid?' Nox snapped. 'Your niece and Bron made a complete mess of the repossession. It's time you sever links to the old way. I beg you, let me end them.'

Shadox silently revelled in Nox's frustrated urge for bloodshed and his unquestionable loyalty to The Dark Lethe's ultimate goal. He had chosen his ward well, and although he knew his apprentice would fulfil his bloodstained destiny, now was not the time. He decided to curb Nox's intensifying ambition temporarily.

'Yes, Rachel and Bron have played by different rules, but they weren't the ones who let Lomax escape,' he hissed. 'But today is not a day for blame, punishment or murder. Today is a moment of celebration. The Dark Lethe is pleased with recent events. As its power grows, so does its focus. I wish you could hear its voice. It sings to me like a choir of fallen angels, cooing and screaming at the same time. It's a sound that combines into one aching, discordant note, threatening to split the silence of space in two. When the harvest of realities is near, The Dark Lethe now knows how to remove those that will oppose it. The Dark Lethe is devising a new form it calls the Vargoed. When the time is right, and the power is fully in our hands, the Vargoed will reap all of Vastrid and then the Earth and finally the entire Universe.'

Nox nodded. 'Until that glorious day, we still have Lomax and the unidentified new threat to contend with, though.'

'We can defeat them just as we defeated their kind before. The Dark Lethe called out to me just prior to your arrival. It appears that this new Child Of The Light is with Lomax as we speak.'

Nox was both excited and alarmed by the news. 'What? Where? We have to destroy them now.'

Shadox's eyes flickered for a moment as he paused for thought. 'Regrettably, their location at this time is unknown. However, all is not lost; though The Dark Lethe may not currently be strong enough to simultaneously hold back the Tide of Light and make a journey to Earth, it can muster up a quick demonstration of the annihilation it intends to bring. Maybe the challenge of destruction will draw out these last champions of life.'

Shadox threw back his head and slowly rose up through his cloud of darkness a further two feet. His body began to pulse and vibrate as his face turned into anguished beams of ash grey and crimson light.

From across the vast stretches of outer space, the Dark Lethe acted upon their servant's request and sent a cluster of their dark sprites out past Shadox VI and towards Earth. Upon reaching the cusp of Earth's exosphere, they changed form, firstly sticking to each other like inky, black glue before tensing into a large rectangular shape.

The shape quickly grew and extended; its inside was a unique shade of flat darkness. It was indented yet shallow like a letterbox that had been boarded up on the inside. It moved towards Earth, steadily and apathetically erasing all meteors and space debris in its path.

Two Shadox troop carriers also fell victim to the dark sprites' rectangular form; the ships, the crew and their terrified screams all disappeared from reality as they drifted helplessly into it.

Seventy-two minutes had passed since The Salvator had left Vastrid. Marcus Hagen and his crew had observed this strange alien shape and what it had done to the previous obstacles in its way.

'I don't know what that is, but we need to get the hell away from it. Take us back to Vastrid immediately,' Hagen ordered the Salvator's two principal pilots, Raina Tash and Jonah Torr.

Raina circled her hand through the ship's holographic flight controls. 'I am trying my best, Captain, but it's no use. That thing, whatever it is, has thrown out all of the controls. Nothing's working right.'

Jonah flicked through a stream of status reports. 'Nothing the ship is telling us makes any sense. It's like that thing has shortened the universe; it's changing the understood physics of space. I shudder to think what it's done to orbit patterns of the planets. The controls to this ship can't seem to correlate to the situation. This ain't just about our ship. I think this is the end of everything.'

Marcus felt something more alarming than fear; he felt a draining sensation of sad, inescapable damnation. He had felt trepidatious about bringing Alex Navin in, and that feeling had grown when Rico captured Kendra Lomax. He couldn't have imagined, though, that the end of all existence would be his undoing.

Marcus' thoughts were interrupted by an almighty commotion at the other end of the ship.

'My friends, it seems our guests have also seen the *rectangle of doom* on the monitors,' he patted his pilots on the shoulder reassuringly. 'You see what you can do to halt our imminent destruction, and I'll go back there and tell everyone to calm down. I really don't want to spend my final precious moments with a splitting headache.'

Hagen raced down the length of his ship to the holding pen. He found his crew attempting to calm and restrain their captives, who had observed the effects of the rectangle on overhead monitors and were now desperately trying to free themselves from their cuffs.

The only two prisoners sitting calmly in their seats were Kendra Lomax and Alex Navin. Lomax was poised as if waiting for a moment to come. Navin, on the other hand, sat back in his seat, smirking at the panic exploding around him. If this was the end, then so be it. He couldn't have planned for a giant rectangular existence-eraser to emerge and destroy him, so he felt no frustration or unfairness at this sudden threat. If the end of the universe was inevitable, then he may as well face it in a calm and dignified manner. He felt that the en masse melodrama was a frankly ridiculous way to face certain death, and he wanted no part of it.

Hagen marched up to Navin and grabbed him by the lapels of his trench coat. 'C'mon then, genius! You're the one with all the answers and a smile on his face. How do we get away from that thing?'

Navin smugly looked down at the cuffs on his hand and motioned with his eyebrows that they would need to be unlocked if he were to help.

'Oh, you'd love that, wouldn't you?' Marcus snapped. 'I set you free so you can stab me in the back. Just so that in the dying moments of all time and space, you can take some kind of pompous pride in winning.'

Alex nodded, taking a long inhalation on his Med-Stick.

'You're pathetic,' Hagen answered before suddenly being knocked out cold by a solid right-hand punch from Big Joe.

Shortly before Hagen had arrived in the holding pen, Caleb Scudder had managed to pick the lock of his cuffed hands. A casual observer may have presumed that Scudder's loosely tied boots were just an element of his slightly scruffy look. Few would detect or indeed suspect that the tips of his bootlaces were, in fact, designed to pick locks. In the hustle and bustle of the situation, Caleb had slipped down unnoticed to the floor and begun to crawl towards the front of the holding pen.

As he was crawling past Kendra Lomax, Caleb heard a 'Psst' noise before a foot hooked through his trouser belt and halted his progress.

'Where are you going to go when you've run out of floor to crawl on?' Lomax whispered down towards him.

'I don't know. I'm going to find a bleakin' escape pod or something,' Caleb whispered. 'Now, let me go before I get caught.'

Lomax pushed down hard with her boot, squashing Caleb close to the floor. 'In case you hadn't noticed, the whole of existence is currently being eaten away. If Hagen's men don't catch you, that scary looking rectangle closing in on us will. If you were a smart man, you'd crawl back to your bench and un-cuff that big fella sat next to you. He can take out the guards while you unlock everybody else.'

'And then what?' Caleb wheezed, still stuck under Lomax's boot.

'And then,' Lomax paused, uncertain of the words leaving her lips, 'hopefully Ryan Tyler will begin to do what's long been expected of him.'

'Ryan? What, *my* Ryan? What's he got to do with all this?' Caleb asked, confused.

'Hopefully, we'll all get to see,' Lomax answered, lifting her boot as Caleb reluctantly began to crawl back to the bench where he started.

'Back so soon?' Big Joe chuckled as Caleb slid under the bench he was sitting on.

'Alright big boy,' Caleb snapped back as he began to pick at Joe's lock with the two metal tips of his bootlace. 'In case you haven't worked it out, I'm setting you free. The plan is, you get un-cuffed and go berserk taking down as many of the crew as you can while I free everyone else to help you. Do you understand?'

'My pleasure,' growled Joe as he heard the lock snap and the tight steel cuffs that had bound his hands fall to the floor.

Joe pounded down the aisle at great speed and, within seconds, had smashed through seven of the Salvator's crew before reaching Hagen and knocking the ship's captain out cold with a swift jab to his chin.

Caleb knew there was no time to waste and quickly worked through un-cuffing all of the prisoners, who one by one all joined the mutiny led by Big Joe. As soon as she was set free, Callie Haywood bolted from her chair, taking down Bad Boy Stevie with a kick to his stomach followed by a palm shot to his jaw, which knocked him out cold. Kurtis Lackner took a slightly more subdued course of action, removing himself from the erupting brawl to stand in the shadows to observe for a while. With the large number of Royal Guards and the various other classes of prisoners forming an unspoken pact and joining forces, they were easily over-coming Hagen's men. Lackner knew if he were to survive this situation, he'd need to join the winning side and threw himself into the melee, knocking down any of Hagen's men that got in his way.

Alex Navin, despite being un-cuffed, decided to remain seated, silently taking in the fight that surrounded him. He caught the ends of occasionally missed punches, but the pain was something he could easily shake off. Alex had no desire to be caught up in the brawl. He took a look around and slouched back in his seat, turning his focus back to his Med-Stick.

Caleb Scudder, meanwhile, was frantically scurrying under and around the legs of the battling mob and finally got to Kendra Lomax.

'Well, you took your time,' muttered Lomax as Scudder began to free her.

'Do you know how many bleakin' locks I've picked in the last minute and a half?' Caleb protested.

'No, but you could have done them all if you spent less time cowering between them,' Lomax replied as the cuffs holding her hands sprung open.

'Right, now go get Ryan. We need him more than anything else going on.'

Lomax sprung to her feet and summoned her bo-staff. Glancing across the ship, Kendra noticed that Big Joe was struggling in combat against Rico Akabusi.

Rico had tightly wrapped one of his nunchucks around Joe's arm and was currently trying to drag him to the ground. Lomax leapt towards them, striking Rico's arm hard with the bo-staff. Rico groaned in pain and shock as he fell to the floor. Joe staggered back as the nunchuck unwound and fell to the floor.

Rico rolled towards his weapons and grabbed them before

springing back to his feet and launching a fierce attack towards Lomax. Using her bo-staff, Kendra managed to deflect the attack; Rico had skills, but his eagerness to attack left his defences wide open. Lomax took full advantage of this, striking Rico hard in the stomach and then smashing him into the side of the ship.

By this point, Caleb had reached Ryan and began un-cuffing him.

'Finally,' Ryan groaned dryly. 'I thought you might have forgotten me or something.'

'Aint everyone a bleakin' critic these days,' answered Caleb as Ryan's cuffs opened. 'Never mind all of that; you've got to go and do your thing.'

'What thing?'

'Old Bo-Staff down the front reckons you can do some-thing to stop the universe being destroyed. So whenever you're ready,' Caleb said, using a sweeping arm gesture to usher in whatever trick or tactic Ryan allegedly held up his sleeve.

Ryan had no idea what Caleb was talking about and looked towards Lomax for a clue, only to see Lomax staring back at him encouragingly. As the freed bounties rounded up all of Hagen's crew, Ryan scanned the room for answers and found every pair of eyes upon him.

Ryan looked at the overhead monitor, observing how fast this dark and destructive rectangular shape was closing into the ship, and felt utterly powerless and weak. 'I can't save the universe,' he thought to himself, 'I've got no useful skills, no secret plan up my sleeve. And my clothes are *still* damp.'

Ryan's mind was blank, and he remained frozen to his spot at the back of the holding pen, looking sheepishly back at everyone.

The Salvator drifted towards the large shape, and a strange form of tension gripped and shook all aboard the ship. The power of the Dark Lethe in its purest form took hold, tightly squeezing the minds of all nearby. Everyone grabbed their heads, trying to relieve the agonising pain; it was as if all of their senses and memories were being torn through their face by a force they could neither see nor comprehend.

The Salvator began to shake and spin out of control. With nothing to hold on to, Ryan stumbled and fell down the aisle of the ship. Callie noticed him flailing towards her, and she thrust out her hand to steady him. The turbulence of the moment caused Ryan to crash into Callie's arms, and he began to feel a sensation that reminded him of the strange events at the Grid and Craydon's Corner. However, this time, the feeling was stronger and more direct; it felt like a beam of pure strength starting in the pit of his stomach and travelling through his heart, centering all of his thoughts and emotions into one focused pulse. Ryan flung his head back as light shone brightly from his eyes.

Everyone aboard the Salvator looked on, frightened and yet in awe of this spectacle. Many of them looked hopefully towards the Vid-Screens to see if this had saved them from being annihilated by the dark shape. Unfortunately, it appeared that it hadn't.

With Ryan's eyes continuing to glow, The Salvator drifted directly into the rectangle's dark form as the crew, and its prisoners, prepared for eternal nothingness.

However, instead of nothingness, there was everything. Inside the darkness, there was light. The brightest light any human life form had ever or would ever see. Suddenly there was change.

Chapter Twenty-Four

A BLESSED MUTINY AND THE DOLPHIN'S SMILE

For two long minutes, everything was silently bound in pure, luminous light.

Lost in a moment of blissful confusion, the crew of The Salvator and its mutinous captives were too perplexed to wonder whether they were alive or dead.

The light didn't fade suddenly to reveal its surroundings; it slowly eased away from the scene like a sheet being removed to reveal a prize that lay beneath.

As the light passed through the Salvator, it caressed, upgraded and transformed the ship's form. The Salvator's battered grey chassis and a lifetime's worth of black market, patched-up mechanics were replaced atom by atom.

As the light receded, it dragged the Medi-Trolley carrying Bandit and the remains of Probot with it. The trolley was pulled with force into the Salvator's cockpit, causing it to crash into the pilot seats, knocking both Raina Tash and Jonah Torr out of their chairs and onto the floor.

Bandit fell from the trolley and quickly scampered under one of the seats, trembling in fear. The light, however, entangled Probot and, by accident or design, thrust the

Mandroid into the ship's control panel just as it was reconstructing.

Light poured through Probot's eyes as he became encased in a new, improved control panel. With the remains of his lower half connected to the bespoke docking pit, Probot felt compelled by the source of power flowing through his body to become one with the technological metamorphosis surrounding him.

The Mandroid lifted his arms and threw back his head. Lustrous energy poured from his mouth as the blue holographic controls of the Salvator faded and were replaced by upgraded versions, each coloured in various luminous shades of green, sapphire, pink, orange and yellow.

With the transformation of the ship complete, those aboard The Salvator who were still conscious stared at Ryan and Callie, who were clutching each other tightly.

'What did you just do, boy?' Kurtis Lackner barked in their direction, disguising his fear and confusion with anger.

Ryan raised his head from Callie's shoulder. The light had faded from his eyes, and although he knew he had done something rather unusual, he wasn't exactly sure what and certainly wasn't in the mood to discuss it.

'I... I don't know,' Ryan stammered. 'I don't think I did anything.'

Before anyone could mention Ryan's glowing eyes, Kendra Lomax stepped forward. 'Actually, he did. This boy here saved us all. He brought the light that destroyed the oncoming darkness. He is the Child of The Tide, the one that my fellow Sentinels and I have been searching for. He is the one that can summon the Tide and harness its power. Take a look around you; just look at what the Tide has done to this ship if you don't believe me.'

Everyone gasped as they looked around the Salvator and noticed the change to the ship's structure. The dirty grey metallic interior had been replaced by technologically advanced alien materials coloured pure white. At the same time, the artificial oxygen and gravity conditioning felt more natural and comparable to that of Earth.

Although impressed, Lackner was also concerned. 'I'm guessing that you're Kendra Lomax and because it appears some cosmic nonsense has occurred around us, you think we'll quite happily let you take charge of this ship.'

'No, not particularly. I mean, it'd be nice if you all just followed me, but I'm not expecting it,' Lomax answered. 'Look at the ragtag variety of people we've got aboard this ship right now. I'd say the first thing we do is get rid of the mercenaries and then sit down like civilised humans and discuss what we do and where we go.'

Callie gently let go of Ryan and looked at him with a mixture of concern and wonder. 'Oh Ryan, what did you do?'

Ryan shook his head. 'I'm really not sure.'

Callie had always felt that Ryan was different from other boys, but this was something else. She didn't know what to make of the strange developments of the previous few days. Callie glanced across the ship and noticed Lomax and the captured members of the Royal Guard had begun working together to round up Hagen's men. 'We'd better go and help them,' she said, if only to break the tension.

Ryan and Callie walked together in an uneasy silence towards the temporarily allied forces of Lomax and the Royal Guard. They were pushing the beaten and battered mercenaries towards a sealed hatch at the back of the ship. Marcus Hagen was still unconscious from Joe's punch and was being carried by Stevie and a dazed Rico Akabusi. The crowd parted for a moment as pilots Raina Tash and Jonah Torr were shoved towards their crewmates.

'Now then, we could be the kind of people that trade on captives for our own gain, but luckily for you and despite what you may have heard, we're the good guys,' said Lomax, pressing the emergency exit button on the hatch. 'Now get going.'

Rico and Stevie lifted Hagen through the hatch onto the escape shuttle, and one by one, his crew followed. Once they were all in, Lomax hit the close button with her fist. With the rumbling sound of the escape shuttle blasting off aimlessly in the background, Lomax looked towards the amassed forces of Guardsmen, criminals and fugitives.

'So we have a handful of very different factions and one cosmically enhanced spaceship,' she said. 'Let's negotiate.'

Callie stepped forward. 'We must take this ship back to Vastrid. I don't know if I believe your hocus-pocus shtick, but it's clear this ship has become something extraordinary. I couldn't give a damn about the politics or the theological wars that raged between our parties in the past; all I know is the Corporation has declared war on innocent people who will need this ship to survive.'

Kendra smiled at Callie, but her tone was firm. 'I can tell you've got a good heart, and I'd like, even at this early stage in our acquaintance, to consider us mutual allies and friends, but I have to disagree about handing this ship over to anyone. We all experienced its transformation; nobody back in Vastrid would ever understand it. Prince Alistair would gladly tear this ship apart on the off chance of understanding how to make a fleet of copies. We must keep this ship out of other hands and act as humanity's saviours independently.'

'What are you suggesting? That all the members of the Royal Guard desert their duty and go traipsing around the universe with you?' Callie replied. 'The last time the Sentry attempted to act as humanity's saviours, it didn't end so well, did it? Ryan, what do you think about all of this?'

Callie looked at Ryan, hoping he would say something to settle the argument, but he had no idea what to say or do. He wished they could all just go home and find that, somehow, peace had been declared, leaving him to get into some dry pyjamas and have a sleep. It was during this train of thought that his spirit lifted as he realised that the cosmic light passing through the ship had also dried his damp, sea-soaked clothes. This realisation brought him happiness; perhaps, considering the situation, too much happiness.

'Well, Ryan?' Callie asked. 'What's that smile for?"

Feeling caught out, Ryan answered, 'I think... erm, there's lots to think about and discuss, so maybe we should all just sit down and mull things over.'

Frustrated, Callie glanced up and noticed the rest of the Guards, apart from Kurtis Lackner, grouping together and making a move towards a hatch leading to a second escape shuttle.

'And where do you think you lot are going?' she asked.

One of the captured Guardsmen turned back and sheepishly replied, 'We're following Prime Directive two-four-eight. You know, that "Any freed or rescued guard must report back to Vastridian service base immediately" rule.'

'But not at the expense of a spacecraft like this one,' Callie protested as they ignored her words and departed in the shuttle.

'And then there were nine,' Lackner cackled.

'Ten. If you count that Mandroid,' Alex Navin finally spoke. He remained seated yet uncuffed. Alex nodded his head to the side, motioning towards a Vid-Screen showing Probot in the Salvator's cockpit. 'I'm not sure why, but I'd wager he's the only thing keeping this ship going at the moment. To be honest, I'm a little shocked that no one else felt compelled to check who was piloting this thing after you crudely dispatched the original crew, but I guess that just serves to prove my instincts correct.'

'And what instincts would these be, Navin?' Lackner answered in a low growl.

'It doesn't matter which of the two factions get this ship,' Alex spoke clearly and calmly. 'Whether you cloak your inadequacies with a uniform or use a fairytale's worth of cosmic clap-trap to cover your true intentions, it makes no difference. Either way, none of you have the nous to harness the unique power this ship almost certainly has.'

Caleb let out a hoot of laughter. 'Oh, get him! The blue fella who did absolutely nothing during the mutiny has all the answers, it seems. What grand plans do you have for this ship then? Other than to sit in a chair like a bleakin' coward.'

'A coward?' Alex slowly turned his head to look Caleb directly in the eye, 'that's fine coming from the man who spent the whole incident scrambling around on the floor like a frightened mouse.'

Caleb was both offended and a little intimidated by Alex's scorn. 'I was picking locks. Including yours! If it weren't for me, you'd still be cuffed.'

'That is debatable,' Alex replied.

Lackner didn't like how this was unfolding, and he was keen to take Alex Navin out of the mix as soon as he could. Lackner wanted to return to Vastrid with this ship intact. Once back home, he'd hand it over to whichever side currently held power and hopefully be rewarded with a comfortable retirement, allowing him to escape the military game before his chequered past caught up with him. Navin was a threat to this plan; a young man thrust into war without allegiance to either side was unpredictable.

Lackner backed towards one of the chairs and concealed a jagged piece of broken cuff in his palm. He decided he'd try to rile up the mutineers into provoking an altercation with Navin, and then, in the fray, he'd use the foreign object to take Navin out for good. 'I say that the little slum rat is right.

You didn't exactly rush in to help. You *are* a coward, and you can't be trusted.'

Alex smirked. 'Really? Would a coward do this?'

Alex stood up and reached inside of his dark trench coat. He revealed a unique looking handgun and aimed it directly at Lackner. 'I believe you've mistaken guile for cowardice. I'm taking this ship. By force, if I must.'

Immediately Lomax spoke, hoping to alleviate the situation before it flared into something unnecessary and ugly. 'I suggest you put that gun down, son. We're all in this together for the moment.'

With his weapon still aimed directly at Lackner, Alex snorted. 'Firstly, I'm definitely not your son, and secondly, we are oh-so-very far from being in this together.'

With that, Alex squeezed the trigger. There was a bang, then a trail of smoke from the barrel of the weapon. Lackner fell to the floor with a blood-spewing hole in his heart.

Callie raced towards her fallen Guardsman and checked for a pulse that was no longer there. 'He's dead. You murdered him!'

'Self-defence,' replied Alex, coolly motioning to the piece of shrapnel that Lackner had in his hand. 'Plus, I heard every word of the plot you two conjured up earlier. I do suggest you don't attempt to *take me out* as planned. Otherwise, the next bullet in this gun will be for you.'

Ryan felt a queasy sense of unease in his heart and stomach. At first, his thoughts dwelled on how Callie could be as cold-blooded as to plot to take out a fellow prisoner. With everything building between them as it had been, Ryan wondered if he'd turned a blind eye to some of her more ruthless qualities or projected some kind of ideal-girlfriend persona onto her. Either way, it was clear once more that Callie was far more worldly than he was, and it made him question once more whether or not she could be interested in him romantically.

These thoughts and fears arrived and left as Ryan realised that he was staring at another dead body. He thought back to the massacre – Jayden's death and the many other corpses that lay at his feet that night. Up until that point, Ryan had never seen a single dead body, but it was now becoming a regular occurrence. He began to wonder whose death he would be next and whether or not it would be his own. Strangely, Ryan didn't fear the situation he was in; as he looked at the blue-skinned off-worlder, he felt an odd sensation of trust and safety.

Ryan looked around at the rest of the mutineers. Most of them looked ready to surrender, except Callie and Lomax, who were both poised to strike. Alex was aware of this and aimed his pistol towards Lomax, believing her to be the more significant threat. However, just as he was about to squeeze the trigger, The Salvator was hit by a flurry of shots.

The ship's hull shook violently, causing Alex to misfire into the ceiling and then drop his weapon. The mutineers looked at each other, confused and surprised.

'Oh, what now?' moaned Caleb.

'Enemy fire from the sound of it. The Corporation must be on to us,'

Lomax advised the group before looking at Callie. 'Do you think you could fly this thing?'

Callie shrugged her shoulders but looked confident. 'There's only one way to find out. Everyone to the cockpit.'

'What about this guy?' Big Joe nodded towards Alex, who was crouched over looking for his pistol.

'Oh, let him scrabble for his gun; we've got bigger fish to fry,' Lomax scoffed. 'And besides, he's not going to manage to aim a shot with all the impact we're taking from outside.' The ship rumbled as more shots struck the hull.

The mutineers ran through the length of the Salvator together, eventually reaching the cockpit. As they stepped through, they were greeted by the newly upgraded Probot.

'Hello. My name is Probot. I have been reappropriated by this enhanced version of the ship. It requires a human crew of at least five. I'm here to act as an interface. We are under attack.'

Another barrage of shots hit the ship. 'Oh, you don't say!' Caleb cried.

Probot scanned the room and fixed his eyes on Callie. 'Ms. Haywood, we were briefly acquainted when I served Prince Alistair in Vastrid. If you could please take the main controls. My filesystem seems a little corrupted, but it suggests you are one of the Royal Guards' highest scoring pilots.'

'Yeah, highest scoring in *test* scenarios,' Callie clarified as she took a seat in front of the new and improved holographic control. She'd never seen anything like it before. Callie eased her hands into the beams of light and was surprised at how responsive they felt. She scanned through the data feeds in front of her to surmise what the threat was and what capabilities the Salvator had.

The radar showed a fleet of eight Shadox drones moving in towards the Salvator, opening fire together and then dispersing in separate directions before regrouping and repeating the attack. The data provided from the radar's tracking system revealed that the unit had already done this several times, with the Salvator being protected by an advanced holo-shield surrounding it. However, the ship's power was starting to fade, and a few shots were managing to snake in through the gaps.

Callie knew she could fly The Salvator in and out of danger easily enough but would require someone to operate the shield, two gunners and someone to provide data updates.

She looked around at the mutineers, scouting for suitable candidates.

'Ok team, there's a fleet of eight attacking us. I can take them out, but I'll need some help.'

'I beg your bleakin' pardon. What do you mean, take them out?' Caleb protested, 'Can't we just hyperdrive our way out of this grief?'

'No way,' Callie replied, 'they'll blow us out of the sky while we're plotting coordinates. Plus, we'd be leaping further away from Vastrid. Deep space is The Corporation's territory; we'd be surrounded and destroyed within hours. Minutes even.'

'She's right,' said Lomax. 'Callie, where do you want us?'

Callie nodded towards Caleb. 'Well, seeing as this one seems most concerned about saving his own skin, I think he'd be ideal to work the shields. They're on that console just behind me, to the left.'

Lomax looked at the young locksmith. 'Well, go on, Caleb, you heard the lady.'

The two prisoners that had been brought on board with Big Joe stepped forward. 'Excuse me, miss,' the taller of the two chirped. 'My brother and I have a great deal of experience on freight ships, fighting off pirates using all kinds of weird, cosmic weaponry. We'd be delighted to blast some Shadox drones out of the sky.'

'Excellent. The weapons hub is on a lower deck, back down towards the middle of the ship.' Callie looked back over her shoulder to check they were listening, but the two brothers had already gone. 'What an odd pair,' she muttered to herself before raising her voice. 'And Ryan, I'll need you next to me – '

Caleb raised his eyebrows knowingly at Ryan as she continued to talk, ' – as I'll need your experience at the library to analyse the data feed as we attack.'

With a slight blush on his cheeks, Ryan took the seat beside Callie. The crushing weight of his heart's romantic expectation was colliding against the fear and confusion of imminent battle, and Ryan felt more than a little nervy.

The strange new holographic controls beaming away in front of him certainly weren't helping.

Noticing his confusion, Callie gently took his hand and placed it directly into a large cylindrical column in front of him. The feeling of closeness amplified as she guided him through the controls. 'It seems simple enough to control. Just move your hand in and out of the light and guide the data feed.'

Ryan nearly became lost in a moment dominated by the butterflies in his stomach but fell back to the harsh reality of the moment when Callie suddenly let his hand go and spun round in her chair to address Lomax and Big Joe. 'And you two, go and find Navin before he murders us all.'

'Ok, let's get this thing done,' said Callie, turning back around to look at the myriad of controls in front of her. 'Ryan? What have we got coming our way?'

Ryan looked at his data. 'There are seven ships coming towards us like a triangle and one ship hanging back.'

'Ok crew, I'm going to drop The Salvator and speed past underneath them. When we get in range of that ship hanging back, I need Ryan to relay range data to the crew,' Callie ordered. 'When he does that, the shield needs to be dropped with the verbal confirmation of the word "clear". Do you get that, shield boy?'

'Of course I get that. I may not have a uniform, but I'm not a bleakin' idiot,' Caleb grumbled.

Callie glared back at him.

'Yes, ma'am,' answered Caleb, giving a sarcastic salute as soon as her back was turned.

The speakers crackled, and the voice of one of the

brothers boomed through the speakers. 'And then when we hear "clear", we blast those drones out of the sky, right?'

'Exactly,' answered Callie. 'Ok, let's shake this place.'

With that, she pushed her right hand forward and down through a lavender coloured holo-control while circling the tips of her fingers on her left hand through a green circular control.

The Salvator dipped and quickly sped past the oncoming fleet and, with all crew members following her instructions, destroyed the lone ship with ease.

Callie spun The Salvator back around to face the rest of the fleet. She was hoping that she'd be able to attack the remaining ships before they had time to correct their position; however, they had begun to turn in unison in preparation to strike.

Ryan looked over at Callie and noticed the uneasy concern on her face.

'What's wrong? Don't you think we can out-gun them?'

'No, it's not that,' Callie responded, concentrating on the controls in front of her. 'That first attack went *far* too well. The controls don't seem to operate solely on manual input. It's like they're bonding with my instincts, deciding the best course of action and then guiding me.'

Ryan was surprised. '*They're*? You're talking like the controls are alive.'

'Exactly,' Callie replied. 'These flight controls appear to have an almost precognitive targeting and guidance system. They somehow influenced my manual use of the controls. This ship was far too easy to fly. I would hazard a guess that the shields and weaponry are similarly influenced. I don't like it; I don't like it one bit.'

'Well, can you just pretend to like it or something?' Caleb snapped. 'Those other seven ships are nearly on us. I didn't sign up to be part of your bleakin' war. It's not like my old mum's going to be getting Vastridian service payment if I get blown out of the sky.'

Ryan was quick to interrupt his new friend. 'Caleb, Caleb, settle down. Look at the display panel. The schematics for the ship have recalibrated, and I've got the upgrades here in front of me.'

Ryan flicked through the holographic data in front of him, delving into the architecture of the ship's control deck. 'The entire workings of the ship seem to be covered with multi-path sensory receptors. From what I can gather, they act upon the actions of the crew and by using data provided by some kind of high-frequency broadcast. I've studied underground information relays at the library when trying to discover rare secret echoes but never heard of anything like this before.'

Callie felt all the more trepidatious about the apparent lack of autonomy. 'A broadcast? Where's it coming from? It could be from a Corporation stronghold in Vastrid or Shadox VI, or even wherever that damn light came from. I don't trust it.'

Probot spun around in his console. 'If I may suggest something, I can trace the signal to its source and then, using one of the many Shadox Corporation surveillance satellites, obtain an image of the geographical location.'

Callie nodded. 'Go for it, Probot, and make it fast. We've got about twenty seconds until those drones reach us.'

Almost immediately, the monitors blinked in unison, and Probot glanced towards them. 'Location data acquired.'

Caleb, Callie and Ryan all looked at their screens. They were shocked and speechless. They had expected to see a Corporation branded satellite dish or some form of communication centre. Instead, the camera feed displayed a cheery-looking dolphin poking its head out of the sea with what appeared to be a smile on its face.

'Well, he's a chipper looking little bleaker, isn't he?' Caleb said wryly.

Noticing the enemy fleet closing in on them, Ryan scanned through his data feeds again. 'According to this, that image is correct. I don't know how or why, but all the data is coming from that dolphin.'

Callie was still unsure. 'Is there any information on how to override it? I'm really not comfortable with trusting this relay method.'

'Trust it! Trust it!' whined Caleb as the attack ships moved faster and faster towards them.

She knew he was right; there was no time to spare. 'Listen up, crew; we're going to do the same thing again, but this time there's seven of them, so we need to hit them harder and faster. Yell "ready" if you're ready.'

Ryan, Caleb and the two brothers hollered in response, and Callie skimmed The Salvator under the oncoming fleet. She quickly spun the ship around, and the two brothers opened fire, taking out four of the drones. The remaining three ships were taken care of equally swiftly as Callie led the charge towards them with all of the Salvator's guns blazing.

'Well done, Officer Haywood. Big Joe and I have brought you a gift to say thanks for saving all of our skins,' Kendra Lomax said, strolling into the cockpit and motioning back at Big Joe, who was dragging a cuffed and bruised Alex Navin behind him. As he reached the cockpit, Joe flung the blue-skinned colonial towards Callie's chair.

Callie stood up and looked down at Alex. 'Thanks, but no thanks. I don't want this murderer aboard my ship.'

'*Your* ship?' Alex cackled. 'That's a bit presumptuous, isn't it?'

'While I'm piloting it and while we're nearer to Vastridian aerospace than any other habitable planet or colony, this ship belongs to the highest-ranking member of the Royal Guard.

Which is me.' Callie's tone was forceful. She was, in fact, surprising herself with just how well she was adapting to all the deep space peril they had been flung into. 'And while I'm in charge, I have no desire to keep someone like you aboard.'

Before Callie could finish speaking, the ship began to shake. She looked over towards the control panel in time to see Lomax quickly remove her hands from a cluster of small orange and yellow coloured cuboid holo-controls. The rest of the crew switched their focus from Callie to Lomax, who slowly backed away.

'What's going on? What's she done to the ship?' cried Caleb in dismay.

'I apologise for my brash action, but I needed to get us as far away from here as soon as I could for all of our sakes,' Lomax spoke quietly. 'Ryan and this ship are precious items which could both be snatched from us without discussion or mercy. We're all involved with this now. If we're to survive the next twenty-four hours, we must band together, and that includes Mr Navin here.'

'I appreciate the concern, but where are you taking us? How did you even work out the coordinates that quickly?' Ryan asked, feeling a bit uneasy about being the centre of all this attention.

Lomax looked pensive. 'I've had emergency coordinates committed to memory for decades. As for our destination? Unfortunately, in the long term, the safest place for you and this ship is, in the short term, the most dangerous place for the rest of us.'

Caleb scratched his head. 'Wait a minute, does that sentence even make sense?'

As confusion and panic spread across the faces of The Salvator's new crew, the ship made a light speed jump, travelling further from planet Earth than any of them ever expected to go.

Chapter Twenty-Five

A SINGLE DESTINATION CAN SERVE MANY PURPOSES

'Ok, so where are we?' Callie was somewhat disgruntled at Kendra Lomax's sudden hijacking of the ship's warp drive.

The Salvator had left light speed and arrived above a disc-shaped colony protected by a biosphere dome.

'Stay calm, everyone,' said Lomax, holding her hands up in an attempt to elicit trust. 'We're approaching Terra Novate, one of the largest and most innovative of the many attempts to colonise the galaxy.'

'I know that place,' Ryan stepped forward. 'I had to pull files on it when I worked at the library. It's one of the Corporation's largest off-world facilities. Apparently, they do all kinds of weird experiments and stuff there.'

'I don't want to go there,' cried Caleb in dismay, turning to Callie. 'Tell her we're not going there.'

'I agree.' Callie answered. 'Why would we risk putting ourselves in danger by going to one of the Corporation's strongholds?'

'I'll be truthful with you. I'll tell you everything you want and need to know. In return, I ask that you trust my judgement and remain loyal to the cause of the Sentry. What I propose we do over the next twenty-four hours will be incredibly dangerous, but if we don't act now, then I fear the whole of existence may be at stake. I need to know you're all on board with me,' Lomax looked down at Alex, who was still cuffed. 'And that includes you.'

Caleb was shocked. 'Why the bleak are you asking him? He was going to murder us all less than an hour ago, in case you'd forgotten!'

'You don't need to worry about this one,' Kendra assured. 'This is Alex Navin, for anyone who doesn't recognise him. The only person to successfully hack into the Shadox Corporation's core data system. If he's smart enough to be able to manage that, then he's surely smart enough to realise that instead of trying to murder us and steal the ship, it's actually in his best interest to work alongside us.'

Caleb's eyes lit up as he realised he could throw some cheeky barbs at the colonial. 'Oh, so you're *him*. I know all about you. You're the guy that got access to everything the Corporation controls for a full ten minutes and still didn't manage to steal a single credit.'

'I didn't do it for the money, you idiot.' Alex replied.

There was a moment of silence while the crew waited for Alex to explain his reasons, but instead, he looked at Lomax. 'You are correct in your analysis of my place within this situation but let me make it clear I'm only tagging along with you for two reasons; increased security, and this ship. Once we're free of the Corporation, I'm taking this ship by fair means or foul.'

'When the Corporation crumbles, we can talk about what happens to this ship,' Lomax unlocked the cuffs wrapped around Alex's wrists. 'You've made the right choice.'

The rest of the crew looked at each other, uneasy with Lomax's actions.

Big Joe stepped towards Lomax. 'Listen, I don't care

about the ins and outs of politics or beliefs. All I know is there are people out there that want to do terrible things to me. When we teamed up and took control of this ship, I felt safer than I had done in a very long time. I'm happy to follow you, but you gotta let me know the score. Why are you taking us to Terra Novate?'

Lomax smiled and looked him in the eye. 'Joe, I appreciate the vote of confidence, especially from you. It can't be easy to trust anyone after all those years spent on a ranch.'

Lomax was referring to the Corporation's soldier farming program, where the strongest young men and women from remote villages would be taken from their homes to be brainwashed and genetically experimented on to become ultimate killing machines. Lomax could tell by the circled R tattoo on his arm that Joe had escaped one of these places, and the sadness in his eyes showed that the horror of his time there hadn't faded.

'I'm taking us to Terra Novate to make contact with a scientist called Abila Sanchez who has been sitting on a sanctuary of sorts for The Sentry. She guards a great source of power. Underneath her laboratory, she keeps guard of a blessed garden.'

'A *blessed garden*? What the bleak is a blessed garden?' Caleb chortled, finding the name far more amusing than anyone else aboard the ship.

Lomax took a deep breath to help tame her temper. 'If you would be gracious enough to shut the *bleak* up for five minutes, I'll tell you. A blessed garden is a small patch of land hit by a direct beam of The Tide's pure light. I need to take Ryan there so the power within him can be brought to fruition.'

'Excuse me, do I get a say in this?' Ryan asked.

'Ryan, it's in your interest. Word will get back to the Corporation that you summoned the Tide, and they will come looking for you. Don't you want to be ready?' Lomax looked towards Alex. 'Navin, I'll need you to access the Terra Novate data streams and remove all trace of our trip there.'

'Easier done than said,' Alex replied.

Caleb still wasn't convinced about this plan. 'And what about the rest of us? What are we supposed to do while you two are off in the blessed garden, trimming the verge?'

'Keep guard of the ship and liaise with Abila and her team. They might be able to help with weaponry, supplies and diagnostics,' said Lomax. 'Once we're done, we'll fly this ship to the edge of the known galaxy and plan our next move. '

Lomax was interrupted by the sound of panting and groaning. 'What's that?' she asked as the whole crew looked around the cockpit.

The moline emerged from her hiding spot under a chair and leapt up onto Caleb's shoulder.

'Eh! Look who I've just found!' Caleb proclaimed, proudly petting the creature's dark fuzzy head. As he did so, Bandit began to rock back and forth, making a pained choking sound before vomiting across Caleb's shoulder, down his arm and all over his hand.

Embarrassed and shocked at her actions, Bandit leapt from Caleb's shoulders and darted back under the chair, shivering and frail.

'Well, that's just charming, isn't it?' groaned Caleb, taking the lumpy vomit all over his hand and wiping it on the pristine white wall of The Salvator. The vomit hung on the wall for a moment before absorbing into the ship.

'Did you see that?' Caleb yelled.

Probot was quick to answer. 'Various status levels of the ship have increased. Full analysis of the ship indicates that it is now powered by waste, dirt and human omissions.'

Lomax was excited yet cautious. 'Not fuel? You mean we're free from using Corporation fuel?'

'Affirmative. The ship is self-sustaining as long as it's oper-ated by a human crew generating bacteria and breathing out carbon dioxide,' Probot reported.

Alex's eyes sparkled with joy for the briefest of moments before he diminished their fire with his well-worn stoic face.

Lomax bent down to look at Bandit. 'And what about you, my furry friend? You don't look so well.'

She stroked the moline gently as Bandit nuzzled into her forearm. 'Abila was one of the lead scientists on the corpora-tion's Life Forms project; maybe she could take a look at you when we get there.' She turned and addressed the rest of the group. 'It will be nighttime in the colony, so we should get some rest.'

Callie crouched down next to Kurtis Lackner's dead body. As the rest of the mutineers shuffled off, Lomax moved beside her. 'Naturally, we'll keep his corpse preserved and hand over the body when we get back to Earth so that his family can mourn appropriately. Were you close to him?'

'No, not really. I mean, I only met him aboard this ship. But he was a fellow guardsman, and he was the only person to speak to me when I woke up bound in one of those chairs.' Callie felt a strange sense of guilt and fear over his murder. 'I'm not sure you made the right decision letting Navin go like that. Do you think we can trust him, really?'

'No, I don't think we can or should trust Navin, but I do know that he wants this ship and that he offered a warning before aiming his weapon at us. From what I know of Lackn-er's reputation, I'm not certain that he would have shown us the same courtesy. Navin needs this ship to live autonomously from the Corporation, and he needs this ship to have a full crew. He's well aware of the range of bounties aboard, so he almost certainly sees all of us as assets that can be traded somewhere down the line. That alone keeps us safe, at least for the short term. While we, like it or not, will need his technical knowledge if we're to stand a chance against the Corporation.'

Callie sighed and nodded, reluctantly accepting Lomax's logic. Running the tips of her fingers over Lackner's eyelids to close them, Callie said her goodbyes silently to her recent acquaintance. She'd never be sure whether he was a potential friend or threat, but she did know that his plotting had helped keep her alert and calm during her time aboard the ship and, to some degree, saved her life. Lomax let Callie know with a glance that she'd take care of the rest and dutifully slung Lackner's body over her shoulder, and began to look for The Salvator's medi-room, praying that it had adequate refrigerated storage facilities.

As the crew of the newly upgraded Salvator explored the ship for suitable cabins, little did they know that they were being discussed and plotted against by Mr Nox and Rachel Stone on Shadox VI.

'Shall I address the elephant in the room?' offered Rachel, her voice pitched with pride and confidence. 'Bron's actions during the repossession were inexcusable. As soon as I've decided when it would best suit the needs of the Corporation, he shall be punished accordingly.'

'So you're saying you had nothing to do with it?' Nox asked.

Rachel leant forward calmly, looked Nox straight in the eyes and sold a lie as only she could. 'I can assure you that I was as surprised and as disappointed as you were. I thought Bron was dependable, and in turn, I put a lot of faith in him. Too much faith. I shan't make that mistake again. In the future, I shall leave the bloodshed side of things to you and focus on what I'm good at.'

Nox grinned. 'Which is?'

'Diplomacy, presence and most importantly: management. You see, as powerful as you and my uncle are, you don't have the required skill set or corporate behaviours to maintain the ever-expanding control infrastructure that our beloved Corporation requires,' said Rachel. 'Your broad shoulders weren't designed to carry these petty burdens. The juggling of resources and the painted smiles of political duties would be as ill-fitted to your skills as marching into a storm of bullets would be to mine. We *can* work together, Mr Nox. We just need to respect each other's boundaries, and,' Rachel smiled broadly, 'a little trust.'

Nox didn't trust her as far as he wished he'd be allowed to throw her, but it was clear he needed her onside while Lomax and the Child of The Light were alive. He also realised that she had come to the conclusion that she had bitten off more than she could chew, and with Bron now out of the picture, would be required to at least half-heartedly toe the line. He had no doubt that she would continue to keep secrets from him and operate within her own agenda. That was fine. He certainly had his share of secrets; when he had earlier relayed how the presence of The Child Of Light had been felt by Shadox himself, he hadn't revealed that the old man had unleashed a force to remove all living matter across the galaxy.

Nor had Nox mentioned that after he and Shadox witnessed The Tide annulling the oblivious force of the dark Lethe, the cocoon of Lethe particles holding Shadox aloft also dissolved temporarily. The frail, rotting husk of the man he actually was tumbled down onto the floor, gasping what appeared to be his final breaths. Shadox was back in his device now and recharging, but it had been too close.

'Indeed, during these testing times, trust and synchronicity in approach will be our most effective weapons,' said Nox. 'To put this new collaborative approach into effect, I have already shared my knowledge regarding Lomax and her protégé. What information do you hold that I should know about?'

Rachel Stone leant back in her chair and smirked. 'Well, firstly, one of my scouting ships has already intercepted a capsule containing Marcus Hagen and his crew.'

'Hagen? Isn't he one of our bounty hunters'? asked Nox.

'Indeed, one of the best. It would appear that he and his crew not only picked up the members of this new Sentry threat but were also aboard the ship when the young Sentry did what he did to get you and my uncle so rattled. Hagen just described the whole incident to me. It was most *enlightening* if you'll excuse the pun,' Rachel replied.

Nox was irritated by Rachel's use of the word rattled but knew her vicious, catty nature and decided to let it slide. For the moment, at least. 'Ok, so we've picked up a bunch of mercenaries? So what?'

Rachel raised an eyebrow. 'Well, my dear, this is where it gets really interesting. Also aboard that ship, as a prisoner, was Alex Navin.'

'Navin? They had Navin on board as a bounty? Why didn't anyone inform me? He is an Alpha Grade fugitive. Is he part of this New Sentry threat?'

'That's what I intend to find out when I bring him in, but luckily for us, Hagen and Navin have quite the past. Alex Navin is no more than a weak colonial survivor trading on the enigmatic aura he has created for himself. It's hard to get any form of upper hand on a man who plays his cards close to his chest and harder still with a man who chooses not to play cards in the first place. He's possibly the most wanted person on our lists, bar Lomax. The Royal Guard has been after him for years; even his fellow Colonist Rebels have a price on his head. When he infiltrated our systems, he could have robbed the Corporation blind if he wanted to. He broke through all of our security and was there traceless for ten whole minutes. What on Earth was he looking for?'

'A friend?' offered Nox snarkily. 'It can't be easy with the whole universe hating your guts. Though from what I've heard, that's how the Rudey Blue likes it.'

'Now now, Mr Nox,' answered Rachel in a mock schoolmistress voice. 'I'm not fond of the off-worlders either, but I would ask you to refrain from using derogatory names like Rudey Blue in my office, thank you very much. Let us not forget that the Shadox Corporation is a caring, welcoming, forward-thinking company.'

There was an awkward silence as Nox tried to work out whether or not he was expected to laugh. While few could deny that Rachel Stone was a brilliant businesswoman, a shrewd financial planner and a deadly viper in the boardroom, it was safe to say that comedy wasn't her strongest suit.

Nox was becoming tired of the conversation and was keen to lead Rachel to her point. 'So you think that Hagen will be able to bring us the fugitives because he knows Navin better than anyone else?'

Rachel leaned forward to deliver her most impressive bit of news. 'Yes, but not only that. Hagen is a very experienced and resourceful bounty hunter. He always makes sure that all bounties are logged and processed when they board his ship. I've just received the results of the cross-reference between his pending bounties and our database. It seems that we put one of Davron's trial behavioural mod chips into one of their brains way back when.'

'So we can track exactly where they've taken the ship. That's useful, Ms Stone.' Nox was reluctantly impressed.

'I told you that Dr Davron's more controversial experiments would yield a reward one day. Unfortunately, the chip isn't attached to anyone of note, just a small-time Baker's End rat.' Rachel's voice was full of vague disgust at the concept of such a person. 'I can't recall his name, something like Colin Scanner. Hopefully, he will remain with the crew when they land. At present, they've just entered the aerospace of Terra Novate.'

'Terra Novate? That's an interesting choice. What do you think their next move is? An attack on our labs? Take over the old Citadel?' asked Nox.

'I have long suspected that Abila Sanchez is a Sentry sympathiser. If I were a betting woman, I would presume that Lomax is heading straight to her lab.'

Nox was surprised by this revelation. 'Really? I've always had Sanchez down as a timid little mouse of a woman, but you've had more dealings with her than me, so I'll follow your lead on this one. I propose we send Hagen and his crew to take down as many of them as possible. We will then set up base in the Citadel and bring the Prince and Vastridian military heads down with us as collateral to draw Lomax and her protégé away from their new friends. I'll handle the Sentry scum. You get to do whatever you please to the rest of them, including Sanchez. Deal?'

Rachel's eyes lit up. She'd never liked Abila Sanchez and had long wished to punish her. A sharp creak in the ceiling above interrupted Rachel's excitement.

'What was that?' Rachel asked.

Nox laughed. 'Just the rickety old air con in this bucket of bolts. As soon as we eliminate Lomax and her friend and nip this sad little rebellion in the bud, I'll have another word with the old man to see if we can finally get the Shadox VII plans pushed through.'

Nox knew the sound had nothing to do with the air conditioning and had witnessed a quick flash of heavily bandaged face pull away from one of the air grilles in the top right-hand corner of the room. He knew it had to be Bron; who else would be as crazed and tenacious as to crawl through miles and miles of ventilation tubing just to gather operational intel. It was clear to Nox that Rachel was oblivious to this fact and that the estrangement between herself and the Colonel was as severe, if not more so, than she had let on. He decided to keep Rachel in the dark about this for the short term at least; whatever crazy plan Bron was likely to hatch could be used to his advantage.

For over an hour, Bron clambered and crawled through Shadox VI's labyrinthine ventilation system. Everyone thought he was insane when he decided to take the job policing the station during its construction, but he learnt every nook and cranny of it. It was a knowledge that was paying great dividends now as he scuttled back to the hospital ward, his head rattling with Rachel's cruel betrayal. The vicious looping chain of events began to play in his mind once more with Rachel's words, 'Shall I address the elephant in the room?' joining the tormenting sequence.

'Enough!' hollered Bron through his bandages, thrusting out his hands as if he were clutching a physical representation of the chain in front of him. He knew that he was on the fast track to becoming an insignificant victim of recent events. He needed to take control of his destiny, and he needed to do it on Terra Novate.

Bron looked around the hospital ward disdainfully. This was where victims came to be dictated to by doctors, as their life and legacy were chipped away from the outside. Bron knew that this was no place for a great warrior like himself and decided to check himself out.

Reaching behind his head, Bron began to unravel the bandages surrounding his mutilated face. The doctors had warned him that it would be weeks, maybe even months, before his face would have healed enough for the bandages to be removed, but by then, it would be too late. Pus, scabs and infected skin all came away with each layer of gauze. Bron grimaced through the pain but made no sound. Free from the bandages, his face felt raw and exposed. He reached over to a medi-tray by the side of his bed and felt around for the proto-type facial mask the doctors had shown him earlier. With one swift movement, he clamped it hard against his face until the tissue adhesive around its edge melded it to the side of his head.

Bron walked towards a mirror to look at the damage. The face he'd developed over the past four and a half decades of his life was now gone, but he was still a soldier, a warrior, a cold-hearted killer. Staring deep into the scar tissue and stitches that now defined his face, Bron smirked, planning the chaotic fury and bloodshed he intended to unleash on the colony.

Chapter Twenty-Six

FASCINATION

After a couple of hours of light slumber, Ryan awoke to find Alex Navin sitting on a chair beside his bed. The colonial fugitive looked deep into Ryan's sleepy eyes and said quietly, 'You fascinate me.'

Alex's tone was cold and detached; he sounded far from interested, let alone fascinated. There was a slightly disconcerting pause between all three of the words, leaving Ryan to consider just what form of unexpected trouble he'd stumbled into now. Ryan also wondered how he'd ended up sharing a cabin with someone who had identified himself as a threat. He had hoped he could spend some time with Callie, to perhaps rekindle that particular feeling of flirtatious oneness that he had felt at the Ball. An hour or two in a cosy starship cabin away from all the increasing danger and peril swamping their lives might just be the place to re-establish that feeling of familiarity.

However, Callie had stayed back to take care of Lackner, and in the mayhem of the new crew of The Salvator calling dibs on the few decent sized cabins on the ship, Ryan had lost track of her whereabouts.

Ryan's second choice would have been to share with Caleb, but the Baker's End locksmith had darted off with Big Joe, both looking for the best and biggest quarters. Unfortunately, in their haste, they had not only found the worst and smallest cabin but then realised that they would have to share it after all the cabins they had rejected were now taken.

Tired and drained, Ryan decided to take a quick nap on the bed opposite Alex Navin before looking for Callie. However, he had drifted into a sleep plagued by his reoccurring dream and had now awoken to find arguably the most frightening member of the crew watching over him.

Ryan wanted to ask why Alex had been watching him sleep and for how long, but could only muster a nervous, 'Sorry, I beg your pardon?'

'I said that you,' Alex threw in another long pause, 'fascinate me.'

Ryan lifted his blanket up against his chest, attempting to provide some kind of barrier from this awkward moment.

He was unsure of the nature of Alex's attention and had no desire to be of interest to someone who had pointed a gun at him just hours earlier.

'Erm, I don't know why. I mean, I'm quite boring all in all,' Ryan said, hoping to defuse the situation.

Alex continued to stare at him for a second or two before answering. 'The thing that fascinates me about you is that nothing adds up. You were brought in with a Baker's End rat, but you don't look like you've lived a rough life amongst the thieves and scoundrels that lurk there. You wear a Guard's jacket – admittedly, an ill-tailored excuse of a Guards jacket, yet a Guards jacket nonetheless, but you don't have the same air of entitlement and superiority that normally comes with the role. And then there's The Sentry element.'

'Oh, I'm not a member of The Sentry,' Ryan answered.

Alex looked around Ryan's eyes, examining them for any

traces of the light that had shone from there earlier. 'Hmmm, somehow, I don't think that you'll be the one to decide that.'

Ryan looked towards Alex's bed and noticed the gun he had threatened to shoot them with earlier, laid out in pieces on a cleaning cloth.

'Speaking of fascinating things,' Ryan said, keen to shift the focus elsewhere, 'how did you manage to get that gun onboard?'

'Now that would be telling,' smirked Alex, sliding off the chair and heading back to his bed to rebuild his pistol. The answer was rather mundane, but Alex knew that a little bit of mystery now could serve him well in the future. As Alex began to put his weapon back together, Ryan noticed some unique symbols etched on the butt of its handle. Alex saw Ryan's glance and moved to obscure the view with his back.

Before Ryan could investigate any further, he heard a familiar voice booming through the corridor outside.

'Ryan? Ryan? Anyone seen Ryan? You know, the one in that guard's jacket, with the eyes that glow. Anyone seen him?'

It was Caleb who, within seconds, stuck his head into the cabin. 'Oh, there you are! I wondered where the bleakin' heck you'd gone.'

'Sorry, Caleb, you went racing off, and I was exhausted. It's been a rather odd couple of days if you hadn't noticed,' Ryan apologised.

Caleb leant forward and whispered, 'You took a bit of a chance sleeping in the same room as *him*.' He threw two arched eyebrows and a nod in the direction of Alex.

'You do realise that I am not deaf, don't you?' Alex asked. 'I presume you're either a complete idiot or an arrogant fool who holds his whispering abilities in too high a regard.'

Caleb rolled his eyes and made a quick flapping motion

with his right hand as if he were attempting to swat away a fly.

'Never mind him, Ryan. I really think we need to get out of this situation. Nothing is forcing us to join up with this lot. Let's just say we appreciate their plans and concerns, but we need to get back to Vastrid and – '

'Caleb, where are we going to go? The Corporation has control of everything in Vastrid. They'll hunt us down no matter who we're with or where we end up. I don't want any of this either, but what can we do?'

Caleb sighed. 'OK, but you promise me if we're about to die, you'll do some of your bleakin' glowing eyes business because I don't want to die. I REALLY don't want to die.'

'I would suggest you quit your incessant chatter then,' Alex interjected, aiming his newly rebuilt pistol directly at Caleb's head.

Caleb was unsure if the off-worlder was joking or not, and a bead of sweat dripped from his forehead. Luckily for him, the moment was interrupted by the arrival of the two brothers. Barging past Caleb as they bounded down the corridor, the eldest of the brothers hollered, 'Come on, you guys, it looks like we're about to begin landing.'

Caleb gave a polite smile and held up his hand in gratitude. 'Thanks for letting us know....'

He had intended to address the older brother by name but realised he had no idea what either of them were called. He wondered if anyone else on the ship knew their names. He presumed Ryan wouldn't know (after all, he couldn't even get a Guard's jacket that fitted), so he glanced over at Alex and considered asking him, but the words paused on his tongue, blocked by a sense of awkwardness.

'I suppose we'd better join them,' said Ryan. Alex nodded in agreement, and the three of them began a silent walk to the cockpit.

Upon reaching the front of the ship, Ryan noticed Callie rubbing her eyes and yawning. Stretching out her arms in an attempt to re-energise her body, she glanced up at Ryan and smiled. 'Hey you! How's the rest of the ship? Is it as impressive as here?'

'I didn't get to see much of it.' Ryan answered, scratching his head as he spoke. 'I mainly just jumped into a bunk and drifted off. Did you find somewhere to crash?'

'Nah, I thought it best to stick around here and make sure the auto-pilot did what it's supposed to,' Callie replied. She frowned a little as she glanced out at the dark skies. 'To be honest, I don't think I could have slept with the threat of being blown out of the stars looming over us.'

Callie's sense of duty made Ryan feel weak and foolish. He gulped a little and managed to utter, 'Well, I'm glad someone on this ship is here to look out for a lazy bones like me.'

'I'm sure you were very tired,' Callie answered before a noisy alarm sounded and flashed brightly in the holo-controls, breaking Ryan's awkward moment. 'Sorry, I have to check this.'

'You and her? It ain't ever going to happen,' whispered Caleb as he walked past Ryan shaking his head in disbelief.

'OK, team,' Callie hollered over her shoulder, 'it looks like we're about to begin a landing procedure. Ryan and Caleb, I'll need you two on the data feed and the shields again. The rest of you should find a seat and buckle down; this may get bumpy.'

Big Joe raised his eyebrows and looked at Kendra, Alex and the two brothers. 'You heard the lady, let's get strapped in.'

The five of them found some seats towards the back of the cockpit and, one by one, strapped themselves in. Alex glanced across at Lomax and noticed she looked nervous. They made eye contact, and Lomax adjusted her posture, rolling back her shoulders and raising her head. Alex realised that despite the trust she'd managed to elicit from the crew, she was as lost and clueless as the rest of them. In time, Alex knew he would usurp them all and take the ship but now wasn't the time. He'd let Lomax's little folly of a plan play out and then take the spoils in the aftermath. All he needed to do was survive, and he'd been doing that unaided since he was a child.

As the Salvator began its descent, Lomax's heart sank. She feared she was gambling too much, too soon with her plan. Underneath her rain cloak, she tightly crossed her fingers, desperately hoping that Professor Abila Sanchez still held the same values that she did almost twenty years ago. Lomax had sent a coded message to Abila a few hours earlier but had yet to receive a response. She feared she had made a terrible mistake leading so many young lives to what might be their premature end.

Down on the surface of Terra Nova, on one of its large, grassy hills, a young technical engineer named Cassandra Braham bounded towards the sprawling laboratory complex that belonged to her mentor, Professor Abila Sanchez.

Cassandra had excelled during her early years at the Royal Academy. The Corporation had soon singled her out as a promising young asset, and they had rewarded her innovative approach with countless scholarships and educational funding. Someone more politically astute might have questioned the Shadox Corporation's keen interest in their abilities, but Cassandra was a happy-go-lucky, slightly distracted kind of girl, especially if she was left able to pursue her advanced academic projects. Her current focus was on the theoretical framework of melding advanced mechanical concepts to artificially created body tissue. She'd always felt that the human body was somewhat limited in capability and was shocked that no one had ever really found a way to enhance it.

Cassandra eventually reached the rusted red tin roof of Abila's main study quarters and lifted it open.

A crackled yet friendly voice came from inside. 'Cassandra? Is that you? Get in here quick and make sure you lock the hatch.'

'Yes, Abila, it's me,' Cassandra called as she climbed down the service ladder. 'You'll never guess what I saw out by the citadel when I was taking my readings. The Corporation is here! Can you believe that? No one comes here! And they've brought the captured Prince! How exciting! Will they ask for our help?'

'I do hope not,' Abila sighed.

The professor was a short woman, only a little over five feet tall, with wild, unkempt hair. She walked over to the entrance hatch's ladder and helped Cassandra down.

'Why? Do they think we're in league with the Royal Family or something?' Cassandra snorted, pushing her rapidly descending glasses back to the top of her nose.

'No. Not as such. Cassandra, there are lots of different reasons why I'm out here on Terra Novate. Most of it is research, and yes, the Corporation funds that, but there is a bigger reason. It's something I've kept from you because you're better off out of it. For your own sake, I suggest you make arrangements for someone from the Independent Scholarship Trust to pick you up immediately.'

'And leave all my valuable work? I'm on the cusp of a major breakthrough!' Cassandra was adamant. 'I can't leave it behind. I won't leave it behind. I'm too close. Whatever your secret is, I'd rather face the fallout of it here amongst my work than go off and live a life built on never knowing if my theories were correct.'

Abila smiled. 'I understand. It's how I've ended up in this mess.'

'What mess?' asked Cassandra. 'Are we in danger?'

'Probably. I owe an old friend a favour, and it's time to repay it,' Abila sighed. 'She allowed me to study a source of great power that, by rights, is hers. I believe she's come back to claim it once more. You may have heard of her. Her name is Kendra Lomax.'

Cassandra was shocked. 'The terrorist?' she gasped.

'Some call her a terrorist. Some call her a miracle. I think she's an interesting case study of both theoretical and theological possibilities. Either way, she's coming here with some allies. I've sent Tiegan out to find them and lead them back here.'

'Tiegan?' asked Cassandra, surprised. 'Is that wise? She's not really what you'd call a people person.'

'True,' Abila replied, her eyes misting up for the briefest of moments, 'but she's going to have to learn to be, sooner or later. And with the universe going the way it appears to be, sooner might be for the best. Now, if you'll excuse me, I have some cultures on a petri dish I need to monitor.'

Cassandra took a step back and began to clean her glasses. She weighed up the various revelations and potential danger she had been exposed to and thought to herself, 'What a fascinating start to the day!'

Chapter Twenty-Seven

TIEGAN

'Oh, so it's changed on the outside as well,' Caleb beamed, taking a look at The Salvator's new sleeker, shinier exterior.

They had landed in a grassy clearing deep within the artificial forest that filled the east side of Terra Novate. One by one, the crew had left the ship and gazed in wonder at its lustrous and shapely new bodywork.

'Ain't she a beauty?' Caleb continued. 'If this landed in Baker's End, it would be chored good and proper within minutes.'

'Chored?' Callie asked.

Caleb shrugged. 'Yeah, you know – chored, taxed, nicked, stolen.'

'Indeed. I hope Probot's security measures are adequate to ensure it's still here when we return.' Alex was studying the ship's exterior and threw a glance back at the group. 'Or should I say, *if* we return.'

'Well, Probot assured us when we landed that the ship had scanned all crew members. We're the only ones who can open and power the ship,' Callie answered. 'Neither the Mandroid nor the ship has failed us this far. I think it's safe to trust them.'

Big Joe followed behind them, carrying Bandit the Moline in a case. The creature's health appeared to be on the wane as she curled up into a crescent-shaped furry heap, only stirring from her sleep to murmur in pain occasionally.

Ryan looked at the surrounding woodland. For as far as his eye could see, hundreds of trees with vast, dark trunks and vivid emerald leaves stretched up to the sky. He'd never seen anything like it before in his young life. In fact, the magnitude of being not only away from Vastrid but also away from Earth began to sink in and make him feel slightly overwhelmed.

'Hey, I hate to sound soft but is this anyone else's first time away from Earth?' He looked around for support.

Except for Caleb, who had never even left Vastrid, most of the crew just mumbled a brief and disinterested, 'No.' Alex didn't bother to respond.

The younger of the two brothers shook his head. 'Afraid not, buddy! Me and my big bro have bounced around the cosmos several times. Though I must declare the last twenty fours have been stranger than even our strangest excursions.'

'And we've had some very strange excursions indeed,' proclaimed the elder brother with a sleepy smile forming as he spoke.

Big Joe looked around the dense forest of trees and leaves that surrounded them. 'So, what's the plan?'

Alex was quick to jump in. With a snarky grin on his face, he turned to look at the increasingly anxious Kendra Lomax. 'Come on, Lomax, let's hear it.'

'Quiet,' said Lomax, looking deep into the forest in front of her. 'Do you see that?'

'See what?' Callie asked, stepping forward.

'There! In the woods, something thin and pink. Weaving through the trees and moving in our direction.'

'Stop stalling, Lomax! Your plan isn't going anywhere. Now let's get back on-board The Salvator and make tracks to somewhere a lot more sensible,' Alex scoffed.

Caleb was getting nervous. 'I agree. I don't think we should hang around here. There's going to be nothing for us but grief.'

'There! I see it,' hollered Big Joe, noticing a flash of pink.

'Keep your voice down. It could be an enemy,' Callie scolded.

'Or a distraction,' Alex replied, drawing the pistol from his trench coat and scanning the area for threats.

'Either way, I think we should all just say that we had a look here, nothing looked promising and go somewhere with less bleakin' peril,' Caleb fretted through gritted teeth.

'Caleb?' Lomax asked, keeping her focus on the pink streak coming closer.

'Yes?'

'Please shut up.'

The pink came closer and closer until it revealed itself to be a streak of hair attached to a girl in her late teens. Dressed in a collection of old rags, she had a unique look that suggested a long family lineage of mixed ethnic backgrounds. Her skin was light olive, hinting at Parnasian genealogy, yet her eyes were bright green, a tone more commonly associated with those from the Outer Islands. As she approached through the woodland, the crew became aware that she held an array of handmade weapons. She carried an expertly crafted bow with a quiver of artisan arrows on her back. An ornate sword hung from a belt decorated with shurikens, and a hunting knife rested in a sheath beside it.

Accompanied by a sleek, grey fox, the girl came to the forest edge and stopped, looking directly at Lomax across the clearing. Pointing her index finger towards them, she made the Sentry's Blessing circular sign in the air before motioning with her head that they should follow her into the woodlands.

'Why should we trust you?' Lomax hollered.

The girl scowled and put her index finger to her mouth, making a shush gesture, then motioned that there may be people watching them. It was too late, though, as red targeting dots suddenly began to appear on and around the crew of the Salvator.

Callie turned and saw that the majority of targeting dots were peppered across Ryan's chest and limbs. Without waiting another second, Callie yelled 'Get down!' and leapt at Ryan, pulling his body to the ground as a flurry of Tranq darts rained down on the Salvator's crew. Although Ryan had landed safely, Callie hit the floor hard, causing her left arm and hip to collide with the rocks beneath her.

Callie felt a sharp jarring pain and howled in agony, realising immediately that her arm was broken.

Ryan scrambled towards her and helped her to her feet. 'C'mon, let's get out of here.'

With tranq darts flying in their direction, the pair hobbled towards the girl and the fox. The girl had begun to return the sniper's fire, shooting arrows into the trees surrounding them, causing hidden Shadox troopers to tumble to the ground.

The girl glanced sideways as Ryan and Callie passed. 'I'm here to guide you to Professor Sanchez. The Corporation got here first, though. I'll help your crew escape this attack. In the meantime, follow the fox.'

The fox by the girl's feet looked up and motioned at the pair to follow him down a muddy trail behind him.

'Thank you,' Ryan addressed the girl with a humble smile and helped Callie hobble after the fox. The gesture took the girl back; most people who came to Terra Novate were far from polite, especially the males. She felt compelled to glance back at the young man to try and flesh out her initial impression of him, but she knew her duty was to get the crew of this ship to her adopted mother.

With the fox leading the way, Callie and Ryan eventually made it to a smaller clearing tucked away under the shelter of a small thicket. Beams of early morning sunshine blistered through the gaps in the leafy branches, infusing the area with an incandescent sense of calm. The fox nodded at the pair to let them know they should wait there before disappearing back down the muddy path to rejoin the girl.

'Are you ok?' Ryan asked.

Callie grimaced in pain as she leaned her weight against one of the larger trees. 'My arm's not good for anything, and my hip hurts like hell. I think the arm's broken, but the hip might just be bruised.'

'Thanks for saving me back there. I feel like a useless waste of space.' Ryan stared at his shoes. 'I'm not sure I'm really cut out for the uniform.'

'That's nonsense,' Callie said, taking in a deep breath and trying to focus on the conversation to take her mind off the pain. 'You've not even had any full-time Guards experience or training yet. If you don't mind me asking, why did it take you so long to join the guards?'

Something about the question triggered insecurity in Ryan, causing him to answer in an uncharacteristically combative manner. 'Well, I wasn't lucky enough to have wealthy parents to ship me off to the academy as a child – '

Callie cut Ryan off, but not before the heavy feeling of thoughtless words and the upset they can cause dropped like a bomb in the clearing.

'My parents weren't rich. They died when I was four years old. My uncle, who preferred to pay the tuition fees than raise me, sent me to the academy. I was sent there alone and heartbroken. I don't think there's anything *lucky* about what I went through.'

As she was speaking, Callie knew that she was taking her pain out on the wrong person, but the loneliness, bullying, forgotten birthdays and cold cruelty of her earliest years had left barely-healed wounds. The agony from her injuries and the unexpected flippancy of Ryan's comments had torn these wounds wide open.

'I... I'm sorry,' Ryan said, feeling terrible about his careless words. He suddenly felt small and naïve.

'It doesn't matter,' Callie replied, making her way to a nearby tree stump. She sat facing away from Ryan and wiped away the one tear she couldn't hold in, then turned to him with the most status quo-resuming smile she could manage. 'It's ok.'

The tense moment was broken by the return of the fox, who, for reasons only known to himself, seemed surprised the pair were still there.

Ryan then heard a sound he was becoming only too familiar with; the sound of Caleb Scudder moaning.

Caleb emerged in the clearing, along with Lomax and Alex. Together, they were dragging the fallen body of Big Joe, decorated with tranq darts like a pincushion.

'It would have to be old big-bones here that got pummeled with tranqs,' Caleb grumbled as he dropped Joe's left leg to the floor.

'He drew their fire, you moron,' Alex replied. 'Without his sacrifice, we would, at this very moment, probably be unconscious, carted off to certain death. *You* certainly wouldn't have made it back here.'

'I wouldn't be so sure of that,' Caleb snapped. 'I've survived worse than that. It was only yesterday that Ryan and me escaped from a Synistrail, for bleak's sake.'

'I'm not entirely convinced that Synistrails exist. Are you

sure it wasn't just one of your many cousins, pale and unkempt from a lifetime of bootleg grog?' Alex replied.

'It's true,' said Lomax, lowering Joe's shoulders to the floor. 'He and Ryan did escape from a Synistrail last night.'

'And how, may I ask, do you know that?' said Alex.

'I had to save them from it,' Lomax replied.

Alex remained cynical. 'You would say that. Monsters, conspiracies, foul play and things that go bump in the night; all part of the fear-trading fable dreamt up to justify what you do.'

'All The Sentry wanted to do is help,' Lomax answered sharply, growing tired of Navin's attitude.

'Ah, but what about you, Kendra Lomax? What is it that you want?' Alex then turned to Ryan. 'Don't you ever wonder how this new friend of yours is still alive after all her so-called Sentry kin perished?'

'I'll happily answer any questions Ryan wants to ask me,' Lomax replied, steadying her temper.

Ryan didn't know what to think, let alone how to respond. Everything had been such a whirlwind; every decision borne out of a need to survive. Now, far from home and with an opportunity to breathe and think clearly, he knew there was some weight in Alex's provocative barb, and it was a consideration that needed to be taken seriously.

Something else was bothering Ryan, too, distracting his thoughts. 'Sorry to sidetrack, but where are those two brothers who were with us?'

'Who bleakin' knows?' Caleb said, shrugging his shoulders. 'They legged it in the other direction as soon as the darts came flying.'

'I doubt we'll be seeing them again, alive at least. They didn't seem the type to survive in the wild,' Alex said with a warm smile spreading across his face as if he actually relished the thought of their death.

'We shouldn't get too cocky. We don't know for sure we're safe at the moment,' answered Lomax.

A female voice suddenly spoke. 'We should be safe for a while. I managed to drive your attackers away from the woods. I left them scurrying towards the citadel.'

The voice belonged to the girl with the pink streak in her hair, who had made her way back to the clearing via treetop.

'It appeared to be a collection of Shadox troopers along with hired help,' she said, hopping down from the tree.

Alex knelt beside Joe, removed one of the many tranq darts from his torso and examined it. 'I know these darts all too well. They're custom made, and there's only one mercenary out there who uses them. It's Hagen and his crew. They must have struck a deal with the Corporation to have found us so quickly.'

'What makes you so sure it's him? The darts don't look *that* unique,' Caleb scoffed.

'Oh, these darts are unique, alright. I was there when Hagen was taught how to make them.'

'And who taught him? Was it you?' Caleb asked.

Alex kept the answer to that question to himself, saying nothing but allowing himself a bittersweet smile as he thought of his father.

'It's never easy with him, is it?' sighed Caleb, turning to face the girl. 'Ok, so who the bleak are you? I do hope you're a bit more forthcoming than old chuckles here.'

'My name is Tiegan,' the girl replied as she tended to Callie's broken arm. 'I was raised by Professor Sanchez. She sent me to escort you to her laboratory. These woods are full of dangers, both natural and otherwise.'

The grey fox that had led the crew to the clearing nuzzled the top of his head against Tiegan's arm to get her attention. 'Oh yes, this is Zam, my loyal partner in crime. He is a good friend.'

Zam gave everyone a respectful nod before sniffing the air and racing back down the muddy track towards The Salvator.

'Don't worry; he'll be back.' Tiegan finished placing Callie's arm in an emergency splint and then asked, 'I have pain relief if you'd like some?'

'That would be great,' winced Callie. The shock of the break had long since worn off and been replaced by a sharp nagging pain. 'My name's Callie, by the way, and I'm extremely glad you know how to use that bow you're carrying. You've got some skill with that weapon.'

Tiegan smiled. 'There's not much to do around here but practice. At a young age, I realised I had no interest in science, and the only thing to do other than hang around the lab was to become one with the great outdoors. I feel happier out here with the tall trees to climb and the animals to protect. Though, there is darkness in these woods. Hunters, troopers and the type of creatures you wouldn't believe. I had to develop my skills with weapons to defend my home and everyone I hold dear against these threats.'

Lomax was intrigued. 'Why only handmade weapons, if you don't mind me asking? I'm sure Abila has access to guns, grenades and all manner of tech.'

'It's too easy,' Tiegan replied. 'I like to give my enemies a chance.'

Caleb was keen to join in. 'And I really like the pink streak in your hair. I think it's a hot look.'

'It's not there to indulge attraction,' Tiegan replied. 'It's a warning. Like I say, I like to give my enemies a chance.'

'You're very sure of yourself, are you not?' Alex replied, instantly disliking this girl; her appearance, her love of nature and the cocksure boasting of her abilities.

Tiegan began to get a little flustered. This was why she hated other people coming to Terra Novate, with their questions, their critical analysis of her answers and the clumsy threat they presented to the safety she had managed to create for Abila and the animals she cared for. 'Well, I know my abilities have nearly killed people in the past, and I am not arrogant enough to believe I have the right to choose the last moment of a creature's life.'

Caleb hadn't picked up on the subtleties of how the line of questions was beginning to annoy Tiegan. Hoping to draw an end to this escalating tension, he asked, 'So, you're a vegan or something?'

Tiegan glared at Caleb, but before she could respond, Zam appeared back in the clearing, carefully carrying Bandit the Moline in his mouth.

'Oh! Oh! Choo left Bandit Moline behind in the broken case.' Zam gently lowered her to the floor. 'Choo left Bandit Moline to get carried off in that creature's filthy mouth when she is already suffering. Oh!'

Feeling guilty, Ryan raced over to her. 'I'm sorry, Bandit; I promise I'll get you somewhere safe as soon as I can.'

Callie approached the creature and began to stroke her furry head. 'Poor little thing. Ryan will take good care of you until we get you to the Professor.'

Ryan felt reassured that his faux pas earlier hadn't completely destroyed any good feeling Callie might have harboured for him, but his heart sank when she walked back towards Tiegan and the rest of the crew instead of hanging back with him.

'We should probably go,' said Tiegan. 'I have a Medi-Trolley hidden nearby. We can use it to get your unconscious friend back to Professor Sanchez's base.'

Noticing Ryan's face fall as Callie walked away, Caleb gave him a friendly nudge. 'Chin up, mate. It probably wasn't meant to be.'

'But the thing is, Caleb,' Ryan replied, 'I have this feeling that it *is* meant to be, and now I'm worried I've blown it by saying something stupid.'

'Calm down! It ain't over until it's over. In Baker's End, we can always tell for sure whether a femme is interested or not. We use the Horrigan Test.'

'What's that?' Ryan asked.

'If she looks back and smiles, it means she's interested. I think it's from an old Flex-izdat or something.' Caleb and Ryan watched Callie continue to take step after nonchalant step away from the clearing before disappearing into the woodland without so much as a cursory glance back.

'Ooh, unlucky,' said Caleb, trying to hide his amusement at Ryan's romantic shortfall with a consolatory pat on the back.

As Caleb strolled on to catch up with the rest of them, Ryan hung back for a moment, feeling crestfallen.

'Maybe she's more concerned with her broken arm. I can't say I'd blame her. It's not that, though; she's angry with me. I've properly mucked things up without even trying,' Ryan lamented to himself.

He stood silently, trying to compose himself. As he closed his eyes and took in a deep, calming breath, fast flickering glimpses of dreams and visions paraded through his mind. He recalled the ever-elusive spark; a tower emerging from scorched earth. A new image appeared briefly of himself and Callie holding hands, each with their free hands held tightly behind their backs. Callie clutched a large assault rifle, while Ryan held a bo-staff similar to Lomax's. They were surrounded by what Ryan presumed were trees darkened by the night sky although when he looked up, he realised that instead of leaves, the branches were tearing through the sky, revealing the darkest depths of the galaxy. As Ryan attempted to focus on this image, he was pulled from his thoughts by a sudden noise.

'Scuse me! Choo carry me, mister man?' Bandit gurgled. 'I am oh-so-poorly!'

Ryan nodded wearily and bent down to pick the little creature up, gently cradling her in his arms and racing off to catch up with his fellow crew members.

Having made his way back towards the Salvator, Marcus Hagen stood amongst the many arrow-pierced and injured Shadox Troopers Rachel Stone had loaned him. He felt uneasy about failing once more; the Corporation would not be happy to discover this outcome.

He looked over at his loyal crew, trying, without success, to obtain entry to the ship they used to call home. It had been a shock to see how different the ship looked when it had landed, but Hagen had presumed he'd still be able to seize it back.

'Well, chief, we've tried everything, but the Salvator won't open for us. I have no idea what all that light and hocus-pocus did to it, but the ship you knew and loved is gone. Long gone,' said Rico Akabusi.

Hagen rubbed his hand over his stubbled chin. 'Forget the ship, my friend. We have more pressing matters to attend to. If we don't get those bounties, Rachel Stone will bring a world of pain to our doorstep. This little cluster of misfits is gaining ground far too quickly. If they hit the Corporation hard, Stone will be looking for people to make examples of. I don't want us to be the ones they use.'

'You think we'll catch up with them?' Rico asked.

'Have no fear. Scout has taken after them. He's currently on their tail, hiding high in the trees. We'll find them soon enough,' Hagen answered.

This news reassured Rico. Scout Engellis was the best tracker Rico had ever known. He'd wondered where the little fellow had darted off to when the arrows started flying but presumed he'd just fled like the rest of them and was taking his time to return.

'And when we find them, then what? I don't like this tranq dart business with this bunch. Let's hit them hard. That's what we're best at. If they live, they live. If they die, they die.'

'My friend,' Hagen smiled, 'I admire your enthusiasm, but Rachel Stone has requested that they be brought in alive.'

Before Rico could protest, Hagen placed a calming hand on his shoulder. 'However, I partially agree. Lomax is a problem. She's too powerful and too big a fish to risk catching. When we ambush them, I want you and Bad Boy Stevie to take her down fast with rapid live ammo headshots. Stone will be annoyed, naturally, but hopefully still relieved that such a threat has been taken out for good. And besides, she'll have that young one with the light-up eyes to experiment on and whatnot. Then there's Navin. I tire of him and our insufferable feud. I want to ensure it ends today. The rest of them pose no immediate risk; they will be tranq darted and shipped to the Corporation, and hopefully, we will be set free from this escalating nonsense.'

Hagen's cuff-Linq beeped twice, alerting him that a message had been received. After keying in a security code, the speaker on the device crackled. 'Hey there, Mr Hagen, this is Scout reporting. Just as Rachel Stone presumed, they headed straight to Abila Sanchez's lab. I'm on my way back to lead y'all there.'

'What is it, chief?' Rico asked as a huge smile spread across Hagen's face.

'Stone despises Sanchez,' Hagen laughed. 'I have no idea why, but it doesn't matter. Hopefully, she'll be so happy that she can imprison and torture the Professor that the deaths of Lomax and Navin shouldn't throw shade on our achievements. Things are beginning to look up, my friend.'

Chapter Twenty-Eight

THE BLESSED GARDEN

'What *do* I look like?' Callie groaned at the full-length mirror in the reception area of Abila Sanchez' laboratory. She was still wearing the tattered ball gown she'd been trapped in since the debutante ball, only now it was complemented by a plaster cast on her broken arm.

Callie couldn't complain about the treatment she'd received from Professor Sanchez's young assistant Cassandra. Her arm had been placed in a cybernetic split and expertly bound in plaster. She was, however, concerned by the cold welcome they had received from the Professor herself. Callie had been expecting a shower of confidence-boosting counsel from Sanchez. Instead, the Professor had greeted the crew with a curt welcome before dragging Lomax off to a side room to thrash out whatever grievances she appeared to hold.

The muffled row between Lomax and Sanchez continued to rage as Callie looked around the room at the rest of her makeshift teammates. Big Joe was still snoozing under the influence of the many tranq darts he'd been covered with. Caleb Scudder was also fast asleep on an adjacent couch; he was tranq dart free and had no excuse for his slumber other than his idleness. Tiegan sat crossed-legged on the floor, sharpening her weapons with her fox Zam standing guard beside her, while Alex Navin was over in the corner with Professor Sanchez's assistant Cassandra Braham. Callie wondered what Alex was up to; he was bombarding the poor girl with question after question. Callie noticed that the young lab assistant appeared to enjoy the attention. 'I wouldn't get your hopes up, love,' Callie thought to herself, considering Alex's apparent lack of interest in forming even a friendly relationship with anyone, let alone a romantic one.

Callie then glanced over at Ryan sitting alone at a table drinking a milkshake. She felt bad about how she'd snapped at him back in the woods. His flippant comments were still playing on her mind, if truth be told, but she knew they couldn't live in the strange vacuous tension created by a half accepted apology, so she walked over to the table and joined him.

'I'm sorry for going off on one back in the clearing,' Callie offered. 'Can we be friends again?'

'Of course,' Ryan responded, 'though you don't need to apologise, it was my fault. I was a careless idiot. I had no idea about your parents, and even without that, I was wrong to be so judgmental about those who get sent to the academy. It's me that needs to apologise. I feel like a dirtbag about it.'

'As well you should, but if you want to make amends, there is something you can do,' Callie replied.

'Name it,' said Ryan.

'Give me a go on your milkshake.'

Ryan smiled and slid his drink over to her. 'All yours.'

Callie grabbed a straw from a cutlery dispenser at the side of the table and stirred the shake. 'So tell me about your family. Are they alive and well?'

Ryan instantly thought of Jayden and how she'd perished, but he wasn't in the frame of mind to move the conversation in that direction. He paused awkwardly for a moment to push back his grief and then answered. 'Yes, my mother and father are still alive. I've got two sisters, one older and one younger. I don't speak to them as often as I should, but we're relatively close.'

'Relatively!' Callie snorted out the sip of milkshake she was drinking with a laugh. 'You're a funny one, Ryan Tyler. You don't look it, but you really are a funny one.'

Ryan had no idea that he had accidentally slipped a joke into his nervy description of his family, but he was relieved to see Callie smile. 'Thanks, I don't know if I'm funny enough to lose milkshake over, but I'm glad I made you laugh.'

As the pair began to giggle and chat, Tiegan glanced over slyly while maintaining her weapons. She wondered what the relationship was between the two of them. She had been hoping that Ryan might come over and say hello, but that seemed out of the question now. Tiegan wondered why she was even feeling frustrated about it. She had been told of amorous feelings before but had never previously been intrigued enough by anyone to experience them. She feared that this might be the sense of attraction that she'd heard so much about. 'All feelings pass,' she told herself over and over again in a mantra as she closed her eyes and began to meditate.

Meanwhile, Alex continued to question Cassandra as she attempted to analyse Bandit's health.

'So this whole facility is powered by Terra Novate's ecosystem?' Alex asked.

Cassandra was busy trying to complete the tests on the moline but welcomed some male company for a change. 'Yes, Professor Sanchez oversaw the implementation of it. She doesn't like to rely on the Corporation, so, fifteen years ago, she adapted some of Earth's ancient geothermal energy concepts to create our own power. Water flows from the oceans on the Outer Ridge directly under this lab, eventually passing over the magma core of Terra Novate. We then take the heated water and use the steam from it to generate electricity. Once the water we've taken has cooled, we pump it straight back into the system, giving us – '

'Complete self-sufficiency,' Alex answered with keen eyes and a self-satisfied grin.

'Well, I *was* going to say a reliable, reusable energy source, but yes, we are self-sufficient. The system is a work of genius. It's automated to manage water flow, which is collected and deposited every hour, on the hour. Would you like to look at the blueprints?'

Alex nodded once and said, 'I most certainly would.'

As Cassandra brought up blueprints, schematics and data about the laboratory's power source, Professor Abila and Lomax left the side room they had been in and walked towards the centre of the main hub of the laboratory.

'Come on, Abila, you know as well as anyone that the situation with the Corporation had to come to a head at some point.' Lomax exclaimed, throwing her hands up every so often to emphasise specific words.

Abila shook her head and continued walking. 'Not like this. Not on the whim and hunch of a Sentry. It was a whim and a hunch that almost got me killed along with the rest of your brothers and sisters after they put their foot down and told me to follow them.'

Lomax gently put her hands on Abila's shoulders to calm her. 'It's different this time, I swear. Like I've said, we were in the ship when the boy over there summoned The Tide. I had my doubts; I'm not a zealot like the rest of them, but I saw it.

It converted the ship, and it drove away something that was beyond evil. I felt its divine power.'

Abila looked over to Ryan with a measured squint. 'So, is *he* this supposed Child Of Light? The one Calvin was always rambling on about?'

'He could just be.'

'Hmmm,' Abila sighed as she walked towards Bandit. 'More importantly, how are you doing, my little furry friend? It's been a long time since I saw you. I was there during the creation of all of the Molines, so we've undoubtedly met before.' She brushed a soft stroke across the Moline's shivering black pelt. 'Don't worry, as soon as Cassandra has the test results, I'll be able to give you something to help your ailments. Cassandra, how are you getting on with the analysis?'

Cassandra frowned at the holo-screen projector in her hand. 'Well, Professor Sanchez, it's actually a bit odd. None of the blood analysis matches your original notes. There are still traces of the genetic structure you mention, but it appears to have changed overall.'

'That's impossible. Give me those results,' Abila said, swishing the holo-screen towards her. Abila studied the data and furrowed her brow. 'Tell me, Kendra, was this moline aboard the ship when what you claim to be The Tide made contact?'

'Absolutely,' Lomax nodded as Abila hit a switch on the left lens of her spectacles, enabling her to scan the internal biology of Bandit.

She took a sharp intake of breath, removed her glasses and looked Lomax in the eye. 'Ok, Kendra, if you're telling me that this Moline was aboard a ship that came in contact with the Tide, then I'm ready to start believing every single thing you, Calvin and the rest of The Sentry have ever told me. This Moline isn't sick. She's pregnant.'

'WHAAAAA'!?!' cried out Bandit, jolted from her weary state.

'I know, it's quite the shock,' Abila said, nodding in agreement. 'The one thing we could never master was the ability to make artificial life forms that could breed. However, it appears that the Tide has corrected the flaw in this creature's DNA and has not only enabled her to breed but also filled the womb with healthy and, I would imagine, fully breedable Moline babies. Six of them, to be precise.'

'SIX!?! Oh no, no, no. Bandit Moline is going to have six babies?' The creature began to pant while pressing her paw to her dizzying head.

Abila gave Bandit another soft stroke. 'Cassandra can take you downstairs to the medical bay and make you comfortable. I'll send down some meds to help you rest.'

'And Ryan, I suggest you come with me,' Lomax instructed.

Noticing the perplexed look on Callie's face, Ryan gave a quick shrug of the shoulders to her, mouthing, 'I have no idea'.

He slid from his seat and followed Lomax down a long staircase located at the back of the lab. At the bottom of the stairs, they came to a large stone tablet, which Lomax rolled aside to reveal an opening. She turned to Ryan. 'Well, here we are; The Blessed Garden.'

Following Lomax through the opening, Ryan found himself in a cave. He gazed around at the dusty shelves holding mysterious glass jars, strange artefacts and hundreds of books. The walls and floor were covered in plant life, and standing in the centre of the cave was a majestic tree illuminated by a pale beam of glistening light.

'What is this place?' Ryan asked.

'As I said, it's The Blessed Garden. Well, I say *The,* but it's actually *a* Blessed Garden, as there's a couple of them scattered about. Abila's been keeping this one safe for The Sentry for years.'

Ryan tried again. 'So what's *a* Blessed Garden then?'

'When fragments of The Tide manage to navigate the universe and develop on small patches of our planet's surface, they create Blessed Gardens, like this one,' Lomax answered. 'How much do you know about The Tide and what it could do for humanity, Ryan?'

Ryan's heart sank - he wasn't expecting a test. He tried to remember all the drawn-out, boring discussions and commentary he'd half-heard in the news about The Tide, The Sentry and the issues and accusations they threw at the Corporation, but it was all a bit of a jumbled mess.

Ryan gulped and hoped he didn't look too silly with his response. 'Well, I guess you believe that it's a force of great power that can do to Earth what that light did to our ship. Transform it into something better?'

Compared to some of the hyperbolic pontifications that her former Sentry kin had provided over the years, Lomax was taken aback by Ryan's simple yet clear explanation. 'In a nutshell, yes, you're totally correct. The Tide is beyond anything we can conceive; it's a life form of sorts, and according to some of the more powerful Sentries who could communicate with it, this life form wishes to merge with and enhance our planet in order to complete its lifespan.'

Ryan scratched his head, unsure what he had to do with all of this. 'So what's stopping it?'

As she prepared to reveal The Child of Light's origin and legacy, Kendra Lomax stood tall, feeling the weight of the moment. 'A nasty little mutation called The Dark Lethe. You see, the Tide is made up of millions of tiny astral sprites − '

The grandeur of her speech was cut short as Ryan gave Lomax a doubting glance. 'Tiny. Astral. Sprites. Really?'

'Oh, come on!' Lomax cried, throwing her hands into the air. 'After everything you've been through over the past few days, you've got a problem with that? If you'd kindly stop your eye-rolling and let me continue, I'll explain everything. Earthborn bacteria infected half of these sprites, and it split the Tide in two. The Tide of Light, which you've experienced and The Dark Lethe, a deadly cluster of dark sprites determined to devour every last particle of existence. It's the Dark Lethe that powers the Synistrails and the Dark Lethe that powers Maxwell Shadox.'

'Wait, so The Corporation is powered by these dark sprites?' Ryan asked.

Lomax rested her hand on Ryan's shoulder to explain. 'The Corporation was built and powered by dark energy harnessed by an ancient Parnasian tower. A faction of those sprites was sent and bound in the tower by the Dark Lethe to help it take an early foothold on our planet. I'm sure most of the Shadox Corporation staff know very little about the dark energy that powers their achievements. I have it on good authority, though, that the Dark Lethe has consumed whatever is left of Maxwell Shadox and is using the Corporation to help further its destructive cause. There's also Shadox's bodyguard and pupil – a vicious and malevolent man called Nox. I'm not sure what his story is, but I've seen him in action, and his abilities are frightening. The Dark Lethe almost certainly fuels him.'

Ryan was starting to worry about where all of this was going. 'Ok, so what does this have to do with me?'

'Just as The Dark Lethe sent through some of its dark sprites to create the initial Synistrails and to build the power source in Parnasia, the Tide sent some of its own sprites down to Earth to choose and merge with humans, to create champions to fight on its behalf.'

'The Sentry,' Ryan replied.

'Indeed. Unfortunately, following the slaughter of my fellow Sentry brothers and sisters, The Tide was beaten back by the Dark Lethe. For over a decade, it was not strong enough to reach Earth in any capacity. In fact, as the years went on and without anyone to challenge Maxwell Shadox, the Dark Lethe grew stronger and stronger, surrounding the Tide and attempting to destroy it.' Kendra walked to the great tree and gazed up at the light through the branches before turning back to Ryan. 'In desperation, The Tide sent its two youngest sprites down to Earth to create a closely linked duo of human champions to help bring Shadox and, in turn, the Dark Lethe's reign to end. However, elements of the Dark Lethe chased and tormented these two sprites separating them in space and sending them down to Earth, frightened and alone. Once they reached our planet, they desperately searched out comfort and kinship by merging with the two loneliest children they could find. One was a bullied orphan girl – '

'Callie.' Ryan was beginning to see exactly where this was heading.

'And the other was – '

'Me?' Ryan murmured, hoping that this was someone else's fate and his part in it so far had been some sort of terrible mistake.

'Spot on. And due to your little light show onboard The Salvator, the fate of all existence now sits in your cosmically blessed yet trembling hands.'

Ryan readied himself for a grand proclamation and asked, 'You mean, I am the chosen one?'

Kendra laughed. 'No, if anyone's the chosen one, it's her.

On the way down to Earth, your sprite was damaged while escaping the clutches of the Dark Lethe – '

'Of course it was,' Ryan sighed, finding the fact that he had bonded with an impaired sprite to be just his luck.

' – meaning the power it contains is unstable, and it's been leaking. It's why you've had episodes like you did on the Salvator and at Craydon's Corner, and at The Grid.'

Ryan's face fell. 'The Grid? How do you know about that?'

'I was there, Ryan. I had to make sure you didn't pass that test and become encumbered by Vastridian duty.'

'You sabotaged the wall that crushed that guy's leg? So I'd fail? That wasn't your decision to make. I wonder what else you've done through the years to keep me on this course.'

Lomax lowered her tone in an attempt to calm the situation. 'A few things, here and there, but you can take me to task over all that once we've saved life, the universe and everything else.'

'Ok, so what do I have to do? Do you need to train me or something?' Ryan asked through a tired sigh.

'I will guide you and can help develop you as a Sentry; however, all the training you need is already inside you.'

'Is this one of those "Just Believe in Yourself" pep talks? I've had plenty of those through the years, and to be honest, they just make me feel more anxious.'

Lomax walked towards the tree in the centre of the cave and broke off a branch. She rolled it vigorously between the palms of her hands, and as she did so, her eyes started to glow. Slowly, the branch began to radiate light and transform into a bo-staff.

'I'm sure your mind wanders, Ryan. Vivid images and feelings, more lucid than dreams and nightmares? More tangible than fantasy or fear? These internal distractions, flashes of inspiration, moments of madness – they have been and will continue to be your training. You've been blessed, Ryan Tyler. You have a fragment of something otherworldly flowing through you, something that is from a different sphere of any human knowledge or wisdom, and it has navigated through time and space to bond with you. Let the beat of your heart drown out the noisy conditioning in your brain. All the training you need is already within.'

Ryan was shocked. 'So I'm ready now? I can use this thing?'

'All you need to do is raise this bo-staff and give yourself to the Tide. The Tide will hear you and unleash your full potential.' Lomax grew sombre. 'I have to warn you, though. To become a member of The Sentry is quite an undertaking. As righteous and honourable as the intentions of The Tide are, the life of the Sentry is one of pain and sacrifice. You will hear every scream, every call for help, and it will hurt your heart until you heed that call. Your life will likely end in sacrifice. Even if you survive going to war against the Shadox Corporation and even if you manage to locate the Dark Lethe's power source in Parnasia, its destruction will take everything you have.'

Ryan couldn't quite believe the small print of Lomax's pep talk. 'So I'll die if I agree to this?'

'Do you think the Corporation will let you live, either way? How long do you think the ones you love will survive? At least if you offer yourself to The Tide, you can fight back and control how your story ends. Who knows, you might get lucky and survive all of the madness that's ahead of us. I'm trying to be straight with you from the start and offer you a choice. Be thankful – when I was in your shoes, such courtesy wasn't extended to me.'

'Well, what about you and Callie?' Ryan protested. 'Why's it up to me to destroy this power source in Parnasia? Or do we all go there, save the universe and die?'

'If I'm still alive by the time we find the tower in Parnasia,

I will gladly share the burden of our fate. However, despite decades of searching, the tower hasn't been found, and I am getting older. It may take decades more to find the damn thing, and I may not make it. Then it will be all up to you.'

'What about Callie?' asked Ryan, out of a sense of protectiveness rather than a wish to deflect responsibility.

'She can never know,' Lomax shook her head. 'She hosts the undamaged sprite and must remain unknown and undetected by Shadox. Should the time come when The Dark Lethe is close to defeat and at its most desperately destructive, only her power will guide the Tide to us. You are the one the Corporation is looking for, so you must act as her decoy. You must live as much of a separate life from that girl as possible, do you understand?'

Ryan felt an unexpected blow to his heart, 'But I – '

' – have feelings for her?' Lomax finished Ryan's sentence. 'Each association the two of you share risks the fate of everything in existence. Believe it or not, I know how strong young love is, and this is why I'm giving you all the facts before you sign up. I guess what I'm asking is, are you willing to sacrifice your chance of a normal life to help ensure everyone else's?'

Ryan was still desperately looking for another way to work through the oncoming conflict. 'But why must I blindly give myself to this so-called Tide. What about the Royal Guard? Surely they can defeat The Corporation and that tower. Callie and I could be happy together. We don't need to be dragged into all of this.'

'But you do! It would take a long and bloody war for the Royal Guard to defeat the Corporation. The cost to civilian life would be horrific. Beyond any gift The Tide may bestow on you is the power you already carry. The greatest power of all: hope.'

'I'm not convinced. I'm sorry,' Ryan said, turning to walk away.

Lomax grabbed his arm and handed Ryan the bo-staff she had created for him, 'Hey, before you go flouncing off, take this. You never know; you might have no choice but to use it. There's a secret exit through that tunnel if you want to go and clear your head. It'll lead you to the top of a hill about half a mile away from here.'

'Thanks,' said Ryan, as he made his way out of the tunnel. As soon as Ryan had left, tears began to well up in Lomax's eyes. She slumped to the floor, buried her face in the palm of her hands and wept. She was hoping for a better reaction than that; she needed Ryan to be stronger and more coura- geous – not only to help defeat the Dark Lethe but also for other, more selfish, hidden reasons. If Ryan was unwilling to become the apprentice she needed, it mattered not whether the universe was saved. To Lomax, all seemed hopeless. Picking herself up from the floor, she walked to the edge of one of the bookcases, reached behind it and pulled out a large bottle of bootlegged ghost.

Clutching the bottle with shaking hands, she made her way to the same secret exit. Abila was well aware of Kendra's past and wouldn't hesitate to cast her out if she suspected a relapse. Kendra began the long walk to find somewhere quiet to drown out the disappointment.

Back in the laboratory, Professor Sanchez noticed something on one of her security camera feeds. Looking closer, she saw Lomax strolling off to one of the high hills to the north of her complex.

'Where is she going now?' Abila asked out loud to no one in particular. Suddenly, the screen and all of the other security monitors began to flicker and lose signal.

Abila looked around at everyone in her lab. 'Guys. This doesn't look good.'

Before anyone could speak, a huge explosion tore through the front of the lab, and the combined forces of Marcus Hagen's team and a squadron of Shadox troopers came marching through, firing tranq darts. Callie and Zam were hit before they could even stand up from the seats they were sitting on. Yet more darts piled into the already unconscious Big Joe while the noise of the attack woke Caleb, who managed a quick, 'What the bleak?' before a shot to his arm took him out cold. Tiegan vaulted over the oncoming fire to grab Abila and forced both of them behind a large metallic storage cabinet to take cover.

Following Hagen's order, Rico and Bad Boy Stevie looked around for Lomax and Alex. Seizing the opportunity, Alex fired off a couple of ricocheting shots from his handgun and darted down a service tunnel.

'After him! Live ammo. I want Navin dead,' Hagen ordered as he and his team gave chase.

With their rifles raised, the remaining Shadox troops closed in on the cabinet protecting Abila and Tiegan.

'Come out with your hands up,' ordered the unit leader.

Abila slowly stood up, pushing her glasses back up her nose with her left hand before raising them both. 'What's all this about? You have no right to barge in here and – '

'Actually, we do,' beamed Rachel Stone, emerging through the hole in the wall brandishing an elaborate walking cane. 'It would seem you've been harbouring fugitives.'

Rachel walked over to Abila's desk and picked up a glass beaker full of a mysterious jade coloured liquid.

'Please be careful with that,' Abila said, 'it's a valuable piece of innovative research. It's a very delicate formula.'

'Really?' smirked Rachel as she began to pour the formula onto the floor slowly. 'We've kept tabs on your so-called innovations here, and I have to say your findings are years behind those of Doctor Davron and his team at the Shadox labs.'

With a spring in her step, Rachel began to trot around the laboratory, smashing various glass jars, test tubes, and samples with her cane.

'Please stop,' cried Abila, 'that's my life's work. It's the basis of long-standing samples. It's – '

' – all worthless,' spat Rachel, before darting forwards and striking Abila hard in the face with her cane.

With a split lip, Abila fell to the floor. Rachel crouched down closely beside her and murmured, 'You're a traitor, a criminal and a failure of a scientist,' before hocking up a warm combination of saliva and phlegm into the scientist's face.

Suddenly, four shurikens parted the air and embedded themselves in the shoulders of the front row of troopers surrounding the filing cabinet.

Rachel looked up to see Tiegan leaping towards her over the falling guards. The next thing Rachel was aware of was a blunt strike to her nose, followed by the sound of cartilage smashing and the squelching damp warmth of blood rushing down her face.

Rachel howled and stumbled back, clutching the tattered remains of her nose. Her vision was blurred from the impact, but she could make out the image of a crimson-stained fist before feeling another strike to her head followed by a swift, winding kick to her chest.

'Seize her!' Rachel gasped in agony on the floor as Shadox troopers swarmed a still-kicking and punching Tiegan to the floor.

'Keep her secure but don't harm her,' Rachel wheezed as she slowly pulled herself to her feet. 'I want her to be in perfect health for what I have planned. Round up every traitor in this room and take them to the Citadel. And that fox. I want them all. If the other scouting parties don't find

Lomax and her apprentice, then maybe this sorry lot will act as bait. They will all pay for their insubordination.'

Rachel began to limp away, aided by two troopers. 'Oh, and make sure this useless place is burnt to a cinder before you leave. Now that the trip has been sprung, there's nothing of value here.'

Up on a hill named Pouk Rise, Ryan sat and pondered his destiny. Lomax's suggestion that Ryan should become a martyr wasn't an enticing career path for the nineteen-year-old who had been hoping he'd find himself living a comfortable and carefree existence at some point. But what else could he do? Walk back down to the lab and tell everyone that he'd rather take his and everyone else's chances that things would probably work out for the best and ask to be taken home? He wondered what Callie would make of that. Ryan tried to dress it up in his mind as the most sensible option, but his heart spoke louder, exposing his doubt as cowardice. He looked down at the bo-staff Lomax had created for him.

'Why has all this happened to me?' he sighed to himself. 'I'm the worst person that sprite could have chosen.'

A strange smell began to rise and soon engulfed Ryan's nostrils; it was a heady mix of smoke and chemicals. Following the trail of fumes, Ryan looked down to see billowing flames tearing through the roof of Professor Sanchez's laboratory and a neat succession of Shadox Armored Carriers driving away from the scene, followed by a prisoner transport vehicle. Realising that his new friends had likely been apprehended, he grabbed the bo-staff and slid down the hill in the direction the Shadox vehicles were heading.

At the bottom of the hill, Ryan hit a trap wire stretched

between two trees, causing him to tumble head over heels into a heap. Leaping out from the trees, a squad of Shadox troops aimed their rifles directly into his face.

'Don't shoot,' said Ryan, letting go of his bo-staff to hold up his hands.

With Ryan secured, the squadron leader, Captain Bradlock, broke away from his men and called the capture in. 'Bradlock, sir. Happy to report we've seized the fugitive. Just like you hoped, he's got a bo-staff with him. We'll make sure he has it for your meeting.'

Two squadron members dragged Ryan to his feet and, with their rifles pressed hard into his back, began to march him towards a large citadel about half a mile in the distance, the rest of the squadron following behind.

Eventually, they came to a muddy bank with a damp and musty tin tunnel built into it.

'In you go, son,' ordered Bradlock, motioning towards the tunnel with his rifle. 'Oh, and don't forget your stick.'

Bradlock handed Ryan his bo-staff and jabbed him with the barrel of his rifle, forcing Ryan to crawl into the mouth of the unwelcoming tunnel.

Once Ryan had pushed himself through the small space, he found himself in a corridor dimly lit by a scant array of candles. An eerie humming noise carried faintly in the air as Ryan edged towards an open door ahead.

Walking through the doorway, Ryan saw a large wooden dining table adorned with elegant silverware, candlelight illuminating the otherwise empty room. The soft hum that had been barely audible began to grow louder as Ryan looked around for any sign of danger or rescue. His instincts were telling him that moving figures surrounded the table, but he couldn't hear any breathing or see even the slightest movement weaving its way through the dark.

Suddenly, he heard the sound of slow, measured footsteps,

each one layered with the creak of tight leather shoes. Ryan's pulse began to race as he gripped his bo-staff tight, terrified about what may emerge from the dark edge of the room.

A tall, confident figure who seemed familiar to Ryan walked into the light and stood at the head of the table. 'So, at last we meet. You, the Child of Light, and me? Hmmm, well, I suppose I'm the Bastard of Darkness. However, you can call me Mr Nox. Please, take a seat. We have so much to discuss.'

Chapter Twenty-Nine

FEAST

Nox's glare burned into Ryan. Despite the palpable menace of the situation, Ryan felt that fleeing the scene would be more dangerous than waiting to hear whatever the infamous Mr. Nox had to say to him.

Once again, Ryan sensed figures other than Nox and himself in the room, swaying slowly in the darkness around him. Subtle sounds of skin against fabric, the creaking of old bones and soft wheezing filled Ryan's ears and shook his heart. Yet despite all of this, Ryan nodded at Nox. 'Ok then,' he said as he pulled out the chair opposite Nox and sat down, certain that something terrible was about to occur.

'Excellent,' Nox beamed. 'I'm delighted you've decided to accept my invitation and that you and I can talk this situation through. A lot of unexpected things have happened over the past forty-eight hours. It's all got a bit out of hand. Don'tyou-think things have got a bit out of hand?'

Ryan did indeed feel that things had got *more* than a bit out of hand, but he had no idea how to answer the question. Was this chat to be a trick or a treaty? He decided to play it as cool as he possibly could and mumbled, 'I suppose you could say they have.'

'Indeed,' Nox agreed, pulling his own chair out and taking a seat. 'I'm sure by the end of our meeting today, we will have put an end to the chaos that has emerged over the past couple of days. But first, let's eat! You must be starving. I believe you've been on the run ever since the unfortunate events at the debutante ball.'

Nox was correct in his assumption. Despite managing to grab some snacks and a milkshake along the way, Ryan hadn't eaten anything substantial since his time stuck on Table 13.

He threw a nod towards Nox. 'You're not wrong.'

'Let's get you adequately fed then,' Nox said, clapping his hands and summoning a squad of apprehensive troopers-turned-waiters to race from the darkness behind him and begin to fill the table with dishes containing an array of hot, aromatic food. The stand-in waiters quickly finished laying the table and looked anxiously over to Nox, who gave them permission to leave with a wave.

'Well then, what are you waiting for? Tuck in,' declared Nox, gesturing across the table to highlight the full range of deliciousness he'd provided.

Ryan scooped a portion of golden roasted potatoes, peas, and carrots onto his plate, as well as four helpings of carved roast chicken breast. He reached across the table and took a jug of rich, thick gravy and poured generously. The food smelled so good. Almost too good. In fact, this whole deal seemed far too easy. Even before the massacre at the Ball, nothing was ever this easy. Ryan glanced across at Nox and noticed that despite his encouragement, he was taking no interest in the food on the table.

Nox raised an eyebrow. 'Is something wrong?'

Ryan glanced down at his food and gave a doubtful look back to Nox.

'Are youseriouslyworried that it may be poisoned? You have reservations about eating a meal provided by someone you've been told is your enemy? Fair enough, I suppose, though I am slightly insulted that you'd presume I wouldn't have the courage and ability to murder you myself. If I did want you dead – and at this stage, I'm not saying that I don't – and*if*I lacked the conviction to do it myself, I would have had my troops put a bullet in the back of your head as they led you to the Citadel,' said Nox. 'So eat without fear, Child of Light. Should a time come for me to kill you, I will be proudly forthright about it. But before such unpleasantness becomes even a possibility, I feel wc should see where we both stand. Man to man, away from the posturing and dogma of indoctrination. For this, I need you to be comfortable and alert. So relax and eat.'

None of this made Ryan feel any more at ease as the creaking and slow shuffling in the darkness on either side of him continued. He sliced into the roasted chicken, but it was out of politeness rather than excitement; any appetite Ryan Tyler may have had was fading with each uneasy second that passed.

From a cell deep within the same Citadel, Captain Dunnell looked down at Prince Alistair slumped on the floor and lost in a fog of desolation. The young monarch had also lost his appetite.

'You should eat,' urged the Captain, motioning towards a tray of cold scraps on the floor beside him.

'Not in the mood,' Alistair snarled.

Dunnell knew that even if the new figurehead of Vastrid had been in good spirits, the sloppy grub on the plate would be a hard sell. Instead, he attempted some hard truths. 'Your highness, starving yourself to death will neither bring your father back nor get us out of here.'

Alistair grunted and stared at the floor. 'Are you worried for my health, or are you worried for your own, Captain?'

'My concern is for Vastrid – for the Kingdom your Father built, and for your people.'

'My people? I have no right to declare myself their King. I had one chance to protect them, and I failed,' the prince snapped. 'As for Vastrid, who knows what's left of it or if we can take it back.'

Dunnell leant towards the Prince and spoke in hushed tones. 'Your Father believed in you. From what I understand, he gave you guidance on how to proceed should an incident like this occur.'

Alistair knew what Dunnell was referring to – the classified data and contingency plans hidden by his father. Alistair was sure that his father would have left ample provision to enable him to fight back against the Corporation. However, the system wasback in Vastrid, and at this point in time and space, that seemed so very far away.

Alistair couldn't find the words to explain his feeling of hopelessness. With a weary sigh, he signalled that the conversation was over. The Captain looked sadly at the prince and prayed that there was someone else on Terra Novate with the spirit to fight back against the Corporation.

Tiegan was bound in handcuffs and restrained by four troopers. As she was frog-marched through the citadel, she had kept a mental note of her location, mapping out her surroundings to develop a strategy that would enable her to rescue Professor Sanchez and the crew of the Salvatore. After a brief time in a holding cell, she had been moved to what appeared to be a laboratory or testing room, complete with Corporation scientists engrossed in their work.

Two of the troopers pressed the barrel of their rifles against her head while another unlocked her handcuffs. A large monitor was positioned directly in front of her, showing what appeared to be a live security camera feed of a long, dark tunnel. The feed was grainy and punctuated by static, and little more than a ladder leading up to a bolted hatch was visible in the dim glow of the emergency lights.

With the guns still pointing at her head, Tiegan turned slowly to follow the sound of Rachel Stone's high heels entering the room. A bandage fixed by two surgical plasters covered the bloodied remains of the nose Tiegan had shattered earlier.

'So it turns out that you're Tiegan,' Rachel said. 'I had no idea who you were when you assaulted me earlier, but now that I think about it, I remember you from when you were a child. Plain and difficult, often poorly, if I'm not mistaken. I'm surprised you've lasted this long.'

'You don't know what you're talking about. You've never met me before,' Tiegan spat. Her anger at the attack on Professor Sanchez's lab, her home, was only increasing with time.

'Oh, believe me, I have.' Rachel looked her captive up and down before staring right into her eyes. 'Looking at how you've grown, it must have been at least ten years ago, possibly even fifteen. You were little more than a weeping orphan back then, clinging to Sanchez's ankles like a pitiful afterthought. She's become like a mother to you, hasn't she? And this is why she's going to die. You may have saved her from a beating earlier, but you've condemned her to something far, far worse.'

'If you murder her, I swear on everything I hold true that you'll pay dearly.' Tiegan refused to break eye contact.

'Oh no, you misunderstand. It shan't be by my hand that Sanchez will die,' Rachel smiled, moving in closer and gently brushing Tiegan's cheek. 'It will be by yours.'

Rachel's declaration and the cruel smile that spread across her face shook Tiegan, and the steady confidence she once held in abundance drained, leaving her mouth dry and turning her usual poker face into a flustered series of anxious glances.

Rachel giggled softly and pointed to the monitor in front of Tiegan's face. 'Take a look here. This is one of the old service tunnels we used when we first built the Citadel. Of course, when the building work was complete, we could have sealed them up, but The Corporation has always thrived on opportunity. Being the busy little thing you are, you may be aware that several experiments have occurred here over the past few years.'

'The faded ones? You create them here?'

'On Vastrid, they are known as Synistrails. And no, we didn't create them. I'm not entirely sure who or what did. However, I do have a need to control them. The sap in their foul claws has the power to consume and remodel the genetic structure of a victim. Each kill, or even successful flesh wound, is another Synistrail roaming the universe, anxious to release the dark tension in their fingertips. It's an army that builds itself.' Rachel paused to study Tiegan's face, then moved in close beside her, feigning an air of camaraderie. 'The problem is that these creatures operate purely to fulfil their insatiable kill-create urges. They're not ones to follow orders or indeed see me as anything other than another bag of flesh to scratch and claw at, so certain experimentation has been carried out on these creatures. It's been a long and largely unsuccessful process; we've gone through hundreds of the creatures, trying all manner of tests, chemicals and devices on them. We've had the most success with those that have only been dead for a short time. You see, after a while, they begin to wither, and we find they're too removed from humanity to respond to any stimulus. Those we have no more use for we dump in the tunnel you see on the screen. And speaking of which – '

With a twirl and a pointed finger, Rachel guided Tiegan's eyes towards the monitor where she saw a beaten and battered Abila Sanchez being thrown through the hatch at the top of the tunnel, down to the damp floor below.

Abila looked up to see the only remaining daylight ebb away as the hatch was closed behind her. Limping back onto her feet, lost and confused in the darkness, she began to panic before opening her mouth wide and screaming out for help. The monitor remained silent.

'Are the cameras down there visual-only?' Rachel asked her guards, who nodded affirmatively. 'Really? Oh, that's a shame. Never mind, I'm sure we will all get the gist.'

Tiegan watched in horror as her mentor and friend scrambled desperately, attempting to feel her way back to the hatch ladder.

'So here's where it gets interesting, my dear,' Rachel cooed, placing her hand on Tiegan's shoulder. 'Your beloved Professor Sanchez is mere moments away from her death. That is an inescapable fate for her, I'm afraid. How she dies is up to you.'

'I refuse to play whatever sick game you've got in mind,' Tiegan snarled.

'Oh, but you will. And enthusiastically so, to boot,' Rachel teased, handing Tiegan a box with a large red button on the top and a long lead running all the way back to the control panel. 'The tunnels are lined with intense radiation grills. One quick blast, and they'll disintegrate anything loitering about down there. A necessary precaution, should our old experiments give us cause for concern. I'm giving you the option of quickly and cleanly ending your friend's life before the *faded ones*, as you call them, find her and make a long and vicious ordeal of her death. It's very dark down there; they'll barely be able to see what they're doing. And besides that, they're hungry for a kill. They'll appreciate her warm, bloodied torso and savour each slice and bite.'

Tiegan looked back towards the monitor, its hum and occasional feedback acting as a surrogate soundtrack for Professor Abila's screams. An outstretched hand flickered into view, emerging from the darkness behind her, its claws extending as the tall, gaunt Synistrail it was attached to moved towards her. A female synistrail, covered from head to toe in scars and stitches, staggered into view, stopping for a moment to judder and twitch before turning her half-shaved head towards Abila and making her way towards her intended prey.

Clawing and scratching through the hungry itch of years lost in darkness, the two creatures edged closer to the Professor. The eagerness and desperation of their excited hissing may have been inaudible to Tiegan but was captured on screen by their frantic jaw movements and twitching expressions.

As the creatures closed in around her, the Professor appeared to slip to the floor once more and start fiddling with the lenses of her glasses. A dozen more Synistrails moved in from the darkness with their claws extended and their teeth gnashing at the thought of fresh meat. It was a hopeless situation. With a deep sense of dread and regret held tightly in a breath that consumed her chest, her throat and her mouth, Tiegan knew what she had to do.

'I'm sorry, Abila,' she whispered and pressed down hard and fast on the button before she could cower out of doing so. With tears welling in her eyes, Tiegan looked at the screen only to find nothing had happened. Her mentor was still there scrambling about on the floor with her fingers tapping away at her glasses and the ever-increasing number of foul and famished synistrails closing in on her.

Tiegan jabbed at the button again, yet still nothing. For someone so secure and confident, the feeling of compromise and the lack of control shook Tiegan. She looked at Rachel for help.

'Oh! I am sorry,' Rachel smirked, holding up the box's cable. 'I completely forgot to plug it in. Can one of you lab types radiate that section of the tunnel immediately? I don't want that wretched woman coming back.'

One of the scientists at a workstation to the right of Tiegan glanced over at Rachel and gave a nod. Tiegan swung her head around to look at the monitor just in time to see Abila once more before a brief bright light removed her and the creatures. Despite her best efforts to remain emotionless, a single stream of tears escaped Tiegan's eyes as she whispered a soft, 'Goodbye, my friend.'

Rachel's ears picked up on it and began to titter. 'I had no idea that this would be so amusing. "Goodbye, my friend?" Priceless.'

Tiegan fixed her gaze on Rachel. 'I will make you pay for this.'

'It's funny; I've been told that by so many people over the years, but guess what, pinkie?' Rachel ran her fingers through Tiegan's pink lock of hair. 'My account remains firmly in the black. Guards, take this wood-rat away to a cell until I have some more free time to toy with her.'

'Excuse me, ma'am, but all the cells are full,' replied one of the Troopers.

Rachel thought for a moment, pondering which of the prisoners provided the least threat. 'Hmmm? OK, put her in with that thief from Baker's End.'

Tiegan wanted to fight back, but she knew now wasn't the time; her emotions were running far too high, and she was outnumbered. As the guards led her away from the control room, Tiegan took one sad look back at the flickering monitor and the empty section of tunnel on the screen. She couldn't help but wonder how much of the life she'd known on Terra Novate was left intact. Abila was gone, and Tiegan knew she had to come to terms with it fast if she was to survive.

Barely conscious, Cassandra Braham lay in the rubble of what had once been Professor Sanchez's lab.

Her torso was trapped between one of the supporting walls from the floor above and a large overturned piece of particle manipulator machinery that had toppled over when the Corporation had detonated their charges. She was confused about what had happened and where she was, but she was aware of a faint, persistent tapping on her cheek.

Her eyelids felt heavy as she attempted to see what was landing on her face. Her vision was blurred, and her body felt numb, so she followed the urge to simply close her eyes again and drift back to the cool, calm darkness.

In this darkness, she began to float without thought or concern for another half minute before she felt further tapping on her face. Only this time, it was harder and faster, escalating in intensity until she had no option but to push open her eyes and confront its source.

'Scuse me,' gargled a little voice as Cassandra's eyes focused on the furry black pelt and bright yellow eyes of the moline, standing on her chest and tapping furiously on her cheek. 'I said 'scuse me. Choo get up now, lady!'

Cassandra looked at the debris blocking her in. 'That might not be so simple, I'm afraid.'

'Sorry lady, but choo must try! Bandit moline is hungee! Choo go and find Bandit something to eat, chess?'

Cassandra looked towards the area where a kitchen once stood and observed little more than some mangled equipment and clutch of small fires amongst the dust and shards of concrete. 'I think that may be an impossibility, Bandit.'

'WHAT? But I am with child,' Bandit hollered in shock, rubbing her tummy. 'Choo said choo would look after me because I am with child. Choo get me some food somehow then, chess?'

It hurt too much to explain why she couldn't just get the creature some food, so Cassandra nodded firstly towards the debris she was stuck in and then the ragged remains of what used to be the kitchen.

As the penny finally dropped, Bandit could offer little more than an embarrassed, 'Oh!'

Bandit scratched her fuzzy bonce for a while as she thought. 'Wait a minute! Bandit knows where there is lots of food! Choo come with me to get it?'

'Well, I'm a bit stuck at the moment, but I do have an idea,' Cassandra replied, as she glanced over towards a protective case lying on the other side of the room. If she could instruct the moline to bring her some of the medical enhancement prototypes stored inside it, maybe she could free herself from the rubble. The moline, still somehow unaware that they were trapped in a bombsite, stared expectantly at Cassandra.

In a cell, deep within the Corporation's citadel, Callie Haywood was hammering on the door, also demanding to be fed.

'Keep it down in there, will you?' hollered a voice behind the door. Callie smirked to herself - her plan was already working.

The voice behind the door belonged to a Corporation

trooper assigned to guard her cell. He had kept a stony silence for the first twenty minutes or so of Callie's noisy requests, but her incessant nagging and thumping had driven him to shout back.

'I need some food,' bellowed Callie. 'By law, you have to keep your prisoners fed and healthy. I know my rights.'

'Listen, sweetheart, in case you ain't noticed, all those agreements between my boss and yours went up in smoke like The Great Hall. Now pipe down before I decide to come in there and take further and nastier liberties with your rights.'

Callie pressed her ear to the door and heard a heavy sigh. She knew it was time to strike. She took several steps back before dashing towards the door and pounding a hard side-kick into it.

'Food! Food! Food!' She bellowed over and over again until the guard finally snapped and, using the external control panel, lowered the cast iron observation shutters on both sides of the door to scold her face to face.

While the guard barked threats and contempt at Callie, she focused her attention elsewhere, studying the steel mesh in the observation section of the door that acted as an obstruction when the shutters were open.

It was all she needed to know and the chance she needed to take. She clenched her fist and hoped for the best. The good news was she knew she could escape. The bad news was that it was going to hurt – a lot.

For all the pros and cons of Callie's plan, at least she had one. Ryan, conversely, was still sitting at a table, dining with Mr Nox. As he finished the food on his plate and mopped the side of his mouth with a napkin, Mr Nox gave Ryan a nod and a smile as if to elicit a positive review of the food.

'Thanks,' Ryan swallowed hard. 'It was delicious.'

It had been a strange dining experience for Ryan. While he had eaten, Nox hadn't touched a single crumb of food and remained seated opposite Ryan, offering little more than an encouraging smile should their eyes meet. Making matters worse, the disconcerting ambience of what may or may not have been lurking in the un-lit parts of the room seemed to be growing.

'I'm glad you enjoyed the food. Look! You're still alive,' Nox beamed, 'although something seems to be bothering you.'

Ryan pondered for a moment how best to sum up his concerns without appearing confrontational. 'It's just, well – it's a bit dark in here. I can't see much further than this table.'

'Too dark? I must apologise; over the years, I suppose I've become acclimatised to lower light levels. Of course, as you are The Child Of Light, it's only right and correct that I illuminate this chamber in your honour.'

Nox tapped his Cuff-Linq, and scattered lights around the outer edge of the chamber suddenly lit up, revealing six tall figures dressed in long dark robes standing on the left and the right sides of the table, just a few feet from the chairs. Their heads were bowed down with decorated white china masks covering their faces.

'What the heck are they?' Ryan cried. He grabbed his bo staff while pushing out his chair and preparing to either run or fight for his life.

Nox motioned with hands that Ryan should calm down. 'Relax, they're just mannequins. Clothes horses dressed in the garments and legacy of my homeland.'

The room was smaller than Ryan had imagined. As he regained his composure and sat back at the table, he also observed a large number of exotic relics housed in the display cabinets that lined the chamber's walls. Ryan had never seen anything like them in any of the library records.

'Your homeland? You mean you're not of Parnassian descent?' Ryan asked.

'No.' Nox replied. The word came out short and cold, yet his face held its warm, welcoming expression.

'Oh sorry, I just presumed,' Ryan apologised quickly, afraid he'd caused offence.

'My name, Udo Nox. It does sound somewhat Parnassian, but that's not my birth name. I don't know and will likely never know what my original name is. Professor Shadox found me when I was a young child, two, maybe three years old. He found me covered in other peoples' blood, alone in a village he'd massacred.'

'He felt guilty?' Ryan leaned forward, keen to hear the whole tale.

'No. I don't think that's it. Apparently, what captured Shadox's interest was the fact I was smiling.' Nox reached across the table and poured himself a glass of dark red wine. 'Of course, he's never told me any of this. I managed to glean that nugget of information from a drunken former guard. It's taken me most of my life to piece together who I may or indeed may not be. An approximation of my true lineage surrounds you in this room.'

Ryan took a long arcing look around Nox's chamber, more out of politeness than any real interest in the various pieces of attire and artwork on display. Unsure of what to say next and fearing a long lecture about each piece, Ryan nodded keenly and went back to the subject of Nox's name. 'So where did you get the name Udo Nox from then, if you don't mind me asking?'

'Professor Shadox decided to name me Udo Nox,' he explained. 'The name always amused him. Udo was someone he despised, and Nox was the name of a boat his father had when he was young. As my reputation grew, he'd often tell me how much it pleased him that those two names were now associated with bloodshed. I've never really understood why it makes him so happy, but the Professor is a man with,' Nox paused and gave a slight shrug, 'certain quirks.'

'So Professor Shadox is still alive then?'

'Oh yes, very much so. And he's not too keen about your sudden emergence in our affairs,' Nox replied.

Ryan sank into his chair. 'Well, I didn't have much choice in the matter.'

'No. No, you didn't, did you? At least up to this point. This is where I offer you that choice,' Nox advised, taking a sip of wine and then standing to address Ryan.

'I'm sure your new friend Kendra Lomax has been filling your head with all kinds of nonsense about light and dark, good and evil, them and us. And while there may be some harsh truths in what she's telling you, I would wager that it's not the full picture. As you've discovered for yourself, the universe is full of strange, unique, wonderful and terrifying things. Things most people would prefer not to deal with. Yes, it's true that the Corporation harvests energy from a form of dark matter – the very substance I believe you experienced when you hijacked that prison ship. Yes, it's true that Synistrails exist and were mutated from unprocessed elements from the very same dark matter. However, we are doing our best to control these creatures. Without the infrastructure of the Corporation intervening, the whole of planet Earth and the colonies above it would be swarmed with Synistrails by now. And yes, we were the real power behind King William's throne. When he decided to instigate a coup against us, we hit back first. At the Ball, I would imagine you were there, we arrived not to terrorise Vastrid but to keep it free from the hands of a potential tyrant. Since the day you were born, the Corporation has, without interference and without tyranny, kept you safe and comfortable. Think, and I mean, really think about your life – has it been *that* hard under our supervision? Have you ever gone days without a meal? Has every home you've lived in had clean running water? Have subsections of the community attempted to turf you out of your dwellings and take your home as their own? The answer, I'm sure, is no. The world was a sadder and more desperate place before we came along. Sometimes the Corporation may rule with an iron fist, but that's only to ensure the stability and order for regular people like you, your friends and your family.'

Ryan bristled at the mention of his family. He knew he was out of his depth, on a strange colony far from home, being swarmed by the words of an intimidating man he'd previously only ever seen on newscasts.

'Do you,' there was a hefty pause before Nox continued, 'worry about your family? Do they know about your gifts? Would you prefer they remained unassociated?'

'Of course I would,' Ryan snapped back. 'All I know is I got born, I got shoved into some damn awful school, and since then, I've felt obliged to keep trying to forge some sort of career out of my limited range of skills. I try to do the sensible thing – I join the Royal Guards, and then all of this Child of Light nonsense falls into my lap. I didn't ask for any of this pressure. All I wanted was a nice, comfortable life. With a house and a girlfriend and maybe someday some children.'

'Of course you do, and there's nothing wrong with that. That's more your level of living, isn't it? I must declare when I first heard talk of the Child of Light revealing his power aboard that bounty ship, I was concerned. But it appears you're not a threat, and I personally see no reason not to let you go on your way and secure the peaceful life you so clearly crave.'

Ryan breathed a sigh of relief that Nox was letting him go, despite a twinge of disappointment at being dismissed so easily as a non-threat. Ryan pondered for a moment how quickly Nox had chosen to rule out his abilities, not only the ones generated from the Tide but also the skills and wisdom that he had obtained making his way through working-class Vastridian life.

Before the chip on his shoulder could grow larger, Ryan began to feel the creeping sense of dread flow through the chamber and into his body once more. This time it was stronger and more distracting. The sinking feeling in the pit of his stomach churned and expanded, wrapping around his bones like damp rags. Nox began to speak, but his voice sounded warped and distant as Ryan desperately attempted to focus.

As his panic intensified, Ryan gripped the arms of his chair hard and attempted to steady himself. Sweat began to pour from his brow as he stared down at his feet, hoping to calm the effects of whatever was happening to him. For a moment, he wondered if he had been poisoned, but the source of the discomfort didn't feel internal – it seemed to be emanating from the chamber itself.

Ryan looked up towards Nox, who appeared to be saying, 'What's wrong?' but his words were lost in an escalating sea of hissing and scraping noises. A malicious sensation of being dragged backwards gripped hold of Ryan's torso as he reached out his right hand and began to claw desperately at the table, attempting to keep hold. Glancing over his shoulder, Ryan couldn't see anyone or anything pulling at his body, so again he looked towards Nox for any kind of clue to indicate what was happening. Through the growing atonal din, Ryan could just about make out Nox asking, 'Are you alright?'

The dark, agonising noise, the unnatural feeling of being pulled backwards by a force he couldn't see and the inescapable sense of dread that surrounded the hooded figures around the table all became too much for Ryan. With no other options available, he reached out and tried to ask Nox for assistance. However, as he glanced at Nox, he realised that something was making his eyes blink. Ryan looked up again, trying to keep his eyelids open, but something kept urging them to shut. Using his fingers to stop them from closing, Ryan stared at Nox in horror; every other second, his view of Nox would flicker between an image of him offering help and an image of him grinning menacingly with crimson red eyes hungry for violence. Ryan now found himself unable to close his eyes, and as the hissing and scratching escalated to a deafening pitch, he was frozen, watching Nox's visage flicker, split and separate between manifestations. The room appeared to fold in on itself, squeezing Ryan's senses until his thoughts became lost amongst a rapid succession of piercing beams of scarlet light, colliding into distorting visuals of people and places he had known. Once more, his recurring vision of chasing a spark emerged, along with the associated feeling that his physical form was being eaten away. Ryan had faced this situation before, but this time, it was different. This time he could feel the pain of being slowly and meticulously torn apart.

Unable to cope any further, Ryan threw himself backwards off his chair and jolted his focus back into the room. He quickly felt his back to check if the slow destruction of his torso had all been in his mind and was relieved to find it had been. However, as he glanced across at one of the hooded figures to his right, Ryan realised that it was making louder, less controlled hissing than the others in the room. A pained creaking noise also began to sound, and as Ryan followed it, he noticed five long, yellow-tinged synistrail claws slowly emerging from the sleeves of the cloaked figure as the hissing noise behind its mask began to turn into panting laughter.

Ryan leapt to his feet. Looking up, he saw that Nox had climbed up onto the table and was striding towards him with his eyes glowing bright crimson and his sword drawn, ready for slaughter.

'Unfortunately, whileIsee no reason to prevent you from leaving,' Nox growled, motioning towards the cloaked figures surrounding the table, 'the committee here see things differently. So today, Child of Light, all your cowardice and compromise comes to an end. Today, you die.'

Through a combination of fear and the urge to survive, Ryan picked up his chair and threw it at Nox. Without breaking his stride, Nox blocked the chair, causing it to crash to the floor. Ryan then launched one of the chairs to his right. This time it missed its target, sailing straight past Nox and crashing into one of the display cases in the room. The shattering of glass caused Nox to stop in his tracks to check what had been broken. This granted Ryan just enough time to grab his bo-staff from the table and flee the room.

With his pulse racing and confusion and fear still rattling his mind, Ryan scrambled out of the hatch he had been ordered through earlier that evening. Away from the hatch. Away from the tunnel. Away from that accursed dining room with the red eyes of Nox and whatever was wearing those robes.

Sirens began to ring out across the fields and marshes that surrounded the citadel. The sound of patrol ships filled the skies while their spotlights began to dance around the area hunting a glimpse of the Child of Light.

Ryan panted and looked around for a way to escape. Glancing back towards the citadel, he saw squadron after squadron emerge in troop carriers, all of them racing towards him. There was nothing to do except run, so he did.

He had no idea where he was going, but he hoped wherever it was that it was safe. Suddenly, Ryan stopped. A realisation hit hard as the bitter truth of his situation sank in. While he had no desire to risk his life, he realised that he wasn't running away because he was afraid of dying; he was running away because he was afraid of failing.

Ryan looked at the gravel and dust-filled quarry that stretched ahead, out to the dense woodlands that could possibly lead him back to The Salvatore if he was lucky. He arched his head back a little and heard the rampaging horde of Shadox Troopers sent to catch and kill him. Surely his cowardice was a more certain way to fail than to stand up and fight. If Lomax's counsel in the Blessed Garden had been true, then Ryan's death would put Callie, and in turn, the entire universe, in mortal danger. And while he owed it to every man, woman, child, animal, particle and molecule to help ensure their survival, he owed himself something too – a gift he should have given himself a long time ago. Ryan owed it to himself to be something more. Something more than the tired result of a life spent second-guessing every move he made. Something more than the weak-willed fool running to the nearest safe place after every conceded misstep. Something more than the unfulfilled reality of other people's perceptions.

He realised The Tide's choice to bless him wasn't a gift or a curse; it was an opportunity.

Ryan knew what he had to do. Taking a sharp inhalation of breath, he gritted his teeth and gripped his bo-staff tightly. With measured pace, he turned around to face the oncoming storm of sirens, spotlights and soldiers.

'I hope Lomax hasn't sold me a fairytale,' Ryan muttered to himself as he raised his bo-staff high into the air.

Ryan closed his eyes as his thoughts stretched out, seeking the Tide's power source like a lost child looking for home. He could feel his thoughts grasping and pulling, emerging from his mind and climbing up higher and higher into the air, through Terra Novate's artificial sky, then firing off through the stars into the deepest realms of space.

Ryan felt loose and disconnected as different fragments of his mind and soul floated aimlessly in space like fishing hooks in a river waiting to latch on to something. With the first dispatch of troops closing in on him, Ryan attempted to prepare for battle, but with his mind scattered amongst the stars, he fell clumsily to one knee. His head felt numb and heavy, and it flopped lifelessly forward.

Ryan wondered where this all-saving, all-miraculous Tide of Light was when he needed it. It was more than willing to show up at Craydon's Corner and on The Salvatore when he wasn't ready, but now at his most desperate moment, it was nowhere to be found.

The rumble of troop carriers approached, and Ryan felt the damning illumination from an overhead patrol ship's spotlight. Still down on one knee with the rest of his body growing increasingly limp, Ryan had no option but to continue pushing his reflexes and control further into the deep reaches of space.

Just as he wondered if the Tide would ever receive his call, Ryan felt his right arm shoot upwards. Clutching his bo-staff horizontally, Ryan began to shake for a moment before his head jolted backwards, revealing his eyes were ablaze, full of brilliant, burning light.

The Tide had answered Ryan Tyler's call, and for the young librarian from Vastrid, suddenly everything had changed.

Chapter Thirty

CONTACT

Ryan stared directly at his pursuers as his eyes continued to glow. The squadrons and vehicles sent to catch him had all come to a halt when they saw the intense flash of other-worldly light shoot down from the stars above and strike their intended target.

As the last traces of this power danced and skittered down his body and then over his feet to the ground, they left a circle of scolded soil around him. The blessing was complete.

The bleak surrender of running into a dusty quarry was gone; the fear and compromise fuelling that decision had been washed away by the majestic light now flowing through him. Areas of his mind that had often felt like dead ends opened up into vast expanses. Aches and grumbles that had once ruled over his tired body faded, while emotional states and auras travelled through his thoughts like an untuned radio. Ryan could sense the crew of the Salvatore were close, and he could feel their fear.

From a hilltop nearby, Kendra Lomax looked down at her newly-blessed apprentice and smiled. She'd spent the past few hours fighting the urge to drink the flask of bootlegged whisky she'd taken from the Blessed Garden, torn between her loyalty to the Sentry and her yearning to surrender to the emptiness. Just as Lomax had begun to prepare herself for the descent of darkness, she had looked to the sky and seen the light flood down from the stars.

With Ryan now blessed, Lomax threw the whisky bottle high into the air and struck it hard with her bo-staff smashing it into a thousand tiny pieces.

'Ok, that'll do for a warm-up,' Lomax said to herself. 'Let's see if I can remember how to do that 'save the day' thing like I used to.'

Ryan was already racing back towards the citadel by the time Lomax reached him. He was immediately at ease with his new abilities; he could run and jump in a way that felt as though the atmosphere around was enhancing his movements. His arms were now limber and strong. Striking targets and deflecting shots felt like scratching an itch – as if he were operating purely on instinct.

Leaping through the air and landing next to Ryan, Lomax struck her staff on the floor, causing all oncoming troops to tumble over.

'I'm glad you changed your mind, kid,' Lomax said with a smile.

'Well, the jam I found myself in did kinda force the situation, but yeah, so am I,' Ryan replied.

'Jam? What happened? Where are the others?'

'Nox and Rachel Stone are here. I got captured and was forced to have dinner with Nox. Things got really weird, and I ran away. It seems that the Corporation has destroyed Abila's lab and kidnapped the others. I think they're being held captive in the citadel. We have to go back for them.'

Ryan looked back to see another wave of Shadox troops closing in. 'I'll tell you the long version after we've got rid of this lot.'

'There's a long version?' Lomax asked, trying to process all of Ryan's updates. 'Well, let's do this, then.'

Ryan and Kendra raced towards the oncoming storm of Shadox troops and vehicles, leaping and swinging their bo-staffs to deflect the enemy fire.

Ryan's confidence continued to grow, and the connection he felt with the Tide swelled. He felt every molecule in his body spring to new levels of heightened existence as his mind cleared of old doubts and a new focus emerged. Feeling the moment, Ryan leapt through the air, bouncing from one troop carrier to the next. He jabbed his bo-staff into the vehicles engines, the impact of the strike overturning them.

Ryan glanced back at Kendra, checking she was witnessing his new talents.

Kendra smiled and rolled her eyes, then threw her staff like a low javelin. She waited until it had cruised beneath a troop carrier and, with a beckon of her hand, summoned the weapon back, causing it to smash through the front of the vehicle as it glided back to her. Ryan had a lot to learn.

As the duo neared the citadel, they were surprised to see the remaining troops begin to retreat.

'What's that all about then?' Ryan asked.

Lomax frowned. 'I don't know, but I doubt they're handing us the victory.'

As the duo's eyes followed the vehicles back to their base, they noticed a tall, athletic figure staring down at them from one of the rocky ridges that stood before the citadel.

The figure gave a slow nod of acknowledgement in their direction before pulling a sword from a sheath on his back. The sky above them began to turn dark as charcoal-coloured clouds smothered Terra Novate's artificial mauve sky. The figure clenched his fingers hard around the handle of his weapon, his eyes turning a savage shade of scarlet.

'You know who that is, right?' asked Ryan, hoping that Lomax had a plan for this showdown.

'Nox,' Lomax snarled through gritted teeth. 'Ryan, you go and free the others and get back to the Salvatore. This isn't your fight.'

Drops of rain began to fall, slowly at first but soon escalating into a downpour. With the rainwater crashing and smashing on the blade of his sword, Nox stood static, poised for action as his crimson gaze burned through the murky air.

'Are you sure? I mean, you will be ok, right?' Ryan shouted over the sound of the crashing rain.

'Yeah,' Lomax replied, flipping the hood of her rain cloak over the top of her head. 'This'll keep me dry.'

They both smiled for a moment before Lomax ordered, 'Now go.'

Ryan nodded and sprinted off towards the citadel. As he did so, he looked back at Lomax. The last of the original Sentry swung her staff halfway behind her back, ready for action, but her face betrayed the confidence of her poise. Ryan could see that his new mentor was afraid, and he wondered if he would ever see her again.

Before Ryan could contemplate any further, he saw Nox and Lomax sprint towards each other. As Nox reached Lomax, he leapt into the air, slashing his sword down towards her. Grey and red shadows traced the movement of the blade as it crashed against the bright arc of colour that followed Lomax's staff, deflecting the strikes.

A sharp jarring pain ricocheted around Ryan's mind as images of The Salvatore's crew crowbarred into his thoughts. Ryan realised that they would need him more than Lomax did at this moment and ran towards the citadel.

. . .

Deep below the surface of Terra Novate and several miles away from the remains of Professor Sanchez's laboratory, Alex Navin leant against a large pillar, waiting for the sound of footsteps.

He had been embroiled in a lengthy game of cat and mouse with Marcus Hagen and his team ever since their grudge had spilt out into the service tunnels.

Alex peered into the opened cylinder of his handgun. He had two bullets left and no desire to waste them in a firefight. Even with his skills as a marksman and his innovative use of mathematics in combat, he had to admit that using two bullets to take out a team of eight would not be achievable.

The idea of being captured or killed in this scenario was unthinkable, and Alex knew he needed to save the two remaining shots for his trek to The Salvatore. He removed both bullets from his gun and placed them safely in a pocket of his trench coat, then closed the cylinder and glanced down at the same etched markings on the bottom of the weapon that had caught Ryan's eye back on The Salvatore. He was ready.

Alex heard the sound of soft footsteps and the faint hum of a tracking monitor coming his way. The steps slowed, and a whispered command followed. He knew it was time to strike; Alex darted out from the pillar he'd been hiding behind, narrowly avoiding the sparks and shrapnel of gunfire.

He raced through the small, winding maze of service passages until he arrived at an opening. Ahead of him was a large trench. Enormous tunnels flanked each side of the cavernous space, and directly opposite him, Alex saw a ladder leading up to a railed maintenance platform. He glanced at a large clock situated above the platform; it read six minutes to eight. If he was going to follow through with his plan, he'd have to be quick. Leaping over the security railing on his side of the trench, he slid down the curve of the deep structure and scrambled to the ladder on the other side.

Pulling himself up to the maintenance platform, Alex stood ready as Hagen's crew emerged on the other side. Before Hagen could give an order, Alex backed away as far as he could, then lay down, pressing his body against the arched edge of the far wall.

'What the heck is that all about?' said Rico Akabusi, pointing across the trench towards the now-horizontal Alex Navin.

'It doesn't matter. Open fire. No mercy!' Hagen bellowed.

His crew pressed down hard on the triggers of their assault rifles; however, the difficulty of shooting at the angle between the verge of the trench and Alex's position on the raised platform was too great. Bullets danced and ricocheted off the railings and the concrete of the ledge but completely missed their intended target.

Alex smirked as Hagen ordered, 'Ceasefire, team. It seems our friend Mr Navin is too far away.'

'Hey boss, how about I lob one of these at him?' Bad Boy Stevie held up a grenade.

Hagen shook his head. 'No, too dangerous in a tunnel like this.'

'Well, let's do this by hand then,' said Rico, wrapping his fingers around his nunchucks.

'I'm not sure,' Hagen answered, rubbing his index finger across his stubbled chin. 'Our friend here is a tricky one.'

Rico shrugged. 'What's the worst that could happen? There's eight of us and one of him.'

'True, but let's proceed carefully,' Hagen advised his team, as one by one, they slid down into the trench and began to walk towards the ladder.

'Alex, my friend,' Hagen called up to the platform above. 'I didn't want it to be like this. I never wanted to kill you, and especially not with my own bare hands. I was hoping to send you off to the Corporation. They were going to keep you locked down. All I wanted was to bring an end to you going after me and me going after you. This cycle of vengeance has to end, and it has to end now. It's time.'

Alex glanced at the clock on the wall as 7:59 turned into 8:00.

'Indeed,' he smiled, as a torrent of water burst through the left tunnel, flooding the trench and washing Hagen and his men through the other side.

As the deluge subsided, Alex rolled back onto his feet and peered over the edge of the platform. Thin rivulets of water trickled from the trench below. He wondered how many of his pursuers would have drowned and where the cooled water might have taken any survivors. Judging by the speed and amount of water that burst through the tunnel, Alex was sure that even if Hagen and his crew had survived, they would have been washed far away from his current location.

Placing his med-stick between his lips and taking a deep inhalation, Alex considered his next move. Ideally, he'd get back above ground and make his way to the Salvatore, seizing it as his own. However, its need for a five-person crew for the vessel to be fully operational would be a problem, as would his lack of piloting experience. He realised that he would require at least Callie to fly the ship and, as much as he hated to admit it, Tiegan would prove useful navigating the woodland area back to it.

Alex had considered all possible outcomes of the Corporation storming professor Abila's laboratory and concluded that they were most likely being held captive and interrogated. Having studied Terra Novate's blueprints, he knew that the Corporation's citadel base stood less than five hundred meters from the service tunnel exit closest to him. He resigned himself to the fact that he would have to be the one to free them. With only two bullets left, the rescue mission would be difficult, but not as difficult as having to endure the sound of their chattering voices again. Because of this, Alex chose to take some time to savour the calm, near-silence of the service tunnel. Apart from the occasional drip of water and the gentle ambience of air passing through the vents, there weren't any sounds to distract or irritate his thoughts. He smiled as he stared at one of the puddles slowly drying in the trench below him. It felt like home.

With no knowledge of Alex's whereabouts or his intention to rescue them, The Salvatore's crew were already attempting to make their escape from the citadel. Within one of the cells, Big Joe was waking up, following a day of being hit with enough tranq darts to kill a lesser human. His mind was foggy and disoriented as a familiar noise roused him further.

'Oh for bleak's sake!' yelled a voice, followed by banging and what sounded like a tool of some sort crashing against metal.

As Joe's eyes focused, he saw a barefooted Caleb Scudder reattaching a series of wires to the edge of a large metal door.

'Keep the noise down, will ya?' Joe groaned, wincing slightly at the noise.

'Oh, you've woken up at last. Nice of you to join us,' Caleb answered, barely taking his eyes from his work.

'Us?' Joe asked, glancing around and noticing a young woman seething on a bunk adjacent to his.

'Yeah, us. Before you got covered in tranqs, you might remember we saw something pink in the bushes?'

'Yeah... sorta,' Joe replied, rubbing his aching head.

'Well, that was her hair, see?' Caleb swung around and, to Tiegan's visible annoyance, pointed with a small electronic screwdriver. 'Anyhow, so yes – this is Tiegan. She's not in the best mood; the Corporation have just killed Professor Sanchez in front of her. She was a bit touchy even before that, so I'm sure you can imagine just how salty she is at the moment.'

Joe glanced over towards Tiegan. 'Caleb, you do realise that she's in the room, right?'

'Yeah, but seeing as how she's already told me twice that she's going to beat the bleak out of me when we get out, I figure I don't have anything to lose.'

Tiegan turned towards Joe. 'Your friend talks too much.'

Before Joe could respond, Caleb continued. 'Oh, and she doesn't eat meat, so you might want to keep how you meet the daily protein quota for those big, bulging muscles of yours on the down-low.'

Turning his back to Tiegan, Caleb folded his arms and began to subtly flap them like a chicken in case Joe didn't know what he meant by protein requirements.

'Nah mate,' Joe replied, 'I don't eat flesh. I ain't munching anything that used to have feathers on it.'

Caleb looked shocked, confused and slightly alarmed at the same time. 'But how then?' he asked, looking over Joe's muscular physique. 'Is it enhancement meds?' he mouthed.

'Enhancement meds? Leave it out. I dunno why I'm so big; genetics, exercise, could be a combination of many things,' Joe replied, avoiding going into the specifics of his Ranch upbringing. 'So, where are we?'

'Well, we're in a corporation cell,' Caleb admitted, in an embarrassed and slightly flustered manner.

'We've been captured? Again? I can't believe we've been captured again. Who gets captured twice in one day?' Joe snapped, glancing down at Caleb's dirty feet, which were covered in blisters and calluses from a life of quick getaways in stolen shoes.

Caleb shrugged. 'Us apparently.'

The answer did nothing to ease Joe's annoyance, and the fact that Caleb's grubby feet were out on display wasn't helping. 'And where's your shoes?'

'Well, don't you turn into a big old grumpy bear when you've been tranqed? None of that loveable gentle giant stuff you were busting out earlier to get into Lomax's good books. I had to break open my shoes to get my emergency lock-picking tools out. I keep them tucked away in the soles, you see? So no need to get all flappy with me, big man.'

Joe got up and began to pace back and forth. 'I'm sorry, I just can't deal with closed spaces like this.'

'Well, if you give me a bleakin' moment,' Caleb said, trying to find the frequency required to open the door, 'I'll have us all out of here, easy-peasy.'

Caleb went back to the device on the floor and began slowly turning a small dial in the centre of it. As the machine started to do its work, a gentle pulsing noise began to sound, gradually increasing in pitch and frequency. Caleb flashed his cellmates a smile. 'It's going to work. It's going to work!'

The group's eyes darted between the machine and the door, awaiting the "click" of the lock release.

The noise stopped suddenly, and red letters spelling 'FAIL' flashed up in the display area.

The cell door remained firmly locked.

'No. No. Step aside, Caleb. I'm gonna bust us out of here.' Joe began to pace back and forth, warming up his muscles.

'You can't just batter down these doors. They're high-grade Corporation security doors. Two feet of reinforced steel. Triple wired magneto-locks that –'

Before Caleb could finish, Joe charged shoulder-first into the door. It held for a moment amidst the sound of structural groans and cracks before crashing down to the floor in front of them.

'You were saying?' Joe asked Caleb with a smile as Tiegan hopped down from her bunk and made her way out.

'Beginners luck,' Caleb snapped, still on his hands and knees as he gathered the various bits and pieces of his lock-breaking kit. With the cold concrete floor nipping at Caleb's bare feet, he hobbled after his two allies, hanging back just far enough to ensure that they would be the ones dealing with any Corporation troops patrolling the corridors ahead.

The two troopers assigned to that sector were made aware of Tiegan, Joe and Caleb's escape from the sound of Joe crashing through the door and arrived armed and ready to take down the escapees.

'Get back in your cell immediately, or we'll shoot,' barked one of the troopers, 'and this time it won't be tranqs.'

'Are you awake enough to do this?' Tiegan asked Joe.

'Only one way to find out,' Joe replied as he sprinted towards the nearest guard and, in one swift motion, tossed him over his shoulder. As if on cue, Tiegan jumped into the air and knocked out the falling trooper with a flying kick to his head.

As the trooper crashed to the floor, Tiegan seized his assault rifle and aimed it at the other guard. She hated using guns, especially ones loaded with live ammo, but this was a do or die situation. Luckily for Tiegan, Joe had grappled the first trooper into a sidewall and managed to knock him out with a hard and fast headbutt.

'Is it clear?' Caleb asked, nervously loitering far back from the action.

'Yes, for now at least. *Thanks* for your help,' Tiegan replied.

'Alright, no need to slate me. I'm a locksmith, not a warrior. And besides, I haven't got my shoes on. How am I supposed to take out highly skilled Shadox troopers with my bare feet?'

'I reckon the smell of them would do it,' Joe smirked.

'Oh very bleakin' funny,' groaned Caleb. 'Let's get out of here before anyone else finds us.'

A loud thudding noise rattled above them.

'Oh, now what's that all about?' said Caleb.

'I think someone has been spying on us in the air vents,' Tiegan replied, arching her neck to follow the sound as it grew fainter. 'Though perhaps it isn't us they're interested in. It sounds like they're moving away.'

Above their heads, Colonel Bron scrabbled to-and-fro gathering intel, forming plans and preparing to strike. He'd pulled a lot of strings to get from the hospital ward on Shadox VI to Terra Novate and had to murder a few of his comrades in the process. He knew Rachel Stone wouldn't look kindly on his actions but was sure he'd be forgiven and rewarded once he rounded up the rebels and brought this supposed Child of Light to his knees.

Despite his increasingly fractured state of mind, Bron remained highly resourceful. Through a combination of torture and cashed in favours, he managed to secure a direct link on a cuff-visualiser to the cross-referenced prisoner data he'd heard Rachel talking about and was now able to scout the citadel, monitoring the whereabouts of each of the fugitives. The three he had just passed held little interest to the colonel; Tiegan wasn't on the list, Big Joe was a low priority, and Caleb had the chip in his head so he could be easily tracked. Ideally, Bron needed to find this new wannabe-Sentry and take him down. Only then could he feel secure about his position in the Corporation.

Big Joe, Tiegan and Caleb continued to make their way through the prison sector corridors. They found themselves at another locked door.

Caleb shuffled towards it, his bare feet still struggling against the cold floor beneath them. As he carefully began to place the wires of his lock-cracking apparatus, he felt a big, strong hand grip his shoulder and gently push him aside.

'Let me take care of this one too,' said Joe, as he prepared to take a run-up to the door.

'No, no, you don't understand! You REALLY can't barge past a door like this; it's – ' Caleb cried out, but it was too late. Joe slammed into the door with a hard thud, and the sound of cracking bone reverberated. As Joe fell to the floor in agony, Caleb ran up to the door, hooked up the rest of the wires, and received a 'PASS' notification on his machine within seconds.

'Like I said before,' Caleb said with a smirk, 'beginners luck.' The door swung open in front of them.

On the other side of the citadel, Callie paced down the corridor, away from the cells. Her broken arm drooped beside her as she walked; the cast cracked and barely held together from where she had punched through the steel mesh of her cell door and knocked out the guard.

Her right arm remained strong, and she carried the unfortunate guard's assault rifle. She had taken the weapon, along with his security pass, from his unconscious body after she freed herself from the cell. With a little skill and a lot of patience, Callie had managed to reach through the hole she'd punched in the observation window and hit the door release with the sole of her shoe.

As Callie made her way along the corridor, she became aware of a faint thudding sound and then growling. She stopped abruptly outside a door to listen, then tried the stolen security pass. The door clicked open, and inside, as Callie had suspected, was Zam, trapped in a small cage. She glanced at the items strewn across the adjacent table and recognised them as the confiscated belongings of The Salvator crew.

'Hey fox face,' Callie said, her presence calming the creature. 'Let's get you out of here.'

Callie unclipped the fastenings holding the cage door closed, and Zam walked towards her, bowing his head in gratitude.

'Ok, now you go find Tiegan and the rest and try to get out of here any way you can. I'll meet you back at the clearing in the woods where we first met.' Callie paused for a moment, realising that she'd not only just spoken to an animal she barely knew as if it was a human but also expected it to follow a precise set of instructions. Despite the ridiculousness of this, Callie felt confident that Zam had indeed understood her. The fox nodded and headed out through the door.

Callie's back began to itch a little as she looked through the items on the table. Eventually, she found what she was looking for. Buried under Tiegan's weapon belt, Joe's gloves and Caleb's collection of stolen identity cards, counterfeit currency and a digital device full of pictures of his favourite Starcuties, Callie found the Cuff-Linq bracelet her father had given to her and was relieved to see it was still loaded with a hidden micro-tranq dart. It was her most treasured possession. Despite the dangers and challenges of escaping the citadel, her greatest concern had been leaving without it.

As Callie slid her right wrist into the bracelet, she heard the sound of troops approaching.

After sweeping the other confiscated items into a large backpack, Callie made her way back into the corridor, carefully weaving in and out of the shadows until she found the Central Control Room for the prison sector of the citadel. Using the stolen pass to open the door and a swift hit with the assault rifle to the head of the trooper standing guard inside, Callie made her way into the room. The room housed an old security system that Callie had studied several times over during her training at the Academy. With a little bit of trial and error, Callie moved through the interface's holo-controls and managed to spring open every cell door in the citadel.

Callie hoped that the fellow prisoners would seize the opportunity of being free. She didn't know who else might be locked up in the cells but prayed that they would be a help, not a hindrance. As she made her way back out into the corridor, Callie, like Tiegan, Joe and Caleb before her, heard a large thud and scurrying in the air vents above her head. She tried to follow the noise, but it grew fainter and eventually disappeared.

On the other side of the citadel, Ryan had begun to battle his way through corridor after corridor of Shadox troopers, trying to get to the cells located deep within the building. As he neared the central staircase, he became aware of a rabble below him.

Peering down the stairwell, Ryan saw two dozen members of the Royal Guards storming up the steps towards him.

As the huddled collective of Guards arrived at the top of the stairs, Ryan saw a familiar figure protected in the middle.

'Your highness!' Ryan cried out. 'Prince Alistair!'

As they approached, he heard the Prince command, 'Hold up! Hold up!'

Alistair stepped past his men and looked deep into Ryan's eyes as their glow subsided. 'Are you still *you*? Are you still that boy from the Library?'

'I'm still me,' Ryan replied, 'just with eyes that glow and a blessed bo-staff. How're things with you? Have you got an escape plan? Have you seen any other prisoners? I've formed an alliance with several other enemies of the Corporation. I believe they may also be held here.'

Prince Alistair's confidence was still low, and he stared at Ryan silently. Captain Dunnell stepped forward.

'We plan to escort the new monarch of Vastrid to safety. I don't know who you are or who you've decided to align yourself with, but I've seen eyes like yours before, and I've seen the trouble that surrounds those who look through them.'

'New monarch?' Ryan asked, surprised.

'Yes, my Father – well, he... he's dead,' Alistair mumbled.

Dunnell put his hand on Alistair's shoulder to comfort him before turning back to Ryan. 'Nox murdered King William. Nox also had glowing eyes, but I'm guessing you wouldn't know anything about that, would you?'

'I'm nothing like Nox,' Ryan snapped back. 'I'm still a loyal Vastridian.'

'Good, then you'll have no problem obeying an order from a captain. Fall in line immediately, or you will be considered a traitor. I trust along with your loyalty to Vastrid that you remain loyal to the uniform and the oath.'

'Actually, I never got to the part where I swear an oath, so the way I see it is that I'm not bound by anything. All I know is that good people are being held prisoner, and surely it's our duty to help them.'

'Good people? A bunch of thieves and dissidents, I'd wager. We have no time to quarrel with a deserter. Troops march!'

Prince Alistair's voice trembled as he spoke. 'I'm sorry, Ryan – your name's Ryan, isn't it? We have to get back to Vastrid.'

'But your Highness, listen to me,' Ryan pleaded. 'You don't understand. One of the prisoners could be Callie.'

The Prince stopped dead in his tracks and, with a raised hand, ordered the guards around to halt. He turned back to face Ryan. 'Callie? Callie Haywood? She made it out alive? Is she ok?'

'The last I saw of her, she was. But if she's trapped in a cell or worse, she might need our help.'

Alistair wavered for a moment, and Dunnell interjected. 'Sir, there could be hundreds of enemy troops down in the lower cells. Nox could be down there. It would be a suicide mission to attempt to rescue her now. For the sake of Vastrid, it's paramount that we get you somewhere safe.'

As Ryan watched the blood drain from Alistair's face, he wondered if the great Prince of Vastrid was guided by duty or fear.

'She'll be ok. Callie's a very resourceful girl,' said Prince Alistair, attempting to push a confident and pragmatic tone through the audible cracks in his voice.

As the Prince ordered his men to continue walking, Ryan shouted after him. 'You coward! You're not fit to be king.'

'The king is not a coward. You, however, *are* a traitor and are not fit to wear the uniform of the Guards,' Dunnell hissed as the troops began to walk away. The Prince acted as if nothing had happened, but deep inside, the guilt and insecurity he was carrying burned fiercely.

Ryan stared down at his ill-fitting jacket. He wondered if Dunnell had a point; was he still fit to honour the duty of the Royal Guards? Did he even want to? As Ryan pondered these issues, a different, more telling question emerged in his mind; had he ever truly wanted to join in the first place?

As his mind began to fill with scattered, drifting ruminations, a clear memory of Jayden telling him to 'CON-CEN-TRATE' before his test at the Grid pushed its way through to the front. A certain melancholy took hold of Ryan's senses as he thought about his cousin, although through the sadness, there was also warmth and reassurance. He knew she was as correct now as she was then. Ryan closed his eyes and let his mind quieten. When he reopened them, they were full of light, and his mind was focused. Ryan set off to find his new friends.

Through the slatted grilles of an air vent above, Bron peered down at Ryan leaving, and between each blink of his eyes, the chain of flashbacks resumed once more. Bron backed himself into a corner of the vent and viciously shook his head back and forth until the images stopped. He forced his breath to slow, inhaling deeply, holding for a moment, then shakily exhaling. Bron knew what he needed: a plan. Something straightforward and easy to achieve. The colonel regained his focus and considered the information he'd just garnered.

'Ryan. Ryan. So his name is Ryan.' The colonel now had not only a name to attach to the catalyst of his downfall but another source of interest as well. 'Callie, eh? Is Callie your little girlfriend, Ryan?' A plan began to form in Bron's mind. From his air vent surveillance and the information from Hagen and his crew, he pieced together that Callie must be the young woman he saw opening the cell doors earlier. Bron had no desire for a straight fight with Ryan. He wanted to see the young man angry, emotional and desperate first, and he now knew how to do it.

Outside of the citadel, the battle between Nox and Lomax raged on. Nox hit Lomax with a kick to the gut and a flurry of snapping punches, forcing her into defence mode. Noticing his shoulder drop, Lomax knew Nox was about to alter his attack and seized her chance. She swung her staff out low, smashing hard into his shins and causing him to crash to the ground. Nox roared in anger and jumped back to his feet, headbutting Lomax. She stumbled to her knees, and the staff fell from her hands, rolling over the edge of the rocky ledge.

Nox raised his sword high into the air then swung it down towards Lomax, missing her by a fraction as she rolled away. He reached down and grabbed hold of Lomax by the collar of her rain cloak. With Lomax in his grasp, Nox began to pummel the back of her head with the handle of his sword before dragging her over to a large, sharp rock. The light beaming from Lomax's eyes began to flicker and fade as Nox clenched his fingers through her hair and smashed her head against the rock.

Nox stood over Lomax's motionless body. Wiping away a thick stream of blood from her face, he pulled back the lids of Lomax's eyes and observed that there were still some faint traces of light glowing and dimming. He cracked her head against the ground again for good measure.

Straightening himself back up to full height, Nox placed the blade of his sword at his fallen enemy's throat.

'You put up a good fight, old girl; I have to give you that. I should kill you now and put you out of your misery. But where is the satisfaction in that? I need you to see what will happen to your young friends if they make it out of the citadel. I've arranged for them to run into quite the surprise. In twenty minutes time – '

Nox's pontificating was cut short when he noticed a bright light reflecting on the blade of his sword, which he followed back to Lomax's eyes as the sound of something whistling through the air filled his ears.

'Impossible!' Nox cried as Lomax's bo-staff flew towards him and struck him in the forehead, sending him flying back down the hill.

'Very possible,' croaked Lomax, springing back to her feet and summoning the staff back to her hand.

Nox, who had been knocked back a good fifty feet by the

impact of the blow, picked himself up and dusted off his suit. His crimson eyes stared back at Lomax for a second or two before they suddenly dimmed as his head slumped slightly to one side. Nox then nodded as if in agreement before tapping some buttons on his cuff Linq and hollering to Lomax, 'We'll finish this next time. Until then, enjoy your new friends while you can. Like I say, twenty minutes. Nineteen now.'

Before Lomax could respond, a corporation hover-ship buzzed over her, spraying a flurry of gunfire to keep her at bay. Watching Nox leap into the ship's cargo hatch and fly away, Lomax pondered what exactly her enemy had planned. Whatever it was, Lomax first had to stop the gash in her forehead that was causing a crimson mask of blood to cover her face. She knew Calvin McGuire would disapprove, but Lomax quickly rolled her bo-staff between her hands until she felt the warm glow. As she rubbed the bright light into her forehead, the wound began to close. Once healed, Lomax staggered backwards and almost vomited. While the process of siphoning Tide energy was effective, it also caused a great deal of discomfort. Lomax steadied herself to deal with whatever Nox had planned and began to make her way down towards the citadel.

Deep within the lower levels of the citadel, Callie pressed her back tight against the wall and hoisted the butt of her rifle onto her right shoulder, resting it against her cheek and fixing her line of vision to the sights. Within moments, a clutch of troopers stormed around the corner. Callie squeezed the trigger, taking care to disarm them by avoiding any vital organs and firing deep into their shoulder muscles. It wasn't pleasant, but it was the only way to ensure that both she and they survived the encounter.

She slumped against the wall and tried to steady her

breathing. The deep, burning pain in her left arm gnawed unrelentingly, and her right arm shook with exhaustion. Callie felt panic and desperation lingering over her, waiting to pounce.

Suddenly, footsteps and the unmistakable sound of a rifle being loaded. Without stopping to think, Callie spun around, saw a Shadox uniform and fired a flurry of shots at the approaching trooper.

The trooper collapsed to the floor, a pool of blood surrounding his motionless body. Callie dropped her rifle and covered her mouth with her hand. She'd never knowingly killed anyone before, and seeing the remains of a life she had taken without question caused a pang of guilt to sear through her gut. Callie didn't recognise the brutal Captain Bradlock lying before her and knew nothing of his cruel nature nor his murderous past. But she had never wanted to be a killer, only a protector, and no amount of justification would have changed where she found herself at that moment − lost in fear and regret, unaware that the air vent above her was softly being removed.

Bron crashed down on top of Callie, wrapping his legs tight around her waist to restrain the lower half of her body and locking his arm around her throat. He gradually tightened the chokehold as Callie coughed and spluttered, desperately trying to break free. Mustering all of her strength, she pushed back against Bron's grip, but with her left arm broken, it was useless. Just as she began to wonder if this was how she would die, Bron let Callie go. She began to crawl away, but Bron had noticed the tattered cast on Callie's arm and stamped down on it several times until the cast was obliterated and her arm suffered a further break. Callie screamed in agony before rolling over and passing out.

Bron smirked and dragged her body to the side of the corridor. Pulling a communications device from his belt, Bron began to speak. 'This is a message for a boy called Ryan looking for a girl called Callie. My name is Colonel Bron of the Shadox Corporation. You took my face, and now I've taken your girl. If you want to see her last breath, I suggest you come and find me by the citadel entrance.'

Bron's voice boomed through every security speaker in the citadel. Rachel Stone stopped in her tracks as she listened. She had received word from one of her sources that Nox had ordered the implementation of a classified procedure called Novate Eximo. Knowing nothing of this procedure or Nox's intention to implement it, Rachel had decided to evacuate Terra Novate and head back to Shadox VI to get to the bottom of the secrecy. Bron turning up in the middle of this was an unwanted complication, although it had occurred to Rachel that if Novate Eximo was as perilous as she presumed, it could do her a favour by taking Bron out of the picture for good.

On the lower levels of the citadel, Tiegan, Caleb and Joe listened in shocked silence to Bron's message. At the same time, several floors below them, Alex Navin lamented the fact that Ryan was going to walk into what was clearly a trap. Ryan, however, wasn't the same boy Alex had met earlier. With his eyes glowing, Ryan gripped his bo-staff tightly and raced off to find Callie, his only fear being that he may be too late.

Chapter Thirty-One

NOVATE EXIMO

With Callie's barely conscious body draped over his shoulder, Coronel Bron made his way to the entrance of the citadel. As he arrived in the reception area, a squad of fifteen armed and battle-ready Shadox troopers greeted him.

Without breaking eye contact with the squad, Bron unceremoniously dumped Callie onto the cold, marble floor and asked, 'Have you lot been sent to try and take me down then? You can try, but I warn you I'm not in the mood. Uniforms or not, there'll be no mercy.'

'On the contrary, sir,' a tall trooper with fair hair replied, 'we're here to help. When we heard your voice over the speakers, we felt it was more important to stand by you than it was to protect Ms Stone. You've always done right by us, and we feel its only fair to repay that loyalty.'

'Good,' Bron smirked. He felt reassured that, despite his mangled face and recent failure in Vastrid, he still had the respect of the troops. He appreciated loyal soldiers in times like these. They'd fight hard for him, carry out his orders without question and ultimately prove to be utterly expendable.

Several levels below the citadel's main entrance, Tiegan, Big Joe and Caleb were still attempting to make their way out of the building. They found themselves in a long, dimly lit corridor that led to an escape hangar situated two floors below ground level.

'I believe that the hangars will have several ramps and service tunnels that should lead back up and out to ground level,' advised Tiegan, drawing on the times she'd spied on the comings and goings of Corporation staff while exploring with Zam.

'Thank bleak for that. We need to get out of here quick,' said Caleb, as a loud alarm began to echo throughout the citadel. 'See?'

'That could be about anything,' Tiegan said, hoping to calm the situation. 'Let's not panic.'

'Let's not panic? That's not a "someone's burnt their breakfast" alarm. That's some big-scale, proper WHOOP-WHOOP-WHOOP let's-get-the-bleak-out-of-here noise.'

Indeed Caleb was correct. The alarm had been activated by Rachel Stone. Startled at the news of both Nox's Novate Eximo executive order and his sudden disappearance, she had thought it best to evacuate the colony and take as many of her most loyal troops and staff with her as she could.

Surrounded by a detail of her most trusted troopers, Rachel had begun to make her way towards the same hangar as Tiegan, Caleb and Big Joe. As the trio of escaped prisoners came to the head of a T-shaped junction of corridors, they saw Rachel and a squadron of troops passing them.

Tiegan and Rachel's eyes met for a fraction of a second. They were shaken and surprised by their sudden encounter before they both yelled, 'Get her!' in unison.

A fierce firefight broke out between the troopers and the members of The Salvatore's crew. With Joe, Tiegan and Caleb pinned down behind a large service ventilation shaft, Rachel took the opportunity to flee.

'Cover me!' Tiegan yelled as she somersaulted over the gunfire in pursuit.

'Fall back!' cried Big Joe as he and Caleb backed away down a side corridor, narrowly avoiding the flurry of oncoming shots.

As they turned a corner, a shot came whistling through the air and clipped Big Joe's already injured shoulder, causing him to drop his weapon

Caleb picked up Joe's rifle and began firing back; however, every shot missed, and he was soon out of bullets.

'Reload it! Reload it!' Joe cried.

Caleb stared at the rifle, hoping for some kind of clue. 'I don't know how!'

Joe noticed the trooper who had clipped him was also reloading, 'Quick. It's got Auto-Load. Hit the left side button just above the handle.'

'My left or your left?'

'We're facing the same way; just hit it!' Joe screamed as the trooper raised his rifle.

As Caleb hit the first button his finger could find, the barrel of the weapon disconnected and tumbled to the floor.

'Not that one,' Joe sighed.

The approaching trooper smiled and raised his rifle, ready to take out both of his targets. Caleb winced and turned to run just as the soldier began to squeeze down hard on his trigger. However, the trooper's shot strayed off into the air as he tumbled to the floor with a bullet wound through his chest.

Alex Navin stepped out from the shadows that filled the corridor behind him, brandishing his personalised handgun.

'So, I presume your conspicuous cowardice is just a mask to hide your incompetence,' Alex sniped at Caleb.

'All right, all right. It's only easy if you know how. I'd love to know how good you are at breaking locks. Ask old muscle-show behind me how hard it can be,' Caleb moaned, walking towards the dead body of the fallen trooper.

'Yeah, OK, you've made your point,' replied Big Joe, tending to his injured shoulder. 'Caleb said you managed to escape when the Corporation invaded the lab. Were you captured, or did you come back to rescue us?'

'Ha, rescue us? You've got to be joking. Don't you remember that time on The Salvatore when he threatened to shoot us?' Caleb scoffed as he removed the boots from the dead trooper's feet and began to squeeze his own bare feet into them, much to the visible disdain of both Alex and Joe.

'I came because I'll need at least Callie and Tiegan if I'm to escape this atrocious decision of a destination. Anyone else is a bonus. Naturally, there are those that I'm less concerned with rescuing,' Alex replied, picking up the trooper's assault rifle and looking directly at Caleb, 'and those that I'd be quite happy to leave here.'

'Oh, well, that's just charming, isn't it?' Caleb answered as the three of them began to follow the corridor system back to the T-junction. 'Well, if you're so keen to find Tiegan, she went after Rachel Stone. Somewhere down there.' Through the winding corridors that lay before them, the sound of gunfire and fighting rattled towards Caleb, Big Joe and Alex.

'I'm guessing she went that-a-way then?' Big Joe answered with a nod in the direction of the noise.

'That doesn't mean that we *have* to follow her, does it?' Caleb asked, but it was too late. Alex and Joe had already begun to make their way toward the noise, and with no other option available, Caleb followed.

They came to the edge of one of the escape hangers. Shadox Corporation bullets bounced off support beams and cargo holds as Tiegan vaulted, ducked and dived from trooper to trooper, making her way towards Rachel Stone. Rachel was well aware of this and hurried along with her guards towards a patrol ship ready for takeoff.

Bouncing over a supply crate, Tiegan wrapped her legs around the neck of one of the troopers and brought him down face-first onto the hard concrete floor of the hanger, knocking him out cold in the process.

Noticing her allies had arrived at the hanger entrance, she slid the troopers assault rifle across the floor to them and shouted, 'Cover me! She's getting away!'

Alex already had the rifle he'd taken from the trooper in the corridor and began drawing the trooper's fire towards the entrance.

Caleb looked down at the rifle that had arrived at his feet. After his faux pas reloading, he wasn't keen to have another go. He looked back at Big Joe, hoping that he would be able to take the weapon but instead found him flexing his muscles and wincing.

'You alright there, muscle-show?' Caleb asked. 'Hows about less flexing and more shooting, eh?'

'I'm regenerating the damaged tissue in my shoulder. One of the few perks of being raised on a Ranch,' he replied, as Caleb watched in shock and wonder as a bullet shell worked its way out of the wound on Joe's arm and the flesh around it began to heal. 'Now hand me that gun, and I'll show you how to use it.'

With Alex and Joe aiding her, Tiegan began to gain on Rachel, who was now just a hundred meters or so from her vehicle. Glancing back, Rachel screamed to her troops, 'What are you waiting for? Get ready to go!'

As the engines of Rachel's escape craft began to whir, the crew on board rolled a cargo net out of the side hatch. Rachel reached out and started to climb the net as the ship gently hovered above the ground. Just as she made it to the door, she glanced back and noticed Tiegan desperately fighting her way through the remaining ground troops.

'Silly girl,' Rachel smiled to herself. 'It'd take a miracle to catch me now.'

'No! No! She's getting away!' cried Tiegan.

Suddenly Zam appeared in the corridor and followed his carer's cries, darting past Alex, Joe and Caleb. Tiegan glanced over towards the fox and cried, 'Quick! That woman on the cargo net. Stop her from escaping, Zam. She murdered Abila!'

Zam looked up at Rachel climbing onto her patrol ship and growled. Abila had created him and had helped nurture him. It was an injustice that required resolution.

With her ship now hovering twenty feet in the air and preparing to evacuate, Rachel was oblivious to the arrival of Zam and had stopped to catch Tiegan's eye.

As Rachel sarcastically waved goodbye, she noticed something furry racing towards her. The creature bounced from stacked cargo boxes to towers of crates. Stone frowned; 'Is that some kind of fox?'

Before she had time to contemplate the situation, Zam had leapt at her with his teeth bared, ready to do whatever would be needed to avenge Abila's death.

Rachel howled in agony as Zam clamped his jaws down and drove his sharp teeth deep into her right foot. As Rachel screamed and kicked, the fox sank his fangs in further until the tendon tore, sending Zam falling through the air, bringing with him a portion of her foot in his mouth.

'Zam!' Tiegan cried as she saw her loyal companion tumbling back down towards her.

'I'm on it,' Big Joe shouted as he bounded forwards, leapt into the air and caught the falling creature.

Joe placed the fox back on the ground. Zam spat out the gnawed chunk of Rachel's foot and watched it land with a squelch on the floor as Rachel's howls of pain trailed away into the sky above.

Tiegan continued to make her way towards the end of the hangar, hoping that she'd somehow find a way to stop Rachel's escape ship from leaving the area, but it was too late.

'Get her out of here before she gets us all killed,' Alex shouted over the covering fire as he ducked back behind a cargo crate

Joe nodded and began to urge Tiegan out of the hangar with Alex backing out with them, still holding off the troops.

'OK, where now?' asked Caleb as he, Tiegan and Zam huddled in the corridor with the rest of the group.

'There's a path leading to a supply door if we follow this corridor to the right,' Alex answered. 'That should take us to the front of the citadel where we might be able to slip away.'

Caleb, Alex, Big Joe, and Tiegan sprinted back down the winding tunnels with Zam following behind them.

Meanwhile, several floors above, Ryan made his way towards the citadel's main entrance in search of Callie. His mind raced with questions: who was this Colonel Bron, and what had he meant when he accused Ryan of taking his face? As Ryan turned through a side door, he saw Bron standing beside a fallen curtain and an overturned glass table. As Bron stepped forward, his strong boots crunched on the broken glass on the floor, and it all came flooding back to Ryan. Despite the plastic mask and the mangled flesh that lay beneath it, he remembered Bron's cold eyes and bitter sneer from the night of the massacre. Ryan also recalled how he had clumsily shot Bron in the face and how his cousin Jayden had sacrificed herself to save him from the colonel's retaliation. Between Ryan and the colonel stood the squad of fifteen troopers who had pledged to protect their leader. The soldiers sprang into attack formation as they heard Ryan's footsteps approaching.

'Easy lads,' the colonel ordered, holding his hand up high. 'Let this boy approach. I want to have a little word with him. Let me see if he's still the quivering little manchild that ruined my face.'

'You said you had Callie. Let her go now, and I'll let you walk,' Ryan said, stepping towards the first row of troopers.

Bron smirked. 'No need to grow a pair, boy. I've got your girlfriend, but I'll hand her over when I choose to.'

'I don't have time for games. Let her go,' said Ryan, as the white light began to shine in his eyes.

'Oh, so you're blessed,' Bron sneered. 'You're the Child of Light that Stone and Nox are so concerned about? Haha, that's a laugh. Listen, son, that might frighten the average squaddie, but I've been around the block. I've taken on your kind and won. I'm guessing that you know Kendra Lomax, right? It's a shame you won't be around long enough to ask her about the prick of my needle.'

'You're the only prick I'm bothered about right now,' Ryan retorted, 'and if you won't tell me where Callie is, I'll just have to make my way through your little pawns and beat it out of you.'

Bron snorted as he reached down and dragged back the white sheet beside him, revealing Callie, half-conscious on the floor next to his feet. Callie attempted to look at her surroundings, but her vision was blurry, and she struggled to focus. She could see Bron was standing over her with a squadron of troopers in front of him and beyond them was something she didn't expect to see - the shadowed visage of a man with brightly glowing eyes. The man she'd seen before in her distractions. Callie was unsure whether he was real or not but knew that this might be her only chance to escape. Before she could put her plan into motion, Bron grabbed her by the throat and dragged her to her feet.

'Is this who you've been looking for?' Bron taunted.

'Unfortunately, you won't have much time with her. You see, I've injected her with a messy dose of poison. A nasty little mix of Strychnine, Cyanide and some of the lab's newest neurotoxins. She's dying in my grasp.'

Ryan clenched his bo staff and prepared to attack.

'Now hold on,' Bron placed Callie back on the floor and reached into his jacket. 'I have an antidote, but you'll have to get through my troops and then you'll have to get through me.'

Ryan charged at the troops, quickly taking down the first five. Bron was shocked at how easily the boy dispatched the soldiers. Making eye contact with Ryan, Bron crushed the vial in his hand, hoping that the action would distract or discourage him, but instead, it only seemed to spur him forward.

Something else was bothering Bron, too, just below his right ear. He wondered if a bug or piece of grit had been kicked his way during his troops' scuffle with Ryan. As he began to fidget and feel around his neck, looking for the source of discomfort, he heard a voice.

'Hey, face-ache.' Bron looked down at Callie as she spoke. 'You should have broken the *other* arm.'

As Bron focused on the Cuff-Linq bracelet on Callie's raised wrist, his fingers located the micro-tranq dart embedded in his neck. His mind began racing through the possible toxins the dart was laced with as a wave of nausea crept over him and beads of sweat prickled across his skin.

Having fought fiercely through the lineup of troops, Ryan launched himself towards Bron, swinging his bo-staff high over his head, ready to strike.

Despite the increasing effects of the dart's toxin, Bron drew his combat machete and managed to block Ryan's attack with his armour-plated forearms. Ryan's second strike connected hard, sending Bron high up to the ceiling before crashing back down on the floor.

Ryan continued raising his bo-staff and striking it down across the colonel's face, knocking the clear protective mask to the floor. Bron lay terrified and powerless as the boy stood over him with a savage vengeance burning through the light that beamed from his eyes.

The memory chain of recent failures began to play in Bron's mind as Ryan attacked. With each strike, Bron felt he was edging closer to his demise. Bron had always hoped for an honourable death, but as he lay helpless on the citadel's cold marble floor, his face beaten to a bloody pulp, his failures consumed his thoughts. A painful realisation rampaged through his mind in what he feared were his final moments; could it be that, despite his rank and his military record, he was ultimately just as expendable as the troops he had placed between himself and Ryan?

As Ryan lifted his staff once more, Bron arched his neck upwards and croakily pleaded, 'No. No! I don't want to die! Please, I don't want to die.'

Ryan heard the colonel's words, but they were jumbled – buried by thoughts of his own life and the last few days. He thought about the compromises of his childhood. He thought about the hard work he'd had to put in just to become a librarian and the work needed to secure a secondment with the Guardsmen. He thought about how Jayden had died and how Callie's fate now seemed to echo that sadness. He thought about how Bron had caused this sorrow and how there was a lack of any significant purpose behind the colonel's cruel actions. It was clear to Ryan that men like Bron existed purely to cause harm. Blinded by the light burning through his eyes, Ryan felt no reason to grant mercy and swung his staff high above his head before bringing it down with enough force to provide a fatal blow. However, instead of feeling his staff crush through the mangled flesh and bone that made up Bron's face, he felt it bounce off something wooden.

Shaking the light from his eyes in order to see more clearly, Ryan was shocked to see he had struck another bo-staff that was hovering little more than an inch over the colonel's face.

Looking towards the door, Ryan saw Kendra. As she approached, Lomax summoned her staff back to her hand. Ryan suddenly realised how far he'd gone and paused in shock. Lomax looked down at the beaten and bloodied Colonel Bron and then turned to Ryan. 'Don't let his blood stain your hands, kid.'

Lomax placed a comforting hand on Ryan's shoulder. 'The Corporation will be looking for a scapegoat for everything that's happened here today. Let it be him. The punishment they dish out will be a fate far worse than death. Especially for the once proud and powerful Colonel Bron.'

Bron rolled over onto his front, burying the remains of his face in his hands, and began to sob like a child as his now-complete memory chain of failures consumed him.

Callie, whose body had lain motionless during Ryan's attack on Bron, suddenly began to spasm and convulse. Ryan and Lomax ran to her side. 'What's happened here, then?' Lomax asked as she gently lifted Callie into her arms.

'Bron,' Ryan replied. 'He injected her with poison. He had an antidote, but he crushed it. Can you do anything?'

Lomax glanced down at Callie, whose head was now rocking from side to side. Foam leaked from her lips, and then she became still.

Ryan took a sharp intake of breath. 'Is she...?' he asked.

Lomax rested her fingers on Callie's neck and detected a

faint pulse. 'No. Not yet, at least. Look, I can save her, but when I do, I'll be severely weakened. The first thing you have to do when she opens her eyes is to get the hell out of here.'

Just as she had done to heal her bleeding forehead upon the rocks earlier, Lomax began to roll her bo-staff between her hands, summoning power from the Tide to her fingers. While she did so, she continued giving instructions. 'You and Callie make your way back to The Salvatore immediately. Don't wait for me. Don't go looking for the others. Nox has something planned, and I don't know what it is, but I'm guessing it's bad news. If you can get to the ship and somehow get it to take off with just you and Callie piloting it, you have to promise me you two will leave. Straight away. Without the rest of us. Also, Callie will be cold, and she'll need to keep her body heat up, so give her your jacket.'

In the background, Bron continued to whimper, howl and sob.

'And can you keep it down, mate? I'm trying to save a young woman's life here,' Lomax hollered back at the colonel over her shoulder. 'I'm using space magic. It's not an easy task, and it's very much your fault, so a little quiet wouldn't go amiss.'

Bron groaned one last time before the effects of Callie's dart and the beating from Ryan finally caused him to pass out.

'OK, here we go.' Lomax glanced up at Ryan as she began to use her now-glowing hands to scan Callie's body from head to toe and back again. 'Now, as I said, as soon as she can stand, help her start walking and get out of here.'

As Lomax's hands hovered over Callie's body, she began to stir, gently stretching out until her eyes opened slowly.

Lomax placed her hands firmly on Callie's heart. As the light from her fingers faded into Callie's torso, Lomax's skin turned a deathly white, and her physical form started to wither, the colour draining from her checks and her arms falling limply beside her hunched body. Conversely, Callie began to stir, stretching out her arms and legs and softly murmuring as her eyes began to open.

'Now, kid. Get her out of here and back to The Salvatore,' Lomax ordered in a weak, dry voice before collapsing on the floor.

Ryan threw Callie's arm across his shoulder and helped her to her feet.

'Ryan?' Callie mumbled, looking up, trying to recognise the face of the person who had come to her aid.

'Yeah, it's me,' Ryan answered with a smile, placing his jacket around her shoulders. 'C'mon, we've got to get out of here. Something's about to go down.'

Together, the two young Vastridians made their way through the citadel's main entrance. Ryan squinted at the gravel path that led back towards the hills, quarries, and eventually the woodland where he hoped the Salvatore would still be waiting for them.

'Wait. Wait,' Callie urged as she took a moment to catch a breath and slipped her arms into the sleeves of Ryan's jacket. 'Sorry, I need to put this on. I feel so cold. I'm so glad you came to find me.'

'It was the least I could do. I mean, I owe you for saving my life back in the woods, and besides....' Ryan paused as a declaration of his feelings for Callie stalled on the tip of his tongue.

Callie continued to speak. 'No, I mean, I'm glad it was *you* who found me. It's led to this terrifying and beautiful moment, and I can't explain it, but it feels right to be facing it with you.'

'Maybe that's what we're supposed to do with our lives.

Save each other,' Ryan felt Callie place her hand in his and saw her lean closer towards him. Callie tightened her grip on Ryan's hand and moved her thumb to brush against his palm gently. 'I have to warn you. Things have become a bit complicated,' Ryan said as his eyes began to glow brightly.

Callie looked straight into the light. 'Complicated bad? Or complicated good? It feels complicated good.' She leant forward, and Ryan began to move his body closer to hers, the pair of them feeling the physical magnetism of a first kiss.

But before their lips could touch, they were shaken by a bellowing voice. 'Bleakin' heck. Look who it is!'

Callie and Ryan turned to see Caleb, Tiegan, Big Joe, Alex and Zam walking towards them through the dusty, grey pebbles of the citadel's forecourt.

Ryan's eyes continued to burn brightly. 'I'm so glad you made it out. Are you all OK?'

'Never mind us. Are *you* alright?' Caleb asked, frowning at the new intensity of the light pouring out of Ryan's eye sockets. 'What the heck did Lomax do to you in the professor's basement? Don't you have an off-switch for those? Or a dimmer? No offence, but it's a bit full-on.'

'Oh, sorry,' Ryan answered as he softly shook his head and squinted his eyes until they returned to normal. 'I didn't realise that my light was showing. But yes, I'm fine. It's a long story, but the Tide of Light blessed me.'

'So, are you an official member of the Sentry now?' Big Joe asked.

'I'm not sure, but I guess so?' Ryan shrugged.

Alex wasn't impressed by the vague answer and looked at Ryan scornfully. 'With that level of insight and articulation, it looks like Vastrid will be getting the hero it deserves. What happened to Lomax?'

'She's back at the citadel. She healed Callie, but it left her weak. She told us to go on without her,' Ryan answered.

'What about Professor Sanchez?' Callie asked.

'No. She's gone.' Tiegan said, staring at the ground.

The group exchanged dismayed glances, and Callie placed a hand on Tiegan's shoulder. They stood in silence, unsure of what to say until Caleb spoke up.

'Look, I hate to say it, but if Lomax told you to leave without her, then we should probably get out of here, pronto,' said Caleb, unable to hide the panic in his voice.

Caleb began to walk away, but Tiegan pulled him back. 'But what about Cassandra? She might be in one of the cells or still stuck in the lab.'

'And Bandit too,' said Callie.

Alex glanced away dismissively. 'I'm not risking my life for a Moline.'

'That's odd; I had you down for being a Moline person,' Caleb chuckled. 'Growing old, all covered in their fur, with just your little pets to keep you company.'

'Compared to your moronic chatter, the gargled ramblings of a moline would be an improvement,' Alex replied, 'but not enough to die for.'

As they bickered, a strange noise caught Tiegan's ear. She could hear what sounded like jets of air popping out of the ground. Turning to see where the sound was coming from, Tiegan saw rows of rivets shooting up from the soft earth around them and high into the air before eventually landing with a thud.

Tiegan stood, pondering what these rivets could be holding down, and her eyes followed the rows back to the citadel. A sickening realisation dawned on her.

'Everyone,' Tiegan said, 'take a look at this.'

The group scanned the ground on either side of the dusty, pebbled path and saw the final few rivets shoot up into the air.

'What's this all about?' Callie asked, looking around for clues.

'I saw something terrible when I was being held prisoner by Rachel Stone,' Tiegan replied. 'If this is what I think it is, we need to get out of here fast.'

The ground around them began to rumble as if the mechanics that held together Terra Novate were coming apart.

'You don't have to tell me twice,' Caleb shrieked.

As the group turned to run, a loud boom erupted around them, followed by the sound of heavy iron crashing down onto the rocks that surrounded the path. Two large, deep trenches had now been uncovered, and their cylindrical iron covers lay discarded by the side of them.

Sounds of scratching and hissing emerged from the deep pits. They filled the surrounding area, building in intensity as sunlight, air, and the aromas of life above ground began to introduce themselves to the long-forgotten inhabitants of the underground tunnels.

Tiegan placed her hand to her mouth. 'Oh no,' she murmured. 'We've got to run.'

'What did you see down there, Tiegan?' Callie asked as panic began to ripple through the group.

Before Tiegan could answer, a hand emerged from inside of the nearest trench and attempted to grab hold of the soil above it. The skin was pale and worn, and as the fingers grasped at the dirt and gravel that lined the edges of the trench, its nails began to extend. Finally, it gained enough purchase to pull the rotting and weathered body it belonged to up onto the top of the trench, where it juddered and screamed.

'Oh great! There's a Synistrail down there?' moaned Caleb.

'Synistrails,' Tiegan corrected. 'There's more than one.'

'Well, how many?' asked Big Joe. 'Ten? Twenty? A hundred?'

The din of the hissing, wailing, groaning and frantic clawing from within the trenches continued to build to a deafening volume.

'I don't know. It sounds like hundreds,' Tiegan shouted. 'As I said, we should run.'

Chapter Thirty-Two

THE FORGOTTEN FIRE

Wrapping her fingers around the frame of the citadel's main entrance, Kendra Lomax pushed her body back outside. Landing on the dusty forecourt, she felt spent. There was no sign of Ryan and Callie or any of the other members of the crew. At this stage, Lomax presumed that her new allies had either escaped back to the Salvatore or died trying. Her vision was blurry, and she could hear a savage din erupting in the distance. The air was dense, as if a dust-filled fog had clouded the skies above.

A small, scuttling creature caught Lomax's eye as it approached her foot. It might have been a cockroach or beetle, but its deformities now made it hard to tell. Lomax struggled to deduce what had happened to it; it almost looked as though it had been chewed by a larger animal and spat out or dunked into a corrosive formula.

Lomax gazed further into the mist and saw a flock of birds, again severely wounded, frantically flapping what remained of their wings.

Glancing down again at the insect, she realised two

things. One was that the creature might be in pain, and the other was that it could be carrying some terrible disease.

'Sorry pal, this is for the best,' Lomax sighed before squashing it under her bo-staff. As she stared deep into the murky horizon, she saw the unsteady but persistent approach of at least fifty Synistrails. She realised that these poor deformed bugs and birds had been chewed, clawed and picked at by the creatures coming her way.

Lomax attempted to swing her bo-staff around to prepare for battle but was still too weak. She slid back down against the door, hoping to either recharge her energy or prepare for the end. As her eyelids flickered, she saw a bright light coming towards her. She wondered if this was what death looked like and whether it would be merciful.

Deep in the woodland beyond the citadel, Lomax's associates fled on foot, attempting to outrun the oncoming swarm of Synistrails. Occasionally Ryan would stop and try to tackle the creatures, but they were too great in number. Tiegan was at the front of the group with Zam beside her, weaving a path through the trees and bushes back to The Salvatore.

Just behind her, Joe, Callie and Alex sprinted past the branches on a dusty path, dried mud from the terrain springing from their heels. Ryan was surprised at how athletic Alex was; Joe's legs had muscles on top of muscles, and Callie's Royal Guards training ensured fitness, but Alex's powerful sprint betrayed the stoic and slouching nature of his usual posture.

Behind them all, Caleb fared less well. Panting and wheezing, he repeatedly found himself tumbling to the ground from exhaustion or clumsiness or a mixture of both.

Ryan looked down at his new friend and held his hand out. 'Come on, we can do this,' he said as he helped lift Caleb back onto his feet.

Despite his survival instinct urging him to keep running, Ryan knew that had he not been blessed, he too would have been down on the floor, panting and gasping. In helping Caleb, Ryan realised his gift; he could protect people that couldn't protect themselves. For the first time in his life, Ryan felt a sense of pride.

Ahead of the group, Tiegan had clambered up a tree to survey the area.

As she dropped back down to the ground, she turned to address the others. 'I'm sorry to say this, but there's no way of getting back to your ship. The western path is full of faded men.'

'Well, what do we do then?' Callie asked.

'I suggest we make our way east, towards the sea.'

Callie frowned. 'The sea?'

Alex was also unconvinced. 'This is a biodome, a chunk of rock floating in a spherical bowl. Where do you propose we swim to? Back where we started?'

'No, no – the faded men aren't keen on the sea,' Tiegan replied.

'Please tell me the saltwater melts them or something,' Caleb said, sounding both afraid and hopeful at the same time.

'Unfortunately no, but the current confuses them. I've studied their behaviour; if they can't get a kill, they'll eventually get bored and find something on the shore to prey on.' Tiegan felt bad about the animals her plan was condemning but realised that their fate was almost certainly sealed whether she survived or not. 'Once they've gone, we might be able to make our way back.'

'You're kidding!' Caleb cried, peering back to see how close the predators were. 'We could be treading water for hours.'

The sound of clawing and clambering intensified as the Synistrails drew nearer.

Callie listened for a moment and realised Tiegan was right. 'I don't think we have much choice. Let's get out of here.'

Everyone nodded in agreement, and they began to sprint eastwards, following Tiegan.

'It's not much further, just down this path,' she urged.

Rushing past the last of the branches and bushes that lined the woodland area of the colony, the escapees felt the texture of the terrain beneath their feet change from damp mud to free-flowing sand.

The sound of Synistrails began to surround them. Glancing back over his shoulder, Ryan could see the mass of hunting creatures swarming. The more agile of the beasts were now using their clawed hands to climb up and move from tree to tree, a tactic that was proving quicker and more effective than trying to navigate on the ground.

Ryan looked to the path ahead and saw a huge drop in front of them, about one hundred metres away. Callie turned to face him.

'No other option. We're going to have to jump,' she said, her voice barely audible over the clamour.

The crew of the Salvatore sprinted across the sandy ground towards the precipice, launching themselves off with all their might as they reached the edge.

As they landed, they found themselves rolling down the gradual gradient of a forty-foot dune that led to the seafront. The sand was deep and fine, making it hard to stand.

As they tumbled down the dune, Callie reached out and grabbed Ryan's hand. The sound of the creatures following them arced over the top of the dune, its din raining down on them like a shower of arrows.

Callie and Ryan glanced back to the top of the dune and

saw a wave of Synistrails leap from the edge with their claws outstretched, ready to feast. The crew of the Salvatore scrambled to their feet, poised for battle. They were vastly outnumbered. The situation appeared hopeless.

However, just as the first Synistrail was about to land above them, the thunderous sound of artillery gunfire erupted, cutting through not only the bodies of the creatures but also the din they had been making.

A squadron of Vastridian Skyfighters sped past the beached crew of the Salvatore and continued their flurry of gunfire, tearing apart the torsos of the nearest Synistrails and sending the others scurrying into the woods,

As Ryan and Callie turned and looked towards the sea, they saw a fleet of Vastridian warships slicing through the water, making their way towards the shore. A familiar face was standing on the deck of a smaller ship leading the charge with his sword held high.

'Alistair?' giggled Callie, partly out of shock and surprise but mostly in amusement at his ridiculous posturing.

'I don't want to play for points here,' Ryan said, 'but I have to let you know he wouldn't stay in the citadel and help me find you.'

'You don't have to play for anything, Ryan. It's not his hand I'm holding.' Ryan looked down and saw his hand was still locked in Callie's.

Ryan and Callie walked towards the seafront as Alistair strolled down his ship's boarding ramp and made his way toward them.

'Callie! Ryan! It's so good to see you're ok!' Alistair's brow furrowed for a moment as he glanced down at their joined hands, but he quickly restored his smile.

'You seem to be in better spirits than the last time we met,' Ryan answered, as a garrison of troops led by Captain Dunnell waded through the water to join the prince.

'His highness acted in accordance with his duty,' Dunnell interjected, pausing to glare at the rest of the Salvatore crew, 'whereas you disobeyed orders and worked to free enemies of Vastrid.'

Caleb glanced furtively at Alex and Joe. 'Oh, I don't like where this is going,' he muttered.

'Me neither.' Alex reached down into his coat pocket for his handgun. He only had one bullet left, but he knew how he'd make it count.

The prince shook his head. 'There's no need to get into all that now, Captain.' I just want to check my friends are ok and get everyone home safe and sound. Callie, are you alright? What happened to your arm?'

Callie looked down at the tattered and cracked cast around her arm and thought about how, over the past twenty-four hours, it had been broken twice, partially fixed once and then fully fixed through some kind of space magic.

'It's a long story,' Callie replied. 'But never mind us. How did you escape Terra Novate? Where did all this backup come from?'

'Oh, I'd love to take the credit for all this, but I just led the charge,' the prince confessed, a huge smile breaking over his face. 'Actually, an old friend of yours arranged this whole rescue mission. And here she comes now.'

A familiar face made her way from the back of the deck of the nearest gunship to the lowered docking ramp and began running through the sea towards the shore, screaming Callie's name.

'Oh my stars,' Callie grinned. 'Tanya? Is that you?'

Sure enough, Tanya Masters bounded up to Callie and hugged her as if her arms were hungry.

'Callie Haywood, you crazy, beautiful thing. I'm so, so glad you're still alive. And still in a ball gown. Let's get you home.

We've got so much to talk about,' Tanya glanced over at Ryan. 'Like him, for starters.'

'Never mind me. Or him. What are you doing here? How did you arrange all of this? How did you find us?'

'We were on a rescue mission trying to find any captured Vastridians from the massacre at the Ball. We came here after I managed to pick up a distress transmission from a Professor Sanchez.'

'Abila? Abila Sanchez?' Tiegan asked, stepping forward.

'Yes, do you know her? Is she here?' Tanya asked.

'Yes, I did know her. I knew her very well indeed,' Tiegan paused and thought back to her last memory of her mentor and friend. She remembered how Abila had been fussing about with her glasses and realised that she must have been sending the transmission in her final moments.'She didn't make it. Rachel Stone murdered her.'

'Oh no, I am so sorry. It's of little consolation, I'm sure, but she sent us a wealth of information on Stone and the rest of the Shadox Corporation. I'll do everything I can to make sure that her legacy lives on by using this to bring down those that wronged her,' Tanya replied.

'Thank you,' Tiegan replied. She was working hard to keep her voice steady. 'It is some comfort to know she went out fighting. In her own way.' Tiegan and Tanya exchanged half-smiles as Tiegan turned away to give Zam a reassuring stroke across his back.

'Ok, so that's how you found us, but how did you arrange all these troops and equipment?' Callie asked as Tanya turned to face her.

'It's all down to the genius of a guy and his crew I bumped into while searching for you lot after the massacre. Hey, Squad 13! Stop hiding back there; come and get the kudos you deserve,' Tanya called out before sticking her fingers in her mouth and summoning the hidden heroes with a loud whistle.

It was then Ryan's turn to be greeted by some familiar faces as Private Rex Ambrose and his three other dining companions at the Debutante Ball came out to the deck of the ship and nervously waved hello.

'Ryan The Little King! Good to see you alive and well, sir,' bellowed Rex from the boat, throwing in a salute.

'I'm only alive and well because of you guys. I owe you one, Squad 13,' Ryan replied with a smile, throwing back a little salute of his own.

'This is all very charming,' interrupted Captain Dunnell, 'but we must address the situation in front of us.'

'Oh, here we go then,' Caleb muttered, rolling his eyes.

'This is ridiculous. There's no situation here,' Callie protested. 'Everyone in this party is against the Corporation. No matter where any of us came from, we're all standing here together because we're enemies of Shadox.'

'Callie, I understand your point but take a look at who you've got standing around you.' Prince Alistair had been briefed on the information provided by escaped Salvatore prisoners on the way there. 'A colonial terrorist; a thief from Baker's end; an escapee from the Corporation's ranch system; and an associate of Abila Sanchez who, from the data we received, appears to have been something of a double agent. These are not trustworthy people.'

'And the boy,' Captain Dunnell added, throwing a nod towards Ryan. 'Don't forget the boy.'

'Yes indeed, Ryan,' the prince said, 'I like you. You seem a good sort – '

Ryan raised an eyebrow suspiciously. 'But?'

' – but you have all this Sentry stuff happening to you. Glowing eyes, connections to criminals like Kendra Lomax.'

'The conflicts between the Sentry and your father were

resolved a long time ago. This isn't about a difference of opinion from before we were born, and it isn't about the fact that my eyes glow. This is about protecting Vastrid. Something we'll do better if we do it together.'

'You there!' Dunnell suddenly hollered across the beach at Alex Navin. 'Get your hands out of your pockets where I can see them.' Using his right hand, Dunnell signalled to his troops to raise their rifles directly at Alex.

'Shouting won't get you anywhere with me, but just to alleviate the tedious nature of this encounter, I will show you my hands. I predominantly had them in my pockets to keep them warm, but I'm prepared to feel the chill and reveal what I'm holding,' Alex replied, slowly removing his handgun from his pocket but keeping it aimed towards the floor.

'Ryan! Callie!' Prince Alistair shouted. 'Tell your friend to drop his weapon.'

'Dunnell gave the order first. You tell your troops to drop their weapons,' Ryan replied. 'Alex is only trying to protect himself. He won't shoot anyone. He knows he's outnumbered.'

'Oh, won't I?' Alex smirked, raising his weapon and aiming directly at the prince's head. 'I've only got one bullet, but imagine the mess it'd make. You're the only heir. If I'm going to die, I may as well stop a treacherous dynasty in its tracks and bring a regime down with me.'

'Guards, ready.' Dunnell ordered.

Before the Guards could react, two large explosions shook the sand on either side of the standoff, and hundreds of green targeting lasers peppered the Vastridian troops and warships.

'What's this?' asked the prince, but his words were drowned out by a smooth whooshing sound from the woodlands behind the beach. All eyes turned towards the noise and watched as The Salvatore rose high above the trees and moved towards them.

The Vastridian soldiers' communication devices suddenly crackled to life, as did the speaker on Callie's Cuff-Linq. 'This is a communication from The Salvatore. We have your army targeted. Please place your weapons on the ground.'

A green dot appeared on the back of Alex's head. 'Alex Navin, I also ask the same of you.'

'Next time,' Alex muttered, holding eye contact with the prince as he placed his beloved handgun down onto the sand.

The transmission continued. 'I wish to address Prince Alistair Hawthorne of Vastrid.'

'I'm here,' the prince answered, suddenly recognising the voice of his childhood toy. 'Probot? Probot, is that you?'

'I am Probot, and I was once in your service. I have been modified. I now serve as part of this ship.'

The prince paused for a moment as the memory of how he had sacrificed the Mandroid during the massacre at the debutante ball flashed through his mind.

Probot similarly paused, analysing the gap between their previous dialogue and their current one. He realised that the prince had left him there. After considering some variables of the situation, he could not accurately determine if the prince was worried by this.

A soft breeze moved across the beach, and the troops, conscious of the targeting dots upon them, stood motionless. Callie looked towards Alistair.

'So then, what do you want to talk about?' the prince asked.

'This ship serves the Child of Light and the group of allies at whom you currently have your weapons aimed. I urge you to give the command to stand down so the crew may talk to you face-to-face and reach an agreement.'

Dunnell leaned in. 'Your Highness, I really must urge you to stay strong –'

'Probot, you have my word,' The Prince answered, brushing Dunnell to one side. 'Troops, stand down.'

Caleb squinted up at The Salvatore as it came in to land. 'If we're all down here, who's piloting that bleakin' ship?'

Aboard the Salvatore, the work of five people was being attempted by just two. Cassandra sat in the main pilot's chair, wearing her latest prototype arm braces. On each shoulder, a small flap had opened to reveal a miniature mechanical arm, both of which now flailed at the ship's controls.

Beside her in the co-pilot's chair was Bandit, her paws in large cylindrical holo-controls, working to stabilise the ship's downward trajectory. Bandit's quest for food had taken Cassandra and her from the wreckage of the lab to The Salvatore, where, alongside Probot, they had put a rescue plan in motion.

From behind them, their first rescuee, Kendra Lomax, appeared from the sick bay. She surveyed the blinking warning lights and eased herself in the seat next to the Moline, quickly taking control of the craft and correcting their descent.

'I have no idea how we would've landed this thing if we hadn't found you outside the citadel. We owe you big time,' Cassandra said.

Lomax shook her head. 'If you hadn't found me, I'd be dead. I owe you my life; I won't forget it.'

With The Salvatore safe on the shore, everyone turned to look as the hatch opened, eager or anxious to see who would emerge.

'Kendra, you made it!' Ryan cried as his mentor appeared on the entrance ramp.

The prince strode forward, though his facial expression appeared a little hesitant. 'Kendra Lomax, I presume. We've never met, but I know who you are.'

'And I know who you are, Prince Alistair Hawthorne. I

have no quarrel with the crown or the Royal Guards. I just want to protect Vastrid.'

'You must understand my position, Ms Lomax. There's a lot of history between your kind and the Royal Family. I can't simply let a fugitive from Vastridian law go free.'

'Am I a fugitive from Vastridian Law, though? Please go ahead, name my crimes! Your father had no faith in my fellow Sentinels or belief in a Tide of Light. We never targeted him or waged war against him for it. We fought only to defend ourselves. Your father took against us because of the lies the Corporation were feeding him. Tell me, after everything that's happened over the past few days, who are you going to believe; the Corporation or me? Can you honestly tell me that the current state of Vastrid hasn't changed what you believe? Your father was King of another time, but that time has gone, and so has he. This isn't about me, or your advisors, or your father or what the people of Vastrid might think. This is about now, and this is about you. Never mind about me, I think it's time that you understood *your* position.'

The prince pondered Lomax's words for a moment or two and then spoke. 'You're right. These are different times. All things considered, I'm prepared to let you all go free.'

Captain Dunnell scowled.'Your Highness! I really must protest.'

'I'm not finished,' the prince continued with his eyes remaining on Lomax. 'That doesn't mean I trust you, Lomax. We'll be keeping a close eye on you and your crew's antics, but as long as you continue to take on the Corporation without hindering the safety of my people, we won't have any problems.'

Callie watched as Lomax nodded in agreement, and a peace of sorts was brokered between the two sides. Her attention, however, suddenly wavered, and her eyes found themselves captivated by the outward current of the artificial sea surrounding them and the arc of the waves that followed it. The water rose high and then curved into a beckoning shape, urging Callie to follow the current far from the shore. For the sixteenth time, Callie felt a distraction begin to take hold as a sensation of submission fell across her eyes, abandoning sight and allowing a separate vision to emerge.

This time the distraction was different. There weren't any Synistrails, and Callie wasn't in her bedroom. She found herself stood amongst the wreckage of a destroyed Vastridian tower on a hill, looking down at hundreds of her countryfolk wading through mud and carnage. Clinging onto the blackened and scarred marble of the building, she sensed something dark and formless many miles in the distance and felt it begin to drag the people away. Flickers of crimson began to overlap and cut through her vision with every heartbeat as clipped, splintered sounds of screams from the people below filtered through.

She felt an urge to go and rescue them but found herself moored to something. As the distraction faded, she looked down and saw she was still holding Ryan's hand.

Callie spoke softly. 'Ryan, I have to – '

' – go back, right?' Ryan said, finishing her sentence as the disappointment in his eyes betrayed the understanding and encouragement he was aiming to convey through his words.

'I need to get back to Vastrid. I need to help save whatever's left of home. Believe me, I'd love to stay here with you, but something, I'm not sure whether it's duty, guilt or a combination of both, would always be pulling me back, and it wouldn't be fair to anyone.'

'It's the right thing to do, Callie,' Ryan sighed. 'I wish it weren't, but it is. Vastrid needs you.'

Just then, Prince Alistair hollered across the shore. 'Come on, Callie. Unless you plan on deserting too, it's time to leave.'

'If ever The Salvatore lands in Vastrid, be sure to say hello, ok?' Callie said, forcing a bittersweet smile to push the sadness from her face. 'Here, I better give you your jacket back.'

'No. No, you keep it,' Ryan replied. 'It looks great on you. And besides, it's been pointed out to me on several occasions that the Guards jacket didn't fit me. Both literally and figuratively.'

Callie laughed. 'Alright then, Ryan Tyler. It's been an honour to have shared whatever the hell you'd call what we've just been through with you.'

'Ditto,' said Ryan as he felt her hand gently leave his.

Following Callie aboard the royal ship was Bandit the Moline. Curiosity had gotten the better of her, and she had decided to make her way down The Salvatore's ramp shortly after Lomax to explore the shore. While Callie and Ryan had been saying their goodbyes, the smell of sweet Vastridian-cooked food emanating from the prince's ship had filled her nostrils and prompted a strong desire to return to her homeland.

'Scuse me, lady,' Bandit said, tugging at Callie's dress. 'Can Bandit have a carry back to the boat? No wet pelt for me, please.'

'Of course,' Callie answered, lowering her shoulder so the Moline could hop up onto her back.

Watching Callie walk into the sea and board the prince's ship, Ryan's mind wandered back to Caleb wittering on about the Horrigan Test.

'Ok, if she likes me, she'll look back,' Ryan thought to himself. 'Please look back. Please look back.'

Callie remained with her back to the shore, and it wasn't until the ship started to fire its engines that she slowly glanced back and locked eyes with Ryan for a series of enchanted seconds. As the ship set off and faded from view,

Ryan knew that his heart would carry the spell cast by the moment forever.

'Let me guess,' Ryan said as he felt Lomax approach, 'if I love her, let her go?'

'If you love her, let her live,' Lomax responded, patting Ryan's shoulder. 'Come on, let's head back to The Salvatore and get the hell out of here before his Highness changes his mind, turns those ships back round and has us all shot.'

The remaining crew of The Salvatore made their way one by one back up the ramp to the ship, unsure of where they'd be going next but feeling a newfound comfort in going there as a group.

Aboard one of the Royal landing boats heading back to the Vastridian warship, Tanya Masters caught up with Rex Ambrose.

Rex greeted her with one of his big grins. 'Well, it took some doing, but it looks like all's well that ends well, eh?'

'You can say that again,' Tanya answered. 'Nice working with you, Private Ambrose.'

'And an absolute pleasure working with you, Private Masters. Say, we're as good as off-duty now, please call me Rex.'

'And you can call me Tanya.'

Rex, as ever, couldn't resist his penchant for revealing his knowledge of name meanings, 'Ah do you know what the name Tanya means?'

'Haha, I do actually — it means 'Fairy Queen', right? Well, I ain't no Fairy, and it looks like the prince and I aren't ever getting married, so that's the queen bit debunked too. Though, Tanya's actually my middle name. It's strange. Technically I'm named after my mother, but for whatever reason, people always called me Tanya growing up, and it stuck.'

'And if you don't mind me asking, what's your mother's name?'

'Aithne.'

'Aithne. Aithne. Aithne,' Rex repeated, rolling the name around in his head. 'Do you know what that name means, Tanya?' He asked, staring straight into her face.

Tanya leant in a little closer to hear Rex rattle off another entry from his encyclopaedic mind, but as he spoke, The Salvatore blasted across the sky above them, drowning out his words.

Tanya decided to nod as if she'd heard what he'd said, then make her excuses and head to her cabin for a well-deserved rest. She'd experienced a lot over the past couple of days and needed some time to process it all. If she could lead a Vastridian fleet, travel across the galaxy and rescue a prince without any forewarning, she wondered what she might be able to achieve if she had time to plan. Tanya smiled to herself, lost in the wonder of possibilities and opportunities yet to be.

Chapter Thirty-Three

REUNION

'Another ball gown, another arm cast,' Callie Haywood sighed, staring at her reflection in the large oval mirror that sat in the corner of her bedroom.

Tanya's voice drifted in from the hallway. 'Firstly, I agree with the palace's medical staff; that cast on your arm is for your own good; you can't trust that Kendra Lomax's space magic healed your arm properly. And secondly, that's not a ball gown,' Tanya appeared in the doorway. 'THIS is a ball gown.'

Callie looked her friend up and down as her eyes took in the lavish silver and purple dress she was wearing.

'A bit much for you, I'd imagine,' Tanya chuckled.

'Well....' Callie struggled to conjure a diplomatic response.

'It's OK. You and I have very different tastes. It's why I like you so much, probably. You don't try to compete.'

Callie frowned, unsure of how to take Tanya's comment. 'Let me just say that I think that dress is very *you*.'

'Thank you!' beamed Tanya, admiring herself in the mirror. 'And the party dress you're wearing is perfect for you.'

'I don't see why I have to wear it.'

'You have to wear it because we're being celebrated. We're the heroes of the day. Toasts will be raised. Pictures will be taken. Eligible men will be eligible.'

Callie sighed and shook her head. 'I'm not sure what happened last month should be celebrated. And besides, I'm on duty tomorrow, so I won't be drinking. Also, I have no interest in being photographed or, indeed, seeking the company of so-called eligible men.'

Are you just sore because *he* won't be there?' Tanya said, throwing a sideways nod towards Ryan's jacket hanging on the edge of a chair. 'I mean, don't get me wrong, he's not my type, but he did have a certain boyish charm. I can see why you'd like him and everything, but aren't you worried about all the rumours? Y'know, hanging out with Kendra Lomax and the stuff about his glowing eyes.'

The truth in the accusation threw Callie a little off guard. 'Well, I've seen his eyes glowing, and they're nothing compared to the dazzle coming off the dress you're wearing. To be honest, I'd just rather stay home tonight. It's been a strange month,' she said, steadying herself. 'I don't think it's the right time for a party.'

'You never think it's the right time for a party,' Tanya said, rolling her eyes. 'Come on; our ride's going to be here soon. As you like to say: Let's shake this place and get out of here.'

'I never say that.'

Tanya threw her arms in the air. 'You say it ALL THE TIME!'

'Whatever. Just give me a moment to grab my things,' Callie said, savouring the last moments of peaceful solitude before surrendering to the cluttered closeness of socialising.

'OK, I'll be outside,' Tanya bellowed as she made her way out of Callie's apartment and down the stairs.

Callie put on her Cuff-Linq, grabbed her purse and walked to the door before glancing back at Ryan's jacket.

She thought about Ryan and how he should be with them to celebrate surviving the Corporation's attack. More than that, she thought about how she wouldn't be able to share the evening with him.

Callie grabbed the jacket and threw it on, rolling up the sleeve to allow for her arm cast. She knew that the combination of Guards jacket and party dress would be frowned upon, but if she had to go to this party, then she was taking a piece of Ryan along too.

Far from Vastrid, Rachel Stone was broadcasting a speech to every Shadox vid-screen in the universe. She had taken time over her appearance and chosen her words carefully. She was keen to let the people of Vastrid know that, despite the Corporation's wishes to seize power back from the royal family, citizens would remain unharmed. After all, the circle of finance created by a healthy populace working for and living under The Shadox Corporation was too essential to jeopardise. The massacre had damaged the reputation of the Corporation for the majority of Vastridians. However, after some proactive public relations work and slashed prices, business was picking up, as was a sense amongst an ever-growing number that they'd perhaps be better off and safer with the Corporation in charge than they were with a royal family.

With her speech over, Rachel stepped down from her podium and made her way backstage. The moment she was sure that she was alone, Rachel let out a groan and slid against the wall towards her cane. Zam's bite had done serious damage to her ankle. Despite two operations, the nerves had refused to heal. Doctor Davron had a few more procedures to try; however, the recovery time would hamper her work to reinstate public trust in The Corporation. After steadying herself, Rachel hobbled over to a mirror and looked at her face in disgust. Some of the finest plastic surgeons in the world had fixed the nose that Tiegan had broken, but Rachel still felt as though her once-perfect face was ruined.

Looking down the hall, Rachel glimpsed Mr Nox stepping from a nearby office and talking to two smartly dressed men in the corridor. Neither Nox nor Shadox had returned her calls since the incident at Terra Novate. At first, she'd wanted to call a meeting to thoroughly scold Nox for opening the Synistrail cages without her agreement. However, over the past few weeks, there had been a shift in the mood within the Corporation. A creeping feeling that she was on the verge of being removed from Shadox's top tier had emerged, and she was keen to re-establish her authority.

'Nox!' she called out, repeating it more loudly when he didn't respond. It appeared he either couldn't hear her or didn't want to. As Nox and the two gentlemen turned and began to walk away, Rachel fell to the floor, causing her cane to rattle and bounce down the hall ahead of her.

Grounded and in agony, Rachel watched as Nox faded from her sight, unaware or unconcerned by her calls.

'If that's how he wants it,' Rachel thought, 'that's how he's going to get it. I need to get on my feet. And I need to make that pink-haired woodrat and her fox pay.'

Rachel slowly pulled herself along the wooden floor towards her cane, finally grasping it in her hand and pulling herself back to her feet.

'That's the first problem solved,' Rachel scowled. 'Now it's time for the second.'

Far away from Rachel's fear and rage, The Salvatore rested on the deepest edges of charted space. After a successful raid on a Corporation storage colony, the crew had briefly joined another band of rebels in liberating the enforced workers of the Terra Herc mining colony. They now gathered over cele-bratory drinks to discuss what they should do next.

'So, have you two made up your minds, then?' Lomax asked Tiegan and Cassandra. 'Are you staying with us, or shall we find a planet to drop you off on?' The former protégés of Abila Sanchez had initially remained with the crew of The Salvatore out of necessity but had begun to feel at home, each for different reasons.

'I'm absolutely staying!' Cassandra piped up. 'I'll admit I'm still not sure about the politics of this situation, and I'm fearful of what this might do to my career. But, the chance to explore this ship and the places we can go to is like candy for my brain. As long as you don't force me to fight, I'll gladly remain here as your medic and all-round boffin.'

Something about the way she said 'boffin' set Alex's teeth on edge. Still, he shook it off and watched Tiegan stare at an oblivious Ryan before making her decision.

'I will also stay,' Tiegan said calmly.

'As if there was any doubt.' Alex smirked to himself.

'I'm here because I want to smash down the Corporation once and for all,' Tiegan replied. 'I do, however, have one condition.'

'Ryan's my cabin mate; you can't have my bunk,' Alex teased.

Tiegan continued, ignoring him. 'My condition is that I feel we should have a change in leadership. Or at least a vote. I don't mean to dishonour you, Kendra, but you brought the Corporation to Abila's doorstep, and it sealed her fate.'

Kendra hid her feelings behind a poker face. It was a disappointing development, but one she had presumed would occur eventually. 'You're right. I made a mistake leading everyone straight to Terra Novate. I was playing with old tactics, old connections, old agreements, and old disagreements. We don't live in that world anymore. We should vote for someone more suited to these times.'

'I couldn't agree more,' Alex said, slithering back to the forefront of the conversation. 'I'm only here for this ship, and I won't be alive to keep it if we follow the woman responsible not only for the losses on Terra Novate but also, through her failings as a member of the Sentry, for the current mess the universe is in. As for my vote? It's tricky. Joe's heart is too soft, but Caleb's brain is even softer.'

'Hey, now wait a minute!' Caleb interjected, but Alex continued.

'Cassandra was happily working under Corporation funding until we came along. I find Tiegan's self-righteousness annoying, and I suppose that nobody here will vote for me,' Alex stopped, then turned to look deep into Ryan' eyes. 'Which just leaves you. I vote for Ryan Tyler. I'm not happy about having him in charge, and I'm not saying I'll follow his orders, but if we must have a leader, then I think he will at least put some balanced thought into any decisions.'

'No offence to anyone, but I vote we stick with Kendra,' Joe piped up. 'She's got the experience of going up against the Corporation. True, things went south on Terra Novate, but who knows how things would have gone if she hadn't taken charge and got a plan together.'

'I agree,' said Ryan. 'Last month, I was just a librarian. I wasn't even in charge there. I don't have any leadership experience.'

'Who the bleak cares?' said Caleb. 'When I was down-and-out on the shore with all those Corporation spotlights flashing about, you put together the plan to get us out of there. When we were all trapped in the Citadel, you came back on your own to rescue us. When we were running for our lives from all those Synistrails on Terra Novate, and I fell, you were the only one to stop and help me up. So I vote for Ryan.'

'I also vote for Ryan,' said Tiegan.

'Of course you do,' Alex chuckled.

'Oh gosh,' Cassandra noticed that all eyes were on her. 'Erm, I'm not really sure about this sort of thing. I think Kendra's done a good job leading us this far. I mean, our last two missions were a success. But looking at the scores so far, it would appear that Ryan's won anyhow.'

Probot sat in the console of the ship, a series of routines within his programming unable to analyse why nobody had considered whether he had an opinion on the matter.

'And so it's decided. Ryan Tyler, the Child of Light, is now the Captain of the Salvatore,' Lomax smiled. 'He can tell us what his first order is tomorrow. I think tonight, while we're out here safe and undetected, we all need to get some much-needed rest.'

As the rest of the crew finished drinks, Ryan and Caleb made their way back to their rooms. Lomax and Alex turned to watch Ryan walk away; they were both glad that he had won the vote to be the ship's Captain, but each had separate motivations and desires to help shape his leadership. A flicker of understanding passed between them as their eyes met, and Lomax's brow furrowed. Alex replied with an insidious smile.

The burden of leadership weighed on Ryan's mind. He has already been questioning whether the life of rebellion he'd found himself in was what he should be doing, and now he'd be the one spearheading it all. There was something else bothering him as well, and Caleb had picked up on it.

'Are you OK? You've been a real glum little bleaker for the past few days, y'know?'

'Have I? I'm sorry, I've just got a lot on my mind,' Ryan said, rubbing his hand over his face.

'Well, ain't we all?' Caleb chuckled. 'But there's something different troubling you. You've got the look of a man with a broken heart.'

They walked for a moment in brief yet agonising silence until they reached a window that looked out towards the clusters of stars that peppered uncharted space.

'Hang on a minute,' Caleb said, stopping in his tracks. 'Are you pining over that Callie girl?'

'I guess,' Ryan said, hunching his shoulders and trying to feign a measure of nonchalance.

'Blimey! I knew you liked her, but I thought you were just looking for some relish.'

Ryan cringed at the term 'relish', unsure of exactly what it meant but aware of the lewd way Caleb delivered the word.

'You don't want to waste your time on that. I mean, she's all the way back on Earth, and you're here. She's a member of the Royal Guard, probably with rank and everything now, and you're the leader of a bunch of rebels. We've got the Royal Guard and the Corporation calling us their enemies, and lord knows what the Parnasians will make of you and your powers. Plus, if Lomax is right, and after everything I've seen recently, I think she is, there's all this light and dark stuff floating about trying to either change everything or destroy it. If you haven't noticed, there's a lot going on.'

Caleb paused for a moment.'I mean, can young love survive the universe?'

Caleb saw Ryan's crestfallen face and took a look around the cosmically altered spaceship he was currently on, and shrugged. 'Well, I suppose stranger things have happened. Anyhow, nighty night.'

With that, Caleb took himself off to his room. Ryan sat alone, looking out of the window; he was as far away from home as it was possible to be, and he felt it. He didn't know how he'd explain all of this to his family and felt nauseous at the thought of them finding out. During The Salvatore's last mission, Ryan had managed to send a message home stating he'd been sent away on an assignment as part of his Royal Guard secondment, but he had no idea how long he'd be able to keep that false alibi operating. Ryan knew what he needed to take his mind off all of this and picked up a device that Alex had created for him. Having overheard Ryan lamenting that he no longer had access to his Flex-izdats, Alex had somehow managed to piece together a machine that would reunite the new captain of The Salvatore with his 'secret echoes'. Ryan was unsure of Alex's intentions in doing this favour for him, but it was a welcome gift, and he accepted it gladly. While the device couldn't store any audio or visual material, it could, via the dolphin, receive and decode encrypted transmissions from sources broadcast from Earth. Christened Relay by Caleb, the creature had been aiding in the delivery of data to the ship.

'I wonder if D'Rekk has a feed going?' Ryan pondered to himself as he rolled the dial on the side of the gadget towards the market trader's usual frequency, A/252. Through a crackle, the faint trace of music eventually emerged. Ryan used another dial to lock on to the signal and slumped back into his chair.

'Thanks, D'Rekk,' Ryan said, 'I really need this today.' His mind drifted back to his days hanging around the market, and he wondered how his old friend was doing.

D'Rekk Creel, however, wasn't at the marketplace at that moment; he was in the Great Hall, putting the finishing touches to the sound system and readying the recently restored Meloquins for the ball. Stepping away from the machinery, D'Rekk smiled to himself.

'And what do you think you're doing hanging around

here?' barked the recently-promoted General Dunnell, striding towards him.

'I'm just finishing up the sound system for tonight's party,' beamed D'Rekk.

'It's not a party; it's a ball. And you should have been finished over an hour ago.'

D'Rekk shrugged. 'Sorry, sir. I just wanted to make sure it was perfect, see?'

'Hmmm.' Dunnell scowled, peering down at the sound systems mechanics. 'I hope you're not running any illegal third-party hardware or software in there.'

'Well, of course not,' answered D'Rekk, his expression turning serious. 'Security at a time like this is paramount.'

'Yes, well, let's see.' Dunnell turned towards two of the Royal Guards operating a security detail. 'Sweep this machine for signals, please.'

D'Rekk grimaced for a second and shoved a hand into his overcoat pocket, hitting the off switch on a remote control for the broadcasting unit he had placed deep within the mechanics of the Meloquin. He watched the two guards run their holotracers over the machine and held his breath until they nodded that it was clear.

'Very well, then. If you're all done here, I suggest you leave before I find something to charge you with,' said Dunnell.

'No worries, sir. I guess I'll be getting credits sent to my account, right? I don't suppose I could be paid cash for this one?'

Dunnell responded with a stony glare, refusing even to dignify the request with an answer.

'Very well. See you around. I hope you enjoy the *ball*,' D'Rekk replied, bowing his head respectfully.

As D'Rekk walked away, he hit the switch on his device

and resumed broadcasting. 'Yeah, you enjoy your *ball*, pal. It'll be a party for the rest of us.'

General Dunnell watched to ensure that D'Rekk left the premises, then turned to see Prince Alistair making his way over.

'Was there a problem?' the prince asked.

'If there was going to be one, I put a stop to it,' the General replied. 'I don't know why you let the likes of him in to do maintenance work. We could just as easily train our Guards to do this sort of thing.'

'If by the *likes of him,* you mean the workers and lifeblood of Vastrid, I let them in because it puts a little bit of our wealth back into the city and maintains a good relationship with them. The security measures my father put in place – the sky scanner, the defensive shield, the re-building of bridges with other countries and communities; these things will help combat the external threat but will all be for nothing if we have internal enemies.'

'I suppose you're right,' the General admitted through a sigh, 'this isn't your father's age. I think everyone here in the palace will need to rethink our concepts of them and us.'

'General Dunnell, could it be you're changing your mind? I can't believe it. Next, you'll be telling me that you're looking forward to the ball,' the prince teased.

General Dunnell buried a final hmph out of respect for rank. 'If that's everything, Your Highness, may I be dismissed for the evening?'

'Permission granted,' Alistair replied with a salute and smirk. The young monarch looked around the Great Hall as the guests began to file inside. The building still bore many of the scars from the night of the massacre, but as the lights danced and the Meloquins started to channel the music, the prince watched the people cheer and felt that tonight was going to be one of much-needed revelry.

· · ·

In the kitchens, the staff were beginning their service, bringing food and drinks to the arriving guests. Keeping one eye on the food was Bandit, resplendent upon a cushioned throne. She wore a luxurious, powder blue cape from which her heavily pregnant and heavily hungry tummy poked out. Since returning to Vastrid, she'd become something of a celebrity. The prince had been publicising her miracle pregnancy to help garner goodwill with the people whilst also diverting attention away from the elements of the Tide that the public may find less digestible. Bandit loved the attention, but right now, she was famished, and her main concern was her forthcoming dinner, her third that evening.

Brushing past the other serving staff, a waiter allocated solely to Bandit arrived. In order to ensure Bandit was happy and healthy, Prince Alistair had decided to appoint a personal assistant for her and enquired whether she favoured any particular member of the palace staff. Bandit, who struggled to remember both names and faces, could call to mind only one person, and that was the headwaiter who had previously delighted in forcing her to serve dishes instead of eating them.

It had been a busy couple of weeks for Gustav, and tonight didn't look like it would be any easier. Being careful not to spill it, the waiter made his way over to the moline carrying her favourite dish - Potage aux Légumes et Poulet. The tired, overworked head waiter placed the bowl down and turned to leave when he heard a small, gurgled cough.

'Erm, scuse me, mishter,' Bandit said, licking some of the sauce from her paw. 'Thish could do with more pepper.'

The waiter tried to pick up the dish and take it away only to receive a smack on his hand. 'Not now! Bandit has already waited too long. Next time.'

'Yes, ma'am,' the waiter sighed before slouching off to the kitchen to fetch her next course.

Bandit stuck her fuzzy face deep into the pot of soup and quickly finished it all. As she did so, she felt a flurry of tiny kicks inside her tummy. 'And you'se lot can calm down too. Thish is mama's food.'

By the time Callie and Tanya reached the ball, it had already been in full swing for the best part of an hour. The ride to the Great Hall had been slightly awkward, with Tanya's disapproval of Callie's attire etched plainly across her face.

As they walked through the entrance of the Great Hall, Callie could feel Tanya nervously glancing in her direction.

'If you've got something to say, can you just say it?' Callie asked.

Tanya stopped. 'I'm sorry, it's just….'

'Yes?' Callie said, urging Tanya to deliver her critique.

'Well, I mean, I picked you out a lovely dress, and you've chosen to bury it beneath your scruffy boyfriend's ill-fitting Guards jacket.'

'Yes, I have,' Callie replied.

'Fine. It's your life,' Tanya replied, craning her neck. 'Oh look, here comes Alistair. Tonight's the night! I'm going to tell him exactly how I feel.'

The memory of Tanya's declaration at the previous ball flashed in Callie's mind, and she turned to her friend. Before she could speak, Prince Alistair's voice arrived, several seconds before he did.

'Ladies,' he boomed, carrying a glass of champagne for each of them. 'It's wonderful to see you here.'

'And it's wonderful to see you too. In fact, there's something I've been dying to tell you, and I feel tonight's the night to do so.'

Callie couldn't bear to see this unfold again. 'I think I'll leave you to it,' she said, squinting vaguely into the distance and edging away from the pair.

'And I have something I must talk to you about,' Prince Alistair replied, turning to Tanya and gazing deeply into her eyes. 'I underappreciated you before. None of us would be here today if it weren't for your brave tenacity. You're the finest soldier in the Guards, and you're the most beautiful girl at the ball. I would be honoured to have this dance.'

Tanya paused for a moment, trying to keep the soft smile she was wearing from turning into a giddy grin. 'Well, you're right about one of those things. I hate to blow my own trumpet, but yes, I agree I *am* the most beautiful girl here. I'm *not* the finest soldier in the Guards, though.'

'Oh, don't put yourself down – ' Alistair hushed.

'Please allow me to finish; I'm not the finest soldier in the Guards because I'm not a soldier in the guards. Well, not anymore, at least. I've just handed in my notice,' Tanya said, finally unleashing her grin and letting it take over her face.

'What?' said Alistair.

'Saving everyone's behinds on Terra Novate made me realise a lot of things. Primarily that if I'm left in charge, I can achieve a whole lot more than being a pawn in someone else's game. No offence,' Tanya smiled. 'So I looked around and landed a role with the HaloHydro energy group.'

Alistair was bewildered by the news. 'But they're in Parnasia! Isn't this all a bit drastic?'

'For you? Perhaps. For me? Not at all,' Tanya shrugged her shoulders. 'I've spent the past few years waiting for a happy ending to land at my feet. Now I realise it'll be easier if I go out and get it for myself.'

The prince stood speechless, holding the two glasses of champagne.

'Maybe I'll catch you on the dance floor later,' she

grinned, taking both glasses and polishing them off, before heading over to talk to Rex Ambrose and the other Table 13 associates who were tucked away at a table in the back.

The prince hadn't expected to be knocked back on both a romantic and a professional level. Still, he wasn't too disappointed. Callie remained the primary focus of his attention. He looked around the hall to see where she might be, but she had gone.

Callie weaved her way through the hall, looking for a corner to lurk in until she either felt like joining the party or found an opportunity to leave without too much frowning from others. As she edged past the groups of revellers, one of her favourite songs began to play. Callie felt it would be a shame to share it with the noisy mass of chattering and laughing around her and so made her way to the terrace doors at the back of the hall. Gently clicking open a latch, she slipped outside and walked down to the large wooden pier that stretched into the sea. Through the music playing in the distance and the smell of bonfires cutting through the early summer night air, Callie could sense all the districts surrounding the centre of Vastrid throwing their own parties.

Standing alone on the pier, Callie felt a connection to all of the parties in the distance – a feeling of unity between individuals that felt freer and more empowering than the suffocating obligation of the event she'd just left. It was a moment that couldn't be captured on film or recreated in ink, but Callie knew it was a warm sense of contentment and clarity, the type of moment that she'd think back to time and again as the years rolled on. She pulled Ryan's jacket tighter around her body and lent forward slightly over a safety rail.

'And where are you tonight, Ryan Tyler?' she asked, looking out over the sea.

Callie gazed at the inky blue water as it edged out further and further and merged with the horizon, leading up into the night sky and lit only by the blanket of stars that rippled upon the surface.

Callie's mind once again began to play her familiar distraction: the curtains blowing in the breeze, the sudden invasion of synistrails in her bedroom, her bed rising high into the sky, and the emergence of a young man with glowing eyes. Only this time, the events replaying in her mind took a backseat to her stare, deep into the voluminous sky and the stars shining above her. As her distraction reached its conclusion, with the young hero who had helped her stepping forward, Callie realised that his identity was no longer a mystery.

Just as the sea led into the horizon and the horizon spread out into the sky, Callie began to understand that no matter the distance, there would always be a pathway to cover it. From his window light-years away, Ryan came to the same understanding. A sense of power and warmth surged through his body as he gazed at the stars, and his eyes began to glow.

Callie's back began to itch intensely but, lost in the moment, she barely noticed it. Reflected on the surface of the water below, two beams of light shone from her eyes, illuminating the pier in a warm glow. Bright sparks of silver, pink and blue began to shoot from Callie's shoulders, arcing above her into wings of pure light. In this moment, both Callie and Ryan realised that no matter the distance between them, they would always be together, united not only by the adventure they had shared but also by the adventures yet to come.

Ryan and Callie will return in
 THE REALITY RACE

***

Aboard The Salvatore, all but two of the crew were asleep, resting as quiet and as still as the space surrounding the ship. Big Joe would have loved to have been among their number, enjoying a restorative slumber, but, to his increasing annoyance, he was being kept awake by the fidgeting and restlessness of Caleb Scudder in the bunk next to him.

After hearing yet another frustrated exhalation of air, Joe heard Caleb's voice whisper, 'Joe?'

Joe chose to ignore it. He liked Caleb and usually enjoyed the excitable declarations that his company brought, but he was tired and needed to rest.

There was a clearing of his throat, and then Caleb spoke again, this time a little louder. 'Joe?'

Joe buried his face into his pillow and hoped that Caleb would drop whatever it was that he wanted to ask.

All stayed silent for ten seconds or so before suddenly out of the darkness, Caleb's voice offered a short and sharp, 'Joe?'

With his face still deep in the pillow, Joe replied. 'What?'

'Joe, are you awake?'

'What do you think?' Joe replied, his voice soaked in salt.

***

'Great,' Caleb said, ignoring the undertone in Joe's reply and jumping out of bed to turn on the lights. 'I need your help. I can't sleep. Something's troubling me.'

Joe sat up and rubbed his eyes. 'What's troubling you, and why do you think I can help?'

'It's just a weird feeling, y'know?' Caleb said, pacing around scratching his head. 'Kinda like we forgot something.'

'It's been a crazy few weeks. It's probably just your mind trying to process it all. Forget about it. Get some sleep; that always helps.'

'Yeah, I suppose you're right,' Caleb yawned. He jumped back onto his bed and fell into a deep sleep, producing the kind of snoring noises that made Joe long for the sound of fidgeting again.

Meanwhile, back at Terra Novate, the source of Caleb's pondering feared that their luck might have run out. The two brothers that had been on board The Salvatore were hiding at the top of one of the largest trees. Surrounding them on the ground were numerous synistrails, desperately trying to climb the trunk to feast on them.

The brothers had managed to survive the past few weeks on Terra Novate by carefully traversing the terrain and living off the resources left behind on the deserted off-world colony. But the number of synistrails above ground had continued to grow as the resources on Terra Novate had dwindled.

Looking down at the vicious hissing sea of clawing, desperate synistrails, the younger brother looked at his sibling and gulped, 'Is this it? Is this the end?'

Before his brother could answer, there was a flash in the sky above them. Looking up, they noticed a dazzling circle of flashing light linger above them for a moment before it descended upon them.

With the intense glare of the light blinding their eyes, the brothers closed them tightly as they became engulfed by this strange and unexplainable sudden luminosity in the sky.

When they opened their eyes ten seconds or so later, they found themselves aboard a spacecraft, sitting in a shallow, circular pit in the middle of a flight deck that was also circle-shaped. A plethora of holographic controls and displays flashed around the forty-foot diameter of the flight deck. To the left of them, they noticed a woman with silver hair flowing from her head to her shoulders. She was dressed in a long, olive green coat and pointing an unusual looking shotgun at them. To their right, a middle-aged man with an anxious look on his face had his arms folded across his chest with his fingertips resting on his shoulders.

'Excuse my husband,' said the woman, nodding in the direction of the man. 'He's what you might call the superstitious type.'

The younger of the brothers recognised the stance of the man on the right; it was how Parnasians held themselves whilst in prayer. He glanced at the symbol on the lapel of the man's shirt – an X which was joined by a straight line at the top with a hyphen crossing each lower line. This, along with the couple's pale skin, would indicate they were indeed from Parnasia, but the ship they were aboard seemed far too advanced for such a small and under-resourced country.

'What's going on? Who are you? Where is this?' the older of the two brothers asked, his voice tight. He had noticed the same clues as his sibling but again struggled to reconcile the conflicting evidence.

'We'll ask the questions thankyouverymuch,' asserted the silver-haired woman, steadying her shotgun towards the two brothers. 'First question; were you two prisoners aboard a ship known as The Salvatore?'

The brothers nodded. The woman glanced over at her husband, who relaxed his arms, answered with a soft nod and proceeded to key some coordinates into a holographic display.

'Excellent,' the woman said, turning to face the siblings with a satisfied smile. 'We need you to help us locate someone who was on board that ship with you. Someone with incredible power.'

'And then what?' asked the older brother, cowering with the expectation that he may not like the answer.

'And then you can sit back and watch them do what they've always been destined to do – ravage the old world and destroy the dynasties; the idol-worshipping turf tribes in Parnasia, Shadox's nepotistic boardroom and this so-called Child of the Light's very own Vastridian masters, the Royal Family of Hawthorne.'

ABOUT THE AUTHOR

Phoenix Phil Morley currently resides in Hitchin with his family and an adopted hamster called Fluffy (who has miraculously returned from 'the dead' on at least one occasion). He works in primary schools by day and creates stories by night.

His stories are predominantly influenced by the daydreams and nightmares of his teenage years with some additional seasoning provided from his love of geek culture and pop n' rock music.

f 𝕏

REVIEWS

If you enjoyed SURVIVE THE UNIVERSE I'd be eternally grateful if you could leave a review on Amazon, Goodreads and anywhere else you discuss books. Here's what others have said about the book:

"Four chapters in and I'm HOOKED!" – **Steve McLean (comedian, writer, Action Figure Archive)**

"5 Stars. This one goes at 100 mph. There are some big characters leaping off the pages here that'll spark your fantasy casting off strongly" – **5 star Amazon review**

"A massive space opera that sort of takes all the cool bits of Star Wars and splices them to all the cool bits of Blake's 7. And it's got this hungry cat thing in it too that I loved" – **Peter Richard Adams (writer, Pod To Pluto podcast)**

"Bought on a whim mainly because I liked the front cover and really enjoyed it. There are some clever touches and good characters, I would recommend it" – **5 star Amazon review**

"I had so much fun reading this book and will miss spending time with the characters. I look forward to catching up with them in the proposed sequel" – **5 star Goodreads review**

"I dug this book a lot. The characters are well considered, the writing is tight and smooth, but it's really the story and the world (or should that be universe?) building which will leave you needing to know what happens to our protagonists. A compelling Sci fi yarn and a great Young Adult/Bratpack type romance story, but doesn't scrimp on either genre. Keen to see what this guy puts out next." - **5 star Amazon review**

"A ripping story, full of well thought out and nicely rounded characters. Someone else (amazon reviewer) referenced Blake's 7 and the Breakfast Club, and I was surprised to find that I totally saw the reference. Really good fun, and well worth a read! Go for it!" – **Mike Hibbert (author)**

'A fun sci-fi romp. Reminds me of the Red Dwarf novels meets Star Wars. Set in a sprawling outer space Universe, a lot of the worlds in Survive The Universe kinda conjure up the futuristic island of City of Bohane by Kevin Barry.' – **Frankie Moloney (DJ, The Bugle podcast, The Face Radio)**

ALSO BY PHOENIX PHIL MORLEY

BITE BACK!

"Despite his pale skin and fangs, teenager Benjamin Cooper doesn't want to be a goth, let alone a vampire. However, one fateful night in the summer of 1995 he catches the eye of Christine, a blood-drinker returning to town having left under a cloud several years previously.

She needs Benjamin for protection. He needs Christine to drag him out of the malaise of his stalling, small-town life. They both have a thirst for vengeance leading to a partnership bonded by blood. As the body count rises and enemies multiply, Benjamin and Christine are cast into an escalating spiral of revenge that they may not escape from.

BITE BACK! is a darkly comedic, lewd and violent teen horror story set in Sittingbourne during the Summer of Britpop, seasoned with suburban drama and offbeat characters."

COMING SUMMER 2024

Milton Keynes UK
Ingram Content Group UK Ltd.
UKHW020347250524
443177UK00008B/17

9 781068 648601